INVERCLYDE LIBRARIES

GOUROCK

INVERCLYDE LIBRARIES

**This book is to be returned on or before
the last date above. It may be borrowed for
a further period if not in demand.**

For enquiries and renewals Tel: (01475) 712323

This Holey Life

Sophie Duffy

Legend Press

Independent Book Publisher

Legend Press Ltd, 2 London Wall Buildings,
London EC2M 5UU
info@legend-paperbooks.co.uk
www.legendpress.co.uk

British Library Cataloguing in Publication Data available.

ISBN 978-1-9087759-7-9

Set in Times
Printed by CPI Group (UK) Ltd, Croydon, CR0 4YY

Cover design by Gudrun Jobst www.yotedesign.com

Author photo © Fiona Riches

Legend **Press**

Independent Book Publisher

Praise for Sophie Duffy

'Sophie Duffy has written a powerful first novel and shows huge promise' **Katie Fforde**

'One book I shall certainly be recommending this summer is Sophie Duffy's *This Holey Life*... By turns deeply moving and funny, the narrative zips along in an appealing and spirited voice. Duffy is particularly good at describing the power of family scripts, the way contact with parents and siblings can have us all travelling back in time to howling childhood, no matter how grown up and competent we look on the outside.' **Kate Long**

'Sophie Duffy is a real find. Sharp as a tack' **Laurie Graham**

'A warm, moving, wonderful read' **Wendy Holden**

'An extraordinary story... A born storyteller with a gift for characterisation, she writes with warmth, lovely earthy detail and a pathos which keeps a lump lodged in the throat... echoes of Victoria Wood and Laurie Graham, it is a cracking first novel' **The Daily Mail**

'Sophie Duffy explores grief and the vagaries of inter-family relationships with her usual blend of warmth, wit and wisdom. A triumph.' **Margaret Graham**

'a brave, bold, warm, rich, amusing, engaging novel which sits well alongside more established authors like Kate Atkinson's *Behind the Scenes at the Museum*' **Hello Magazine**

'Deftly written, very moving' **The Bookbag**

'A book you just can't put down' **Western Morning News**

Reader reviews

'So glad I had this recommended to me... I enjoyed every bit of this book, the characters are excellent, the local references (I live in Devon), the highs and lows, it was so gripping and easy to read I found myself carrying it around the house with me, literally unable to put it down! And the ending... well, you have to read it for yourself... Highly recommended!' **Miranda**

'I loved this book. The characters were well drawn and likeable. I felt I knew them and was part of their world. I was so engrossed in reading it one day that I forgot to get off the train - so Sophie you owe me £5!' **Anne Burnett**

'This is a wonderful read. The flow of the story line combined with the great characters gets you hooked. Born in the same year as the heroine, I found myself reliving so much of my childhood through this story, so many memorable dates, events and TV shows! It made me laugh out loud and sob uncontrollably. What a great first book, I can't wait to see what will come next.' **Jules**

'The novel is heartwarming and beautifully written... A heartwarming tale, this is a book with broad appeal although several issues are dealt with in a sensitive and engaging way.' **A.J. Dugdall-Marshall**

'The story is well told, there's plenty of twists and turns, and the characters are wonderful. I know it's a cliché to say that I couldn't put this book down, but in this case it's true. I can't remember the last book I read which had me so completely and utterly absorbed. So absorbed that I suddenly realised I'd been reading until 3am. Oops!' **Jacqueline Vincent**

'What a fantastic first novel. I couldn't put it down and became completely engrossed in the lives and experiences of all the compendium of characters... A wonderful read. Funny and sad, uplifting and moving. All my book club are reading and raving about it.' **Nicky Bowerman**

'I read *The Generation Game* over two days. I started it on Saturday afternoon and didn't stop reading until 2 the next morning... I loved the flashback to the 70s and the 80s and I also loved the crazy and wonderful family that Phillipa acquires in Torquay. For me this is the real charm of this book - I challenge you not to fall in love with Wink and Bob. You won't be able to help yourself any more than I was.' **Glenninexeter**

'*The Generation Game* was one of our book club books and I'm so pleased we all had the pleasure of reading it! What a great first novel, the twists and turns throughout were captivating and I couldn't put it down.' **Paula**

'What a lovely, heart-warming novel! For anyone who remembers the 1970's when Saturday night television was Bruce Forsyth, Larry Grayson and Morecambe & Wise rather than Sir Bruce, Ant and Dec and Gary Barlow, this is the book for you.' **SRJ**

'If you don't have time to read anything else read this - you won't regret it. It was recommended to me by a friend and so I bought it to take in holiday with me. I couldn't put it down... the story grips you in such a manner that you want to know what happens next.' **Book Bug**

'Well, didn't Sophie Duffy do well! I thought this was an excellent book, a real trip down memory lane. I found I could really relate to this tale - it was an entertaining, amusing, at times moving and nostalgic read... So, to coin a couple of phrases, it was nice to read it, to read it, nice! And I will not be shutting the door on any future work by this author, in fact I am eagerly looking forward to Sophie Duffy's next book.' **Vanessa**

'There were moments where I cried but more times where I laughed out loud. Growing up in the 70s, I totally related to the popular cultural references and it brought back my own memories.' **Deb**

'I also enjoyed the story itself & found myself reminded in places of one of my favorite authors, John Irving, who also skillfully weaves his books around the lives of his characters, often with very thought provoking results. High praise indeed! If you belong to a book club, I recommend this for your short list - it will get you all talking for sure.' **VCP**

'A friend recommended this book & as soon as I picked it up I couldn't put it down & I totally welled up at the end. It is a great story about life and all its twists & turns, about love, loss, forgiveness & hope. I also agree that if you enjoyed *One Day* you will probably enjoy this more, primarily because of the social references & the gentle humour.' **Louise**

'This is an astonishingly assured and intricately plotted novel from a debut author. It held me in its narrative grip from the first page to the last, as the heroine Philippa unravelled the mysteries of her past and worked out what (and who) she wanted in life.' **Lally**

'I believe that *The Generation Game* is The Book to read for 2011. I recently read it during my holiday and completely loved it. Sophie Duffy tackled many subjects in her debut novel. Relationships, marriages, birth, parenthood, friendship and death - but all were done so in a feeling and often amusing manner that just kept the reader turning the pages.'
Michelle Rutter

Acknowledgements

Big thanks are due to the following for their support, encouragement and help:

To Elaine Hanson, Luke Bitmead's mother. And to Pip Cantwell, a keen supporter of the Bitmead Bursary. For walking with me on my writing journey.

To the Legend Press trio, Tom Chalmers, Lauren Parsons and Lucy Boguslawski for their unstoppable enthusiasm and energy.

To Broo Doherty, my lovely agent.

To the Harry Bowling Prize. And to Harry Bowling who said 'above all, write from the heart'.

To the Romantic Novelists' Association, in particular to Katie Fforde. To the amazing Exeter RNA local chapter.

To Margaret James and Cathie Hartigan for early reads and invaluable feedback.

To all those vicars' wives (and husbands, of course) for shining a light, day in, day out. This includes Louise Stenner, Karen Wilson and Liz Redfern. And the once reluctant curate's wife, Harriet Ryan.

To my large, extended family near and far for their love and good wishes.

To my two big brothers: Rhys, for teaching me to write my name, ride my bike and bowl overarm. And Peter, for teaching me to be tough by holding me upside down by my ankles over the stairwell and using me as target practice for his air rifle (though not at the same time).

To my two awesome mothers-in-law.

To Mum for continuing to look after me.

To Amy Ford, my partner.

To Johnny, Eddy and Izzy, my three teenagers, for keeping me on my toes.

To Niall, for putting up with much and giving me more than I deserve.

To Mum, with love.

"How can you say to your brother,
'Let me take the speck out of your eye' when all the time
there is a plank in your own eye?"

The Bible, Matthew 7:4, N.I.V.

In the Beginning...

It was during the Eurovision song contest of 1978 that I first realised something fundamental about my big brother, Martin. Well, two things actually:

1. He was always going to be better than me. He was always going to be quicker, stronger, smarter, taller, richer, cleverer, smugger, more manipulative, more cunning, more self-assured.

2. I didn't really like him.

We'd all picked our country, the way we did every Eurovision, a family tradition. Mum went for Greece because she liked the costumes and had a thing for Demis Roussos like Alison Steadman in *Abigail's Party*. Dad, ever the clown, took Norway. Martin and I had our usual tussle, which, of course, he won. He got the United Kingdom. He got the favourites, Lynsey de Paul and Mike Moran with the classic 'Rock Bottom.' And me? I got a French woman singing in French about a bird and a child.

But I was to have the last laugh that night. By some blip in history, 'Rock Bottom' was beaten into second place by the French woman, Marie Myriam. I could've kissed her. In fact, I do seem to remember rushing up to the telly and pressing my lips against the screen.

'Don't do that, Vicky-Love,' said Mum. 'You'll go blind.'

Then she left the room to go and put the kettle on. She was always leaving the room to go and put the kettle on.

If I had been struck blind, I wouldn't have seen the look Martin gave me. A death threat look. Victory had been cruelly snatched from his hands by his puny little sister with the buck-teeth and frizzy hair.

But 'L'Oiseau et l'Enfant' was my one and only taste of glory *vis à vis mon frère*. And in some weird way that evening, my minor win somehow made me realise I was destined to forever be the underdog. The little sister. That was the role I would have to play until the end of time.

We grew up and this was confirmed. Martin was still quicker, stronger, smarter. He was more successful, too, in every way imaginable. A better job (his university lecturer to my primary school teacher), a better house (his semi to my terrace) in a better area (his Dulwich to my Penge). He married up a class to a beautiful woman (I married Steve), and together they spawned the ecologically correct number of children (his Jeremy to my Rachel, Olivia and Imogen). Martin had it all – career, wife, house, location, son – but there was only one thing he had that I coveted. His boy. Because once I had a boy too.

Then one Boxing Day, thirty years after that Eurovision, Martin turned up on my doorstep with only a duffle bag, a beard, ten-year-old Jeremy and a three-quarter-size cello.

'Hi Vicky-Love,' he said, his mock-Mum voice. 'We've come to stay.' And without waiting to be invited, he ushered in Jeremy who proceeded to dump his cello in the hall, ensconce himself on the sofa, and steal the television remote from a gob-smacked Rachel.

That was the point at which I should've put my foot down. Stamped it hard. Stopped the past repeating itself. But what did I do? I did what Mum used to do in times of crisis. I left the room and went to put the kettle on.

Chapter One: *Wednesday December 26th*

'So, are you going to tell me what this is all about?' I hand my brother his tea, sit myself down in the armchair and take a good look at him.

He has already made himself at home on the sofa, my new leather sofa (usurping Jeremy who has commandeered Rachel to find him turkey sandwiches). He is red-faced above his revolting beard, wheezy from forty a day, and his legs are splayed to leave little to the imagination. I want to throw satsumas at him.

Martin takes a tentative sip and winces. How dare he? There's nothing wrong with my tea. I make good tea. I am a curate's wife. It's in my job description. The one that's not actually written down anywhere but that I am expected to know by heart. And soul. 'Don't you have any sugar?'

'Yes, funnily enough, we have sugar. Would you like sugar in your tea, Martin?'

He lifts his eyebrow. His bushy eyebrow. 'Why are you being arsy?'

'I am not being arsy.'

'You are being arsy.'

'If you think I'm being arsy, it's only because you've turned up at nine o'clock on Boxing Day evening when we're in the middle of putting the kids to bed and you haven't even told me why.'

Steve has quietly fetched the sugar bowl and handed it to Martin. Martin shovels in three heaped teaspoons and stirs it frantically. He evidently has anger issues.

'I mean how long are you planning on staying?'

'That's the whole point, Vicky. None of this has been *planned*.' He sighs, all dramatic, and tugs at his beard. I want to rip it off. 'Claudia's kicked me out.'

'I see. And you took Jeremy?'

'No, I didn't *take* Jeremy. She kicked him out too. Said it was time I shared the childcare responsibilities.' He takes another slug of tea. 'Any biscuits?'

Steve slips out to fetch the biscuit barrel. He returns, holding it aloft in the manner of one of the Magi. He gives it to Martin.

'You've got a biscuit barrel,' says Martin. 'How retro.' He helps himself to a Bourbon, completely oblivious to how patronising he sounds or to the biscuit crumbs he's scattering over the new leather sofa, the only new thing this house has seen in a very long time, apart from baby Imo.

It's at this point, when he notices my fists begin to clench, that Steve finally decides to speak up. 'Would you rather have a beer, Martin?'

'Now you're talking,' Martin smiles back at Steve, a small boy offered sweets.

Steve disappears again to the kitchen. We can hear rummaging in the fridge. Clanking and fizzing.

'You'll have to sleep on the sofa,' I tell Martin, trying to sound like a grown-up – this is *my* house – but I suspect there are undertones of that puny little girl with the buck-teeth and frizzy hair. I thought I'd shrugged her off with the combined efforts of an orthodontist and ceramic hair straighteners but she has come back to haunt me. She must have been hiding in Martin's duffle bag. 'And Jeremy can have the zed-bed.'

'Zed-bed?' Martin doesn't even bother to stifle a laugh. 'Sorry, am I in a time warp?'

'No, Martin. You're in my house.' I underline this statement by flouncing out of the room, which is good timing because once I am in the hall – our poky hall, made pokier by the wretched cello – I can hear little Imo whimpers coming from above.

My breasts are tingly and heavy. I feel like marching back in there and telling Martin that, to see him squirm. But unfortunately I can't bring myself to mention the word 'breastfeeding' to him. He's my brother. He's Martin.

I climb the stairs, slowly, wearily. Maybe things will be better in the morning. That's what Mum always used to say.

Then I hear his voice call out to me: 'Night, night, Vicky-Love.'

Hours later, all is quiet. Steve lies next to me, warming his cold feet on my legs, smelling slightly of beer. 'I had to keep him company,' is his excuse. 'You left me to it. I had to listen to his story. It's a mess.' He tries to squash a hiccup. 'And this can't be good for poor old Jeremy.'

Poor old Jeremy is wrapped up in a sleeping bag on the zed-bed in the back room. Martin is on my new leather sofa with a Pocahontas duvet and pillow set kindly donated by Rachel. (*I'm too big for Disney, Mum. Disney's sad.*) I don't have to see for myself how Martin looks. I can picture him perfectly well, no different now at six foot two with a paunch and a beard than he was at fourteen with spots and smelly feet. He somehow takes over any room he enters. He has one of those 'big' personalities, which wouldn't be so bad if he were charming, nice even. But he's neither of those. I can only wonder how it's taken Claudia so long to take this latest action. A lesser person would have done it years ago. And yes, if Steve had access to my thoughts, he would tell me to be more understanding. More forgiving. But when it comes to Martin that is quite impossible.

'Do you think you could stop huffing, Vick. I'm trying to

get some kip. Imo will be waking us soon.'

'He's got me all stressy.' I sit up in bed, adjusting my breast pads and disentangling my nightie from the duvet.

'I know.' Steve uses that tone of his he reserves for the kids or a parishioner with learning difficulties. 'Just relax.' He makes a half-hearted attempt to rub my back. 'Claudia will be begging him to go back before you know it,' he goes on, stifling a yawn. 'She's besotted with him.'

'Mmm, maybe. I'm not so sure.' I wriggle his hand away and lie back down, trying some deep breathing, the way Steve's always encouraging me to do.

Maybe. Bizarrely, Claudia worships the ground Martin treads on with his big, flat, still-smelly feet. Worships the very air he hogs. Well, she did. Maybe she's simply proving a point: she's not the pushover he thinks she is. Or maybe – please, no – maybe she's... serious?

Thoughts for the Day: Why do women always follow men? Look what happened when Pocahontas came to England to be with John Smith. Will Claudia cave in and crawl after her husband, plucking him from the perils of Penge? And what will become of me? I thought I'd be a plumber's wife till Steve retired. And now look. Steve's a vicar, a curate. And I'm a curate's wife. Only I don't want to be. I want to be me again. Only I'm not sure I actually know what that is anymore.

Chapter Two: Saturday December 29th

I am locked in my bedroom. Not from the outside, barricaded by a makeshift Berlin wall of Encyclopaedia Britannicas, craftily constructed by Martin as he used to do when he'd had enough of my 'whining', but from the inside. Why? Because Martin is still here, downstairs, sprawling his over-indulged body across my new leather sofa, amongst the ravages of a cold meat lunch, three days on from his unexpected arrival. And Jeremy is practising the *Harry Potter* theme tune on his cello. Or is it *Lord of the Rings*? Or *The Simpsons*? They've all blurred into one mournful dirge over the course of the last few days. Whatever happened to Elgar?

Steve's disappeared to the park with the girls, rather more quickly and enthusiastically than usual, to get some fresh air, leaving me to deal with Martin and Jeremy and *Top Gear*. I lasted five minutes before having to storm up here with a gin and tonic, two aspirins and the remainder of a giant Toblerone. The giant Toblerone was a Christmas present from Rachel who spent her pocket money on me, wrapping it carefully (*You'll never guess what it is, Mum*), and putting it under the tree – only to discover her cousin Jeremy would eat half of it for breakfast a week later. Imo is too young for pocket money. At six months, she's too young for most things except milk. My milk. And Olivia got me a pack of dusters. Yes, dusters. *To help with your cleaning, Mummy.* At three years of age, Olivia is the one to get my cleaning genes. The ones that came from my grandmother, bypassing my mother, whose fondness for tea-making was the height of her domesticity.

So, to pass the time, I've treated myself to a long overdue tidy-up, which is something I could thank Martin for, if thanking Martin wasn't a task that went against the grain. But I can't help that feeling of martyrdom creeping through my bloodstream like malaria, knowing that while Martin is slobbing away to his heart's content on my new leather sofa, I am performing household duties usually reserved for springtime. But then I would never have tackled the contents of the bottom of the wardrobe. I would never have found the box.

Mum had given us one each, me and Martin, a box, the night before her bunion operation. She must have felt herself in the chilling grip of Death, vulnerable and scared, worried for her children, wanting to make her mark on their history, their future. They were only two old biscuit tins – his Jacob's to my Family Circle – but she made a big song and dance about them. Mine still had crumbs in it that I had to wash out.

Put all the things you treasure in here, she said. *And when you're older, if you're sad or lonely* (ring any bells, Martin?), *you can look back at all the important times in your life and see what you've done with it.*

Her eyes were glistening as she said this. She thought she was going to die and leave her two children behind with Dad, who had even less of an idea how to work the washing machine or clean a toilet than she did.

She didn't die. It was only a bunion operation after all. But she hated hospitals. And she had good reason in the end. Poor Mum.

I sit on the bed, the tin in my lap. I don't know what Martin has done with his, probably chucked it out years ago – he doesn't do sentiment, being a scientist – but mine's been at the bottom of this wardrobe ever since we bought it for our first flat.

It's been ages since I've had a root through it. Stubby baby teeth tucked in a matchbox. A ticket to a Wham! concert from the days when it was still possible I could marry George Michael. A train-spotting book from one mad summer. Foreign pre-Euro coins. A photo of Alice, my solo friend. Three pink baby nametags. And a blue one that makes me catch my breath. My poor little Thomas. I hold it in my hand briefly, but it is still too painful, even though it's been six long years and I'm supposed to have 'moved on'. Tucking it away with his sisters' tags, I make myself look at something else and I see the diary. 1978. My last year at primary school; the first at secondary. All those forgotten days.

But I haven't forgotten what it's like to live with Martin. How did I ever manage to inhabit that life, sharing a home for the whole of my childhood, until he left to go to university when I was thirteen? The past few days have taken me back there; I don't need the diary to remind me that some things never change. Martin is different to me. It is absolutely impossible to beat him at anything. Savings accounts, Boggle, the perfect boiled egg. He can do it all better than me. And right now he's downstairs with his slightly strange child on my leather sofa while I am sitting up here cross-legged on the newly-cleaned bed. How did I let that happen?

Except for marriage. He hasn't beaten me at that. He was in the lead for a while having got married the year before me and Steve. He had the full white cathedral wedding, the hypocrite, with bullet-sleek cars, fields of flowers, and sugar-icing bridesmaids. I had to make do with Lewisham register office, mini-cabs, and a buffet at Lee Working Men's Club. But now, Martin's marriage to the beautiful Claudia looks somewhat shaky. She has kicked him out, *like a fishwife on Eastenders*, according to Martin. And who can blame her? Certainly not me. Us fishwives have got to stick together. Though, despite him being my nephew, I wish she'd hung onto Jeremy. And the cello.

The cello. Jeremy is cranking it up again.

I swallow two more aspirins and crawl under the duvet with my diary. Perhaps I'll fall asleep. Perhaps when I wake up it'll all be a bad dream.

January 1st 1978

Martin is really annoying me. He got Space Invaders for Christmas and he's hogging the telly. I wanted to watch Black Beauty *because I love horses even though they are a bit smelly and I have never actually sat on one except for that manky donkey at Weston-super-mare last summer. I asked him very nicely and even offered him the Marathun from my selection pack but he thumped me and told me to get lost. And he took my Marathun. So I got my own back and put itching powder on his stinky sheets. Just wait till later – ha ha.*

Chapter Three

The story according to Martin:

I work hard. Long hours. Early starts. Late nights preparing for overcrowded seminars with thick, dumbstruck students and marking essays for aforementioned thick, dumbstruck students. When I come home all I want to do is have a cold beer and watch Newsnight. *Claudia wants to go out. To talk. To have dinner parties. Overseas holidays. Skiing in Klosters. Shopping in Paris. Well, it's alright for Claudia. She only works part-time from home, 'freelance' she calls it, cutting-and-pasting grubby celebrity 'stories' on her Mac. She's being completely unreasonable. Unrealistic. These things cost. I'm a university lecturer. A senior lecturer, granted, but I'm not exactly minted, not with the whacking mortgage payments we have to churn out every month, despite the in-laws' handouts. And I've slipped behind on my research. It's embarrassing. All these younger academics creeping up on me with designs on my job. I'm only forty-five. I'm in my prime. And then there's Jeremy. Claudia's too soft on him. Insisted on Dulwich Prep. I should've put my foot down. He would've been fine at the local school. More streetwise. Wouldn't have opened his big mouth and One Small Incident* (he pronounces these last three words with capital letters) *wouldn't have got blown out of all proportion.*

Martin bombards me with this 'story' once I've woken up

to reality and ventured back downstairs to the kitchen. He is smoking out the back door, exchanging our heating for an easterly.

'And where's Jeremy gone now?' I ask him, ignoring the One Small Incident because I can't go there right now. There's washing up to be done.

'To the park to find the others,' he mumbles.

Claudia would have hysterics if she knew her innocent son was walking the streets of Penge un-chaperoned. But he's obviously had enough of his father, so high on caffeine and sugar he's stuck to the ceiling... and oh my goodness look at the cobwebs up there... must get Steve onto them, though Martin's half a foot taller. There's no way I'm asking him. He'll call me suburban and obsessive. I like being suburban and obsessive. I like keeping a clean house. But he sneers at me. Has no idea how important it is to keep on top of things, to keep busy.

'Can you get a move on with that, I'm freezing.' I snap on my rubber gloves and make a start on the stack of dishes in the sink. 'Have you tried Claudia again?'

Martin blows a smoke ring, screwing up his eyes, Mum's eyes, spilling ash on the floor, my nice clean floor. He knows I know he's talked to Claudia again and again but it is not in either of our remits to draw attention to this.

He lobs his butt into a puddle (must get Steve to clear the storm drain), and slams the door shut. Then he stands there, watching me. I can hear his rasping breath, feel his beady eyes on my Marigolds, half-submerged in detergent bubbles. Does he offer to help? No. He just says: 'Why on earth don't you have a dishwasher?' then helps himself to a beer from the fridge. My fridge.

The story according to Jeremy:
Mum and Dad are always arguing. Then they like moan at me for 'skulking' in my room and listening to my iPod and for

playing my cello too loudly. How can you play a cello quietly?
It's a big instrument. And I've got my Grade 4 coming up.
They should be proud of me. Not annoyed. It's not my fault
I told Mum about the student. The one with the hair like
Christina Aguilera. The one I saw having a frothy coffee with
Dad outside Starbucks in Greenwich when we went on that
school trip to the maritime museum. I was only saying.

Jeremy tells me this on his return from the park, messy-haired and rosy-cheeked, sitting down at the kitchen table, cracking open a can of Coke. (Several of these death traps have appeared in our fridge despite being a zero tolerance house. Thank you very much, Martin.)

'Can I have a packet of crisps please, Auntie Vicky? I'm starving.'

What I should do is refuse his request; tea's nearly ready and if Rachel or Olivia catch a whiff of the possibility of heavy salt intake they'll be clamouring for crisps too. But I feel a whoosh of sympathy for Jeremy, motherless at this point in time and space. And at the mercy of his father.

'Help yourself,' I tell him. 'They're in the pantry. Only do you mind eating them outside? You can go in the shed, if you get cold.'

He gives me a look. A familiar look that says, 'Even though you are related to me I don't know what planet you're from'. But he does as he's told, putting on his coat, crisps hidden in his pocket, and hops his way across the stepping stones to the shed at the bottom of the garden, looking younger and younger the more he shrinks into the distance.

It is then that I hear heavy breathing in the room. A smoker's rasp.

'Stepping stones? Dad would be proud of you but where will this end, Vicky-Love? Gnomes? Budgies? The WI?'

The story according to Steve:
This was always going to happen. They have that kind of

relationship. Tempestuous. Her Elizabeth Taylor to his Richard Burton. It'll blow over in a few days, just you see. Don't worry. You worry too much. Take a deep breath and enjoy your bath.

Steve tells me this while having a whizz while I am trying to enjoy my bath. You'd think he'd have more decorum now he is a man of the cloth, but no.

The story according to Claudia:

He's been having it away with one of his students. Why didn't I listen to you when you warned me not to marry him?

Claudia tells me this on the phone, on the one and only occasion I get through to her mobile. Otherwise she is unreachable. She has gone away. She doesn't even ask about Jeremy, she is so angry. Not so much as a thank you for taking in her family. On Boxing Day. All she says is, 'Make sure Jeremy practises his cello.'

Yes, I did warn Claudia not to marry Martin. She should've listened. Steve says marriage is a sacred institution, a gift from God, but what sane person would enter into such a contract with my brother, the prince of darkness?

I wish I could go away. I wish I was unreachable. But I can't and I'm not. I am a breastfeeding mother. I have a baby, a girl of three – then a gap, a big black hole of a gap – and another one of nine. I have a good husband who loves me and my girls. Unfortunately, he also loves his parish and lives in hope that I will do likewise. Tonight – despite supposedly having a few days off – he has gone to the church hall to show his love to the Ladies Fellowship by speaking to them on the topic: 'Identifying Your Gifts'.

Come with me, Steve said. *Martin can babysit. We should make the most of this situation.*

But I could not leave my children with Martin. Not because I don't trust my brother – which of course I don't – but because Martin chose that moment to sneak out the house. We heard the front door close and looked at each other.

He's gone to the pub, Jeremy informed us, eyes fixed on the telly, grimy hand gripping the remote. *He could be gone for some time.*

So Steve went to the cold church hall to drink tea with the women of the parish and I stayed in and baby-sat for four children, drinking Horlicks with Jeremy on our new leather sofa, watching *Emmerdale.* I never knew so much went on in Yorkshire.

It's been raining but, thanks to the stepping stones and some very faint solar lighting, I can pick my way in the dark across the sodden grass without sinking. I wish I could call the sodden grass a 'lawn' and make Dad proud of me but that claim would be reckless. We have a typical South London garden, a long, thin strip backing onto the railway track. Not long enough to stop the back windows juddering (double-glazing would fix that – must get Steve onto it), but the toot-and-chug of a train at night is reassuring, knowing that other people are working, making a go of things, carrying on, while the household sleeps.

Though I'm more often than not awake, breastfeeding. I don't mind. I like feeding Imo, the two of us alone in the small hours. The screech of a fox. The cat-flap banging on Sock's re-entry. Steve's nose whistling a chirpy tune. The fridge humming. The house creaking... Though this closeness is tinged with guilt. That I am with her. And Thomas is gone.

So... the shed. Steve's pride and joy, lovingly constructed a few years back when he was still a Corgi gas fitter, before his Dartford moment. Finding time for DIY is not so easy now he has to care for the souls of the parish. That's a big ask of anyone, especially someone as conscientious as Steve.

'Jeremy? It's Auntie Vicky. Are you alright in there?'

Nothing. The wind howls its way up the track, wrestling the scrubby trees that back onto the cutting. Looking up the garden at the house, I realise that all the lights have been switched on. Every one of them. Our poky terrace could be seen from outer space. Maybe an alien will come down and kidnap Martin and beam him away to another galaxy. If he ever gets back from the pub. And where's Steve? What can the Ladies possibly be talking about at this hour? What previously undiscovered gifts have they unearthed?

It's late. Jeremy should be in bed. I knock tentatively on the shed door. 'Jeremy? Can I come in?'

Shuffling. The door swings open. His face appears, backlit by a torch, ghoul-like. 'Alright,' he says, retreating into the shadows.

As my eyes adjust I can see that he has made the shed into a kind of nest. He has stowed a stash of prawn cocktail crisps and a packet of Penguins in a flower pot. He has found a sleeping bag from somewhere and a cushion from the armchair where Socks likes to sleep. He slumps onto it, banging his head against the wall as he does so. He doesn't flinch; he's used to crashing into things, having inherited the clumsy genes from Mum, via Martin. Mum was always stubbing her toe, dropping her keys, spilling her tea. Dad used to joke about it, *there she goes again*; Mum would roll her eyes, a quiet smile playing at her lips. And although Martin can catch a cricket ball at a running dive, he might just as well pour his food straight onto the carpet without bothering to attempt to eat it first.

Jeremy is looking at me, waiting.

'I should watch your asthma with that cushion, Jeremy. It'll be covered in cat hairs.'

'I'm alright with cats,' he says, solemnly. 'It's dogs that like make me sneezy and that. Which my allergist says is unusual.'

'I'm sure it is.' I reach up for the camping chair that hangs from a nail and sit myself down, trying to sound casual when I say: 'I didn't know you had an allergist.'

'Mum made me go and see this woman.' Jeremy picks the dirt out of his nails with a bit of twig. He may be able to pluck deftly away at his cello but he is likely to cut himself and get lockjaw.

'A doctor?'

'A voodoo doctor Dad called her.'

'I see.'

'What's a voodoo doctor, Auntie Vicky?'

'I shouldn't worry about that, Jeremy. Dad was probably only joking.'

'Mum didn't laugh.' He starts snapping the twig into little pieces. I take it off him.

'No, I don't suppose she did.'

A train rumbles past, vibrating the wooden floor. When it's gone, I suggest we go in for a snack.

'Please may I have a Pot Noodle?'

I have to resist the temptation to say yes you can have a Pot Noodle. I can't believe we actually have Pot Noodles in our house but they have started appearing in the pantry.

'How about some nice toast and jam?'

He looks doubtful.

'It's homemade jam.'

'Did you make it, Auntie Vicky?'

'Yes.'

'What flavour?'

'Raspberry.'

'Alright,' he says. And he gets himself up, comes out into the night garden.

I follow him across the stepping stones. The back of his head is at once annoying and pitiful. He is so like Martin. And so different.

Thoughts for the Day: Did Richard Burton ever have a beard? What are my gifts, other than cleaning?

Chapter Four: Monday January 31st

New Year's Eve. Time to look forward but I can't help reverting to the gawky, awkward Vicky that lived in the house in Catford with Dad the gardener, mower of lawns and planter of bulbs, pruner of hedges and mulcher of vegetable plots. And Mum, the housewife, the sidekick, the woman in whose eyes you sometimes glimpsed other lives. Other possibilities.

Martin broke out from there, escaped to university to study some kind of science. Got a first. Then an MSc. A PhD. A lectureship. A fellowship. Got Claudia, social commentator, beauty, family money, envy of every one of his peers. Ended up just a few miles from where he began. But what a few miles they are. Dulwich Village. Claudia finally persuaded him to move there when Jeremy was little, and my brother is in his element, despite his whining. He loves being surrounded by wealth. It reminds him how far he has come from our humble beginnings.

And me? I'm a few miles in the other direction, standing at my kitchen sink peeling carrots to be sliced into crudités to dunk into dips for a few friends (not parishioners) that we've asked round for drinks, seeing as Steve's not doing the midnight mass. That duty's down to Desmond, the vicar, the one with the superior vestments – usually spattered with grease stains.

Tonight is to be shared with our old mates. Friends from

school, the plumbing days. Neighbours. This past year has been mad what with Steve's new career and Imo. Steve thought it would be a good chance to catch up, to let them see he's not become some kind of weirdo. Not that Steve's an embarrassing Christian. He doesn't have Jesus Loves Me car stickers or wear socks and sandals. But he has changed from the man he was. He's still Steve but he's got something extra. And it's more than the conscience that makes him fork out for *The Big Issue*. It's more than the dog collar or the 'Revd' that's transformed him from plain old 'Mr'. It's something inside that's changed.

It's called the Holy Spirit, Vicky, Desmond's wife, Amanda, informed me.

Amanda is a proper vicar's wife. She'll be in church tonight with Desmond, sitting enraptured in the front pew while her husband appeals to the congregation to turn over a new leaf in the coming year.

Amanda has an open house, a very nice vicarage in a tree-lined street with a large garden that doesn't back onto the railway. There's a constant pilgrimage of waifs and strays passing through, eating her enormous beefy stews and hunks of granary bread.

Amanda gave Desmond four sons who are all worthy men, settled down with worthy wives in Greater London and the Home Counties and every few months a new grandchild is paraded in St Hilda's to the delight of the congregation. Their photographs fill the vicarage with cherubic baby faces on every shelf, every surface. Which at least has the advantage of hiding the dust.

The Lord doesn't love me for my cleaning, Vicky.

Just as well.

Amanda escorts Desmond everywhere, making sure he is never alone with a single woman. For his protection, not theirs.

We learnt our lesson early on, Victoria. When Desmond was a curate in Plymouth, women were always falling for him. There was one particular woman who thought Desmond was so in love with her that he would actually leave me and the boys and run off with her into the sunset. She was very convincing, had the vicar doubting Desmond's integrity. They saw through her in the end, once she started attending the Methodist church, oh but gosh it was a close shave for a while.

The poor woman must've been deluded. Who would fall in love with Desmond? Except for Amanda. Though maybe he didn't always have a round belly and comedy hair. And how would dozy Desmond ever manage without Amanda?

I'll never be like Amanda. I'll never be a proper vicar's wife.

The carrots are done. My dress is ironed. The kids are in bed. Martin was supposed to be making himself scarce, going down the pub or something but he's still here, lurking in the kitchen, eyeing my food display with derision.

'Is there a problem, Martin?'

'Yes, there is, Vicky-Love.' He swipes a carrot and crunches into it with his great big teeth. 'I'm skint.'

'Oh?'

'So I won't be going out after all.'

'Oh.'

He reaches for another carrot but I am quick off the mark and get the dish out of his way. He opts for his fag packet instead, watching me strain to keep my mouth shut.

'Unless, that is, you can lend me some money.' He gets out his lighter. 'I'll pay you back as soon as.'

'How come you're asking me for money? You're the one that's loaded.'

'Cash flow,' he says, as if I'm an idiot. 'Go on, Victoria. Twenty quid should do it.'

A moral dilemma: Do I lend Martin money – money we haven't got – to go boozing? Or do I let him stay and ruin our evening?

Martin looks out the window, unlit fag in mouth, lighter in

hand. It is raining heavily. Big fat drips chasing each other down the panes of glass (must give them a going-over). He sighs like a dog. He hates the rain. Hates getting wet. Sets his eczema off, the poor diddums. I can guess what's coming.

'The pubs'll be full of students and chavs tonight.' Another dog-sigh. He's stalling, feeling sorry for himself that no-one's invited him anywhere. 'I suppose I shouldn't really leave Jeremy anyway.'

Pitiful.

'No, you shouldn't leave Jeremy, Martin,' I wag a carrot stick at him. 'But why change the habit of a lifetime?'

'Now, now, Vicky,' he retorts. 'Show some of your *Christian* ideals.'

I ignore this bait. I might not have been overjoyed when Steve confessed he wanted to go into the Church but I won't have Martin make fun of the unexpected turn our life has taken.

'You can stay but you'll have to make yourself useful.' I make a point of thinking about this. 'You're on peanut duty.' I get a large packet of KP nuts out of the pantry and slap it into his hand. 'You should know where the bowls are by now.'

'But you should know I'm allergic to peanuts. And I've left my EpiPen at home.'

'Oh dear, of course. You'd better go and get it then, hadn't you? Better safe than sorry.'

Martin eyeballs me for a few moments. If this were a cartoon he'd have steam coming out of his ears. But he's not going to put me off. I've hit the ground running and I won't let him catch me. Ha!

'You should go and see Jeremy's voodoo doctor. She might be able to weave her magic on you.'

If this were a cartoon Martin's face would be pillar-box red. No, wait, Martin's face *is* pillar box red. He lights his cigarette in the kitchen, my kitchen, and as he stomps his way out of the room, he skids on a carrot baton which, had it been a banana skin, would have completed this cartoon moment.

He swears, loudly, as he hobbles down the hall and for once I am grateful for the eardrum-rattling volume of the TV so the kids don't hear his disgusting expletives. But no-one can miss the bang of the front door as Martin exits (must get Steve to install rubber stop).

Two minutes later, our first guest arrives. Perfect timing.

My moment of triumph is short-lived. Unfortunately Gerry the carpenter is the one and only guest to arrive. Over the following half hour the phone rings no less than eight times with various excuses ranging from babysitting problems to the flu. There's even an RTA thrown in for good measure. Our tentative venture back into our old world with a little soirée has been a complete failure. We are left with a mountain of carrot batons and no washing up. We force ourselves to stay up till midnight to see the New Year in with the TV, watching the fireworks and our council tax go up in smoke. I phone Dad to wish him a Happy New Year. He doesn't answer. Steve phones his mum and dad. No answer. We turn in at 12.15. No sign of Martin who must've had a wad of cash somewhere up his sleeve. Or crashed the party of some poor unwitting soul.

What a depressing night. It would have been better to be in church with Desmond and Amanda rather than spending our evening 'listening' to Gerry's tales of dovetail joints. Whether we have been struck by a vengeful God for my lack of brotherly love or whether we are now too cringe-worthy for company is for me to fathom as I lie in bed, listening to the rockets zoom into the night sky and the shouts of drunken camaraderie echoing on the London streets.

Happy New Year, Vicky-Love.

Thoughts for the Day: Do I actually have any friends? Why do our parents have a better social life than us?

Chapter Five

I have finally inched my way towards a fitful sleep when the phone rings, cracking the night-quiet wide open. My heart thuds, like I've been stabbed in the thigh with one of Martin's EpiPens. Something must be wrong... While I am pinned to the bed in a state of paralysis, Steve has jumped up, phone in hand, all sticky-up hair and skinny legs.

'Yes, yes, I'm Reverend Butler. Is he alright?' He puts his finger in his ear, turns away – is that me shouting hysterically? 'Yes, yes, of course, I'll be there as soon as I can.' He sits on the bed. 'Thank you, officer.'

Officer?

'What's happened? Is it Dad? Is he alright?'

Steve puts the phone down beside him and turns to me. 'It's not your dad.'

Thank God! It's not my dad. Oh the relief. But then... 'No!' I leap out of bed and start pacing.

'Calm down, Vick,' Steve grabs my hand and guides me gently back to the bed, like I'm sleepwalking. Perhaps I am sleepwalking. 'Don't worry.' He rubs my neck.

I shake him off. 'What's he done?'

Steve scratches his stubble, considering how to break the news to me.

'Just tell me, will you.'

'He's been arrested,' he says, as if he doesn't quite believe his own words.

'ARRESTED? WHAT THE HELL FOR?'

'Ssh, Vick, be quiet. You'll wake Imo.'

'Sorry. What for?'

'Breaking and entering.'

'BREAKING AND ENTERING?' I am flabbergasted. Is Martin that skint he has to resort to burglary? 'What do you mean breaking and entering? Where? Why... ?'

'Vicky, ssh, calm down,' Steve grips my shoulders, gets me to look at him, eye contact, body language. He's been on a course. 'I don't know the details... only that they feel I ought to get down to the station sharpish.'

'Why?'

'Apparently Martin's agitated.'

'Agitated?'

'Agitated.'

'I'll give him agitated.' I'm off the bed again, agitated myself.

'No you won't, Vick. You have to stay here. The kids, remember.' Steve starts throwing on clothes, the nearest to hand.

The kids. That's when I think of Jeremy. Is it wrong for me to race ahead of the situation and hope for his father to get a custodial sentence? One way to get him out of here...

And then there's Claudia. I slump back onto the bed. 'Shall I call Claudia?'

'Best wait till we find out what's going on,' he stoops to kiss me. 'I'll phone as soon as I know more.' He's about to go out the room when he turns back and puts on his shirt and dog collar over his vintage Anarchy in the UK tshirt.

'What are you doing?'

'You never know,' he says. 'Could come in handy.' He fiddles with the collar. I can't quite believe he's my husband. A vicar. It seems ludicrous somehow. I keep expecting him to turn back into Steve the plumber. To get my old life back.

'Poor old Jeremy,' Steve says as an afterthought as he goes out the bedroom door, leaving me stranded in the middle of the bed until eventually I manage to get some control over my thoughts and turn them back towards my nephew, innocently sleeping on the zed-bed downstairs.

Yes, poor old Jeremy. I shouldn't be wallowing in self-pity right now. I should be concentrating on him. He'll be mortified. His dad, a criminal. Happy New Year, son.

Chapter Six: Tuesday January 1st

'Wow, cool!' exclaims Jeremy, eyes bright with excitement. 'Can we go and see him, Auntie Vicky? It's like *The Bill*. Is he banged up in a cell?'

This is the most animated I have ever seen Jeremy so I should be thankful for small mercies. He has appeared in the kitchen, where I have been force-feeding Imo baby porridge. I have had to explain the absence of his father. I thought about lying but Steve wouldn't go a bundle on that.

'It's not "cool", Jeremy. It was a very foolish thing to do.'

'But it was our house. He only wanted to get some stuff but Mum's like changed the locks. That's what you said.'

'Your mum changed those locks for a reason and your father should have respected that and gone down the proper channels.'

'You sound like one of those police officers off *The Bill*. How did you learn that, Auntie Vicky?'

I've obviously been watching far too much TV since Jeremy's arrival.

'I have no idea.'

I am being a good mother and aunt. I have gathered the four children together (i.e. dragged them away from CBeebies), and we are busy at the kitchen table making biscuits. Even Imo is on the table in her car bucket, kicking her feet in encouragement. The table and the children are covered in flour but they are smiling and so am I.

Then the door goes and in walks a bedraggled Martin accompanied by a slightly crumpled curate.

'Morning all,' says Martin, bending his knees like Dixon of Dock Green. This goes right over the kids' heads but annoys me right off that he can be so blasé about the havoc he's caused.

'Right, I'll put these in the oven while you lot go and get cleaned up. And don't touch anything with your sticky hands.'

'I'll wash the bowl,' volunteers Olivia, rushing to the sink before I can get rid of her and find out exactly what's been going on.

'Steve, do you think you could supervise while I have a little chat with Martin?'

Steve expresses concern at the prospect of me having a little chat with Martin. 'Are you sure you want to do that now?'

'Yes. Definitely now,' I squeeze Steve's arm in a display of marital harmony and support (must encourage Steve back to the gym; church doesn't tone the biceps the way a tap wrench once did). 'Then I'll make you some breakfast. You must be famished.' I drag Martin out the back door into the garden before Steve can intervene.

It is freezing outside so I button up my cardy. 'Don't even think about mentioning the stepping stones or gnomes. Tell me what you've done, Martin.'

He looms over me in his Martin-way but I will not be made to feel small. His little sister. 'It would never have happened if you hadn't forced me to go round to retrieve my EpiPen,' he whines, colour returning to his cheeks from the cold. There is an arrogant jut to his chin that lurks somewhere under his increasingly skanky beard.

'So it's my fault, is it? Ha! I should've known.'

'I didn't say that. Only I wouldn't have been at my house

otherwise, would I?'

'Do you seriously expect me to believe that you went round to retrieve your EpiPen just because I put you on peanut duty?'

Martin kicks at a bit of gravel on the patio, probably imagining it to be my head. 'I was going to pick up a few more things. For Jeremy. He's got Nintendo Withdrawal Syndrome. You wouldn't appreciate that, having girls... ' He tails off, not sure how to get out of this.

I turn away from him, like he's slapped me in the face. Because I haven't always just had girls. And I don't need him reminding me of that.

'Sorry, I mean... You know what I mean.'

I pull my cardy round me and take a very deep breath, filling my lungs with Penge's finest morning air. 'So girls can't play on Nintendo wotsits? Is that what you're saying?'

'Well, not your girls. This isn't exactly a technologically advanced household, is it? You haven't even got Sky.'

'What a come-down it must be, slumming it in such a deprived house.'

'Yes, it is,' and he smiles. Which annoys me even more than if he didn't smile. He's trying to pull me off the trail of his arrest. It's not going to work.

'Forget Sky-Nintendo-Wotsits. Tell me why you got arrested.'

'If you stop interrupting me I'll get to it,' he takes out his fag packet. More delay. It's empty. He puts it back in his pocket. More delay. More deviation. The deviant.

I take a packet of Polos out of my cardigan pocket and offer him one. Not to be nice; to keep his concentration up.

He crushes it immediately upon entry into his mouth. No thank you or anything but at least his voice is less spiky as he goes on. 'I went round there all prepared to be nice to Claudia and yes, before you ask, I admit there was an ulterior motive.'

'Which was?'

'I was hoping the dawning of a new year might make her

rethink our situation.'

'What, the One Small Incident situation?'

'Do you want me to tell you or what?'

The less spiky voice didn't last long so I nod in vague encouragement, trying to get Martin back to a level of calm. Calm that I don't feel. But I really want to know what happened. And I really want to know if last evening's events have taken Martin further away from the day he will move back in with Claudia and out of my house.

'Are you listening, Victoria?'

'Of course. Fire away.'

'Right, well, I rang the doorbell. Nothing doing. I went round the back and peered through the lounge French windows and the kitchen door. Nothing. Then I came back round the front and got out my keys. Tried the lock. Tried all the locks. They'd been changed. Can you believe it?' He snatches the packet of Polos out of my hand, shovels three into his mouth and starts crunching them aggressively.

'Yes, Martin, I most definitely can believe it. You've got yourself into trouble and Claudia's not happy.'

He ignores this and gobs instead into a nearby flower pot. Some of it remains in his beard, glistening in the weak morning sun.

I practise heavy breathing. 'And what exactly did you do then?'

'Nothing.'

I raise my eyebrow.

'Well, I went round the back again and tried the utility room. There's an old sash there. I've been meaning to get a lock for it. It was a bit of a squeeze – you've been giving me far too much fat – but I managed it.'

Breathe, Vicky, breathe.

'Only then the alarm went and I couldn't switch it off because she's changed the code. I tried every sequence I could think of – even the date of our wedding anniversary, which, yes, alright, is an unlikely choice under the circumstances – and then next thing I know there's a torch in my face and two coppers grabbing hold of me.' He relives this moment of disbelief. Like the time the French lady won the Eurovision. Disbelief that he could lose control over the situation. His life.

'Go on.'

'I told them I live there and to go and ask next door for verification. Only I should've been more specific. I meant next door at Giles' house. But they went the other side and got Bella. Bella hates me. Even more so since Claudia's told her the gory details of our marriage. She denied that she knew me. Can you believe it? Surely that's perjury.'

'Did you tell them that?'

'Yes, of course I did.'

'And?'

'They arrested me and bunged me in the car. One of them put his filthy hands on my head just like on the TV.'

'Yes, *The Bill*, I've seen it.'

'Really? I didn't have you down as a *Bill* fan.'

'There's a lot you don't know about me, Martin.'

At that moment the sun skulks off and a gust of wind blows up the railway track, wrapping itself around us as if to emphasise this enigmatic point I am making to my brother. He watches me pull my woolly sleeves down over my hands to try and keep warm. As if it weren't his fault we were out here in the cold. As if I wouldn't rather be inside in the warm with my family, breathing in the comforting smell of baking biscuits instead of a great hulk of a man who has spent the night in the cells.

'I've heard that cardigans are back in fashion,' he switches the focus, deftly, onto me. 'Were you aware of that, Victoria? Isn't it lucky you hung onto that one from the Wham! years?'

'At least I don't have a beard.'

'Give it time, Vicky-Love. Give it time.'

If I had itching powder on me, now would be the time to

throw it in his cantankerous, eczematous, beardy face. But I don't. Instead, I turn on my heel and leave him to it. I need some of those biscuits. Even if Jeremy's slimy fingers have been all over them.

Thoughts for the Day: Why don't we own a house that requires an alarm? Will we ever?

January 10th 1978

Martin has a girlfriend. Yuck. She is called Heidi like on that programme where the actors' lips move in different time to the words they are saying. It's called 'dubbing' Martin told me. Know-it-all. He said Heidi *was a book as well – as if I cared. I'd rather watch the telly.*

Martin's girlfriend, Heidi, has big bosoms. Bigger than any grown up I know and she's only 14. Martin has taken her to the cinema tonight to see Star Wars. *Again. I think Heidi would rather see* Watership Down. *I would. But Martin always gets his own way.*

Heidi came for tea first. Mum gave us fish fingers (burnt), mash (lumpy) and peas (hard). Heidi ate it all up without complaining. She likes her food Dad said when they'd gone to the cinema and we were watching Tomorrow's World *(Dad is interested in technology, especially when it is Judith Hann talking about it).*

Mum went to put the kettle on. Dad said Heidi must like Martin. He sounded surprised. She'll soon learn I said. I have inside knowledge. If anyone knows, it is me. I know what it is like to be alone with Martin. He sits on your head and blows off. He is a disgusting pig.

When I am 14 and have a boyfriend and hopefully big bosoms, my boyfriend will take me to the roller disco and spin me around like he's Robin Cousins or John Travolta. My friends will be amazed. They will be jealous of me, Vicky. Ha-ha!

47

Chapter Seven: Friday January 4th

Olivia sits amidst an array of shoeboxes and tissue paper, her leg up on a foot-stool, like Cinderella, waiting to try on the glass slipper. Only this is not your fairy tale ending. She is adamant she won't have a T-bar as recommended by the haughty young assistant called Melanie.

'She's got narrow heels and the bar will stop the shoe slipping,' Melanie states firmly.

'No,' Olivia states, even more firmly. She quite clearly isn't having any of it; her cheeks are flushed and she is tossing her hair like a diva. She'll be demanding her own stylist and a basket of exotic fruit next. 'I want those shiny ones, Mummy. Femi's got shiny ones like that. Her mummy let her. I hope you're going to let me.'

I look at Imo for help, but Imo is busy sucking her big toe as thankfully shoes are still a way off for her. Why did I think it would be a good idea coming to Dulwich to buy the wretched shoes? I should've stayed in Penge and gone to Shoe Zone.

Deep breath. Count to ten.

This is one of those situations when I should put my foot down. (My own feet haven't seen new shoes in a very long time.) Martin would laugh if he saw me floundering like this, a grown woman being manipulated by a three-year-old and an uppity shoe-fitter.

Olivia is coveting the shiny shoes. Melanie is barely

concealing her disapproval, looking at her watch, and tapping the shoehorn on her long skinny leg. But like Steve is always saying, you have to pick your battles. And I don't have to live with Melanie. Thankfully. There's something about her that sets my teeth on edge.

'We'll have the shiny ones.'

There. That is decisive. I think.

Olivia claps her hands and gushes *you'rethebestmummyin thewholewideworld*. Imo gurgles in her bucket, kicking her chubby legs like a bulbous frog. Melanie is not so appreciative; she tuts, smoothing her long blonde hair before beginning to laboriously repack the discarded shoes in the boxes.

'You wait till you're a mother,' I tell her, before I can stop myself. 'Things will seem completely different.'

Melanie looks doubtful. But then I would've looked doubtful at that age. In my early twenties. With my adult life in front of me and London all around me. I never for one minute thought about having children. And then, when the time eventually came, and the prospect of kids edged into our radar, I never thought about the consequences of having children. Real children. Snotty, pooey, crying, three-dimensional children. I didn't see beyond the holding-the-baby-in-your-arms stage. I didn't consider the fact they would keep growing. They would have their own opinions. They would voice their own opinions. Or that those opinions would be more forceful than mine. (I should've known though, growing up with Martin.) But what I never foresaw was that life could be so fragile. That a baby could be here one minute, and gone the next.

'I suppose you're going to let her wear them home,' Melanie sighs.

I want to tug her long blonde hair. Pull out great chunks of it and scatter it over the plush red Dulwich carpet. What does she know about anything?

It takes much self-control to muster up my primmest curate's wife voice and push out a basic response through clenched teeth: 'Yes. Please.'

I pay for the shoes (*How* much?), not convinced I'm doing the right thing but Olivia is doing her very own version of *Riverdance*, a big smile on her face, and there's no way I'm giving high-and-mighty Melanie the satisfaction of back-tracking.

I am a good mother. I make sure they have their five portions and a bath every day. I sew nametags on their school clothes. I read with them. Even Imo. I try to remember to tell them I love them. I teach them right from wrong, their Ps and Qs, their table manners. I even pray with them sometimes though technically that's Steve's department seeing as I'm still not too sure about this whole God thing.

So why does this pair of shiny shoes make me feel like such a failure?

The reason I chose to come to Dulwich – the real reason – was so that I can call round at Claudia's. I had a text message this morning.

Back home. Sorry to land family on you at Xmas. Wot a mess. Missing J loads. Is he OK? Can u come & see me? Don't tell Martin. Cxxx

How can I not go? I feel bad for Claudia, even worse that I couldn't bring Jeremy as Martin had a rare moment of guilt and whisked him off to the golf course. He persuaded Steve and Rachel to accompany them. Anything to avoid being on his own with his son and having to explain his actions to him. Wimp. Wuss. Scaredy-cat stinker.

After getting over her initial disappointment that Jeremy is not with us, Claudia pulls herself together and becomes the hostess-with-the-mostest. She would make an admirable vicar's wife. If she believed in God.

'Nice shoes, Olivia,' Claudia says, showing us into the vast kitchen at the back of their double-fronted Victorian villa.

She clacks across the slate floor in her own expensive shoes. I think they are called kitten heels.

Olivia's new shoes shine as she skips after her auntie, deeper in love with her than before. But, as is her nature and her age, she cuts to the chase. 'Why is Uncle Martin living with us?'

The question bounces around the echoey kitchen like a runaway tennis ball. I can feel my arms straining to catch it and hide it away, though Olivia has a point. Why is Martin living with us?

Claudia might also be taken aback by this question but she doesn't show it. She touches Olivia on the shoulder and says: 'Because your mummy is a great big softie.'

'Believe me, Claudia,' I say. 'If he hadn't brought Jeremy as some kind of human shield, my brother would be confined to a Travelodge right now.'

Claudia smiles grimly and puts the kettle on the Aga as if Dulwich Village were not actually in South London but somewhere in rural Devon.

I sit at the enormous distressed pine table but leave Imo strapped firmly into her bucket, next to my chair; she'd crack her skull open on these unforgiving tiles. Olivia's skipping is on the verge of mania and I can visualise a trip to Kings College Hospital. She needs distraction. She needs television. Martin owns the biggest set in Christendom so that should do it.

'Olivia, why don't you ask Auntie Claudia if you can watch the TV?'

Olivia considers this idea and asks in her sweetest voice: 'Have you got *Pimp my Ride*, Auntie Claudia?'

'Oh dear,' says Auntie Claudia, blushing, recognising Jeremy's hand at work. 'How about you go up to my room and try on my shoes?'

Olivia disappears sharpish before her auntie overcomes her guilty conscience. Claudia meanwhile busies herself making coffee, grinding beans and frothing milk with gadgets I didn't know had been invented. Finally, she joins me at the table, offering posh organic biscuits as a softener.

We talk about her mother, where she has been staying since Boxing Day until finally returning home last night. (Claudia's mother is quite possible royalty; she lives in a palace; I have seen the photos.)

Then we talk about Jeremy.

Claudia says she misses him like crazy but she doesn't feel she can let Martin off the hook where his son is concerned. I ask her if she wants to talk about what happened. Three cups of coffee later – boy, this family likes its caffeine – and I have all the major details:

Martin is a pain in the arse to live with (nothing I didn't already know). He has long since broken all their wedding presents, including the Dartington champagne flutes, which didn't even make it to their first anniversary. He is loud. Takes over any conversation whenever they have a dinner party – on the rare occasions he agrees to one. He is facetious. He is patronising. He is a pig.

Martin is having a mid-life crisis. He downloads 'silly music' for his iPod and has grown 'that disgusting excuse for a beard'.

Martin worries over his job and takes it out on Claudia, belittling what she does. Claudia believes the world wants to know about Posh and Becks. She is fulfilling a need. Martin says she is vacuous and facile.

Martin moans about Jeremy going to Dulwich Prep. Claudia believes Dulwich Prep is the best place for a boy as 'sensitive' as Jeremy.

Jeremy saw Martin with a younger woman. A student. In Starbucks. I ask if that is really a reason to suspect him of adultery. Apparently that isn't the only time he's been spotted with her.

'So I'm sorry, Vicky,' Claudia sniffs, the tip of her pretty nose tinged pink. 'I can't have him back. Not after what he's done. Not to mention the attempted break-in.' She sits up straighter in her chair. I know her well enough to see there is something else. Something that will affect me. 'Actually, I've agreed to go to LA to cover a story. A two-week trip. It'll be great for my career. And great for me.'

Ah.

'Do you mind?' she asks, a little sheepish.

Yes. I mind. I mind very much. But I am the Good Auntie. 'No, of course I don't mind.'

'Another coffee?'

'Best not. I'm still feeding Imo.'

'Gosh, Vicky. How old is she now?'

'Only six months.' I hoik Imo out and plonk her on my lap. She weighs a ton.

'What a devoted mother you are,' Claudia whispers, tears crowding her eyes. Then she actually starts crying. Really snotty, dribbly, mascara-running, shoulder-shaking crying.

I pat her hand. I do a lot of hand-patting in my new role. I may not have been on a course but hand-patting usually does the trick.

Claudia's sobs recede and she gives her nose a good blow on the clean hanky I always have up my sleeve. 'Maybe it's because you have girls,' she says, then looks horrified. 'Oh, sorry, Vicky, I didn't mean... well, it's just that Jeremy's so like his father. He's so... big. So... bulky. He takes up too much room.' She searches for understanding while I snatch a look around the vast kitchen – the Aga, the hulk of an American fridge, the army of cupboards and acres of granite worktops – wondering just how much room a three person family needs. Wondering why so many human beings, plus a cello, are crammed into my poky terrace. 'Why can't he take after me?'

I look at Claudia. Petite, refined, delicate Claudia. Jeremy can wade his way through Middle Earth on the Playstation-DS-Nintendo-Wotnot, but he will bang into door frames as he passes through. That is, when he actually manages to get himself vertical. When he's not sitting on the new leather sofa watching *Cribs* – which, I have discovered, has absolutely nothing to do with the Baby Jesus.

Yes, Claudia's right. Thank Heaven for my little girls. But it's harder to be thankful for my little boy. How can I be?

Thoughts for the Day: I wish I lived in Middle Earth? Anywhere but here and now.

Chapter Eight: Sunday January 6th

Epiphany

Sunday. Traditionally a day of rest. In our world there's not a whole lot of rest going on. It's a whirr of to-ings and fro-ings and trying to keep the children quiet and smiling and small talk and roasting parsnips and tea and hand-patting.

Being a curate's wife doesn't come easily. Being a curate's wife wasn't what I signed up to all those years ago when I said: 'I will'. What I meant was: I will go out to work and help pay off our mortgage. I will share the cooking and washing-up but am more than happy to do the bulk of the cleaning because that's the way I like it and I know you, Steve, are much happier, and more proficient at, wielding a power tool. I will have your children if and when the time comes – which it did, on four occasions. That's what I meant.

I didn't mean this. I didn't mean Steve to swap his copper pipes for a surplice. I didn't mean to swap my old life for this one. I was happy being a teacher, a mother, a plumber's wife.

But how could I say no to Steve? I promised him, didn't I? Said I would stick with him for better, for worse. And while he believes this life is better, I still have to be convinced. And it's going to take nothing short of a miracle to do that.

Not that it's all bad. Sometimes I open the front door to find a package left by a good-intentioned parishioner. A marrow. A jar of chutney. Once, generously and anonymously, a voucher for a day's pampering at The Sanctuary (which I still haven't used, surprise, surprise). And sometimes, when I pop into the church to polish the lectern – it's really tricky with all the engravings and twiddly bits – I feel something surround me. I'd like to say it was God's love. His peace and understanding. But it's probably the silence that is so elusive at home.

Jeremy has agreed to come to Sunday School. He actually agreed quite readily which surprised me as I assumed he'd be as resistant as Martin – a worshipper of Richard Dawkins – to the idea of a loving God. Or, perhaps like the rest of us, he wants some space from his father who has been acting strangely since his dealings with the long arm of the Law. He is spending a lot of time with Jeremy for one thing. Just the two of them. Playing chess. Going to the park. Golf. Even shopping for clothes. Martin hates shopping for clothes. He's always left that to Claudia. He always left everything to Claudia. And now that he's actually rising to the challenge, I am shocked. And I am suspicious.

St Hilda's is like many of its regular attendees: grey and dusty, which, I know, is not a Godly thought for me to be having. But then God knows that I'm not exactly His whole-hearted follower. Unlike my husband.

I have to admit I am sort of proud watching Steve perform, at my sparkling lectern, speaking to his flock. But then I used to be proud of him when he lay with his head under the sink twiddling his ratchet. He is a good man who does a job well. It's me that's struggling.

Today I have to sit on my own – on a less than perfectly polished pew seeing as they are Amanda's responsibility – trying to keep four fidgety children quiet while Desmond and Steve do their double act. We've sung the embarrassing children's song with actions. Jeremy was strangely enthusiastic about it, waving his arms about like a Charismatic. It was quite infectious. Even Rachel, known for her disdain of anything infantile, joined in a little. I actually caught a glimpse of a smile hanging about her lips. Olivia was more interested in flaunting her new shoes, which haven't been off her feet yet except for bath time. Now we just have to get through the children's talk. This is when I always struggle to keep my lot from heckling.

Today isn't so bad because some of the drama group are doing a sketch and at least the kids can focus on something. Like Mr Maynard's shoes which, according to Olivia and commented on in her loudest voice, are like Jesus' shoes. I pretend I have dropped something vital on the floor so that I can duck down behind the pew. It is warm down by the heating grill, with the comforting smell of beeswax. I'd like to stay there for the rest of Mr Maynard's amateur dramatics, in fact for the duration of the service, possibly for the rest of the day but alas I am a grown woman and must act accordingly.

At last: relief. The children file out to Sunday school and I can lug Imo to the crèche. (She's definitely fat. Must go to clinic and be reprimanded by health visitor.) Soon I can creep back into the rear of the church and concentrate on important matters i.e. my list of things to do for tomorrow. For tomorrow is school.

I had every reason to be suspicious. The reason Martin has been spending all this so-called 'quality time' with his son is so that he can toughen him up. And why? In order to send him to a new school. Martin is taking Jeremy out of Dulwich Prep and sending him down the road to St Hilda's C of E. He's been in to see the Head and, using his connections to Steve and his overbearing powers of persuasion, has wangled a place. And to make things worse, Claudia is clueless on the other side of the ocean. He's had this planned for a long time, gave the correct amount of notice so he didn't have to pay the term's fees. That's the money he was going to be coming into. The flow of cash. He is calculating and despicable. And very stupid. Does he really believe this will help win Claudia back? If I know Claudia, this is the very thing that will stop dead any chance of mediation.

I am telling all of this to Steve in the brief respite we have late Sunday afternoon, me at the ironing board, with a heap of white polo shirts, Steve going over his preparation for the evening service.

'Do you think we should let Claudia know?' he asks me, gripping his pen the way Rachel grips hers. All wrong.

'I've been trying her phone on and off all day. There's no ring tone.'

'We could leave a message at the hotel asking her to call,' he suggests.

'I don't want to worry her. She'll think something dreadful's happened.'

'From her point of view something dreadful has happened.' He shuffles his revision cards and takes off his glasses.

'I don't know what to do, Steve. I'm not sure I want to get involved.'

'We are involved. They're your family.'

'But I didn't choose that family. I chose this one. You and the girls.' I look at Steve in his dog collar and try to remember what he used to be like in his overalls. I feel tears wash my eyes and I'm not entirely sure why.

'I'll have a word with Martin if you think that'll help,' Steve suggests. 'Otherwise, you're right, there's not a lot we can do for now.'

'He won't take a blind bit of notice. I'll speak to Rachel's teacher though. Get her to keep an eye on him.'

'Rachel's teacher?'

'They're going to be in the same class.'

'Well, that's a God-incidence for you.'

'A what?'

'A God inspired coincidence,' Steve beams. Life is simple for him these days. He hands over his worries to God whereas I gather mine all around me like a class of small uncontrollable children. 'Stop fretting, Vick. It'll work out. Trust in the Lord.' Then he pats my hand and it is a real struggle not to let the tears fall.

Thoughts for the Day: Should I go on a counselling course? Or should I go into therapy? And just what is an epiphany exactly?

January 20th 1978

I hate school. Mr Harris, my teacher, has grease marks on his trousers. They must come from his hair, which looks like it would catch fire if you got near it with a match. Only one more year at this dump and then I will be going to another dump. Martin is at the Grammar but I didn't get put in for the eleven plus because I am not brainy like him. It is so unfair. I work much more than the lazy slug but he always gets 'A's. Even when I try really, really hard, the best I get is a 'B'.

Heidi goes to a private school because her Dad is a financier, whatever that is. Heidi met Martin at a public speaking competition. Martin's team won of course. Heidi said his speech on the rules of cricket was inspiring. She is a big fat liar. Martin told her she looked like Olivia Newton-John. He is a big fat liar too. Heidi looks more like Dolly Parton. I wish someone would tell me I look like Olivia Newton-John. I look more like Leo Sayer. With a brace.

But I shouldn't call Heidi a big fat liar because I like Heidi. She is nice to me and smiles a lot and last night she helped me with my French homework. I have no idea why I need to learn French. Mum and Dad will never take us to France. They never take us further than Worthing or Weston-super-Mare. Heidi is going to Egypt for her next holiday. She is going to see the pyramids and the Sphincter. I wish I was Heidi.

Chapter Nine: Monday January 7th

Packed lunches. For Jeremy and Rachel. Not for me as I still have a few months reprieve until Imo hits her first birthday and I return to teaching. Not for Steve who no longer has to eat his sandwiches in his van. He comes home these days. Which is nice. Usually. Though sometimes I'd like to sit down and watch *The Little Mermaid* DVD with Olivia in the hope of twenty minutes shut-eye, instead of listening to how the diocese works and feeling guilty for not being as enthusiastic as Amanda about the new prayer books.

Guilt. Must have caught it off Claudia. I can feel it snapping at my ankles like the Jack Russell the children are always nagging us for. Guilt at the extent of my joy that Rachel and Jeremy will be out of the house for six whole hours. No *American Idol*. No monosodium glutamate. Back to *CBeebies* and rice cakes (unsalted). And guilt because this is Olivia's first day at playgroup and apart from buying her a pair of shiny inappropriate shoes I haven't prepared her for stepping out into the world without me. And now I have to step outside. Into the garden. The shed.

'I'm staying in here, Auntie Vicky,' Jeremy mutters as I try to coax him out, his father having disappeared to work. Typical.

'What's wrong, Jeremy?'

'I'm going to get beaten up and that cos I'm a posh kid.'

'You're twice the size of an average ten-year-old. They wouldn't dare. Besides, Mrs Lake is a really good teacher. She won't stand for any teasing. Certainly not bullying. There's a school policy.'

'Dad says school policies aren't worth the paper they're written on.'

'Well, your dad's not a teacher. Now come on. There's a bacon sandwich waiting for you.'

'With tomato ketchup?'

'With tomato ketchup.'

The door swings open and Jeremy steps outside. 'At least I don't have to wear a tie anymore.'

'Exactly. Every cloud has a silver lining.'

Monday is Steve's day off so he drops Jeremy and Rachel at school and leaves me to deal with Olivia. I am not actually worried for Olivia. I am more worried for the playgroup workers who may not have previously encountered a child quite in her league. I am a little concerned they will have her down as one of those eccentric children, possibly on the autistic spectrum as she is quite fanatical about some things – namely shoes and cleaning.

I have managed to persuade Olivia not to wear her Snow White dress and am trying to convince her that leggings and a fleecy top will be the most practical outfit for painting and going on the trikes outdoors.

'But I don't like leggings, Mummy. You never wear leggings.'

She is right. I never wear leggings. What sane adult would wear leggings? Except for petite refined delicate Claudia who has neither hips nor bottom.

'How about your corduroy skirt? That's really pretty.' Really hardwearing and I can wash it at sixty degrees and not turn Steve's underpants a shade of purple.

'How about Tinkerbell, Mummy? I could go as Tinkerbell.

That's really pretty.'

I kneel down and look her in the eye, woman to woman. 'Olivia if you get paint on Tinkerbell it will never wash out however much Vanish or Cillit Bang I use and you will never ever be able to dress up as Tinkerbell again and that would be very sad indeed.'

'Okay, Mummy, I'll wear the courgette skirt,' Olivia says as if I have just pulled her back from the edge of a hidden precipice.

'Good. The courgette skirt it is.'

Hallelujah.

I watch at the door of the church hall. A familiar place for Olivia but these are different kids to the ones she knows from Sunday School. These are un-churched kids. London kids. She's a London kid but I suspect she is a little cushioned from London life. Will she be alright? At least she knows this space. The smells. The quirks of the ladies' toilet. She has even cleaned the toilet when it's been my turn on the rota. Thankfully she doesn't have to battle with the urinals. I wouldn't want her to share them with the boys in this room. (Thank Heaven for little girls.)

She has already muscled in on a group having a tea party with plastic cup cakes and foam French fries and has insisted on being mother. 'I'll just go and put the kettle on,' I hear her strident voice ring out above the cacophony. While she waits for the kettle to boil (she is very realistic in her role play), she takes a doll out of a Moses basket and changes its nappy.

Nappies. Rachel knows how to change a nappy. For real. She'll do Imo if I'm desperate. If I'm stuck on the phone with a parishioner, for example. If I pay her. 50p a go. Olivia would love to change Imo's nappy but at the age of three I draw the line.

Rachel. I wonder how she's getting on at St Hilda's C of E. With Jeremy. She has to put up with a lot, my big girl. My too-old-for-Disney girl. It wasn't so long ago I was changing her nappy. Her skinny legs with the softest pearly skin. And then there was Thomas.

'Come on, Imo,' I say. 'We've got loos to scrub and food to buy.

Imo starts crying, furious because I'm dragging her away from all the fun. Olivia looks up at me about to leave. Looks at Imo. It dawns on her that maybe she will be missing out on something too but then one of the assistants asks who wants to do some cutting and sticking. She turns away from me, grabbing the assistant's hand with surprising fervour. (Does she realise messy glue is involved?) Then, throwing me a scrap of a smile, she is gone.

As I'm putting the shopping away, the door goes and I know straightaway it's not Steve back from his Monday prayer run. 'Martin?'

He creeps into the kitchen in a most un-Martin-like way. Imo is delighted to see her uncle, banging her highchair like a deranged member of parliament in a frenzy of adoration. 'I'm glad you're here,' he says, ignoring her.

'Oh?'

'I've had a phone call.'

'Jeremy?'

'No. Not Jeremy. Why would it be Jeremy?' Martin waves his arms about, perilously close to a vase of flowers on the dresser. He can see I'm waiting, a clutch of Pot Noodles in my hands. 'It's Dad.'

'Is he alright?'

'He's in hospital.'

'What?' I hold on tighter to the Pot Noodles and feel my face grow hot.

'Nothing serious. A fall.'

'A fall? Where? Has he broken something?'

'His wrist. Stop getting all worked up. We should just go

and see him and then we'll be able to assess the extent of the damage.'

'The extent of the damage?'

I am about to launch into a rant about his legalistic choice of words when Steve comes in, all sweaty and puffed-out, looking like Steve of old back from the gym. But this is the new Steve who combines running with praying for his neighbourhood as he paces the streets of Penge. Steve, the rock, the peace-maker. Steve who listens calmly, telling me to breathe. Who says he will collect the kids from school and give them tea and for us to get going and not worry. It will be alright.

'But what about Olivia?' I think of my daughter waiting to see her mother's face appear at the door of the church hall. 'I have to collect Olivia. She comes out soon and I promised her I'd be there. I can't let her down. She might never believe anything I say to her ever again.'

'We'll all go,' Steve says. 'We'll take both cars. You can say hello and then get straight off. Just give me five minutes to have a quick shower.' And he's gone, leaving a sweaty Steve smell behind him.

Martin gets himself a glass of water and sits down, watching me pack up the changing bag with nappies, wipes, water, spare clothes. He uses his stunning scientific mind, gathering hard evidence, to fathom what I am doing. 'Are we taking her with us?' He looks at his niece, sitting in her highchair, wearing her lunch of mashed banana.

'Of course.'

'In my car?'

'Of course in your car. We've only got the Espace, remember? Steve's going to need it.'

'Can't you leave her with Steve?'

'No.'

'He can give her a bottle, can't he?'

'No.'

Steve *could* give her a bottle. It's about time he gave her a bottle. But I'll decide when we give her a bottle. Not Martin. 'Your precious leather seats can always be wiped clean, can't they?'

He looks at my daughter, doubt all over his face, the way banana clings to hers. 'Well, bring a towel then,' he says, grudgingly. 'A large absorbent one. I've only just had the Saab valeted.'

I resist the temptation to bash Martin repeatedly over the head with a Pot Noodle and concentrate on wiping down Imo as quickly as possible so we can get to see Dad. Poor Dad, down in Worthing all on his own. I wish Mum were here.

'You might want to get changed, Victoria,' he says, offhand as he heads for the back door for a quick smoke.

'Why, what's wrong with this?' My Tesco's economy jeans and old top might not be up to Claudia's fashion standards but Steve's not on plumbing wages anymore. Clothing is not a priority.

'You look like you're entering a wet tshirt competition,' he says. 'You've got two circles around your – '

Martin doesn't get the chance to describe the part of my anatomy that has the two wet circles, because a Pot Noodle leaves my hand and flies through the air, towards the back door – to the amazement of Imo – and whacks my venomous brother in the face, wiping away his snarl and squashing his words. Ha!

Chapter Ten

After the obligatory snail-crawl out of London, we eventually make it into fifth gear, once we get beyond Coulsdon. Martin makes the most of this, as if the very hounds of hell are on our tail. Or even the four horsemen of the Apocalypse. The A23 rushes beneath us and I'm grateful after all for the large absorbent towel on my lap. We don't say much to each other; it's difficult with Jazz FM coming at you from every angle.

'Since when have you liked jazz?'

'I've always liked jazz.' Martin starts boopity-boopitying along to prove a point. Or to wind me up.

At least the discordant notes have the benefit of lulling Imo off to sleep. I'd love to sleep but I can't stop thinking about Dad, what sort of state we're going to find him in. Plus I need to keep an eye on my brother. I need to imaginary-drive the car to prevent us from crashing.

Finally, we cross the Downs and head along the A27. When we see the gothic Lancing College chapel, the end is near. Soon we are entering the windy flatness that is Worthing. We don't even see the sea, the prom, the pier, or any of the town's delights, as we have to get to Dad. I'm really worried now. Feel like spewing all over Martin's highly-polished dashboard.

I used to like hospitals. I liked the idea of people whose job it was to take care of you. Qualified people who'd trained and studied and taken exams and were putting their theories into practice. People who had a vocation, more than a job. Like Steve, I suppose. Would it be easier if Steve were a doctor? A doctor's wife could have her own career without guilt or comment. She could spend her own money without accountability or tithing. She could run her own home without the fear of parishioners dropping round in need of offloading. She could enjoy a certain amount of anonymity.

As we walk down the corridor, following signs for Dad's ward, it comes back to me, the memory, hard and fast like August rain, the ground under my feet unable to take the deluge so that I have to stand still, breathe deep, stay close to the wall as the tide of people wash past me.

The memory. The bunion operation. Mum in her tired old nightie with the button missing. I'd picked her some primroses, from the garden, and tied a ribbon round them. Dad bought her some juicy black grapes from the greengrocer's. Martin got her a car magazine, from under his bed. She smiled when she saw us, a smile of relief, her family all together. If she could, she would have kept us like that, close, tied up with ribbon.

It was a relief for us too. After the biscuit tins. There she was, in a scrubbed-down place, in her nightie, smiling at us. Alive.

The matrons have been replaced with hand gel. I feel sick at the thought of Dad being vulnerable to superbugs and deadly infections, though he must have a tough immune system, living in the near-squalor that is the norm for him. It's even worse since Mum died and it wasn't exactly great before. Perhaps he can come back to Penge? We'd fit him in somehow. Martin will have to leave.

Dad is propped up, looking odd in a single bed. And washed-out. But he's alright, not nearly as bad as we thought. We can tell straightaway, by the way he nods at us, the reserved, no-nonsense half-smile. The way he slips back into being our dad.

'Have a chair, Vicky-Love. The kids been running you ragged, have they?'

'Hi, Dad,' I kiss him on the cheek. Stubbly. The familiar smell of potting sheds overlaid with hospital.

'Alright then, Martin?'

They shake hands, awkwardly, and Martin takes the chair next to me, near Dad's covered feet. He looks like he'd rather be on the operating table than about to embark on small talk duty.

'How's the wrist?' Martin manages to ask.

So we talk about the wrist. The X-rays. The break. The cast. The physio he's going to need. It's a relief. He's alright. And at least while he's here he's had some decent meals inside him. And nurses to fuss around him. He's like Martin in that way – commands the focus of a room. A hospital ward. There's noise and comings and goings and colour and I imagine it's difficult to feel lonely surrounded by all this. Though you can be surrounded by people and be lonelier than ever.

'Grape, Vicky-Love? You're looking peaky.'

'No thanks, Dad. I'm fine. It's you who's looking peaky.'

'I'm anaemic,' Dad announces with pride, fiddling with the cuffs of his grubby pyjamas. 'That's why I got dizzy and fell over my spade. They've put me on iron tablets. Warned me I might get constipated. I'm already constipated. I'm all backed up so I can't go. It's hard enough in communal toilets as it is.'

'The grapes should help with that, Dad. And drink plenty of water. Let me pour you some.' I reach for the jug on the bedside cabinet, trying not to check for dust behind it whilst ignoring Martin's sighs of discomfort. He hates all this talk of bodily functions. We're in a hospital. What does he expect? Debate on Sharia law in Western society?

'Little Imogen's coming on nicely,' Dad says, like she's a

ripening tomato in his greenhouse.

I bob her up and down on my knee, good for the biceps, whilst stealing a glance at Martin, daring him to mention the breastfeeding. He won't go there again. It makes him feel too queasy. 'Grape, Martin?' I ask him sweetly.

He throws me a dirty filthy MRSA of a look. I pop a grape into my mouth, chewing it casually so he knows I don't give a monkey's.

'And how are the other kiddies?' Dad asks.

I tell him about Olivia's first day at playgroup. Hand over the collage she greeted me with when she came out at the end of this morning's session.

'That's... er... nice and colourful,' he says.

'She got a bit carried away with the glue. But she wanted you to have it.'

'Well, then, I'm honoured.' He relinquishes it to the bedside cabinet, wiping his sticky hands across the hospital blanket. 'And how about young Rachel?'

'Young Rachel is growing up.' I can't help sighing when I hear myself say this.

Dad chuckles. 'You've got it all coming then.'

'What?'

'The teenage years.'

'I wasn't that bad, was I?'

Martin snorts.

Dad chuckles some more.

I bob Imo up and down slightly too hard and fast so that she starts grizzling. Martin, meanwhile, swipes Imo's collage off the cabinet and examines it with the patronising, unattached demeanour of an art critic. 'Are you sure you've looked into the educational provision at the playgroup? Are the leaders qualified?'

'Yes, of course. They offer a broad curriculum. Lots of varied activities.'

'So you think cutting and sticking from the Argos catalogue

is going to spark Olivia's creativity?'

I snatch the picture back off him and examine it more closely. Under the lumps of glue I can see a montage of sovereign rings and camping equipment mixed in with Bratz dolls and dog baskets. But I won't let him take the moral high ground. I know more about early years' education than he ever will. 'Cutting and sticking is excellent for developing her fine motor skills.'

Martin ignores me, reads the *Top Gear* magazine he bought to go with my grapes. I can tell by the way he emits a dog-sigh every few seconds that he's wondering why he missed the afternoon off work. He obviously believes I could have managed on my own, that reports on Dad's fall have been greatly exaggerated. As if my maternity leave is not as important as his floundering career. Maybe he and Jeremy Clarkson were separated at birth... Before I can beat him about the head with his wretched magazine, a nurse in creaky Crocs joins our happy family group and takes Dad's blood pressure. She should try taking mine.

'What a bonny baby.' She squishes one of Imo's thighs. I wish people wouldn't do that. 'What have you been feeding her?'

'Pot Noodles,' Martin says, deadpan, sizing up the nurse's vital statistics.

Her eyes widen for a second then she notices Martin and goes all silly, tittering in that annoying way my school friends used to do whenever they encountered him. She finishes her job, still giggling, and then sashays off.

'And how about Jeremy? You never told me about him. How's my grandson?' Dad blunders on.

'He's fine,' says Martin. The liar.

Dad doesn't pursue this. Switches on *Neighbours*. Martin's got away with it. And I'm finding it suffocating in here.

'Actually Dad, we ought to be getting off now,' I start gathering my stuff together. 'Leave you with your programme.

I'll try and get down at the weekend. It sounds like you'll be home by then. I can get you some shopping. Make sure you're settled back in alright.'

'Can't you stay a bit longer?' He looks disappointed, older suddenly, vulnerable. Exactly what's been worrying me: that he won't be able to take care of himself.

'Sorry, Dad. We've got to get back to the kids. It's Jeremy's first day at the new school.'

'New school?' He zaps off *Neighbours* and transfers his attention to Martin.

Whoops.

'Didn't I mention that?' Martin asks casually, studying a photo of a car even he will never be able to afford.

'You mean he's left Dulwich? Oh dear, I am sorry about that.' Dad is on the verge of crying, which makes me feel weepy only I'm too angry for tears. Angry with my dumbo brother. So what do I do? I pat Dad's hand.

'I was so proud of my grandson going to Dulwich,' he says, quietly.

There's a pause. No-one is quite sure how to respond to this. Imo lolls her head from side to side in her bucket, looking from face to face, wondering what's going on. Then Dad pulls himself together, shuffling upright in bed, fixing Martin with his watery eyes before breaking the silence: 'Has he been expelled?'

'No, of course he hasn't been expelled.' Martin flaps the magazine shut. 'Why would you think he's been expelled?'

'Well, you were nearly expelled that time. Or had you forgotten?'

It's funny, I had forgotten. But now it's coming back to me: the fireworks, the park, the girls from the Grammar.

'It wasn't working.' Martin tries to sound like this isn't the big deal Dad's making it out to be. 'It wasn't the best place for him. He was turning into a spoiled brat.'

'I'm not sure you can blame that on the school,' Dad says,

watery eyes all dried up.

Martin is bright red in the face. He's the one who needs the blood pressure check now.

Dad changes tack again, moves back from assertive to defenceless. 'I thought you'd be able to stay until I had my tea. Can't Claudia manage till you get back?'

'Claudia's in LA,' Martin mumbles.

'LA?'

'Los Angeles.'

'I know what LA stands for thank you, Vicky-Love. I was wondering why it is Martin hasn't mentioned the fact his wife is in LA. Is she on holiday?'

'She's working.' Martin says this under his breath, as if he's swearing or talking about something embarrassing. Dad has never really understood that Claudia doesn't just work for the money. That she needs to work the same way I need to clean and he needs to grow tomatoes.

'Well, that's a strange thing.' Dad rubs his head, like he's checking he's still got some hair left. 'Sending Jeremy to Rachel's school. In Penge. And Claudia going to America. Is there anything else I should know?'

Martin stares at me, willing me to keep my mouth shut. One looks says so much. Time to make myself scarce. 'I'll find somewhere quiet to feed Imo while you fill in Dad on what's been happening.' I plonk Imo in her bucket and bend down to Martin's ear. 'Otherwise,' I whisper into it, 'I will.'

Martin staggers across the forecourt of the petrol station towards the car, loaded down with Coke, crisps, sweets and an air freshener. He chucks the junk food in my lap and proceeds to hang up the smelly-tree-thing from the mirror so his Saab looks like a minicab. And now the banana has finally worked its magic, it smells like a mini cab, after a long Saturday night.

He leans across to retrieve some aftershave from the glove compartment. Squirts it all around so we can't breathe at all.

It's a shame he doesn't worry about the cleanliness of my house as much as he cares about the cleanliness of his car.

'I thought aftershave aggravated your eczema?'

'Jeremy gave it to me for father's day. I couldn't say anything. So I keep it in the car. For emergencies.'

I'm not sure I can follow Martin's logic. It's been a long day. But it makes me think of Jeremy.

'I hope he's alright,' I say.

'So do I.' Martin must be tired too. For a second there, he sounded like he cared.

When we get home we walk into the front room to discover we were right to worry. Jeremy has been crying. There are scrunched-up damp tissues all over the new leather sofa, the TV has been muted and Steve looks exhausted, like he always does after a marathon counselling session, the twinkle absent from his eyes, his skin grey to match his hair. But it is Jeremy who is really suffering. Jeremy has had a horrible day, plunged in at the deep end of change. Too much change in one go. He is drowning.

I gather up the tissues while Martin takes him into the back room in an attempt to get him to bed.

Steve shrugs helplessly, lost for once, as we listen to our nephew cry. I wish I could hear what Martin has to say to his son but the only words I catch are 'zed-bed' and an adjective that isn't suitable for ten-year-old ears.

But that's not all. Claudia has phoned and Jeremy has told her everything. She is catching the next flight home. This might work out after all.

Thoughts for the Day: Why is Dad anaemic? Is there some underlying problem he has not told me about? What is the best way to clean a leather sofa?

Chapter Eleven: Friday January 11th

Claudia did not catch the next flight home. Instead I managed to speak to her and persuade her to finish the assignment. We'd sort things out at the weekend. Jeremy's place at the prep school would still be there if he wanted to go back. *Of course he'll want to go back,* she had said. *He'll never survive at that grotty school.* At which point I felt myself bristling and sticking up for that grotty school which is good enough for my children and all the other children living down our street. I was beginning to feel some sympathy for Martin's cause. Shock, horror.

It was only when I put the phone down that I realised I could have let Claudia get on that plane and then Jeremy and his cello would have been out of my hair. Then it would only be Martin to get rid of.

Olivia does not go to playgroup on a Friday. This is her favourite day. On a Friday she comes to St Hilda's and helps me with the cleaning. Steve is working on this Sunday's sermon at the kitchen table but he said he would keep an eye on Imo who is sound asleep in her cot. I make sure he can hear the baby monitor and tell him to bring her to the church if she wakes for milk.

'She'll be alright till you get back. You can normally do it in under two hours. Can't you?' He tries not to betray the anxiety

I know he's feeling at the prospect of lugging an inconsolable hungry baby down to the church. I know he thinks she'd be fine on the bottle but he wouldn't tell me that. Unlike Martin.

It's peaceful kneeling in the nave, polishing the pew ends, the brass umbrella stands. The smell of Brasso. The ache of elbow grease. My middle daughter absorbed in wiping the floor grills with one of Steve's old tshirts. I've missed her this week. She's going out into the world. Rachel has already gone. The gap that's been there for six years has suddenly got bigger. Blacker. He comes back to me. His small perfect face. I want to lie down on the cold stone floor and weep for him. But I can't do that. I am still a mother. To the big girl at school. To the baby at home. To the little girl beside me who never even knew him though she has seen the photos. The handprints. The headstone in the churchyard. I reach for my hanky instead.

'It's dusty in here, isn't it?' Olivia is kneeling up, like a cherub, smiling at me in her simple way. 'Not everybody cleans as good as you and me, do they Mummy?'

'No, darling, they don't all clean as *well* as us. You're quite right.' I take in her young, eager face. Her cheeks shiny from exertion. Her front tooth discoloured from an accident involving the pushchair and the front step. One day that tooth will wobble and fall out and be put to rest inside the matchbox, in the biscuit tin, in the wardrobe. She will grow up.

'It's all sparkly, Mummy, look,' she indicates St Hilda's with her little hand. She'd make a good estate agent. She's good at spin.

And actually it does look at its best. Light pushes its way in through the stained glass of St Hilda's dress and spreads itself over the swept floor. The edge is rubbed off my grief and I can let myself feel the quiet contentment of a job well done. A moment shared with my daughter. This daughter, here and now.

'Shall we go to the cake shop on the way home and get

something for tea?'

'I'd rather have a Pot Noodle, Mummy.'

While I am slicing up the Madeira cake for Olivia and Imo, the front door bangs open and someone falls through it. Jeremy. He crashes his way down the hall to the kitchen, barges straight past me and the girls and is out the back door heading for the shed before I can ask how was school.

Steve comes in a few seconds later, harassed, a grumpy Rachel in tow.

'What's up, Rach?' I ask. 'It's Friday. You should be smiling.'

'Smiling?' she grunts, sending her bag skidding across the table so it knocks Olivia's pencil pot over. 'What've I got to smile about?' Then she kicks off her shoes, one of them skimming the fluffy hair on Imo's still-frighteningly fragile head.

'Watchit, young lady,' I say. 'I think you'd better cool off in your room for a bit.'

'My room?' she huffs. 'That's a joke. How can it be my room when I have to share it with Little Miss Duster?'

'Who's Little Miss Duster?' asks Olivia, busy collecting up her scattered pencils and rearranging them in the pot. 'Is she coming to stay as well?'

'Never mind, Olivia,' says Steve. 'It's just Rachel trying to be funny. You get on with your colouring.'

Olivia gets back to her book, a present from Amanda for starting playgroup. Scenes from the Bible. I'm not sure of the scriptural accuracy of a purple and pink striped ark but at least it's keeping her amused. At least it's not *The Jeremy Kyle Show* or *QVC*.

Meanwhile, Rachel spies the cake. 'Can I have a piece?' she asks, tentative, mellowing.

I know what Steve would say. Steve would say, 'Stick to your guns and send her to her room. Now is not the time for cake.' But I beat him to it, in a shiny-shoes moment. 'Alright, but you'd better wash your hands. They look like they've been dipped in oil.'

'Great,' she says, which is such a positive word I want to hug her. But I have to catch her off-guard for a hug these days.

'Do I get cake as well?' Steve asks.

'Of course,' I smile sweetly before adding: 'If you don't mind putting on more weight.'

He looks at me, looks at his stomach – the one that used to be taut and lean and lovely. 'Best not then,' he sighs. 'I've got to get round to Desmond's anyway. There's an Alpha meeting.'

'And what about Jeremy? What was all the sulking for?'

'Apparently he fancies Jessica Talbot. Rachel told him he was embarrassing.'

'Fancying? At his age?'

Steve shrugs his shoulders as if it's quite normal. The only person I fancied at that age was Starsky. And he wasn't real.

I'm trying to put my thoughts into words but I'm not quick enough. Steve has kissed Olivia and Imo and dashed off again. Another call-out. Around the clock. Only he can't charge extra these days. He does it for a pittance. He does it for love.

Back in the shed, Jeremy is scoffing a packet of Monster Munch. He has rigged up some Christmas lights that he must have swiped before I put the decorations back up in the loft, tidied away alongside the plumbing manuals and teaching resources.

'You've got it all nice in here,' I say, bright and breezy.

'I've got to have somewhere of my own.'

'Of course you do. It must be hard camping out on the zed-bed. You must miss your bedroom.'

'I miss my mum.' He sounds younger than Olivia when he says this. And I'm so angry with Martin and Claudia for doing this to their child. Their son.

'Oh, Jeremy. She'll be back in a couple of days.'

'I want to go home now.' Tears slide down his cheeks – cheeks like Imo's, hamster-like – and I want to hug him too but I've never done that before. He's never been a huggable boy. At least Rachel was huggable when she was little and still is, in weak moments. Martin and Claudia should have spent more time with him. Nurtured him. Hugged him. And I feel bad, guilty, that I can't just do it for them. I pat his hand instead. I even manage to leave my hand on top of his for a bit without too much awkwardness. He is my nephew after all. But I can't shake away the knowledge that he is Martin's son. I have never hugged Martin in my life.

'Come back in the house when you're ready. There's cake.'

'Could you bring me out a piece, Auntie Vicky?'

I am about to tell him to come and get it himself when I stop. The least I can do is bring the poor boy a piece of cake.

But I'm not happy about the situation. I shall have strong words with Martin tonight. He must take Jeremy back to his mother on her return on Sunday. And as for Martin, he's going to have to make it up to Claudia or find somewhere else to live. Ha!

Several hours later, when the kids are fed and bathed and pyjamaed and absorbed in *Coronation Street*, Martin finally returns home. He enters the living room with a banana box full of papers and his laptop, which he dumps in the middle of the room, the children moaning at him to move away from the telly. I'm not going to ask him what's taken him so long, or what the papers are for.

'Research,' he says, anyway, moving reluctantly to one side. As if I care about his research. He thinks he's someone important. We're all someone important according to Steve. Each one of us unique and special to God. I don't feel particularly special or unique with tea tree hairspray in one hand and a nit comb in the other, knowing there are mothers all over South London in a very similar position.

'Have you got nits, Vicky-Love?'

'No-one has in this house, I make sure of that... though I haven't checked your fine head of hair. Or that beard.'

Martin starts scratching his head. Then, realising what he's doing, he stoops to pick up his 'research' and crashes out of the room. I listen to him pinball down the hall to the kitchen, to the echo of his loaded box as he dumps it on the kitchen table, recently cleared and wiped down ready for breakfast tomorrow. Then the fridge door. The familiar clank and fizz that announces Martin's return home. Martin making himself at home. My home.

I need to talk to him.

But first Imo needs her bedtime feed. She's holding up her Popeye arms to me from her place on Rachel's lap and grizzling in that way of hers that I can't ignore. I wish Steve were here to help out but he's got a confirmation class.

'Rach, can you keep an eye on Olivia, while I sort out the baby?'

Rachel nods, happy to get her lap back.

Jeremy sings along to the adverts.

Olivia says: 'I don't need looking after, Mummy. I'm three-years-old and I go to school now.'

'No, Olivia, you go to *pre*-school,' says Rachel.

Olivia starts to cry. Then so does Imo. I have to choose Imo. I know how to stop her crying. Olivia will pull herself together in a minute. Once *Coronation Street* comes back on.

Half an hour later and there are no children crying. The two little ones are tucked up in bed; the two bigger ones lost in the next instalment of *Coronation Street*. I can tackle Martin with strong words.

Martin is drinking beer at the kitchen table, reading through a sheaf of paper, randomly highlighting stuff, in an irritatingly intense fashion. He ignores me as I set up the ironing board.

Ironing will help me focus and avoid eye contact with him.

'We need to talk.'

'Do we?'

'Yes, Martin.'

'Do we have to do it now? I'm rather busy.'

'Busy? You don't know the meaning of the word busy.' I grab an item of clothing from the washing basket to illustrate my point.

He puts down his pen and scrutinises me the way he must do his students. Professor Martin Bumface. 'Well, of course I'm not as busy as *you*, Vicky-Love. Everyone knows you epitomise Busy,' he smirks at this little gem of his, 'but have you ever thought that you might be able to organise things slightly better? Rope in some of those parishioners?'

'To look after *your* child?'

He doesn't reply to this, considering his comeback, unless he's actually listening to me for once. Either way, we're both silent as he gets up to help himself to another beer from my fridge. He doesn't offer me anything, just leans against the fridge door, knocking off a collection of magnets and pictures, and cracks open the can. (*Cans, Vicky-Love? Haven't bottled beers made it to Penge?*)

I carry on, forcing myself to ignore the mess he's created on my floor, tackling the mountainous pile of Daz-white clothes (though not as Daz-white as I would like, seeing as Martin has forbade me to use biological washing powder which aggravates his eczema).

'Are you worried about Dad?' he asks eventually. 'Is that what this is all about?'

'Of course I'm worried about Dad, Martin, but that's not what this is all about, no. It's – '

'Olivia starting playgroup? The works of art?' He looks at his feet, at the latest collage. 'I suppose you've examined this one?'

'No. It's – ' Actually I haven't.

He plucks it off the floor and hands it over.

It's crinkled with dried glue and half of last week's *Heat* magazine. Some celebrity is pregnant again. 'Who on earth are these people?'

'I have no idea. But I know a woman who does.' He takes a double slug of beer and a wave of sadness washes away his haughtiness. He slumps back down on his chair at the kitchen table, head in his hands. He starts scratching.

'Nits?' I ask sweetly.

'Eczema,' he snaps. A drift of dead skin flutters towards the table. My table.

Eczema. How many times have I heard that excuse over the years. *Martin can't do the washing-up, Vicky-Love. You know how it gets him all itchy. Run down the chemists, Vicky would you and pick up Martin's prescription. He's all agitated, poor lamb.* I've always resented him for it. Thought it was all one big con but looking at him now I can see the patches on the back of his hands. Cracks across his knuckles. Dried blood. I hadn't noticed. I try to quash a feeling of guilt. I haven't got enough energy to spend any on him.

'She's back on Sunday.' I hear a note of sympathy in my voice. 'Maybe you'll be able to sort things out then.'

So much for strong words. I pick up the iron again. The backwards and forwards motion is soothing.

'So what was it you wanted to talk about?'

'Oh... nothing. Except... well, do you think we should get rid of the TV?'

'The TV?' He's thrown for a moment. Then he ponders my suggestion. 'Are you that brave?'

'No, I'm not that brave.'

'And one more thing, Victoria.'

'What?'

'Isn't that beyond the call of duty?' He points at the object in my hands, ironed to perfection.

And I realise with horror that I am holding his underpants.

Thoughts for the Day: Why didn't I just throw the nit comb at him and be done with it?

January 28th 1978

Mr Harris doesn't like me because I am Martin's sister. It is so unfair. He always says, 'Victoria Wright. Don't think you can get away with it like your brother.'

Mr Harris likes Alice. Alice is my best friend. She has a private tutor because her parents think education is really important. My parents think gardening is really important. Dad always wanted to be a gardener ever since he was taken to Kew Gardens as a little boy by his grandmother. So that's what he does. That's what he is. A gardener. He would have liked to be a gardener at Kew but actually he only does the gardens of Catford. Though he has a couple of big gardens out in Kent. He takes Mum along to help with those ones. She loves gardening as much as he does. Only Mum doesn't get paid for it. Dad just buys her a fish and chip lunch. She spends all her time out in our garden when she's not helping Dad. When she should be cleaning the kitchen floor.

Alice's mum has a cleaner. Alice's mum does the ironing. Alice's dad washes his car on a Saturday morning. Alice will go to a good school. I will go to the dump.

Chapter Twelve: *Saturday January 12th*

Steve's day off and we are spending it in Worthing. Steve, Rachel and Imo are settled with Dad watching the final scores while Olivia and I are upstairs in Dad's bedroom. She is dusting Mum's knick-knacks on the dressing table and windowsill while I sort through Dad's smalls. There's no way I'm ironing these. Too much even for me. Still, it's satisfying putting things in order. I miss Mum but if she were here I'd be forbidden to help out. *We like things how they are, dear. Stop fussing.*

Olivia, job done, sits tidily on the bed and watches me folding and smoothing. 'Are you going to die, Mummy?' she asks cheerfully.

'Oh... well... not for a long time, darling, don't worry.' Though as each day goes by with Martin in my house, a year is most probably slashed off my life expectancy.

'Good,' she says. 'Cos I don't think I could do all this on my own.' She surveys the room, shaking her head at Granddad's mess.

Suddenly the room is depressing. All Mum's trinkets untouched since she died. The Isle of Wight sand layered in a glass tube. The china pomander that still smells of old rose petals. A three legged china cat. A brass lady that doubles up as a bell. All these knick-knacks that I used to play with when I was little, that Olivia has spent the last thirty minutes playing with as she dusts. It's like Mum's still here, stuck in the cupboard or hiding under the bed. Until now, Dad has forbidden me from coming in here too. But he didn't bother arguing today. Now he's less mobile he can't exactly chase me up the stairs. Why they didn't buy a bungalow when they moved down here is anyone's guess. There's plenty to choose from. But they went for a terrace house almost identical to the one they left.

All the bungalows are out of town. We want to be nearer the centre of things, Dad insisted.

So why leave London?

London hasn't got the sea.

It's got the Thames.

Now you're just being daft, Vicky-Love.

Mum didn't have much to say on the subject. *It's nice and flat,* was all she could come up with. Poor Mum. So flat they couldn't even see the sea from their house despite being only a couple of streets away from the prom.

I look at Olivia, searching for my mum in her. All that shared DNA. I wish they could have shared some time together. Time is what matters.

'Let's go and get a drink, darling. This is thirsty work.'

Olivia nods and reaches for my hand. We go down the narrow staircase, flicking on lights as no-one has bothered downstairs. They are all in the lounge, sitting in the gloom, the hushed stillness of 4.45. I switch on the overhead light and they turn to me, blinking like moles.

'I've put clean sheets on your bed, Dad,' I announce.

'Ssh,' he says, the Millwall score not in yet.

I go on, regardless. 'And Olivia's cleaned the bath. But you ought to consider putting in one of those walk-in showers. I don't want you slipping and breaking something else.'

'Ssshh,' more aggressive this time.

'Yeah, ssshh,' Rachel adds her two-penn'orth, bolstered by her position, between father and grandfather on the sofa.

'Yeeess!!' Dad's suddenly on his feet but has to flop straight back down, his weakness taking him by surprise. A cloud of dust billows out of the sofa on impact.

'Dad, honestly. Be careful.'

'Stop fussing,' he says, swiping his hand at me. 'I'm fine.'

Steve can see I'm almost hyperventilating so he suggests I sit down with them. I avoid the dustbowl of the sofa and choose the least mucky chair, near Imo who is prostrate on her blanket, shielded from the tacky carpet.

Finally, the football over, Dad turns his attention to me. 'I like that bath,' he says. 'There's nothing wrong with it.'

So he was listening.

'It's very deep, Dad. And it doesn't even have handrails. I don't know how you manage.'

Well, I do know. Dad doesn't exactly bathe regularly. He's been using the bath for propagating his seeds judging by the amount of soil Olivia had to sweep out of it.

'And where's our Jeremy today?' Dad deftly changes the subject.

'With Martin.'

'Not Claudia?'

'She's not home till tomorrow.'

'And will they move back in with her?'

'I hope so. Believe me, Dad, I hope so.'

'Been getting on your nerves has he, your brother?'

'What do you think?'

Dad chuckles and it's so nice to hear him laugh that I join in though it's not at all funny.

'Shall I send Steve to the fish and chip shop for tea?'

'Oh you don't need to worry about me, Vicky-Love. I'm alright. You gave me a grand lunch. A whole field of broccoli.'

'But you need to eat a proper tea as well. You're anaemic.'

'That's all in hand.'

At that moment the doorbell rings. Steve gets up to answer it. I'm still looking at Dad, wondering what's going on, why he's blushing the colour of one of his ripened tomatoes, when in walks a woman. A woman of a certain age. Older than me but quite, quite younger than Dad.

'This is Pat,' he says. 'We met through the library.'

Pat doesn't look like the sort of woman you'd meet through the library. She looks like the sort of woman you'd be accosted by down a dark alley. She has a tattoo. And an ankle bracelet. And her skirt's just a bit – well, a lot – on the short side. No wonder Dad is blushing. And to think of the fuss he kicked up when I got my ears pierced aged sixteen.

'I answered her advert.'

This gets worse.

'She wanted to meet you so I said she should pop over. She's my home help.'

Home help. Good. That's good. She might not exactly look like a home help but you shouldn't judge by appearances. And Dad's home needs all the help it can get.

'I've brought you some liquorice, Jim. Thought it might get things moving.' She hands Dad a paper bag with black sticks poking out the top. 'Get your laughing gear around that.'

'Ta very much, Pat,' says Dad. 'Sit yourself down.'

Pat sits herself down on the pouffe. 'What a bonny baby,' she says. 'May I?' And she hefts Imo off her blanket on the floor where she has been trying, unsuccessfully, to roll over. While she does This Little Piggy, Olivia squats down next to Pat, mesmerised by her stilettos. Pat kicks them off. 'You want to try them on?'

Despite the dubious appearance of Pat, Olivia tries them on and struts up and down the room like she's at an American beauty pageant.

Even Rachel is transfixed. 'What's that picture on your arm?'

'Oh, that old thing.' Pat pushes up her sleeve for a clearer inspection; a dolphin, caught in a net of sun-damaged skin. 'I got it done when I was a young girl. Had a bit too much to drink,' she shrieks with guttural laughter.

'When I have too much to drink I wet myself,' Olivia announces once the laughter has subsided. 'It's 'gusting. It goes all cold down my leg and into my shoes. But I don't do that anymore. I am three-years-old and I go to school.'

'*Pre*-school,' Rachel corrects.

'Come on, girls,' Steve cajoles, jumping up, all jolly, clapping his hands like a mad vicar. 'How about a five-minute run around the garden before we get back in the car?'

'Mind the beds,' Dad shouts after them.

Yes, the beds. The beautiful flowerbeds. Not a weed in the garden but dirty dishes in the sink and scum in the bath. That's the way it's always been. And I can't see things improving with the addition of Pat. Not with those nails.

On the journey back, the children sleep, three girls in a row, three peas in a pod. A tug at my heart. A quickening in my stomach. Where has he gone?

Steve is silent, not so much concentrating on the roads, as on his sermon. I can see him preaching internally, tomorrow's expressions already across his face. That leaves me with my own thoughts. So I turn them forwards, to the evening ahead: tea, chores, a bit of telly. A slushy film would be good; anything to stop me worrying about leaving Dad with that woman. Without me. Without Mum. Anything to stop me thinking about my baby boy. My Thomas.

Martin and Jeremy are playing chess at the kitchen table, listening to something classical when Steve and I struggle in with our three hungry, grumpy children.

'How's Dad?' Martin swipes Jeremy's bishop, not bothering to ask if we need a hand. A cup of tea. Anything. Though I think I can detect a note of interest in there somewhere despite the fact he doesn't lift his eyes from the chequered board.

I tell him all about Dad, all about Pat, not sparing any

detail, while I jig a grotty Imo up and down. She's flushed and grabbing at her ear. Teething. Time for a feed and bed but Martin has other ideas.

'I've booked a table at that dodgy-looking Italian round the corner,' he says. 'By way of a thank you for having us,' he adds, so quietly that perhaps I'm imagining it.

'You're planning on leaving tomorrow as well then?' I don't bother keeping the surprise out of my voice.

'Course,' he says. 'Why not?' And he moves his queen with a flourish of his big fat hand, without noticing the quiver of his son's lower lip. 'Check mate.'

There's no way Claudia's going to take him back that easily. She'd be mad. Still, Martin's blind faith means we have to forgo our usual Saturday night routine. I hope we don't regret this. Sunday is Steve's most important day – not that he doesn't work hard every other day of the week, like people think. We all need an early night but I shouldn't throw Martin's offer back in his face. And, I have to say, a nice bowl of spaghetti would go down a treat. And a glass of Chianti. Maybe some garlic bread. We'll have to skip pudding obviously; it'll be way past the kids' bedtime, which has already come and gone. Maybe they do take-out. If only Imo would stop crying. Where's the Calpol? The Bonjela? The teething ring? Anything but my nipples? The prospect of teeth makes me want to cry too.

Imo doesn't stop crying. We have to endure the noise throughout our starters. People are beginning to stare. The waiters – astonishingly stereotypical baby-loving Mafia types – keep coming up to her and patting her on the head which makes matters even worse. In the end it's Martin that stops the crying. He takes a breadstick out of one of those plastic packets and says: 'Here, Imogen, get your laughing gear around that.' She looks at her uncle, quiet suddenly, shocked at being noticed by him. Then she reaches out her chubby little hand and grasps the breadstick. After a moment of examination she manages to aim the stick at her mouth. Then with an after-shudder, she begins to chew on it, grinding her gums, with a satisfied sigh.

We finish the rest of the meal with no crying. The children love their pizzas, my spaghetti is divine. A family meal out with no fuss from the children. It should be bliss. But there is a horrible taste in my mouth. Martin. What made him suddenly do that? He's crap with babies. How come he's the one that managed to stop her crying? I should love him for it. But I don't – Martin yet again interfering. Yet again doing better than me.

Claudia has to take him back tomorrow.

Thoughts for the Day: Do not judge others. But how can a woman like Pat help Dad? How can a man like Martin know what's best for my baby? Do moles blink?

Chapter Thirteen: Sunday January 13th

Jessica Talbot, Rachel's best friend and the girl next door, must reciprocate Jeremy's feelings. Why else would she follow us to church? Jessica Talbot never comes to church, being scathing of anything that doesn't involve football. She only ever enters St Hilda's for the school Christmas concert, despite me often asking her on a Sunday morning, hoping Rachel might think church cool if Jessica Talbot wanted to come along too. Of course whenever I mention church to any of Rachel's friends she gets the hump. And I understand. It's embarrassing for her. If Steve had always been a vicar it might be easier. But Rachel can clearly remember the day, way back in Year Two, when Steve met her at the classroom door at the end of the day and was collared by Mrs Hughes.

Could you take a look at my boiler? she asked. *The pilot light keeps going out.*

And Steve, who would normally have fit her in, being well-acquainted with the lot of a teacher, said: *I'm sorry, Mrs Hughes but I'm not a plumber anymore.*

Have you been struck off or something? she half-joked.

No, he said. *The Corgi inspector has always been happy with my work.*

So why the change?

I'm training to be a curate. I've got a calling. And Steve scribbled out a name and number, a bloke he knew from a

City and Guild's course. (Craig was doing well out of Steve's calling.) *He'll look after your boiler. But if you want help with your soul, then I'm your man.*

Mrs Hughes didn't look so sure. Rachel was left feeling subdued. Her dad had always come to her rescue. Now it was less certain what he actually did. It was that hazy area of God where people blushed or coughed or sometimes got inexplicably angry at the mention of His name. Mrs Hughes blushed and coughed but thankfully didn't get angry as that would have been unprofessional.

So yes, I do sympathise with Rachel. To have to admit to your friends, to every adult that ever asks you, that your dad's 'got God' and that you're expected to go to church every Sunday – not just to get into the school – can create a few problems. Rachel still maintains it caused less of a stir when Jessica's dad, Bob next door, found a Thai bride on the internet.

The Thai bride is actually a big improvement on the first Mrs Talbot, who went to Lanzarote for a friend's hen do and did a Shirley Valentine. She sent for her stuff – her clothes, shoes, handbags, make-up – but not for her daughter, believing dubiously that she'd be better off with Bob.

Tamarine, the Thai bride, is not as young as the stereotype would suggest. She knows exactly what she is doing, has the measure of Bob and seems to enjoy being his wife. He must have hidden talents. Very well hidden talents. Tamarine's talents are more obvious. She keeps the house clean and even sweeps the street outside which is something you don't see these days. And the smell of cooking that finds its way into our house is quite enticing. I would say Bob Talbot has landed on his feet. As has Jessica, who now has clean clothes and help with her homework.

Tamarine told me that although she herself is a Buddhist, her country is tolerant of other religions and therefore she would be happy for Jessica to come to our church anytime.

Bob would be happy for Jessica to be anywhere other than in his back garden kicking a ball against the house.

So this week, during the embarrassing song, Jessica, in her Crystal Palace away kit, joins in with the actions. 'This is cool,' I hear her mutter to Rachel and Jeremy. 'Normally Sundays are *sooo* boring. I have to wait for Dad and Tamarine to get up and then we like go shopping.'

'We don't go shopping on a Sunday,' sparks up Olivia. 'Unless we run out of milk.'

'Lucky you,' says Jessica.

Olivia beams, Jeremy drools, and Rachel tries not to smile at the triumph of bringing a friend into her world and it not backfiring.

And there is Steve, up at the front, singing along to 'Shine, Jesus, shine' and I envy him. For his lack of worrying. He says there's no point in worrying. Worrying changes nothing. Only hope can do that. And faith. And love. But most of all love.

But it's alright for Steve. Steve has thick skin and inner strength, a tough combination to crack. I, on the other hand, am like an egg. Knock me and I am likely to end up all over the floor, broken, in a hideous mess.

After the usual – to-ings and fro-ings and trying to keep the children quiet and smiling and small talk and roasting parsnips and tea and hand-patting – Steve and I are alone again in the kitchen. He used to catch up on the odd jobs. I used to do my preparation. Schemes of work and lesson plans. Not anymore.

The doorbell goes. Claudia. Steve looks at me and I'm pretty sure I catch a hint of worry as he gets up to answer. I check my list. Jeremy's clothes are washed, ironed and packed, waiting in the hall along with his cello (hallelujah!).

'Darling!'

I get to the hall in time to see Claudia embracing her son. He lets his mother kiss him, both of them slightly awkward, but there is relief there too. Things may finally be getting back to normal. Normal? Can I let myself dare to hope Martin may be welcomed back home?

Martin appears out of the shadows and smiles feebly at his wife.

'Oh, hello,' she says, as if she'd forgotten he'd be here which of course she hasn't, because I can see she has put on her going-out face. Cover-girl eyes and killer-red lips.

'Good trip?' he asks, impersonating someone who cares about his wife's career. But I can tell he's taking her in. The new shoes, the power suit. The just-stepped-out-of-a-salon hair.

'Very profitable yes, thank you.' Claudia has morphed into another woman. A woman of power and strength and even more drop-dead beauty than before, all fired up, hurrying Jeremy along. 'Must get going. Cab's waiting.'

Martin follows his family outside, hands in pockets in forced nonchalance but he's fooling no-one. We troop after my brother, standing in a huddle as he watches – a pained expression on his bearded face – the cabbie wedge the very expensive cello into the boot of a battered Astra. 'Where's the car?' Martin asks his wife.

'I was too tired to drive.'

'It is safe around here you know. My Saab's still got all four tyres.'

'Of course.' She looks unconvinced, horrified in fact, her power and strength evaporating in the toxic Penge air. As if our street was in Kabul or somewhere. She's probably wearing a bullet-proof vest under her Karen Millen suit.

'I could've dropped him back if you were worried, I mean tired,' Martin goes on.

'And let you worm your way back in?'

'Would I have succeeded?'

'I wasn't prepared to risk it.'

'So there's a chance then?'

'Don't sound desperate, Martin. It doesn't suit you.' Claudia turns away from him and focuses her attention back on her son. 'Jeremy, say goodbye to your father.'

'Can't he come too?' Jeremy begs, as if Martin's a Labrador.

'You can see him during the week,' she says, fastidiously ignoring the Labrador who's begging for crumbs. Any crumbs. 'Wednesday would be good. I've got a late meeting in town. He can pick you up from school. Dulwich, that is. It's all sorted out. I cleared up the confusion with them today.'

Then, before anyone can answer this, she flips her attention to me. 'Thanks Vicky. You've been an angel.'

You don't know the half of it, I want to say but I am trying to be gracious.

'And thanks Steve. You really are a holy man,' she kisses him. He blushes.

And suddenly we are watching the cab retreat down the street, a dirty emission pluming out of the exhaust, which appears to be held in place with masking tape. Martin is watching his family leave him behind. For a moment he looks on the verge of crying like a baby. But then he turns away and goes inside, telling me to get a life. Me? What a cheek! I have a life. Maybe not the one I was expecting but it looks a darn sight more appealing than his right now.

The evening is very, very quiet. The house quieter still. Even Martin can't fill it with his noise. He has shut himself in the back room. He'll be grateful for that zed-bed, you mark my words. Meanwhile I'm grateful for our marriage bed with the clean sheets. For the chirpy snoring so close to my ear. I'm grateful that we've stuck with it, me and Steve, even though we're different people to the ones who stood in Lewisham register office, pledging our troths. Even though there have been times – bad times, serious times – when I've wanted to go out into the garden, walk across those stepping stones, climb over the fence and up onto the railway cutting and hurl myself under the 10.26 to London Bridge.

Marriage. That's one thing I'll do better at than Martin. Ha!

Thoughts for the Day: Why aren't I the sort of woman who makes men blush?

Chapter Fourteen: *Monday January 14th*

Steve has encouraged me to take Imo to the parent and toddler group at St Hilda's this afternoon. Olivia has already been to pre-school there this morning and has the collage of Katie Price and Peter Andre to prove it. I don't really want to go back but Steve said it would do me good, as if I'm ill or something.

Olivia, the big girl for once, has a congregation of smaller children about her, while Imo, still trying to roll over, has managed to wedge herself under the baby gym. As I am prising her free, a familiar voice assaults me.

'Vicky! How lovely to see you.' It's Amanda, swooping down on us, scarves swishing, beads jangling. 'I was wondering when you'd make it down here to see us with your tots.' She looks at my tots, one with her entourage, the other with her Beryl Cook thighs. 'I hear Olivia is establishing herself at playgroup.'

'She seems to have found her feet,' I say, cagily.

We look at Olivia's feet, encased in her plastic Cinderella shoes. She has now seated a group of toddlers on a mat and is reading *Where's Spot?* to them in a sing-song teacher voice, slapping their wrists if they try and lift the flaps.

'She can certainly command an audience,' Amanda observes. 'Following in her father's footsteps.'

I get a picture – a vision – of Olivia as a grown woman, in

a dog collar, standing in the pulpit, delivering a sermon on tidiness. Even Jesus folded his grave clothes before leaving the tomb, I hear her say. And the angels who attended him were shining white.

'Vicky? Are you alright, dear? You look a little peaky.'

Maybe anaemia's catching. Maybe I need a stint in hospital, being looked after, being cared for. Three meals a day. But no. I'd never sleep. Not in the knowledge there were deadly germs all around me, waiting to pounce.

'You need a pick-me-up,' Amanda proffers a plate of Rich Tea.

'I need a double gin and tonic.'

Amanda laughs, worried.

'But I'll make do with a biscuit and cup of tea.'

'You must come for lunch soon. And bring that clever brother of yours,' Amanda blushes.

I need that G and T now.

On the way home we collect a subdued Rachel from school.

'Can we go to the sweet shop?' she asks, a long shot.

'No, it's not Friday. But there's some delicious homemade shortbread from Mrs Gantry. You could have one with a glass of milk.

'Alright,' she says, no fuss.

'Are you okay, Rach?' She normally puts up more of a fight. 'Bad day at school?'

'Yes. No. It's just sort of like, weird, without Jeremy. I kind of got used to having him around and stuff.'

'We all did, darling. But you can see him soon. Wednesday probably. I expect Uncle Martin will bring him back here after school.'

'It's not the same, though, is it?'

'No, Rach. Things change. It's just part of life.'

She winces and my stomach pulls. It's a hard lesson to learn but an important one. You go along in life and you get used to it, the way things are, day by day. And then gradually, little by little, bit by bit, things change and it's only when you look back that you see those changes. Like your hair growing. One day you step out of a salon, all sleek and groomed and coloured and you manage to keep it up, the sleekness, the grooming, the colour, and then one day you look in the mirror and your hair has got away from you. It is a wiry, straggly mess (actually, bad analogy; my hair's always like that). But sometimes change comes more quickly. Unexpected and out of the blue. One day something happens and your life changes forever.

Rachel slips her hand in mine. For a second. Long enough to get my attention. 'Can I have Nesquik in my milk?' she asks.

Steve is out. Another meeting. Martin and I are in the kitchen. He is battering his laptop with his fat fingers. I am ironing cassocks. If I could have prophesied this as a young woman at college...

'I miss him,' Martin cuts into my reverie. I almost scald myself on a jet of steam I am so taken aback by this revelation. Not just that he misses his son but that he should confess this human frailty to me. Wise words are needed.

I breathe deep, move the iron back and forth. 'Well... maybe you needed this to happen so you could get to know him.'

Martin stares at me, deadpan. I'm not sure if he has heard me or if he is even aware I have spoken. But then I notice his fat fingers twitching on my table, like the hairy fat legs of a tarantula, and it dawns on me that he is angry.

'What?' he says, almost spitting at me. 'Maybe I needed to be turfed out and move in here?' He shoots a venomous look at his surroundings. At my MFI sale kitchen fitted by my husband who could turn his hand to anything, whose wife never in a squillion years thought this would extend to weddings and funerals. 'High life living in Penge?' My brother pronounces the 'P' explosively.

'Oh, shut up, Martin.' One squirt of steam in the eyes and he'd be sorry.

He abandons his laptop, standing up and throwing back his chair in a way my floor will not appreciate. Then he announces that he's going to the pub. 'Don't blame me if I get very drunk,' he says, petulant, harvesting a wad of notes from his wallet and stuffing them in his back pocket as he heads out the door.

'No, of course I won't, Martin. Cos you getting drunk would be my fault, wouldn't it?... Martin... I said, "Wouldn't it'?"'

My question lingers in a swirl of steam. I am speaking words to empty space. He has gone. And I am left alone with a half-ironed cassock and a bad mood.

Much, much later, after checking on the children, watching for the rise and fall of their chests, their pink colour, their warmth, I glance out the landing window to the street below. Tamarine is putting out the rubbish. Mr Khan from number 12 is just back from his shift at work, pushing his spotless Raleigh down the passageway. A cat, black and sleek, leaps onto a wheelie bin as Ray from the dry cleaners walks past with his collie. Who says London's anonymous? All these people, their comings and goings, are part of my life.

But hang on. There's Martin. Staggering up the street with a woman in tow. Not Claudia... someone else. She looks vaguely familiar. A little like... Christina Aguilera. I should know. I've seen her on one of Imo's collages. But that's not why she clicks something in my brain. As she stands under the lamplight, gazing up at him, talking earnestly to him, the way Heidi used to be with him, she looks ridiculously young, barely out of her teens, maybe scraping twenty.

I feel sick.

Not because I'm witnessing my revolting pig of a brother

being unfaithful on my doorstep but because I now realise who this young woman is. Melanie. From the shoe shop. With the long blonde hair like Christina Aguilera. The student drinking frothy coffee outside Starbucks. The One Small Incident. And Martin is stupid enough to make it more than that. Two, three, four, five, six, who knows how many small incidents? Who knows how far these incidents have gone? How big they've become? Claudia's worst suspicions are being confirmed before my very eyes.

I'd better wake Steve. I won't be held responsible for my actions.

That is how I come to be in the car, at eleven thirty in my slippers, ferrying a celebrity looky-likey across South East London. Martin, true to his word for once, got rip-roaring drunk, banging and crashing into furniture and walls even more than normal. 'Ssshheeee's come back for a coffee,' he slurred, diving onto the sofa and falling spectacularly asleep just as the baby started caterwauling. My instinct was to feed Imo, get her straight back off, but I stopped myself from running up those stairs and grabbing her out of the cot. I went to the fridge, took out a bottled of expressed milk (waiting for this moment), and handed it to a bleary-eyed Steve. Much better if I disappeared for a bit, according to Miriam Stoppard. Less confusing for baby. As much as I would've liked to stay and have it out with Martin, I left that to Steve. He's been on the courses. He's got the words whereas I've only got a big sack full of anger and bitterness.

I volunteered to drop Melanie home. Melanie whose job in the shoe shop is part-time. Who is indeed one of Martin's students. A PhD student. Older than she looks. And who stood, ten minutes ago, horrified in our front room, whether at being in Penge, or in our poky terrace, or at Martin's disgusting prostrate form, or at the newly-ironed cassock hanging from the door frame, or all of these, I am not sure. And where does

Melanie live? Dulwich, of course.

After a silent journey – apart from my huffs and sighs, which are supposed to communicate my disapproval – I pull off the South Circular, passing Martin and Claudia's family home. I go this way on purpose. Melanie doesn't even flinch.

'Just here,' she says, after a few more of my huffs and sighs, indicating, with a hair advert flick of her hair, one of the biggest houses in the Village and that's saying something.

'You live here?' I can't help myself asking.

'My mum's place. I'm crashing while I do my PhD.'

I want to ask why she needs to work in a shoe shop. With that kind of money surely you and your offspring need never work again.

Melanie unfolds her long legs out of my very old and modest Espace and stands up straight, all ready to slam the door (please don't fall off). I don't think she is going to thank me for the lift somehow.

'Don't be fooled by him,' I say, before she can vanish up her drive, so big it has an entrance and exit so you don't even have to bother with three point turns or reversing.

'I'm no fool.' She bends down to look me straight in the eye, then closes the door with deliberate self-control so at least it doesn't fall off and make me look like Del Boy.

But I can see through her. Despite her staggering self-assurance and apparent lack of conscience, I don't believe one word of it. She is a fool. Martin is a fool. Somewhere back down the road, sleep a woman and child who, somewhat against their better judgement, love that man who happens to be my brother. And that man happens to be staying in my house, eating my food, raiding my fridge, breaking my crockery, breathing my air, passed out on my new leather sofa. And what am I doing? Driving home this idiotic young woman.

Just who's the fool here exactly?

Thoughts for the Day: Why can't we leave London? Why can't we live in some Dibley-esque parish in the country with stone cottages, a village green, a local pub full of eccentric characters and yet child-friendly and welcoming of incomers. A pretty church with a prettier vicarage and a smart, flat lawn. Daffodils and honeysuckle. Apples and plums. A proper Harvest Festival with those wheat sheaf loaves and giant marrows with Hallelujah! carved into the side. Somewhere far away from the hustle and bustle, the noise and the grime. Far, far away from my brother, Martin, and his messy, dirty, filthy excuse for a life.

Chapter Fifteen: Wednesday January 16th

I haven't seen Martin for two days. No opportunity for strong words. Yesterday morning he left for work before even Imo woke. He never suffers from hangovers – so unfair as he really, really deserved the mother of all hangovers. He deserved my wrath and all of God's judgement. But Martin being Martin has so far got away with it. And tonight Jeremy, the human shield, is coming over. I need to tread carefully.

Playgroup pick-up. Waiting outside, Imo perched on one hip, a hip that will need replacing before its time. I am one of many, part of a multitude of diverse mothers, child-minders, and one solitary dad, most of us with a baby or toddler in tow, in slings, pushchairs, on reins, with dummies, organic grapes and snot bubbling out of nostrils.

The doors open and we begin our shuffle inside, to wait in the foyer for the children to be matched to adults. When it is finally my turn, Olivia greets me proudly, leaping up from the carpet and waving a trademark brightly-coloured collage. I kiss her on the head. She smells of biscuit. 'That's lovely, Olivia.' I use my bright, happy, shiny voice, talking slowly, trying to think of something positive to say. 'What careful cutting out.'

'I know,' says her key worker, a young girl called Shelley. 'She's ever so good with scissors. We never have to worry about her.' And then Shelley laughs in a way that suggests they have to worry about other children and what they might be inspired to do with a pair of scissors.

I grip Olivia's hand and shepherd my girls briskly out of there into the fresh air. I'm feeling a bit faint, fighting off the possible catastrophes leaping about in my head, struggling to do my one woman band thing with two infants, a handbag, car keys, plus a sticky collage of what looks like Alan Sugar's head pasted onto David Beckham's body.

Just as I've bundled them all into the car, I notice her: Natasha's mother. She's always late, got her head down, avoids eye contact, gives off a don't-get-too-close vibe. But I don't think it's rudeness. It's something else. Shelley told me she is *one of them Poles or summink, keeps herself to herself.* And then she added, as if I'd be interested: *But watch her, she's a man-eater.*

Mmm.

If I was a true Christian, a proper curate's wife, I'd talk to her. Ask her round for a cup of tea. But something stops me. Life stops me. Rushing around and chasing my tail stops me. I may not be a true Christian but I'm not a bad person. I'm a mother. A daughter. An auntie. A sister. A wife. A curate's wife. Like Olivia I wear all these different pairs of shoes but none of them fit properly. I feel as if I've been forced into them, like the black clumpy lace-ups Mum made me wear to school so I wouldn't get the bunions that gave her so much gip. I've been forced into these shoes and they're pinching. I want to kick them off and run barefoot across the car park. Might be a bit chilly though. There's a nasty wind up out there.

As I drive away, slowly into the lunchtime traffic, I catch a glimpse of Natasha emerging from the hall with her mother. They hold hands and bow their heads to the wind, walking home, their home from home, wherever that is, just the two of them.

I'm not getting very far with my anti-television campaign. So far my children have watched their weekly quota in one evening. If Steve were here I'd have some back-up but yet again he's out. I am left on my own trying to trick Imo – rigid in her bucket on the coffee table – into opening her mouth for some pureed veg. She ignores the spoon heading her way, cunningly disguised as an aeroplane, concentrating all her efforts into staring at my overfull breasts. I'm not giving in. I'm hanging on till her bedtime.

'Why don't you go and play in the garden, girls?' I suggest, once the jar is finally empty.

'Don't be silly, Mummy. It's dark,' Olivia says, lining up her Barbie shoes on the arm of the leather sofa.

Brain cells. Dead.

Rachel drags her attention away from the screen, sensing her mother is not quite on the ball and using this to her possible advantage. 'We want to watch *Hollyoaks*,' she says.

Hollyoaks hasn't got anything to do with David Bellamy. It is full of rampant sex-crazed young northerners. Another world that is certainly unsuitable for children. That is why I throw Imo's blanket over the telly. That is why Rachel is sulking in the shed, Christmas lights twinkling in the window, when Jeremy turns up with his father at seven. When I explain this to Jeremy, much to Martin's amusement, he takes himself off, with the remains of a KFC family bucket, to join his cousin in the shed. I leave them to it.

Now is the time to pin Martin down and ask him what his intentions are. Yes, I'd really like to pin him down and stuff peanuts in his big gob.

The smell of deep fried chicken is making me queasy. Or maybe it's the sight of Martin with grease in his beard. Will he ever shave that thing off?

Apart from a desultory 'hello' he has ignored me, plonked his laptop on my kitchen table and attacked it with much aggression. I don't care if he's not in the best of moods. I'm not in the best of moods. Steve would say you have to choose the right time. I would say I've tried doing that and it leads nowhere.

'When are you moving out?'

'Fed up of me already, Victoria?'

'It's been weeks, Martin. You turn up Boxing Day, unannounced, and now we're halfway through January. You said it would only be a few days. You need to sort yourself out and move on.'

'I see,' he says, like he's a psychiatrist and I'm his delusional patient. 'I didn't realise it was such a pain having me here.'

'Stop patronising me, you idiot. I'm being serious.'

Silence while my brother processes this concept.

'Really?' he asks.

'Yes, really.'

'I see.' This time he says the words like they're a revelation. He looks genuinely surprised, which in turn surprises me. Is he that thick-skinned? Does he really not know he's getting on my nerves? I thought it was his *raison d'être* to get on my nerves, to persecute me.

'But I'm your brother,' he says, a slight wobble in his voice. Alright, now he just sounds pathetic. This isn't right. He's not playing by the rules. Our rules. Our commandments that were set in stone long ago at the beginning of my life.

'I'm quite aware of that. But the days when we had to share a house are long gone. Or at least they should be.'

He closes his laptop, puts his fingers together in a prayer-like gesture, gathering his strength before moving in for the kill. *Pop down to the chemist's would you, Vicky-Love.* 'I'm not sure what Mum would've thought,' he says, his voice still containing a wobble but now with an edge to it.

'Don't bring Mum into this.'

'She would've expected you to help me in my hour of need.'

'Probably. But you seem to have forgotten the circumstances

– the One Small Incident – that brought you into my house on Boxing Day. I think it entirely probable that Mum would have stuck up for Claudia, despite you being the golden boy.'

He ignores this, changes the subject, rubs his beard in a way he knows will wind me up. 'And what about Steve? Does he know you want to kick me out? He doesn't, does he? Well, well, well, Vicky-Love. Keeping secrets from your holy husband. The vicar. Tut tut. And I thought you two had the perfect marriage.'

'You did?'

'You mean you don't?'

'We have our moments like everyone else,' I mumble. 'But, hang on, Martin. This isn't about my marriage, it's about yours. How do you explain Melanie?'

'Melanie is... she's... it's none of your business who she is.' He waves his arm at the thought of Melanie, catching a pile of his papers and sending them skidding to the floor. My floor. Waving her away like she's an irrelevance. An annoyance.

'How can you say that, Martin?'

'I just did. I opened my mouth and I said it.'

'Oh shut up, smart arse.'

'Now now, Vicky-Love. Language.'

'Arse is a rude word, Mummy,' says a third unexpected voice. Olivia has appeared in the kitchen, clutching a threadbare Tinky Winky by the aerial thing sticking out of his head. 'Say *bottom*.'

'What are you doing out of bed?'

'You were making a big noise. Are you arguing with Uncle Martin?'

'Yes, Olivia, I'm afraid I am.'

She looks at her Uncle Martin with eyes so serious I want to cry.

'Be nice to each other,' she says. 'That's what Jesus would do.' She leaves us then and we listen to her little feet, bare for once, as they pad softly back up the stairs, neither of us sure how to follow this up, all strong words, all regressive behaviour quietened by a three-year-old.

'I'm going to tuck her in,' I say eventually, to the table.

His voice follows me out of the kitchen, unexpected and detached from its owner. 'Fancy an omelette?' it asks.

I don't know if my brother is making amends or if he's manipulating the situation but I am too tired and too hungry to turn down the offer of food. 'That would be... good,' I tell the door.

Bedtime and it's only ten o'clock. In the old days I'd just be thinking about going out. Not that I went out that often. But still, in London – young London, single London – the night is only beginning to get going.

What would Mum have thought if she'd been here? Would she have wanted me to let Martin stay longer? Or would she understand how hard it is for me? He never got on her nerves. I'm not sure she actually had any nerves. She didn't notice the banging and crashing because he was so like her. She didn't notice his mess because she didn't notice any mess. *A little bit of mess never did anyone any harm, Vicky-Love*. She and Dad and Martin had spent the day at one of Dad's big gardens out in Sidcup. Martin was working for pocket money because he wanted to take Heidi out. I spent the day at home tidying and cleaning, wanting to surprise them when they got back. They trod mud all through the house, all three of them. Only Dad was contrite. I think deep down he wanted a bit of clean and tidy but he had long since accepted that that wasn't to be. Not with Mum as his wife.

But she was wrong. Look what happened to her. She'd still be here now if people had taken more care. If they'd been clean and tidy.

Thoughts for the Day: Whatever happened to Heidi?

February 4th 1978

I had a go at spring cleaning today. It isn't spring. But the house is dirty. And I want to ask Alice round for tea after school one day next week. Mum and Dad were busy up on the allotment. Martin was out with Heidi somewhere, a bus shelter or Wimpy. So I had the house to myself.

I began with the lounge. It took an hour just to clean under the sofa and down the back of the seats. I found:

5 of Martin's socks (none of them matched but they all stunk like Dad's fertiliser)

2 of Martin's school ties (both with tomato ketchup stains)

Some Lego bricks (Martin hasn't played with Lego for at least five years)

A half-chewed Wagon Wheel

£4.61 in loose change, including some old money

A slipper (Dad's, I think, though it is hard to tell as it has been there so long, possibly since before I was born)

A Tufty Club badge (mine, stolen from Martin years ago)

Dried-up Satsuma peel that smelt of Christmas

And a photo.

I put everything back in its proper place, apart from the money. I have kept the money as it is impossible to know who it belongs to. This is called 'redistribution of wealth', according to Mr Harris, who is a commie, according to Dad.

I have kept the photo too.

It is a black and white photo of two young men, a bit older

than Martin is now. One of them is Dad. He looks quite a lot like me but with shorter, straighter hair. The other, it says on the back in Mum's scribbly writing, is Jack. I don't know who Jack is but I think I've seen him somewhere before. It's hard to tell. He's shielding his eyes from the sun but you can see his big grin.

I will ask Mum about it later. See if she's got another picture. I don't know why but I want to get a proper look at him.

Chapter Sixteen: Friday January 25th

Sainsbury's. On my own while Steve watches the girls. What's usually a dreaded chore is now a refuge, a luxury, wandering the aisles and daydreaming about being a domestic goddess. No bored baby. No obsessive three-year-old.

Today's a special day: Rachel's birthday. I should feel celebratory every time one of our children becomes a year older, to know we've had a part in shepherding them further along the road. They know how to be polite, how to lay a table and stack a dishwasher. Rachel has avoided getting into trouble at school. Olivia is settling into playgroup. They don't embarrass Steve too much at work or me when I'm taking them down the high street. They answer the phone to parishioners. Sometimes they pass on messages, occasionally with accuracy. They are good kids. But this knowledge is tinged with loss. Panic rises up within me so my chest could burst with the pressure and an unstoppable torrent come flooding out of me. I have to keep it tucked up safe inside.

So, what party food for a girl who's eleven, still a child but on the cusp of adolescence (though actually, Rachel's been poised right there since she was able to talk)?

Last year, for Rach's birthday, we used the church hall. We hired a clown who juggled with knives whilst standing on a plank rolling back and forth over two barrels. The kids screamed with excitement and begged him for more. Last year there were boys and girls who jumped up and down to music and we had sandwiches and crisps and fairy cakes and all the usual party food.

Rachel doesn't want any of that this year. *I'm too old for jelly and ice cream,* she said when I suggested a repeat performance. *But you love jelly and ice cream,* I replied, pathetically. But I knew what she was saying. She's moved up a party level. This year it's a few select friends for a sleepover. I preferred it when it was all over and done within two and half hours. And not in my house. And now I have to put up with Jessica Talbot overnight. Bob was delighted when he saw the invite. *Great,* he said. *I'll take Tamarine for a night out.* Poor Tamarine. I hope she likes Status Quo tribute bands.

Is this the time to move from triangle sandwiches to slices of pizza? Is Rachel really that age? I can't believe that in September she'll be at secondary school. She'll look tiny again and I'll want to protect her, to change her back into the baby she was a decade ago, when television quotas and Pot Noodles were not on the agenda. I want her to be small and warm and attached to me the way Imo is. The way Thomas was.

I remember the last evening I held him. It was summertime. A Friday. There were peaches in the greengrocer's and Rachel had one for tea and got juice everywhere and Steve cleaned her off in the paddling pool when he'd got in from a job in Bromley. She was allowed to stay up and watch Wimbledon with him. A Henman semi-final. *Come on, Tim,* she'd shout, though she didn't know why she was shouting except that was what her daddy was doing. I left them together to go and bathe him upstairs. It was still warm and the sash window was open at the top so we could hear the 19.49 to London Bridge as he splashed about trying to catch water in his little hands. Hands that were just beginning to reach out. Then I scooped him up and wrapped him in his towel with the hood and when he was dry I smothered him in cream before putting him in a white cotton babygrow. I think he had Martin's skin. Sensitive and a bit blotchy. I thought I'd take him to see the health visitor who is good at eczema, much better than the doctor who sees you as a fussy mother. I sat in the chair with him up in the box room. His room. The nursery which was still pink as we hadn't got round to changing the colour. We listened to a blackbird in the old cherry tree in the garden and the occasional shout from downstairs and the sound of mass clapping reaching up to us. Henmania. I sat with him in my arms in the box room, the evening sun all soft and apricot above the railway line, feeling him quietly drop off to sleep, and thought of all these little joys and snippets of life, enjoying our time together, knowing these moments were precious. But I didn't know then how precious that particular moment would become.

'Vicky, isn't it?'

I hear a voice from somewhere, muffled and distorted like I'm underwater.

It's her. Natasha's mother. The young Polish woman.

'My name is Karolina. Our children go to the playgroup together.' Her English is far better than Shelley would have me believe. She rummages in her bag and pulls out a tissue. 'You are crying,' she says, as if I didn't know this. Actually I didn't know this. But she is right. I am crying. 'Do you want coffee? They have restaurant.'

'But my shopping... '

'Your trolley is empty.'

'What about yours?'

'There is nothing freezing.'

Even through my tears and embarrassment I manage to be impressed that she is not the sort of mother to buy frozen dinners.

I follow her to a table and we sit down, a little awkward.

'Tea or coffee?' she asks. I reach into my bag for my purse but Karolina shakes her head, and says she invited me, she will pay.

'Thank you. I'll have tea, please.'

'Of course,' she says and queues up, leaving me contemplating why I am sat here instead of shopping and wondering why the hell I am feeling so foolish. For crying in Sainsbury's? Or for crying in front of someone I felt pity for only a short time ago?

When she returns I manage to smile and say thank you, I'm not normally like this. Then I tell her I'm a bit tired. A bit stressed. I tell her about the prospect of the forthcoming sleepover.

She looks blank, takes a slug of her cappuccino, confirming my foolishness. She thinks I am stressed over a sleepover. She thinks I am a silly, trivial woman. A neurotic mother, that all I have on my plate is the usual mundane day-to-day stuff, not the stuff of Shakespearean tragedy.

She has no idea.

After I have drained my tea I thank her politely, saying I have to get going.

'Good luck,' she says. And I must look confused or worried so she adds: 'With the sleepover.' Then she smiles. But there is something not quite right with the smile. It is trying too hard.

Jessica Talbot is wearing a skirt. I have never seen Jessica Talbot in a skirt. Admittedly this one is a bit on the short side, revealing rather too much of her muscular footballer thighs, but at least she has made the effort like Bob is always nagging her to. I think Tamarine must have taken her shopping because it is the sort of skirt she favours. But then Tamarine has lovely legs. Bob is always ogling them, even after a couple of years he hasn't got bored.

The other girls who have been picked to come to Rachel's sleepover are from her class. Three girls who are all trying to be 'with it', but somehow miss the mark. And that's coming from someone who buys her clothes from supermarkets.

The girls are upstairs, looting and pillaging Rachel's bedroom, when Martin turns up with Jeremy – the guest of honour – banging and crashing their way through the poky hallway, voices ricocheting off the ceiling. The girls stampede downstairs, fiddling with their hair and sniggering as if the band members of McFly have walked in. Only Rachel is not sniggering. She looks put out, observing the way her friends act around her cousin. A feeling I learned to live with long ago whenever my own school friends came round. Not only did I have to worry about our embarrassing dirty house, but that they would fall hopelessly in love with my pig of a brother. I had to warn them off and then they took offence, thinking I thought they weren't good enough for him. As if. But fortunately Martin never looked their way. They were just his kid sister's friends. Dross. Scum. Microscopic life form.

Jeremy, however, is lapping up the adoration. 'Come on, then,' he says, forcing himself to sound casual. 'I'll set up my Wii. Then I'll whoop you at bowling. I'm a pro.'

This is all another language so I leave them to it and head to the kitchen, familiar territory. I could do with some time alone to sort out the pizzas but Martin can't deal with the 'zoo' and so after just a few moments of getting down with the kids, he joins me at the fridge. My fridge.

'Pass us a beer, will you?'

'If you chop up this red pepper.'

'Give us it here then,' he says.

I have to admit, he cuts very well, like one of those TV chefs, but I do worry about his fat fingers. One of them could easily be sliced off and end up on the Margarita.

'So,' he says, cracking open a bottle. 'They seem like... nice girls.'

'Yes,' I say, wondering why he's trying to make polite conversation. 'They are. On the whole.'

'I wouldn't know about girls. Not really. I often wonder what it would've been like if Jeremy had been Jemima. Would I have been a better father?'

'Do you think you're a bad father?'

'I've not exactly made good decisions lately.'

'That's big of you to admit.'

'Are you being facetious?'

'No, I mean it.'

He swallows back half the can, belches, and then goes all quiet. 'Vick, do you ever wonder... ' he starts, falters, fiddling with a bit of pepper, edgy, if indeed he is capable of that emotion.

'What?'

'Well... ' He starts again and then plunges into uncharted territory. 'Do you ever wonder what it would have been like, you know, if he, Thomas, was still... here?'

Thomas.

You'd think I'd want to cry but somehow hearing his name on Martin's lips is unexpectedly beautiful. I feel a warm rush of love – not for Martin, obviously, but for Thomas. To remember that he was here. He was my son. Is my son, even though I can no longer sit with him in my arms on the chair in the pink box room, listening to the trains pass by. He's still around me, with me, every moment of the day. Yes, I wonder all the time.

'Sorry, Vick, I just, well, you know, you never talk about him. It can't be good, keeping all that inside.'

'I don't want to talk about it. Him. I can't. Not now. I've got a party to think about. And anyway, stop changing the subject. We were talking about you. You need to put things right with Claudia. What were you thinking, messing about with that silly girl?'

He doesn't get the chance to answer this. Bob has appeared from nowhere, carrying a six pack of Carlsberg. 'Have one of these, Martin,' he says. 'Not one of those poncey bottled beers you go in for. It's a party.'

Martin is lost for words for once and accepts a can off Bob. Seeing him slumming it with Penge's finest makes up for not finishing – barely even beginning – what could've been our first ever heart-to-heart.

Thoughts for the Day: It is hard to have a thought for today, knowing that in the bedroom next door lie four tweenies, whispering about make-up and music and boys and all the rest of it. All the things that eluded me at that age. All the things that still elude me at this age.

Chapter Seventeen: Sunday January 27th

Here we go again. Sunday used to be the last day of the week as far as I was concerned, the working week over, Saturday shopping and cleaning done, and then finally Sunday, a day for resting and taking it quiet, a roast dinner and a trip to the park or a day out to see Mum and Dad. And then after Mum had gone, just Dad, helping him get his life back on track.

I never got why some people said Sunday was the first day of the week. Now I do. This is where it all begins, not where it all ends. If I were a theologian I might have more to say about this, beginning and endings, alpha and omega and all that. But I'm not a theologian. I'm a theologian's wife. And my husband likes to say that being a Christian isn't just about going to church every week. Being a Christian is how you live your ordinary life, your everyday life, going about everyday ordinary things. And, if I could say I was a Christian, that's how I'd want to be one, through and through and all the time. Not just on Sundays. But I don't know if I'll ever be able to say that.

This Sunday is different. I've invited Claudia to church, bringing Jeremy who is quite the convert. I thought she'd be as resistant as Martin but she said she was up for it, which was refreshing for Steve to hear as he likes to think he is 'seeker-sensitive'. Just as well it's Steve taking the service; Claudia would shudder at the state of Desmond's vestments.

So it's quite a crowd of us squashed up together on a pew as Jessica has followed us along the street and up the church path as well, squeezing herself unsubtly between Jeremy and Rachel. Jeremy is not complaining though Rachel tries. Jessica has thicker skin than even Martin or Steve so she takes not a blind bit of notice.

Claudia is dressed for church 1950s style, only missing the white gloves. To my knowledge she only ever goes to church for the usual rites of passage, which is more than most people. And exactly as often as Steve and I in the old days. Before he got the call to go to Dartford.

We stand for the embarrassing children's song. Claudia joins in reticently, keeping half an eye on her son who is as enthusiastic as ever, bright-eyed and concentrating on hand-eye coordination. Even Jessica Talbot is captivated by something other than Crystal Palace FC. Or Jeremy. It's only when we sit down and the children file out that I notice Karolina and Natasha, sitting quietly in the row behind. I'm surprised to see them here. I thought Poles were Roman Catholics. Steve's mother is a nominal Roman Catholic though she never took him to church. She says religion causes too many problems. Steve says religion might cause problems but God solves them.

I turn round and smile at them in what is supposed to be an encouraging way. She looks distinctly unfriendly at first, till I remind her who I am and then she breaks open that smile again, and apologises, saying she was dreaming.

'Anything nice?'

'Yes, very nice, thank you.' But she doesn't elaborate.

I ask her if Natasha would like to go out to Sunday school. Natasha is on Karolina's lap, clutching handfuls of her mother's bleached blonde hair in her dimpled hands. Natasha doesn't look like she'd want to go out to Sunday school. Natasha doesn't look like she'd want to move an inch away from her mother who gives a shrug – a shrug that says, what do you think, stupid woman? – in answer to my question. I give her a knowing smile that is supposed to say kids, eh? But I'm not sure how effective it is or how she will interpret it.

I turn back then, having done my bit (Amanda would be proud), and try to focus on Steve who is drumming up last minute business for the Alpha course starting this week. Maybe I should do it. I need to discover the meaning of life. But I have more pressing matters. Like discovering when Martin is going to leave. I will corner Claudia later. Meanwhile, she is looking in horror at Mr Barratt's shoes.

Sunday lunch is a success as far as the Yorkshire puddings are concerned, beautifully light and fluffy, but not so regarding the atmosphere at the table, which is somewhat tense. Martin is trying too hard and Claudia is ignoring his cringing efforts. We finally make it through to the end of pudding – a rather nice blackberry and apple crumble brought by Claudia via Waitrose – and then disperse to various parts of the house: Rachel and Jeremy to the shed, Imo to her cot, Olivia to the telly, Steve to the back room to go over his sermon, Martin to the understairs loo with the *Observer*. Only Claudia and I remain in the kitchen, clearing up. Well, I clear up while she sits at the table glugging wine.

At last we are alone, the dishes are done, and this is my chance. I make a cup of tea and join her at the table.

'What is it, Vicky? Do you want to tell me something? Have I got spinach stuck in my teeth or something?'

'No, no it's not that. You look fine. You always look immaculate.'

'What is it, then? Is this when you try to convert me?'

'No, no, that's Steve's job, not mine.' I'm glad Amanda's not here to witness my poor witness. I take a sip of tea and go for it. 'But I did want to tell you something, Claudia. Well, ask you something really.'

'Is it about Martin?'

'Yes, it's about Martin.'

'I suppose you want to know if I'm taking him back.'

'Well, yes.'

'You've had enough of him.'

'Well, yes.'

Claudia does one of those laughs that are not about humour. 'He's only been here a few weeks,' she says. 'I've had to put up with him for nearly fifteen years. Can you imagine that?'

Now it's my time for the humourless laugh. 'Yes, Claudia. If anyone can imagine that, it's me. I grew up with him, remember?'

'That was different.'

'How was that different?'

'You weren't locked to him by wedlock.'

'I was locked to him by Mum and Dad. And it was quite clear who was the Chosen One.'

At this point, just when I have somehow managed to drive the conversation off course, in walks Martin. He stands still for a while, raspy-breathed, weighing up Claudia with her Pinot Grigio, me with my PG Tips.

'What about mine?' he whines.

'Oh, sit down and I'll pour you some tea,' I snap at him. He might as well stay and hear what I've got to say or I'll be waiting forever to get to the bottom of this. Eternity is a long time as Desmond likes to point out.

He does as he's told and sits down, in relative safety, two seats away from his wife. 'So what have you been talking about?' He accepts the tea off me, heaping in the sugar. 'I presume it's me.'

'You presume too much,' I say, sitting back down at the other end of the table from him, still within spitting distance.

'But I'm right though.'

'Yes, Martin. You're always right.'

'Thank you for acknowledging that.'

'Actually,' Claudia interjects, looking from him to me and shaking her head, 'your sister was asking me if I was going to take you back because she's had enough of you. I hadn't given her my answer but I might as well tell you at the same time, kill two birds and all that.' She sips the last of her wine. Dutch courage. 'I'm not having you back. I've found someone else. Nothing serious. A bit of fun but I realise there's more to life than you. And if you can do it then why can't I?'

Silence while Martin and I absorb this new information.

'I'm sorry, did you say you've found someone else?' Martin cracks the silence, his voice roller-coasting like an adolescent boy's. 'Where exactly did you find someone else?'

As if that's the most important question.

'Well, if you want precise details, it was in LA. In the lift of the hotel. I dropped my earring and he picked it up and then we got talking and he asked me to dinner and I accepted.' She pours herself more wine and goes to drink it when Martin reaches over and swipes the glass from her hand, necking it back in one. Claudia leans back in her chair and folds her arms.

Quiet. All that can be heard is the muffled cries of Olivia in the front room shouting at the TV, a reminder of what this marital breakdown has brought into my house. An obsession with the worst of popular culture. We used to be happy with *Blue Peter* and Bill Oddie.

Martin lights up a cigarette, right there in front of me in my kitchen, at my table, seizing advantage of a situation brought about by his own doing, confident I won't tell him where to go at this crucial stage in negotiations. 'I suppose you're going to tell me he's an actor,' Martin says, exhaling smoke down his nostrils. His big fat nostrils.

'No actually, you're wrong. He's a writer.'

Now Martin does the laugh-thing.

Claudia carries on regardless, retrieving her glass and helping herself to yet more wine. 'He's a very talented writer who's all set to be the next big thing.'

'That's what they all say.'

'It's better than being a washed-up has-been who has to take his thrills from his students because he can't cut it anymore in Academia.' Claudia is on her feet, flinging her glass around rather worryingly. It might not be Dartington but it is unchipped and part of a set of six.

'That's where you're wrong,' Martin says, banging my table with the palm of his fat hand, like he's a prosecuting lawyer, though the effect is spoiled with his B&H. 'I'm onto something big. Research. Vicky will tell you.'

Vicky's keeping quiet.

'Research?' Claudia jeers.

'The God gene. I'm researching the God gene.'

'Well, I can tell you now I haven't got that gene. I can't believe in a god that would create you in his image. And anyway, I thought that idea had run out of steam.'

'That's where I come in.'

'Oh, the big I Am.'

I'm half-expecting Steve to come in and ask them both on an Alpha course at this point. But Jeremy beats him to it. There is a very loud crash. A terrible splintering of wood. A very expensive splintering of polished wood, handcrafted in what used to be Czechoslovakia. When the three of us rush out into the hall, into the hushed quiet that follows the cacophony, we see Jeremy standing over what used to be his precious cello. But from the dark expression on his face and the sparks in his eyes, it is clear this was no clumsy accident.

'I hate you both,' he says. 'I hate you more than I hate my cello. I want you both to go. I want to stay here with Auntie Vicky and Uncle Steve. They're a normal family. I just want to be normal.'

He whispers this, but his audience – Claudia, Martin, me, and an inquisitive Olivia who has foregone *Bid TV* to watch her big cousin fall apart in our poky hallway – we hear every word. Despite the significance of what Jeremy is saying, I still find time to think how nice it is to be seen as normal. But most of all, my heart is filled with a sadness that wants to explode my body into tiny pieces against the wipe-clean walls. If I had a son – if I still had a son – I would value him above all else. More than jewels, more than temples, more than the air I breathe. More than the sun in the sky or the moon that stands guard over his grave at night. And the wind that blows in the trees. That blows and blows but can never blow my grief away.

Thoughts for the Day: If any of my children express a desire to take up a musical instrument, I will suggest the penny whistle.

Chapter Eighteen: Monday 4th February

Monday morning. A week has passed since the cello-smashing incident. Jeremy is back at St Hilda's C of E as part of the process he believes will give him a normal life. Despite his initial dodgy start there in January, he has found that he actually quite likes it. Being back at Dulwich for that brief period of time has shown him where he'd rather be: with his cousin and Jessica Talbot.

This means – and Claudia is surprisingly happy about this – that Jeremy is staying with us during the week and back to Dulwich for the weekends. So somehow things didn't work out the way I planned. Instead of getting my house back, the poky terrace is still overflowing. Only the cello is missing.

Claudia wanted to go out and buy another one. A thousand pounds and the rest, just like that. But Martin, for once almost sensible (though probably being tight), suggested they wait. He said that Jeremy couldn't go round losing his temper without there being consequences. This led to Claudia losing her temper at Martin for being a hypocrite and the consequences of this are that they are now even more at loggerheads than before. Whereas, unusually, I'm with Martin on this one; I'm all for waiting if it means my hall stays clear.

It is only eleven o'clock and already I am dreaming of bed in a way only sleep-deprived mothers can dream. I have had to dispatch two sullen children to school, one chirpy small one to playgroup, and I still have to heave a fat baby to clinic. No help from Steve because although it's his day off he has had to shoot off to Plumstead to see his mum who's got herself in a tizz over his dad. And no help from my brother, obviously, because he is at work, chairing an 'important departmental meeting'. Hard to imagine when all he does around here is eat, drink and slouch. Though there has been more battering of his laptop lately. Not that there's time for me to waste imagining. Must get to the clinic where a telling-off from the health visitor awaits.

It is bedlam in here. Naked babies everywhere you look. All shapes and sizes and colours but none quite as fat and pink as mine. Fat because apparently, according to Eileen the health visitor, Imo is naturally this size. I shouldn't fret, it'll come off when she starts to crawl (must get Steve to get stair gate out of attic). And pink because she objected fiercely to the humiliation of being made to lie down, nappy off, in cold scales with Eileen looming over her. As I squeeze Imo's limbs back into her clothes, I feel relief that I haven't been told off. I'm not a bad mother.

The clinic is held in this cavernous room – for maximum sound effect – which also serves as a waiting area for patients to see their doctor. Sick people sit alongside babies, perhaps in an effort by the NHS to keep their immune system in working order.

'Are you alright, Vicky?' It's Eileen. Eileen has been doing the job forever and ever, possibly since the time of Dr Spock. She has seen thousands of mothers over the years. Every sort: blissed-out, euphoric, lovey-dovey, confident, know-it-all, knowing-nothing, anxious, neurotic, weepy, frightened, depressed, shattered, grieving. She has seen even more babies and toddlers and pre-schoolers, crying and gurgling and weeing and feeding. Imo is just another baby but Eileen takes time to talk to her and smile at her and I feel assured that my little girl is alright. We're doing alright. Despite everything. Despite Thomas.

'We're alright,' I say. She hands me back my red book, the pink graph filled in. And that's when I drop my shoulders, clutch Imo to me, and start crying. When I think of the blue graph and the line that was following its centile beautifully. That suddenly stopped at three months.

'It's alright to still be feeling sad, Vicky. There's no specific time limit on grief.' Eileen pats my hand.

I take a deep breath and ask the question I haven't been brave enough to ask anyone else. 'But will it ever stop?'

She thinks about this, pausing briefly in her hand-patting as she does so. A toddler wobbles past us, aiming for the Little Tikes car that needs an MOT. He is wearing dungarees.

I had a pair of dungarees that were so cute. I'd bought them on a whim from a baby shop on Lordship Lane. I was waiting for Thomas to grow a bit more, he was nearly there... And then, after, I hung onto them for ages, folded up in my chest of drawers along with my cardigans and jumpers. But every time I opened the drawer they stared at me. Every time I closed the drawer, they cried out to me. So I put them in the trunk at the foot of the bed but at night, as I lay there next to Steve, listening to his sighs, his silent tears, I could feel them there, folded up carefully in tissue paper so they wouldn't crease, lying there, empty, in the dark. And I could feel Thomas, his hot little body lying next to mine. I could hear him breathe. I could smell his milkyness. And my breasts filled up and my tears overflowed and my heart wanted to stop beating. In the end I could bear it no longer so I sent the dungarees to Romania with a pile of blue baby blankets. I used to imagine a little Romanian boy toddling around in them, cosy and handsome, the pride of his mother.

The patting starts up again. Eileen has thought about her answer. 'Not completely,' she says. 'It *will* get better.' She plucks a tissue from thin air and pushes it into my hand. 'But you might like to think about talking to someone.'

'I'm not depressed. I'm just tired, you know, with this one.' I look down at Imo, who is avoiding eye contact with Eileen. 'And Rachel and Olivia. And Steve. And then there's my brother.'

'You've got a lot on your plate.' She shakes her head and reminds me of Mum who always got exasperated with how much I took on. 'You need to make sure that *you're* okay. Phone me any time you feel it's too much. Any time.'

I pull myself together – I Can Do This – and let Eileen return to the scales. The queue is lengthening and the noise reaching a crescendo. Despite the chill of the day, it is hot and stuffy in here. I need to get us out into the cold air. I need to breathe. I concentrate on Olivia's buttons so I don't have to face any of the other mothers. Not that any of them are aware of my pain. They are all wrapped up with their own babies. But I feel one pair of eyes on me. I look up, blinking fast to hold back any stray tears.

It is Karolina. She is clutching a prescription, gazing at Imo rigid on my lap. She smiles a quick smile in my direction when she realises she has been spotted.

'She is lovely baby.'

'Thank you,' I say. These words are what I want to hear. What I need. But that's all I can say in return. Thank you. I can't manage anything else and before I get the chance to offer something better like 'do you fancy coming back for a cup of tea?' she has gone. I watch her through the streaky double-glazing, a lone figure walking through the grey London morning, the wind pushing back her bleached blonde hair. She makes me think of Steve's mum. Not that to my knowledge Dorota ever had bleached blonde hair. I think hers has always been henna red. But once, long ago, she was young and alone here too. I hope whatever this tizz was about, Steve has sorted it.

Steve's idea of sorting it was to bring his mother back to the poky terrace. Once I've put Imo down for a well-deserved nap, I join them in the kitchen to find out what has happened.

What has happened is this: Steve's mother has had a falling out with Steve's father. This is nothing out of the ordinary. They do it regularly, about every five years or so. Dorota finally has enough of Roland and the only way round it is to keep them apart, separate them for a bit, like naughty children, the way Mum used to do with Martin and me. Usually this strategy works for them. They soon start pining and are running back into each other's arms. Well, limping what with Roland's dodgy knee and Dorota's weight.

Dorota's weight seems to have increased further since she was last here – as it does with each visit. I can judge by the length of time it takes for her to get her breath back after she has made the marathon journey from the car to the kitchen table. Each time it is a little longer, the breathing a little louder. Louder even than Martin's after a packet of Benson and Hedge's. Like Martin, she foolishly blames it on her asthma.

Dorota has a cup of tea in front of her into which she deposits a cascade of sweeteners, a new departure from her standard three spoons of sugar. 'My new friend,' she says, rattling her Hermesetas. 'They come everywhere with me.' She puts them back safely in the handbag, which never leaves her lap.

The sweeteners allow her to have a piece of Mrs Webber's walnut and date cake without worrying. Not that she worries. It is Roland that worries. Roland has begged her to go back to Weightwatchers, not because he doesn't want a fat wife but because he is afraid her lungs will give out. But Dorota doesn't like going to Weightwatchers. She says the woman, Valerie, cheats. She is suspicious of anyone in a position of authority. Police, doctors, solicitors, vets, dentists, bank managers, teachers, priests – which means she has always been suspicious of me and, of late, she has become suspicious of her son.

Why do you want to be a priest? she asked when he'd first broken the news about his vocation.

It's what God wants me to do, Steve said with his new-found simplicity.

How do you know it is God speaking and not voices in your head?

I've been through a scrupulous selection process.

She tutted. She knew all about scrupulous selection processes. This had happened with Steve's Eleven Plus. He'd failed, despite scrimping and saving to pay for tuition.

And my calling has been confirmed from the bishop to the cleaner, Steve went on, rather corporately, it has to be said. *The decision wasn't taken lightly or overnight. It was taken prayerfully and over a long period of time.*

Dorota scoffed at the mention of prayer. In her experience you were told what to do by the priest, not by God. The priest would intercept the channels of communication to the Almighty. So unless you were going to pray to the Virgin Mary who might bypass the priest for you, there was no point. Of course Dorota believes Roman Catholicism is a load of superstitious nonsense but if there has to be a church then it is the only option. As for Steve wanting to join the Church of England, she cannot understand it. Dorota is a woman of mystery. And there is as much mystery about her as there is woman.

But there was one word she picked up on that day: cleaner. She softened a little when she heard it. In Dorota's eyes, cleaners are good honest workers, doing a good honest job. *Well, if it's good enough for the cleaner...* you could hear her thinking. My being a teacher is outweighed by me keeping a clean house. Dorota is proud to have a daughter-in-law who hangs her husband's shirts so nicely in the wardrobe. It makes up for filling children's heads with knowledge. Dorota is deeply suspicious of knowledge. She will not have a book or a newspaper in the house. This ban on intellectual property does not extend to TV, which she loves. It isn't education; it is entertainment. As are her two hobbies, bingo and dog racing.

'Please can I have another piece of this delicious cake?' she asks me now, ignoring Steve's muffled tut. 'A tiny piece.' She indicates the size she would like – her idea of tiny is quite different to mine – with her jumbo sausage fingers which are even fatter than Martin's. Her wedding ring has virtually disappeared. In fact it has disappeared. Steve notices this too.

'Where's your wedding ring, Mum? Things aren't that bad between you and Dad are they?'

'Reggie cut it off.'

'Who's Reggie?'

'Madge's husband.'

'Who's Madge?'

'You know Madge,' she looks incredulous that Steve does not know Madge. 'Madge Madge,' she says as if that clears up the matter and when Steve still looks blank she sighs impatiently. 'From the bingo.'

Too exasperated to carry on with this, Steve gives in and lets it be understood that of course he knows Madge Madge from the bingo. 'And is Reggie qualified to cut off wedding rings?'

'You do not need qualifications to cut off wedding rings. Reggie is odd-jobber. Very handy. He is a good honest man.'

'Why did you have it cut off?'

'It was too tight.'

'Mum.'

'Do not look at your mother like that.'

'I'm worried.'

'Tell your father.'

'He's worried about you too.'

'He's worried about himself. He wants me to stay the skinny girl he married. I was skinny because we had no money for food. We have money now so we can buy food. He wants to go out with me on his arm and show me off. I do my best for him. I do my hair nice and I put on make-up but it is not good enough. I am no girl. I am old.'

'You're not old, Mum.'

'I am a pensioner. I have bus pass.'

She's never set foot on a bus.

'You're only sixty-four, Mum. Sixty-four's young. Sixty-four's the new fifty-four. But you need to take care of yourself. You're not well. Listen to your breathing.'

We sit quietly, listening to her breathing. Despite a police car hurtling up the street, the crackle-and-wheeze is unmistakeable.

'You've got years left on this earth and Dad wants to share them with you.' Steve takes her hand, the one with the missing ring, and holds it still in his own. No hand-patting. 'He doesn't want to be alone. He wants to be with you, Mum, doing good things together.'

She huffs at this. 'Like what?'

'Like being a grandmother for one thing.'

Dorota clutches the locket at the mention of her grandchildren. I know what is inside the locket. A tiny, crumpled and faded black and white photo of her parents on one side. And on the other, Thomas, in all his beautiful, glorious colour.

I make my excuses and leave, citing Imo. I shut the kitchen door behind me and stand alone in the poky hall. The walls seem closer together than ever, even without the wretched cello. Like my mother-in-law, and my brother, I am finding it hard to breathe. It must be catching.

If only I could relieve the symptoms with an inhaler and a strictly observed calorie-controlled diet.

I suddenly want to be anywhere but here, my house, which is usually my shelter, my refuge. I want to be with new, different people who have nothing to do with my past because then they can't bring him up in conversation. They can't remind me. I can forget. Just for a while I can be normal. Because Jeremy is mistaken, we are far from normal. If we could be normal, then maybe we could even be happy. And that is the thought that makes me weep and feel sick. The thought that I could possibly be happy without him.

Thoughts for the Day: Eggs, lemons, caster sugar, golden syrup, chocolate, frozen raspberries.

Chapter Nineteen: Tuesday 5th February

Shrove Tuesday

Dorota has stayed the night, which at least got rid of Martin who sloped off to impose on Bill, a boffin from his department. Dorota slept in our bed. I didn't want to risk the springs of the new sofa already knocked about and finally vacated by Martin. So Steve got the sofa. I got the bottom bunk in the girls' room, top to toe with Olivia.

And while we play musical beds, where is Jeremy's mother in all this? Has she made an effort at reconciliation? Not with Martin, no. Not that I blame her. And not so as you'd notice with her son either. She's only had him for the weekend. Half a weekend because on the Sunday, Jeremy wanted to come to church and Claudia conveniently 'had things to do'. Apart from that, she's called in to see him a measly, miserly once. When she left she looked slightly forlorn but not enough to persuade him to come home with her. After she had convinced herself he hadn't become overly evangelical, she scurried away, dodging the bullets that are commonplace down our street.

But no time for bad thoughts. Must get down to the church hall to check up on things for tonight. The first Alpha meeting. Thankfully I'm not helping with the food, being excused due to childcare responsibilities (children come in handy sometimes). But I need to make sure everything's shipshape. Church halls don't have the best image, being the sort of place you go to for AA meetings or badminton. I don't want our hall to be seen in that light. I don't want it to smell of old socks and mould. I might not be a theologian but even I can see that old socks and mould are not conducive to discussing the big questions of life and death. There aren't many opportunities in this day and age, in our culture, to discuss these things. Apart from *Big Brother*.

I haven't got a lot to work with, hall-wise, but I can spray round with Febreeze and put some flowers in a vase. None of those churchy crysanths. Something white and simple. Something cool and fresh and modern. After all, that's exactly the sort of statement Steve would want to make about St Hilda's – to counteract the appearance of Desmond's vestments.

'Can I make you a cup of tea, Vicky? You look so tired from carrying the baby around all day.' Dorota manages to make a kind offer sound like a criticism of my child-rearing.

But I will be gracious. 'That would be great, thank you.' What I really want to know is when is she going back home. Like Martin, Dorota takes up too much space, physically and in every other way too.

She must pick up on my thoughts because she asks: 'Where is that big hunky brother of yours?' She loves that word 'hunky', always says it with a giggle, making you catch a glimpse of how she was as that lone girl in London, so far from home. When I pretend not to hear, she persists, astutely. 'Are you hiding him from me?'

'No, no, he's working. He was at a friend's last night.'

'Oh, that is nice,' she says. 'A sleepover.'

A wave of nausea pours over me. A sleepover? I assumed this friend of his was male. But this friend could just as easily be female. It could be Melanie... if her parents are away... or liberal... or completely barmy.

'Are you alright, Vicky? Would you prefer something stronger than tea? I have my sherry. Would you like me to pour you a little one?' She indicates the size of a little one, which would put me over the limit straight off. Why doesn't she drink vodka likes she's supposed to?

I'd jump at the chance of one of those, topped up with cranberry juice. That would be cool and fresh and modern.

Teatime. We are all here, the usual suspects, though Dorota has stepped into Martin's shoes, which she fills easily. Steve is tossing pancakes while I sort fillings. My shoulders have relaxed and my neck un-tensed – an experience I haven't had in a while. Even Imo joins in, entering wholeheartedly into the celebratory atmosphere, squishing the soft batter in her hands and squealing with pleasure. It makes a change to see the world through her eyes so I can remember the potential for happiness. For joy.

The front door crashes open. My brother thunders his way down the hall and stands in the doorway taking in this scene of family life that includes his son. His son who earlier announced he'd had no idea as to why we were having pancakes. The only time he has had pancakes was at a Little Chef.

'Ah, Martin,' Steve says as if it's the return of the prodigal. 'Come in and have a pancake. There's plenty to go round.'

'I'm not stopping. Just wanted to pick up some stuff. And check on Jeremy, of course.' He looks at the munching going on around the table and his tongue is virtually dropping out of his mouth. 'I suppose I've got time for one.' He sabotages a chair, taking over the room. 'To be sociable.'

Dorota hands him the sugar bowl, smiling sweetly. Martin smiles back at her, charm personified, cascading sugar over the pancake Steve has presented him with. 'I wish I could stay longer and enjoy the party only I've got a meeting,' he says, tucking in.

'A meeting?' Dorota makes it sound like Martin is about to do something dangerous and brave. Unbelievable. I know for a fact she thinks the British waste far too much time in meetings. Dorota never reacts like this when Steve goes out to a meeting. She usually sighs or shakes her head. And, studying my husband, I catch a glimmer of affront in his eyes, but he quickly blinks this away.

Martin changes the subject deftly, so as not to engage in work-related discussions with 'Dotty Dorota' as he refers to her. He puts us off our stride by asking what we are giving up for Lent.

'We-ell,' Steve rubs his hands together for this is the sort of challenge he relishes, his earlier negative feelings wiped clean. 'For me, it's got to be cake. There's always so much of the stuff in this house and, as Vicky likes to point out, it's not doing anything for my figure.' He pats his stomach. The one hidden under his black vicar shirt but not so well hidden that it can't be seen pulling at his buttons.

'I think you look so much better for a little fat on you. You were always too thin,' Dorota says, refilling her sherry glass.

'Anyway,' Steve goes on, 'what about you, Vicky? What are you going to give up?'

'Breastfeeding,' I state confidently, out-staring my brother who has taken a sudden intense interest in the cocoa content of the Fairtrade dark chocolate wrapper. 'If Imo agrees to do that too.' I look at Imo then, her small plump fists full of pancake-goo, 70% cocoa Fairtrade dark chocolate smeared round her face.

'Really?' Steve asks. 'Are you sure?'

He knows that I know this is not exclusively about giving up breastfeeding Imo. This is about not having any other chances to breastfeed. There'll be no more babies. We agreed Imo would be our last. Unless God has other ideas in the future, Steve was sure to tell me. But, at this point in time, we are both pretty sure another baby is more than either of us could handle. The strain on the house, our finances, nerves. Brittle, fragile nerves that could snap if pulled too taut. We have produced three healthy girls and poor little Thomas. Let's leave it at that and be thankful. That's what we tell ourselves. Again and again. Let's be thankful.

'And Rachel. What about you?' I ask, to stop thinking, to keep going.

'Well, seeing as you've both chosen like difficult stuff and that, I'm going to give up TV.'

'Really?' we all chorus.

Rachel looks around the table at her waiting audience, realising the import of what she has promised. 'Well, not all TV, obviously, that would be dumb,' she says, as if this is what she had meant all along. 'Just the American crud.'

'So no more *Pimp my Ride*?' I ask.

'No more *Pimp my ride*.'

'No more *Cribs?*' Jeremy asks.

'No more *Cribs*.'

'Give me a high five,' says Steve.

Rachel gives her father an extremely embarrassed high five and blushes the colour of the defrosted raspberries. Her dad, the vicar.

'If you can do that, Auntie Vicky,' says Jeremy, bolstered by his cousin and looking to up the ante, 'then I can give up Pot Noodles.'

Sensing a chink here, I venture: 'Just Pot Noodles?'

Jeremy sighs. 'And McDonald's, I suppose.'

'Does that mean more expensive pizzas?' his father asks. I think he's joking. I hope he's joking. Surely he doesn't begrudge his son the odd trip to Pizza Express?

But Jeremy takes his father seriously, at his word. 'Not if you sort things out with Mum. Then we can have homemade pizzas. In Dulwich. No offence, Auntie Vicky,' he adds quickly.

'None taken,' I reassure him. Jeremy can offend me as much as he likes if it enables his family to have another go at being a family, in their own home, a few miles and another world away from here.

Having wolfed down his pancake, Martin has become twitchy, pulling at his revolting beard and bouncing his leg up and down like a schoolboy in need of the loo. 'Would you excuse me while I have a quick shower?' He addresses this question to Dorota. He'd never normally ask permission to leave the table but he is obviously keen to perpetuate the myth of the charming gentleman. But I know the truth: he is a coward who will not answer his son's question. Dorota isn't quite taken in by his charm but she will forgive him anything because, bizarrely and like all those deluded souls before her, she thinks he is 'hunky'.

With Martin conveniently gone, that leaves Olivia and Dorota, who have both been very quiet, to finish what he started.

'What about you, Olivia?' asks Rachel. 'Can you think of anything you can give up for four weeks?'

Olivia thinks about this, twirling her hair around her finger (it'll need washing tonight). 'How long is four weeks?'

'Twenty eight days,' says Jeremy, pouncing on the question like it's a quiz.

Olivia considers her cousin's answer, still twirling. 'Is that a really, really, really long time?'

'No, darling,' says Steve. 'Though it can seem like it.'

'Well, then,' she says, taking a deep breath. 'My sticky pictures?'

'Your sticky pictures? But you love doing your sticky pictures,' Steve says, an expression of amazement on his face that his middle daughter could sacrifice so much.

We all look at her sticky pictures, stuck all over the fridge. My fridge.

'I do love my sticky pictures,' she agrees. 'But they are a bit, um, sticky, aren't they, Mummy?' She looks at me for verification.

'Well, yes.'

'And we don't like sticky things, do we, Mummy?'

'Well, no.'

This is the moment when I should be encouraging Olivia's creativity. But instead I feel relief that we'll have a break from the barrage of celebrities. So I don't dissuade her. Besides, everyone is now waiting expectantly for Dorota who has just poured herself another glass of sherry.

She meets our communal gaze. 'Okay, okay, I give up the sherry. It won't bother me at all. Not one little bit.' Then she downs her glass with a back-flick of her hennaed head, on the off chance we start Lent right now.

In the silence that follows, ballooning up around us, as we each consider the consequences of what we have put on the line, we can hear Martin overhead, banging about in the bathroom. Martin who started this off but isn't here to offer up his own sacrifices. Typical. One rule for him. Still, it would take time for him to pick a vice. There's such a long list.

And who's he sprucing himself up for now?

Later Steve tells his mother he's going out. 'I've got a meeting.'

Dorota says nothing.

'An Alpha meeting.'

She shrugs her shoulders.

He stoops to kiss her anyway. 'And maybe you could think about giving Dad a ring?' He says this gently, a hopeful smile on his slightly harassed face. The smile broadens briefly when she says: 'I'll think about it.' Then it goes again when she adds: 'I've thought about it and the answer is no.'

I go into the dark garden, all the way up to the end, and take a deep, deep breath. Foxes. Then I howl like a vixen and the scream is caught up by the Sutton train, hauling it off to Kent.

Thoughts for the Day: If Jesus came back to earth, would he make it into the pages of *Hello*?

February 5th 1978

I showed Mum the photo. She was repotting a spider plant in the front room and there was soil all over the rug. I wanted to get out the carpet sweeper but I wanted to know about the photo more.

Who is this with Dad? I asked.

Mum turned away from me and yanked off a brown leaf. I wasn't sure if she had heard me but then she said it's Jack. Your Uncle Jack.

I said I didn't know Dad had a brother. She said not a real brother but like a brother. I asked if we'd met him and she said no. I asked her why not.

She rubbed her hands on her skirt and looked out the window like he might be standing out there in the street waving at her.

I looked too but then I felt silly because she said he's dead, that's why.

Chapter Twenty: Wednesday 6th February
Ash Wednesday

My breasts are being attacked with miniature knives dipped in molten lava cutting and scorching every time I even think about moving. I woke this morning, on the floor of Rachel and Olivia's room, having started my Lenten fast straightaway last night, to find engorged, twin peaks of burning, curdling milk.

But it's alright. There's a plan, carefully constructed last night between Steve and myself to help Imo and me through the first day of Lent and making use of Dorota whose appearance yesterday, if not exactly welcomed by me, was, according to Steve, another God-incidence. While Steve is at the early Ash Wednesday service, Dorota is on standby, armed with a bottle and an iron will, so I won't give in if Imo kicks up a fuss when she realises she has to forgo her morning feed.

As for me, I'm leaving the house, keeping out of the way for the whole morning. Steve is going to work from home, not that he'll get an awful lot done with Dorota and Imo battling for his attention. But maybe, hopefully, he'll get the chance for a heart to heart with his mother. He'll manage. It's me I'm worried about. A morning off and for the first time in a decade I am at a loss. Steve gave me some options, wrote them down on the back of an envelope, in his scrappy, plumber capitals to make them seem more real.

SWIMMING (I'll never get these breasts into my swimming costume and even if I got that far and eased myself into the baths, I would prove Archimedes theory on water displacement for all to see.)

SHOPPING (We have no money and window shopping is depressing.)

A WALK (There's only Penge High Street and the park and I spend most of my life in these places and can't walk an inch without being spotted so why would I go there of my own accord?)

VISITING A FRIEND (I no longer have any friends.)

CHURCH (The service is nearly over and if I go down there now I'll be cornered by well-meaning, nosy, demanding parishioners.)

DAD (I can't bear to go that far away. When I know Imo can survive a while without me then yes, maybe a day in Worthing on my own, checking up on the tattooed lady, would be possible. Not that I like to think my baby will be able to survive without me. What mother does like to think that?)

So that leaves the last option:

A CAFE (But where? KFC, Burger King, Southern Fried Chicken. No thanks. Seeing as Steve has kindly offered me the car, I will go to the place I feel most comfortable. Try something new today.)

Is it really the coffee that drew me here? The ambient lighting? The colour scheme? Or is this the limit of my world?

Today I must drink my machine-dispensed latte alone, reading *St Hilda's Parish News* as that's all I had in my bag. Though not quite alone. Here comes Amanda, pushing a trolley, laden with bread and fish, enough to feed the mouths of Penge, not a cleaning product in sight. Too late to hide under the table.

'Vicky! What on earth are you doing here? All on your own!'

Customers look up from their eggs and bacon and take in Amanda's presence. She is not what you'd call discreet. Not one of those people who blend into the background. But she's even more conspicuous with the smudgy grey cross on her forehead, the visible reminder that she has done her duty and gone to the Ash Wednesday service. *Remember you are dust and unto dust you shall return.* If I didn't know this I could be forgiven for assuming she was the local mad lady. Or just dirty – which, of course, she is.

Amanda is used to seeing me with a child attached to my hip, my hand or my skirts or following truculently in my wake. She is not used to the idea of me, Vicky, alone, drinking a latte. At least the sight of me clutching the *Parish News* must assure her I am not sliding down that slippery slope. But the idea of Vicky, woman in her own right, has thrown her usual composure all over the floor, which incidentally needs a scrub. There's a splat of spilt ketchup, like a crime scene.

'Can I get you a coffee, Amanda?'

She is tempted. For a brief moment. But then she gets a grip and tells me with some determination: 'I've given up coffee for Lent.'

'Tea, then.'

'Haven't got time.'

'No time for a cup of tea? Really, Amanda, you must make time for yourself every now and then.'

Amanda says nothing. She has never been offered advice by her protégée before and is unsure what is happening to the status quo. The status quo is having a machine-dispensed latte, reading the *Parish News*. To coin a phrase of Rachel's: 'big wow'. But it is a big wow, clearly. Amanda abandons her trolley – if you can't beat 'em, join 'em – and fetches herself a hot chocolate. It's what Jesus would have done, I know. I saw her checking her WWJD wristband. I'm not sure he'd be in Sainsbury's. I think he'd be where the needy are, at Lidl.

She eases herself onto the plastic chair, jewellery clanging, an assortment of colourful scarves wafting 70s style perfume over me – Tweed or Charlie, something Mum used to wear – and attacks her hot chocolate with gusto. She proffers me a doughnut. 'Thought I might as well be hung for a sheep as a lamb.'

Not sure that's the official Church of England view on sin but I let it go.

'Thanks. I didn't get round to breakfast.'

She stops chewing, watching me navigate the mound of sugar on my doughnut, waiting for me to elaborate. Which I decide is probably the best thing to do or she'll never leave me alone and part of the plan devised by Steve and I was that I would have some time alone. He said it would do me good. This wasn't what I had in mind. Under different circumstances I would've used that Sanctuary voucher but ironically, at the point when I most need to be pampered, I'm not in a fit state.

'In a couple of days, she'll have forgotten all about your breasts.' She says this very loudly, with dramatic expression that could get her a job on the stage and to the great amusement of the builders on the next table whose ears prick up at the mention of my breasts.

I slump in my chair, shielding myself from the inevitable checking-out. But Amanda's words are registering in my pain-addled brain. 'A couple of days? I can't disappear for a couple of days!'

'Be strong, Vicky. Don't give in.' She pats my hand (I knew I'd picked up that tip from somewhere). 'I'll pray for you,' she adds, fiddling with her WWJD wristband. Then she downs her hot chocolate with amazing speed and leaves me to it, assured of my soul.

The doughnut is doing bad things to my insides so once I'm sure I won't bump into her again, I make my own departure, picking my way around the young man mopping the floor (I'd be impressed if I had the energy), heading where, I don't know. I'd like to go to the loos and try and ease some of the milk out but that will only encourage more in its place. Be strong. Don't give in.

As I pass the builders' table, one of them catches my eye, telling me – as if I'd be grateful for his thoughts on the matter – that he wouldn't forget my breasts in a hurry. If only he knew the reason they were this size. Perhaps I should enlighten him, put him off his breakfast. Or perhaps I should give him a swift kick in his double eggs and bacon.

After a random drive, up to Crystal Palace and down again, round in circles and along back-doubles, the pain is too much. I feel hot and flushed, a taste of sick nestling in my gullet, possibly the onset of mastitis, just to make my day. While I'm debating going to the doctor's to get this checked out – surely only mothers of newborns have this problem? – I find the car taking me on its own magical mystery tour, right past the surgery and Eileen and all the possible help in there, help that I do and don't need, straight past the school that is educating my daughter and nephew and we, the Espace and I, end up in the car park of St Hilda's and for once the shoppers of Penge have spared us a place. Hallelujah. After several moments of careful manoeuvring, I am free of the car, and I let my feet take me onto hallowed ground, not into the church, but round the side, skirting the hall so I have to duck down below window height in case I am spotted by an eagle-eyed Olivia. Thankfully it's too drizzly for the children to be out in the yard on scooters and trikes and so I am safe, but I wish I'd brought my cagoule, not that I'd have won the battle to get it over my towering infernos, and then along a red-bricked path cleared of weeds only yesterday by Miss Brooke, onto the damp grass, past the headstones and pots of wilting flowers and bare-leaved shrubs, over to the corner where, under the shelter of an ancient Yew, is a small, simple headstone that tries to sum up a short life and a sudden death. The unknown depths of what it is to be human.

My Thomas.

Remember you are dust and unto dust you shall return.

And thinking of him, I get the let-down reflex, that feeling a man can never know, the tightening in the breasts, the contraction in the womb, the sensation of milk flow, the leaking when there's no baby. What I would give to have one more time with Thomas. One more feed. To hold him in my arms and feel his gummy mouth working hard. His eyes closed in concentration, his breathing, deep and contented. What I would give.

All I can do for him now is tidy his grave, keep it moss-free, and make sure the letters of his name stay bright and clear.

Thomas.

Knowing I can go home to another baby, to my precious Imo, knowing I could go and feed her right now and stop this physical pain doesn't help me. It doesn't change a thing. Whatever I do, wherever I go, I can't shake off the clinging, persistent, incurable ache. *Time is a great healer.* When I walk away from here I can't bring him with me. I can't bring him home with me like I did that first time, a day old, bundled in a blue blanket in the bucket. We brought him home, Steve and I, from hospital, clean and new, to a full house waiting expectantly for him: his big sister, Rachel, and a full set of proud grandparents, Mum, Dad, Dorota and Roland. They couldn't have been more taken with him. His deep murky eyes, his tiny hand that would grab your finger for all he was worth.

Now all we have of him are photos. In albums that are too difficult to open. In lockets that hang next to hearts. Memories of a sweet little boy. I have to leave him here, wherever he is.

I would give my soul.

A hand on my arm. I don't jump because I was half-expecting it; there's always someone lurking around this place, waiting to pounce on you from behind a gravestone. I thought it would be Amanda, still in hot pursuit. Or Desmond. Or Miss Brooke back to her weeding. But it is Karolina.

'Gosh, we keep bumping into each other.'

'Coincidence,' she says and I can't help a small smile to myself when I think of Steve's take on coincidences. 'Is this your little boy?' she asks, so far out of the blue that I don't see it coming.

I nod, feeling light-headed. The ground appears to be moving, like one of those travelators at Heathrow, though I know I am standing perfectly still, concentrating on my breathing, the dark green needles of the yew above my head. 'How did you know?'

'Shelley has big mouth.'

'Ah, Shelley. Yes, she does. Very big.' I watch Karolina's hand fiddling with the crucifix round her neck. 'And what else have you heard about me?'

'You are vicar's wife.'

'I'm not as important as that. I'm just the curate's wife.'

She looks none the wiser so I fill her in on C of E hierarchy. 'So you are training to be vicar's wife?'

'You could say that, yes.'

'I did many years training to be dentist but it is not so important job as looking after souls.'

'My husband does all that, not me.'

Karolina shivers and then I realise I am shivering too, standing here in my next-to-useless cardigan, in the shade of the yew under a slate-grey sky, the February morning biting hard.

She looks at me, up and down.

'I have too much milk when Natasha was baby. I must return to work when she is only few weeks old. I must go in toilets and get rid of it. All that good milk washed away.'

We should both be excruciatingly embarrassed, strangers talking about intimate details. But it isn't embarrassment in the air. It is something else that I am not yet certain of.

'I am sorry,' she says.

'What for?'

'I am sorry you lose your baby.' Her words float there, quietly, the Penge traffic, going about its business on the other side of the high church wall, almost smothering them.

'I can't let go,' I tell her, unexpectedly, for I have told no-one this, not even Steve.

Her hands clutch her bag. 'You are not ready,' she says.

'I'll never be ready.'

She has no reply, not in her bag, or up her sleeves so I don't know if she agrees or what. But 'never' seems an awfully long time to feel like this.

'You could get help maybe?'

'I don't want pills. I've been offered pills and I know if I took one that would be it. Hooked.'

'I did not mean that. I mean for the breastfeeding. A doctor. Or that health visitor I see you with. She can get you through this, maybe. Then you can deal with your... loss.'

'I'd rather just go home.'

'You have good husband. Nice home. You will be okay, I think. But some men can't wait around forever.'

Karolina then says she has to go. And she slips back down the weed-free path and disappears round the side of St Hilda's, her words hanging there before me.

Some men can't wait around forever.

Back home. I let myself in, on tiptoes, easing the door open and closed. But Imo has the nose of a highly-trained sniffer dog and the howl of a Baskerville hound. Before I have made it to the stairs, Dorota appears in the poky hallway, blocking out the sunlight but not enough so that Imo can't fix her eyes on me, reach for me, desperation in her little chubby face.

Be strong. Don't give in.

I grab her from my mother-in-law who is so surprised to see me move so fast, yelping in pain, that she relinquishes her granddaughter and lets me take her upstairs.

'You are making the rod for your back,' she calls up after me. But I don't hear anymore. I don't know which feeling is stronger: the pain of Imo's furious sucking, the relief of the milk flow, the sense of failure that I couldn't even manage a morning, a few measly hours, or the guilt... because it is Imo lying here, curled up next to me on the bed, and not Thomas. He is left behind in the churchyard. He is not with me. He is gone.

Much later, long after the end of playgroup, after the kids have been collected from school by an efficient Tamarine, after the sun has sloped off behind the rooftops of Penge, after Imo has consumed her own body weight in milk and I have applied hot flannel after hot flannel, after self-recriminations and explanations to Steve, to Dorota, to anyone else who thinks they have a valid opinion, Martin shows up again. For a bath. Apparently this friend of his has run out of hot water. (What a shame Steve can't go and fix the boiler.) Dorota insists Martin stay for tea, which she is concocting. I don't suppose he'll be too impressed with her baked bean and turnip lasagne, but tough. He should have politely declined and left. Got a pizza. A kebab. A bucket of nuggetburgerwings.

Still, Jeremy is pleased to see his dad and even drags himself away from *Neighbours* to come to the kitchen and make him a cup of tea. Then he gets out his RE homework to show. The Sermon on the Mount. Hovering at the kitchen sink in case I am needed – which I am, judging by the amount of washing-up my mother-in-law has generated – I notice my brother wince. Our household produces many winces from him. He only has to look in a cupboard or listen in on a telephone conversation to pull that contorted face that reminds me yet again how it felt to be that buck-toothed, frizzy-haired girl. How anyone can wince at the Sermon on the Mount is beyond me. But Martin is an angry atheist, another of Darwin's Rottweilers, a Dawkin's Labrador, getting in a doggy stew at the faintest whiff of faith. Mother Teresa, Julian of Norwich, Terry Waite; he lumps them all together under the heading of 'God Nutter'.

'Why don't you show your dad the makeover you've given the shed?' I suggest, trying to make some breathing space in the kitchen, which is full of hot air.

'Yeah, Dad, come on, it's wicked.' Jeremy leads the way authoritatively, physically pushing his father out the back door.

Not that Martin is reluctant to be ejected from the kitchen; it has the dual function of getting him away from two mad women and giving him the opportunity to light up.

And what about me? I'd like to lock the shed and douse petrol all around it. Then accidently on purpose, light one of his fags. Not with Jeremy in there, obviously. I'd let him back in the house to watch the end of *Neighbours*. Good old Auntie Vicky.

'Vicky?'

I hear a distant voice. A glass is prised into my scrunched-up hand.

'You look like you want to punch your brother's lights out.' Dorota beams at her cockney expression. She has a whole collection of them, quite endearing with her Polish accent, still thick after decades in this city. 'Remember you have one brother only. I have none, no-one who remembers my mother or father. Martin is the only one who knows your childhood. And your daughters... well, they have Jeremy. They are lucky to have such a cousin.' She manages to stop herself saying that my girls will never have a brother. And she is right; they do not have a brother. But they did. And I do. Is that supposed to make me appreciate Martin?

I move away from the washing-up and stand at the door, which has been left ajar to release the steam from the root vegetables Dorota has been boiling to a pulp. The physical pain is easing, thanks to the cabbage leaves she's stuffed down my bra. So I'll forever smell of school dinners. But the lower, underlying, persistent ache is still there. You'd think I'd be used to it by now but it still takes me by surprise.

And there is Martin, loitering on one of my stepping stones, in the dark garden, marked out by the red tip of his stinky cigarette, bringing a whole new meaning to Ash Wednesday. *Grant that these ashes may be for us a sign of our penitence and a symbol of our mortality.*

Do I really wish Martin was dead? Burnt to a cinder? A pile of ashes to be spread on the garden? No, I just wish he was back in Dulwich, drinking bottled beer from his very expensive American fridge and winding up his own family, his wife and his son, putting up with *Pimp my Ride* on his vast plasma screen, so I can finally have my space back. That is, once Dorota has returned to Roland.

And Roland? Has anyone other than Steve given him a moment's thought today? Poor Roland. Where is he in all this? Down The Bull, according to Dorota. Maybe I should join him. But something tells me an early night is required. But if I'm to get any sleep I need Imo to relieve me of some of this milk. Just one more feed.

Thoughts for the Day: Steve is a man of patience. And he is a man with all the time in the world. All the time in eternity. So he will wait around forever. Won't he?

Chapter Twenty-one: Friday 8th February

Dorota is still here, at my kitchen sink, scrubbing yet more cabbage leaves, having taken on the challenge as if she were my personal trainer. She'll be massaging my shoulders and giving me pep talks next.

I turn my attention to the fridge, removing half-eaten jars of chutney and olives. It needs a thorough clean. It is deeply satisfying, allowing me to zone out and think of nothing but the task in hand, but then I become unsteadied by the sight of one of Martin's Stella Artois bottles lurking behind the tomato ketchup. I hear Mum's voice echo again – *Pop down the chemist's will you, Vicky-Love?* – but elbow grease soon gets rid of that.

Dorota and I work in companionable silence and I smile to myself, thinking how much my mother-in-law and I have in common despite her being from Gdansk and all her petty annoyances. Mum wasn't annoying. She was just a mess, couldn't keep a household. But it didn't matter. It gave me a place in that family, as I could never live up to Martin.

Dorota has stopped scrubbing now, and peels off her rubber gloves. I look up at her from my position on the floor and see the slump in her shoulders, a characteristic she's handed down to Steve for when he's tired, or Charlton has lost, or when he's facing the Bishop. Is she crying?

'Dorota, what is it?'

She starts fully-fledged bawling and I wonder just how many tears will be shed in this house this year.

'I miss my Roland,' she says. 'But I can't go back.'

'Why can't you go back?''

'Because I am silly old woman.'

'No, Dorota. You're not. You are a wonderful woman and Roland is lucky to have you.' I had no idea these words were going to tumble out of my mouth but there they are, floating in the steam of the kitchen and I am rather proud of myself for saying something kind, that I know is actually the truth deep down. She might be my mother-in-law but she is the only mother I have now. I'm even more surprised to find myself getting up and hugging her, far more meaningful and restorative than hand-patting has ever been.

She takes a huge sniff and blows her nose into the clean hanky I offer. Her shoulders straighten. 'The drawers in the girls' bedroom need sorting out,' she says. 'There are plenty clothes you can pack up and send to Romania. They are still very poor there. Not like Polska. We Polish work very hard. We are intelligent people.'

I'm really not sure how to answer this, so I let her go.

Late afternoon and Roland is on the phone. He has been calling several times a day, trying to get his wife to speak to him but she is not ready yet. So I let Roland waffle on; he is lonely, all on his own and I feel sorry for him. I half-wonder if I should go over but daren't leave the house right now, not in my physical state, not with Dorota all upset. Besides, from past experience I know this will be done and dusted soon. Until the next marital crisis five years down the line. I try passing him onto Steve but he shakes his head and holds up his left shoe as an excuse. He's polishing his vicar shoes – plain black Doc Martens – on the kitchen table, having first carefully covered it with Martin's *Observer*, being well-trained. He's not joining in his family's unusual reminiscing today. Dorota, still labouring over the girls' clothes upstairs, isn't one to hark back over her past; she says 'it is what it is' and talking about stuff won't change it. But she has mentioned her mama and tata today. Her Polska. Being apart from Roland must remind her of how cut off she is from her mother country.

'Why don't you come over?' I ask Roland, ignoring Steve's more energetic head-shaking, and turning away from him. 'Or Steve can come and see you.'

Steve sighs, then clears away the shoe kit and, after a grudging goodbye peck, sprints off for a confirmation class. His first one. Desmond is finally relinquishing some responsibilities, now Steve has proved himself to be more than a plumber. He's still got a way to go with me.

'Roland? You still there?'

'Still here, love. I'm alright. Just give the old girl a hug from me.'

And I can't help smiling to myself as we say our goodbyes.

As for Steve, he needs to put his family first, his mum and dad. Us. I feel like I've been pushed to the back of a very long queue. I know I should be pleased he's found fulfilment in his life – six years ago I would never have thought that was possible as he was falling to pieces, breaking up before my eyes and I could do nothing about it except be the strong one. But now my strength is sapping. I am so very tired. And he's off out with a bunch of willing Christians, prepared to take that extra step of faith and be confirmed into the church. Teenagers mostly, from the local private school. And, surprisingly, Karolina. She talked to Steve after the service last week and said she was seeking God. Always one to encourage a search, Steve invited her to Alpha but she said she was beyond that. She knew where God was, she just wanted to get to know him better. She wanted to be baptised. She was very keen, which goes to show you never know about people. He said she was really friendly and everything, which I should tell Shelley at playgroup. Shelley should be the one that Dorota aims her speeches at. She's a right little Enoch Powell. Not me. I married a half-Pole, didn't I? I married a plumber.

Eastenders is finished and by some miracle all the children are in their beds – whether they are sleeping or not I don't care, as long as they are quiet. Dorota is having a bath. Thankfully Steve upgraded the central heating with a combination boiler before quitting his old life or we'd have run out of hot water. Every time Dorota changes position in the bath it makes a rocking sound, like the groaning of an old ship tossed about in a stormy sea.

Finally, when I am really worrying about the structural support of the ceiling, Dorota pulls out the plug and a gush of water can be heard, followed by more creaking floorboards. Hopefully she'll take herself off to bed and I can wallow in front of the telly. I won't have to listen to her commentary, her tuts, her exclamations of disgust. And no Martin either. Heaven.

But no. She's coming downstairs, trying to do it quietly but unsuccessfully. She appears in the doorway not wrapped up in her fleecy kaftan of a dressing gown but dolled up in her smart outfit, make-up, the works, so I catch a glimpse of that young girl out on the town, dating Roland at the Locarno.

'I miss my Roland,' she says. 'When is Stefan coming back? I want him to take me home to his tata.'

Thoughts for the Day: Will Steve love me when I am a fat pensioner?

Chapter Twenty-Two: Sunday 10th February

First Sunday of Lent

Early morning and I'm already exhausted despite Imo sleeping through. It was me that lay awake, listening to every little noise. Even the familiar ones sounded different: the creaks of the house, the chirpy snore, the train, the late-night home-comers trudging past. They all had an edge to them.

But it was the silences in between, waiting for Imo to cry out to me. I crept in to her at three, to check on the rise and fall of her ribcage. She'd wriggled onto her front and I placed my hand on her back. Felt her warmth. She snuffled and sighed and I was tempted to pick her up and hold her close. It was the hardest thing to leave her there, to walk away. I stayed for a few minutes more, standing there, watching over her, my ears tuned in to her sleeping breath. Then I managed it. I tiptoed out of the box room and went back to bed, slipping between the cool sheets. I lay there for ages, stiff and alert, the early morning light strengthening slowly through the curtains, hearing those first birds, the early shift workers leaving home and heading for the station. I must have drifted off eventually because suddenly there was Steve, nudging me awake, placing a cup of tea on my bedside table.

'Where's Imo?' was my first response.

Then I heard a raucous giggle coming from next door,

Rachel and Olivia's room. But it was neither of them shrieking. It was Imo.

'I've given her a bottle. Hope you don't mind.'

For a moment I did. But I swallowed any negative feelings down with my first glug of tea, telling myself Steve had every right to do this. He's her dad. Not her wicked uncle.

And when I got myself out of bed and peeked into the girls' bedroom and saw my baby with her big sisters, rolling around the floor together, I put my trust in my husband. Just a little bit.

Steve's turn up the front this week, standing there in his neatly ironed choir dress behind my polished lectern. St Hilda's doesn't have a pulpit, being a modern church without architectural significance. The old St Hilda's was flattened by the Luftwaffe, though not one life was lost. The lectern, along with a few other cherished items, was salvaged from the ashes and, like a phoenix, it has lived again in this new church and so every time I polish it, even the annoyingly tricky bits, I think of the Blitz, the Londoners who had no choice but to go to war. Gdansk had it far worse, I know that, flattened by the Nazis and the Soviets and even the Allies. But that's just the snippets Roland's told me.

So the vicars and curates of St Hilda's no longer float above the congregation, looking down and telling them how to live their lives. They are on our level. Steve likes to move around, using gestures to support his words and giving his arms a vague workout. Today he's particularly animated, speaking on a subject he's passionate about: our church should be a place of community once again, where everyone is welcome – the poor, the rich, the sick, the exercise freaks, the dispossessed, the possessed, the workaholics, the alcoholics, the young, the old and those in between. An inclusive church pouring out love on those who come through its doors, whether they are looking for God or have simply walked in by mistake – which is a possibility as St Hilda's looks more like a job centre than a place of worship.

While we sit in this sacred place, the traffic slugging past outside, I think of the people trapped in their pod-like cars, on their way to visit friends, to football matches, to IKEA, and wonder about this word, 'community'. It's something Londoners pride themselves on. As long as they are born-and-bred Londoners. A certain type of Londoner. But what about the Karolinas and the Tamarines? Are they part of this community? Steve sees beyond Penge, beyond London, far beyond the M25 as far as the kingdom of heaven, ever since that day he headed towards Dartford in his van, his tool box at his side rather than his Bible.

I feel something hearing these words, possibly pride. When I look around at the people I am sitting amongst to see what they are thinking because it has gone very quiet – none of the usual coughing or fidgeting or hassock knocking – all the faces are pulled in the same expression of concentration (except for Mr Maynard who is deeply absorbed in picking a scab on his elbow).

And there is Karolina. She must be taking it all in too; she has what I can only describe as a rapt expression on her rather heavily made-up face. Normally she gives off this hostile vibe that says 'keep away from me' but today, right now, she is all beatific smiles. Even her bleached blonde hair looks less aggressive, softened somehow. That's it: her usual hard edges have been softened. Steve has that effect on people.

I take all this in with a glance. And not just because my mother brought me up in the knowledge that it is rude to stare, but because my attention is grabbed by a man sitting over the far side, near the back, scribbling frantically in a notebook like a journalist at a trial. It is not out of the ordinary for a churchgoer to make notes while the sermon is being given – Bible verses, pertinent points, recommended reading – but this is not what I have seen before. Not since his wedding.

I turn away from him quickly, a funny feeling gurgling

round my stomach. What the hell is Martin doing here? Why is he writing? I take another quick look, from behind Margery's bouffant hair. His hand is still. He is staring at Steve who seems completely unaware that his brother-in-law is scrutinising every word he says. What is he up to?

We stand for the final hymn, pulled from our mesmerisation. There's a fluttering of pages and a waft of perfume as coats are flapped and scarves flung about. Make me a channel of your peace. When I get up courage to look again at my brother, he is gone. But the space where he was sitting seems to radiate a glow. As if his very presence in church was something other. Something that can never be included.

Roast chicken, roast potatoes, roast parsnips, mashed swede, green sprouts, carrot sticks, a mountain of peas, stuffing, gravy, the works. Some people only bother with a meal like this at Christmas but I will do it every Sunday till I am no longer able to use a vegetable peeler or wield a masher. This is my contribution to our Sundays and I may not have thought as a young woman at university that this would be satisfying, but actually it is a triumph of achievement. Every Sunday this meal says 'Look at us, we are a family and by my efforts we will stay a family. Despite our losses, we will be victorious'.

'These sprouts are like golf balls, Victoria. Did you forget to cook them?' Martin gulps down half a glass or Merlot as if it will save his life.

I ignore him. I have other concerns, like trying to coerce a cocktail of mashed-up parsnip and carrot though Imo's gritted gums.

Martin makes a point of pushing his sprouts to one side and continues chomping his way through his meal, refilling his glass several times so that there's only a thimbleful left when Steve goes to top up mine. He goes to the larder and quietly uncorks another bottle.

'You should really let that breathe,' says Martin to his

patient brother-in-law.

Only I notice my husband take a slow inhalation of breath, his patience being tested by Martin who is somehow more obnoxious than ever. Why isn't he stuffing his face at some other sucker's house? Or down the pub? He was supposed to drop Jeremy back to Claudia's after church, but Claudia is busy until later – conveniently, after lunch. At least Jeremy is eating my sprouts, quite surprising as they are green and healthy. Jeremy – unlike me or the baby – is fanatically sticking to his Lenten promise, even managing his five-a-day. God moves in mysterious ways.

'Must get on. Come on, son. Eat up. Your mother's due back soon and I want a word.'

'What about pudding? Auntie Vicky's made lemon meringue pie.'

'Has she now?' Martin turns his beady little eyes on me. 'Have you been at the Fanny Craddock recipes again, Vicky-Love?' He snorts at this 'joke' of his, shrugs on his jacket – denim, I ask you – and informs Jeremy his auntie will save him some for later.

Which of course she will do, being a good auntie. But that doesn't stop me wanting to be a bad sister. Wanting to tie him to the railway track at the end of the garden, like in those silent movies. Only I'd like the sound on. So I could listen to his blood-curdling screams.

A moment of peace. That dip on a Sunday afternoon after the children have been run ragged round the park by Steve and me, after we've washed up together proving I'm not the fifties-style house drudge Martin thinks I am. Steve has done his sermon and has a rare free hour. I put him to work on the draught excluder for the back door.

The phone goes. It is answered immediately which means Olivia has picked it up. She will make a very good PA one day, though I can't see her settling for anything less than director general of the world. She appears at the kitchen door dressed in one of Steve's surplices. She looks like she belongs to some weird American cult but I don't say anything as it's not one I've ironed. 'It's that lady with the dolphin on her arm,' she says, holding out the phone. 'Granddad's friend.'

The tattooed lady. Pat. Why is she ringing?

'Don't worry,' is the first thing Pat says. 'He's not dead or anything, though if I hadn't come when I did he might be for all we know.'

If I could form coherent thoughts and transform them into words, I might ask her where she got her superb telephone manner from. But all I can do is demand, rather fiercely, so that Steve sits up from his prostrate position by the back door: 'What happened? Tell me what happened.'

So Pat does as she's told and tells me what happened.

The story according to Pat: *I'd just been down Lidl to get your dad some bits for the freezer and jam – he's got a sweet tooth hasn't he, he'd have jam with everything given the chance – so it really wasn't my day to see him but I reckoned I'd pop the things round, there and then, rather than putting them in my freezer to be going on with. I suppose you could call it female intuition or a sixth sense – I think I'm a bit psychic, there's gypsy blood in me somewhere down the line – I felt I needed to go round and check up on your dad...* At this point, call me psychic too because I sense a thinly-veiled accusation of neglect being channelled down the fibre optic cables to be snagged on my guilt-antenna... *which was just as well as he didn't answer when I knocked so I used my key and let myself in.* Finally there is a pause while I wonder how she came to have a key and, of course, what she is about to say next. I wait while she catches her breath, suspecting that she is taking the opportunity to have a drag on one of her dirty roll-ups. *He's only lying on the floor of the living room sprawled in front of the* Jeremy Kyle show. *I know for a fact* *he can't stand Jeremy Kyle – I'm more of a Trisha girl myself – so I realised something was up. He's had a fall and the silly bugger can't move.* I blanch at this expression. If anyone's going to call my father a silly bugger it'll be me, thank you very much. *I'm a trained first aider you'll be pleased to hear, so I checked all the vitals and then called the doctor who said he's alright, but they want to find out why he keeps dropping, I just thought you'd want to know but he's asleep right now and he needs his rest.*

I am torn between gratitude and annoyance that Pat found him when she did. I'm sure he'd have got help somehow but then you never know. I tell Pat, graciously, that I'll speak to him once he's woken up and sort out a visit. She tells me, smugly, that she will keep an extra eye on him. I want to ask her where she keeps that extra eye – in her tobacco pouch? But of course I don't. I am good Vicky. Patient Vicky. Bad daughter Vicky.

The story according to Dad: *I was getting up to switch the channels – Pat had tidied up the remote control – when I somehow tripped over my own legs. Don't ask me how. It only took a second. Suddenly I was on the floor with a sore shoulder and no energy to get back up again. The floor was the only place I wanted to be. Though I could've done without that Jeremy Kyle lecturing all those ill-nourished people. Where's a gardening programme when you need one? After enduring several lie detector tests, and all the boos and hisses like the panto at Christmas, I was beginning to wonder if I should try and crawl to the phone when I heard the door go. For a moment I thought that was it. I was being burgled. I was going to be done-over. But then I heard the clip-clop of Pat's shoes and I've never been so glad to see those legs come into view.*

Dad tells me this on the phone when Pat finally lets me speak to him. I can hear her squawk with fake annoyance in the background at the reference to her legs and I do my best to swallow the violent feelings that this generates. I inform Dad that we will be coming down on Saturday for a few days. Half term has come in the nick of time. Vicky to the rescue.

But what about Martin? When is he going to offer up some filial duty?

Thoughts for the Day: Being shipwrecked, alone, on a desert island, with only the birds of the air, the creatures of the sea and the odd wild animal for company, has got a bad press.

February 14th 1978

I didn't get any Valentine cards but I don't care. All the boys I know are dirty little youknowwots.

Martin got a card from Heidi. He was embarrassed because it was ginormous with a massive Snoopy on the front holding a bunch of roses. Mum wanted to put it on the mantelpiece but he said no way and hid it in his stink bomb room.

Dad said Heidi is very keen and Martin said they all are, and Dad said you better be careful. Then Dad went out to sort out the compost and Martin went to rugby practice.

I tidied out the cupboard under the stairs and found 57p. Finders keepers. I am not a commie. Mrs Thatcher would be proud of me.

Alice is coming for tea tomorrow so I have to tidy the front room and remind Mum to go shopping. I will ask if she can get an Arctic Roll. Maybe Heidi will come too then Alice will know not to go silly over Martin if she sees him with his girlfriend.

Alice is clever. She should know better. But then Heidi is clever too. She should know better than to go out with my brother. But then he's never buried them in the sludgy sand at Worthing and forgotten about them.

Chapter Twenty-Three:

Saturday 16th February

Half-term. Hallelujah! No packed lunches, no school uniforms. A leisurely breakfast and then down to Worthing for a few days. The car is packed, courtesy of Steve who has made car-packing into an art form. I wish he'd take the same care over his sock drawer. What is it with cars? Martin treats his Saab better than he treats his fellow human beings, even his wife. Especially his wife. Not that she's in my good books, having asked if Jeremy can 'tag along' to Worthing. Apparently Claudia can't take time off to look after him. I suspect she can't take off time from her new boyfriend, Harold Pinter.

Martin calls by with some money for Jeremy and to say sorry he can't make it down but he's snowed under. Surprise, surprise. As we pile in the car, fiddling with seat belts, Martin stands watching Tamarine who is washing Bob's woebegone Rover. He has a smile on his face as she stretches on her tiptoes to reach across the roof with her sponge.

I lower the window to pass on final instructions. 'Thanks for feeding Socks, Tamarine.'

Tamarine waves her sponge regally and gets back to her task.

'And Martin.'

'Yes, Vicky-Love?'

'Keep your phone with you in case I need to get hold of you.'

'I can give you Bill's number if you're that worried.'

The empty house stands behind us. I know I could offer it to Martin in our absence. But no. He'd trash it. Let Bill (or, if Bill's anything like Martin, his wife), clean up after my brother.

'Go on, then. You'd best give it to me.'

Martin scribbles on a business card of his. Since when have academics had business cards? Professor Martin Bumface. I snatch it off him and shove it in my purse. Just in case.

'See you, Dad,' says Jeremy, a small voice with undertones of Oliver Twist. A well-fed Oliver Twist.

'Bye, son.'

Is he going to offer more than that? No. He's already transferred his attention to poor Tamarine. As Steve pulls away I notice Martin speaking to her. Whatever it is Tamarine says – and I'd love to know what – Martin quickly turns away from her and trudges back down the street to his Saab.

I look at the three girls, lined up across the back seat like Russian dolls, and try to fill the hollowness boring away inside me with thoughts of the week ahead. Of Dad, Worthing, tattoos.

I feel Steve's hand on my knee. His plumber's hand. His vicar's hand. The hand that has fixed washing machines and baptised babies. That I held at our wedding, squeezing on a ring that was too tight as it was such a hot day. I sometimes wish I could go back to the start, just me and Steve. Back to our old flat, my biscuit tin in the wardrobe, minus its hospital name bands and scan photos. Back to a time when there were no babies, no worries. But time cannot go back or stand still though I must replay that night over and over. Time goes on and we move forward leaving that day further and further behind though never far enough away to lose any clarity. Time goes on and I keep breathing. I go to bed at night, I get up in the morning and in between I do all the things I'm supposed to do. And now, right now, the car wheels of our Espace turn round and round and move us on. We leave our home, travelling slowly through the streets of Penge, the Saturday shoppers, the comings and goings, to-ings and fro-ings. It's my home but I'm disconnecting from it. I'm being cast out into a world of fear where I have no control. And this panicky feeling is down to Martin. He's the one who's made me stand outside of myself, forcing me to examine an unwelcome picture of my life.

My husband's hand squeezes my leg and I'm pleased to report my leg is not made of wood. Blood moves through it. Pulses throb. My breath comes and goes. My heart beats. I am alive.

'Don't worry, Vick,' Steve says. He is always saying this to me, probably because I am always worrying. But then he says something unexpected. He says: 'One day your soul will sing.'

I don't know what to say to this. I am trying to visualise this soul of mine, singing, when Imo starts up a whimper, a tell-tale sign that vomit is on the horizon and all visions of souls are blotted out and obscured by the things of this life. This holey life.

The Worthing wind, as usual, is bracing. It bowls along the flat coast and knocks the London grey from us. We take the kids to see the wood slick that has washed up from the shipwrecked Ice Prince since we were last here. It is quite a sight. Dad has told us about it but we had to see it for ourselves. Five minutes of this attack on the senses and then we'll regroup and grapple with whatever Dad has in store for us.

'So, Vicky, what's it like being married to a vicar? D'you have to watch your Ps and Qs or are you all religious?' Pat has called round to check me out. I am a novelty, somewhere between the Holy Mother and Meggie from *The Thorn Birds*.

Steve comes to my rescue and asks her what it's like being a home help, telling her he's humbled by her job. Pat is not won over this easily and switches her attention to Steve instead.

'So what d'you reckon to that *Da Vinci Code*? Have you read it?'

When Steve says yes, he's read it, her eyes widen enough to show how jaundiced-looking they are, as if nicotine-stained by her constant smoking. She has already 'nipped outside' twice and she's not been here an hour, though the clock is ticking slowly and I'm hoping her curiosity will be satisfied soon and she'll leave. Today is supposed to be about family. I can feel Mum's eyes on us, from her photograph on the telly. Poor old Mum. She'd hate to be missing out on this, her family here, drinking tea with a strange woman, in her house by the sea. If only they'd stayed put in London, her and Dad, I could've kept an eye on them, made sure things were done properly. Who knows how things might have turned out then?

'How come you've read it?' Pat perseveres. 'It's not exactly church-friendly, is it?'

'Maybe not, but I need to know what's out there. What everyone's talking about. How else can I come alongside them?'

Pat is quiet. For a blink of her yellow eyes. Then she excuses herself, says she's got to make Dad's bed.

Dad's bed? How can he let her touch his bed, their bed, where he lay down each night with my mother for nearly forty years? I had the party all planned but it never happened. The anniversary came and went and Mum wasn't there to celebrate it... and now there's this woman.

I should be relieved, a burden lifted and all that, but I feel put out. It's always been my job, tidying up after Dad, cleaning out the bath, wiping up mud, sweeping the floor clean of dead leaves dragged in on his wellies, scrubbing work surfaces, sluicing out loos. That's me, Vicky. That's what I do, how I am Dad's daughter. He moans and tells me to stop fussing and

I carry on regardless, like he expects me to. Only now here is Pat, teetering overhead on her heels, in Mum's bedroom, messing with her things. And there is Dad, watching the football, oblivious to how I feel. All my life I've followed him around with a dustpan and brush, ready to pick up every crumb, every speck of dust. My job. My role. And now.

'Put the kettle on, Vicky-Love.' Dad indicates the ceiling above. 'Pat must be parched.'

Eight o'clock and Steve is putting the kids to bed. They are flushed from a long walk along the prom, from hide-and-seek, from baths and sitting in front of the fire. They'll be no trouble, they're whacked, so I can stay put in the front room with Dad, watching Saturday night rubbish.

Dad is fidgety. More than usual.

'What is it, Dad? You're making me nervous.'

'Sorry, Vicky-Love. It's just there's something I need to tell you.'

'Is it Pat?'

'Pat? Why would it be Pat?'

'I don't know. She seems to be here a lot, that's all. She's cleaned everywhere and you know... ' I run out of steam and Dad's anxiety has turned to confusion.

'Is it a problem, her being here? Don't you like her?' He asks this like she's a beautiful exotic flower that everyone would love to have in their midst. How could anyone not possibly like the tattooed lady? But this exotic flower has been transplanted into a cottage garden, sitting there amongst the foxgloves and the roses.

'She's fine, Dad. Salt of the earth. She's setting things in order.'

'I thought you'd be pleased.'

'I am, Dad. Really,' I lie. But it's a white lie because I know I actually should feel pleased. 'What is it, then? That thing you wanted to talk about?'

'It's you, Vicky-Love. I wanted to talk about you.'

'Me?'

He turns down the rubbish a notch but keeps his eyes firmly fixed on the telly. 'I'm worried about you. I don't think you're doing as well as you should be and if your mum was here she'd be saying the same thing. I only wish that brother of yours would get his backside into gear and do something for you.'

'Martin?'

'He's your brother. He knows you.'

'He doesn't know me at all. He knows nothing of people. He only cares about himself. Martin. And his big ideas.'

'That's not fair, Auntie Vicky.' Jeremy has crept downstairs, somehow managing to negotiate the obstacles that usually jump out at him only to find his auntie bad-mouthing his dad. Whatever I feel about Martin, I don't want Jeremy to be influenced. He already has to contend with Claudia's point of view.

'It's alright, son.' Dad pats the dustbowl and Jeremy sidles over and perches on it. 'Your Auntie Vicky's a bit cheesed off,' he goes on. 'Brothers and sisters, they're always arguing. You know what it's like.'

'No,' is Jeremy's small powerful answer. There's a moment's silence that I'm unsure Jeremy will fill, but he does. 'I don't have a sister. And my cousins are all girls – they don't have any brothers. So no, I don't know what it's like.'

Dad finally looks at me, shifting in his seat, fiddling with his trousers.

A picture of Thomas floats into view, obscuring Dad's worry, obscuring pretty much everything. As always, this picture threatens to floor me but I am sitting on the dustbowl and Dad is there ready to catch me with his big earthy hands.

'Take it from me, son,' Dad says to Jeremy, 'if you did – if they did – there'd be arguments galore and that's normal. It doesn't mean they think any less of each other, your dad and Auntie Vicky. Why do you reckon she's so happy to have you come and stay?'

I want to tell Dad that has nothing to do with Martin, that I think a lot less of my brother than anyone will ever know, but I realise this is faintly ridiculous. Jeremy is, after all, Martin's son. They are connected. We are connected. But at any moment, if I wanted, I could get out a pair of scissors and... snip.

Jeremy's not that easily fooled. 'But my dad upsets you, doesn't he, Auntie Vicky? And he really upsets Mum. So it must be Dad, not you.'

This boy is astute.

'It takes two to tango,' Dad chips in. 'Six of one and half a dozen of the other.'

'Thanks, Dad, for that Cockney wisdom.'

'You're welcome.'

Jeremy ignores this exchange between father and daughter and takes a step towards me. I find myself getting up and meeting him in the middle of the room where he is beginning to sag. I find myself putting my arms around him, holding him up, holding onto him. I find myself giving him a hug that both he and I are crying out for.

'Can you move a bit,' Dad calls out. 'Only I can't see the box.'

Thoughts for the Day: Maybe we could replace the dustbowl. DFS must have a sale on. They've always got a sale on.

Chapter Twenty-Four: Sunday 17th February
Second Sunday of Lent

Last night there was a fire. All that wood on the beach, what arsonist could resist? Maybe it was Martin, creeping down from London in the night with his lighter. A shame, though, all that wood gone to waste. It would have made lovely decking for all those seaside gardens.

I go down and have a look. The smell of it. The fire crews are still there, on the beach, with noisy diggers, shifting planks and dousing down. I leave them to it and walk the back streets. I remember them well. We used to come here every summer when I was a kid – apart from that one holiday to Weston-super-mare where Martin made me go on that smelly old donkey. Two weeks out of London to get the air and lose the stress. Not that Dad was ever stressed as a gardener. The holidays were far more trying, being cooped up overnight in a B&B with Martin, banished from the house from ten in the morning till five in the evening by the landlady. That's stress.

Most days we'd sit on the beach for a few hours, a picnic of sausage rolls and crisps, or fish and chips, trying to ignore the smell of rotting seaweed. Sometimes for a treat we'd have a bite to eat in a café: the Connaught, the Denton, Macari's. Or maybe afternoon tea in one of the seafront hotels. Martin would sit there, morose, shovelling heaped piles of food into his big gob, every now and then eyeing up the girls. Any girls. Mum would try and engage us in some kind of discussion: Northern Ireland, school, our favourite pop bands. It was excruciating. At home we managed to avoid all this. At home Martin would be out most of the time, playing cricket or rugby or slouching around with friends. Mysterious friends without Christian names. We rarely saw them because Martin was even less keen on bringing them back than I was my own friends. My small group of select friends. Mainly Alice. I thought I was going to lose her after primary school but her parents sent her to the dump after all. Something to do with their socialist principles. But she was always going to shine, wherever she went. She got into Oxford, took a degree in chemistry and I went to teacher training college. Alice had rooms to herself in a quad. She met her future husband at a May ball. I shared a bedroom with Stacey from Woolwich. It overlooked the dustbins. We had a black and white telly and a leaky radiator and when I complained about it, that's when I met Steve and I didn't have to go on any more family holidays.

Family holidays. When it was raining or it wasn't one of our days to eat out, we had to walk around the shops – unless we were at Arundel castle or Bignor Roman villa. I found this bookshop. It was small and cosy, the way bookshops are supposed to be. The old chap who worked there didn't mind me going through his stock. He didn't mind that I never bought anything more than a bookmark.

The shop has gone now. Time marching on again. I am left behind, wondering what happened to my childhood. Wondering what happened to my mother. Just another story with an unfortunate ending. Not a *Da Vinci Code* thriller to be made into a film with the likes of Tom Hanks. But an important one nonetheless. It stars a woman: Pamela Stanton. She marries a gardener, Jim Wright and becomes Mrs Wright. They have two children, a boy and a girl, Martin and Victoria (aka Professor Bumface and Vicky-Love). Pam lives a good, honest life, working alongside her husband, weeding, hoeing, raking. She has bad feet. Bunions. She has an operation and her feet get better.

It's only later when her kids have grown up and produced kids of their own that she gets bad knees. Years of kneeling, carrying and fetching. Keep your back straight and bend your knees, that's what the Health and Safety gurus tell you. Health? Safety? Forget your back. What about your knees? What about my mum's knees? They got bad. They got really painful so she would have to stop herself crying in pain because it upset Dad too much. She forced herself to get out of bed in the mornings to make Dad a cup of tea the way she'd done every day of her married life except for birthdays and Mother's Days. That was her job. That's what she did. Never mind all those other roles she might have played had life dealt her a different hand. All those other shoes she might have worn.

So this woman goes to see her doctor. Unlike a certain Polish woman with hennaed hair, she trusts her GP. The doctor says she needs an operation and writes off to the specialist, the knee man, who is in agreement about the necessity of putting my mother under the knife. She gets a letter in the post with a date and my mother, unlike the time with her bunions when she made up a biscuit tin for Martin and me, is not at all anxious. She is grateful to have the prospect of an end to her pain so that she can once again spring out of bed and do somersaults for Dad in his gardens.

Only this time she has every reason to be anxious. The matrons have disappeared and a new breed of germs has crept into our hospitals, worming their way along floors, sidling up walls, clutching onto door handles and swarming around toilet bowls. We cannot see these germs but they are there, waiting to pounce on the sick, the old, the frail. They lie in wait for my mother. They come and get her in the middle of the night and they take her away to a place from which she can never return. The same place they took my Thomas. Two years before. They come back for her, not the same germs exactly, but another deadly battalion with the same deadly intentions.

This is an important story. One I want to tell the whole wide world. Only whenever I open my mouth to speak, the words melt in my mouth and I am mute. Dumb. I have nothing to say. So I let my hands do the talking. My hands clean and scrub and brush and wash so that one day my life will be free of germs and my family – what is left of it – will be safe.

Afternoon. While Steve and Dad are out in town hunting for treasure in the pound shops with the older kids, Imo naps in her travel cot on the landing. I tiptoe past her, moving between bedrooms, sorting things out, Dad's stuff. Tatty old clothes that charity shops these days would turn away. The bin is the only place but Dad struggles with the idea of throwing away stuff he believes to be 'perfectly good'.

Every now and then I pause in my sorting and watch my baby sleep. She is pink-cheeked. A good colour. I don't need to worry. I shouldn't worry. Jesus tells us not to worry.

I have a go under Dad's bed and for once I can see through to the other side. Pat's been here. Where's she put the tin... ?

I find it eventually on the top shelf of Mum's wardrobe, which looks intact, her clothes still hanging there, empty. Maybe Pat does have some idea of boundaries after all. I take down the tin and feel Mum surround me, like she's in the room, watching me, telling me not to fuss, to leave things be. But I don't. I take the lid off. Inside, amongst her important documents, letters, postcards and mementoes, is the photo I was hoping to find. Uncle Jack.

This photo has always held a fascination for me, ever since I first found it, stuck down the back of the sofa. Jack was not an actual uncle but Dad's best mate. It was his friendship that earned him this title. Dad's other friends were known by their surnames, Mr Brown and Mr Slater and all the rest of them who met down the pub or spoke on the street or maybe came round for a tipple at Christmas. But Jack was Uncle Jack. Only we never got to call him that to his face because Uncle Jack was dead before we were born.

Two men in a photo. One got married and had children, the other died. Never got old and retired to Worthing. Never lost a wife. Or had a tattooed home help. Time marched onwards for Dad but it stopped for Uncle Jack and though we never met, I somehow can't forget him. As if I don't have enough to fret over without adding Uncle Jack to the ranks.

Still, I can't help wondering why this snapshot taken on a sunny day of two best friends never earned the right to a frame, a place on the mantelpiece amongst the wedding photos and goofy school pictures. How did it get lost in the sofa? Why was it put away in Mum's tin, hidden away in the dark? Why did Mum look out in the street like that when I first asked her about him? What did he do that was so bad? Someone with a smile like that.

'What are you doing, Mummy? Can I help you?' Olivia has appeared by my side, creeping in without me even realising they are back from their bargain hunting.

'Hello, sweet pea.' I give her a kiss and feel the cold of her skin burn into me. 'Did you have a nice time?'

'Not really. We spent ages in these smelly shops. You're going to be really cross with Granddad. He spent twenty pounds in the pound shop, which means he bought twenty things. I don't know where he's going to put them all. But I had an ice cream.'

'An ice cream? In this weather?'

'Granddad says it will put hairs on my chest. I don't want hairs on my chest. Will I get hairs on my chest?'

'No, you definitely won't get hairs on your chest. That's just a joke of Granddad's. He used to say it to me as well and last time I looked I didn't have any hairs on my chest.'

Olivia sighs with relief and then spies the tin in my hands. 'Ooh, Mummy,' she breathes. 'What's in there?' She starts to go through the contents carefully, somehow knowing these are special things.

'This is Grandma's tin,' I tell her. 'Like Mummy's tin back home.'

'I miss Grandma,' a voice says. It is Rachel. She has crept into the room as well, shuffling onto her bottom and sitting alongside us.

'Can you remember her, Rach?'

'Course,' she says, as if it's the most stupid question she's ever been asked. 'She had curly hair like grandmas in books and she gave me chocolate buttons and cut the crusts off my soldiers. You always make me eat the crusts on my soldiers.' Rachel's not one for letting anything go.

'They're good for you.'

'Well, I miss her.'

'Me too, darling,' I tell her, gently, squeezing her cold hand. 'I miss her too.'

Olivia carries on studying the postcards and letters and then she stops for a moment and leans back on her heels, looking from her sister to me. 'Are you sure you're not going to die, Mummy?' she asks.

'Not till I'm very old.' I give her a smile, which I hope is full of reassurance. I don't know if I can promise such things. Is it right to make her believe this? Or should I prepare her for the fact that life is fragile? That it can crack and shatter in a moment.

Rachel is holding the photograph of Dad and Uncle Jack, handling it delicately as black and white means precious.

'Very, very old, Mummy?' Olivia is still in need of reassurance, her eyes wide and dark and full of uncertainty.

'Very, very old, Olivia.' I squeeze her hand tighter and grab hold of Rachel's too. Reassurance of my own.

'Who's old?' asks another voice. Dad has climbed the

stairs and is standing holding onto the door handle, breathing heavily. 'Are you talking about me?'

'No, Dad, don't get paranoid. We were just talking about, you know, stuff.'

'Oh yes, Stuff. I know all about Stuff.' He winks at the girls, who giggle, which makes Dad stand up tall, chest back and head held high. He's still got it, whatever it is he thinks he's got. Whatever it was that made Mum giggle like a girl all their married life. You could hear it at night, as the house settled to sleep, Mum's giggles drifting like snow. Magical Christmas snow. It wasn't embarrassing, cringing giggling, giggling you don't want to associate with your parents. Giggling like Dorota. It was what he said to her, summing up the day, a way with words, a silver tongue to go with his green fingers. He misses his audience, his captive audience that used to hang on his every word, even when she was shattered from a day out in the open, shovelling and digging and pushing wheelbarrows. She always had a last scrap of energy to muster up a giggle. I'm not the giggling kind but the girls do their best to make up for this whether they mean to or not.

As I watch Dad watch the girls, I see a flicker of something cross his brow like a cloud passing overhead on a fine summer's day, unexpected and unwanted. Then as soon as it's come, it disappears, replaced by the smile, but the smile doesn't quite do it this time. It doesn't quite brighten the eyes or wrinkle his brow. I look back at the girls. Maybe they're up to no good all of a sudden. Not taking care.

But no, they are still sitting as well as they can, Olivia holding the tin like it's the Ark of the Covenant, Rachel still with the snapshot in her hand. Turning back to Dad I realise that it is Rachel he is watching, her hand. He is looking at the photograph, remembering his old pal, Jack.

'Do you want to have a look, Dad?' I ask him, reaching for the photo but he waves me away.

'No, no, you're alright, Vicky-Love. I need a cup of tea.

Jeremy was supposed to be putting the kettle on. I can look anytime I want. Make sure you put it away safely.' And he's gone, shuffling off and breathing heavily like his son. Martin.

Thoughts for the Day: Perhaps we could deck over our garden – then I wouldn't have to worry about the weeds.

Chapter Twenty-Five:

Wednesday 20th February

Time to go home. Relief combined with regret. I should have talked to Dad more but it's been tricky with the kids and Pat and the 'stuff' and trying to spend some time with Steve. Right now Steve is outside packing up the car, assisted by his new apprentice, Jeremy.

Inside, the girls trail after Pat while she does her chores, asking her intimate questions that she answers with more honesty than I feel comfortable with.

As for me, I am sitting on the dustbowl with Dad who is watching the box, for a change. I am giving Imo a last feed. We've been doing pretty well, just mornings and bedtimes but she needs one for the road. I'll knuckle down once we're back and our routine gets under way again.

Imo drifts off and I tip her up and pat her back gently, her soft warm back, gathering the energy to speak to Dad, last chance for a while. 'So you'll be alright with us going home? You'll manage?'

'I've got Pat,' he says, matter-of-fact, eyes on the screen.

'Yes, you've got Pat.' I wind Imo a little more vigorously. 'And what about the anaemia? What have the doctors said about that?'

'They said I wasn't eating properly. They said proper grub

and some iron tablets will sort me out.'

'You sure?'

'I'm sure.'

'Well, insist you get another blood test soon. To make sure your blood's back to normal.'

'Nothing wrong with my blood. Pat's doing me some liver and bacon later. Special treat, she said.'

I bet she did.

I'm about to say something to this effect when Dad zaps off the telly, rests the remote on his knees, sitting still like he's in church, waiting for the right moment to speak. It's suddenly very quiet. The clock ticks on the mantelpiece. Rachel and Olivia screech somewhere upstairs, like baby gulls.

'You can get help, you know,' he says, a slight tremor in his normally assured voice.

'With the kids... ?'

'No, not the kids. You're doing a grand job with the kids. For you, I mean.' His knees jig up and down; the remote wobbles.

'What... a cleaner?'

'You really think you need a cleaner?' Dad tries a smile.

'No.'

'Well then. No, I mean for your... for Thomas. You can get help to get over it.' The remote falls to the floor and as I reach down for it, clutching a heavy Imo, Dad stops me, grabbing my hand and holding it the way I held my daughters' yesterday on his bedroom floor, Mum all around me.

'Get over it?'

He lets go of my hand, hearing the sharp note in my words.

'I mean "him". Get over "him".'

'I don't want to get over him, Dad. Why should I get over him? It's all I've got left. This... thing.'

'It's called grief, Vicky-Love and it's been going on long enough. I know you'll never get right over him,' he goes on, 'I'll never get over losing your mum. But... look at me,

184

Vicky... you can feel better about things. I feel better about things. It doesn't stop me missing her, mind, but I don't wake up and wonder what's the point in getting up no more. I want to get up and have my cuppa and listen to the radio. I want to get out in the garden and smell the sweet peas, pick the runners, sow the potatoes. See spring and autumn come and go, the year passing. It was winter for a long time but now the sun's shining.'

We look out the window at the flat grey Worthing sky.

'Not brilliant sunshine, granted, but enough to lighten your day every now and then... ' He catches his breath. 'Steve must know someone. You get all sorts in churches.'

The phone goes, grabbing our attention. Here's my chance to avoid carrying on this conversation. I plonk Imo on his lap, rush over and pick it up.

'Vicky, you coming home today?'

'Tamarine?'

'Yes, yes, is me, Tamarine. You coming home today?'

'We're leaving any minute now. Is everything alright?'

'There is problem with your brother. He had fight with my Bob. And my Bob better fighter than your brother. Your brother he got brains somewhere I guess though I can't see them but my Bob he got muscle. Your brother he's in your house. I let him in with your keys. I try to keep him out of Bob's way. You better come back and sort him out.'

Tamarine's gone before I can ask what the fight was about. Instead I kiss Dad goodbye, peppermint and compost, ignoring the exasperated look he tries to pin on me, telling him I'll phone him later, there's a problem at home with Bob.

I don't mention Martin. Not till I know more. Not to protect Martin, to protect Dad. He doesn't need this. I don't need this. But I need to go home. My home.

We reach Dulwich around lunchtime. Indeed Claudia is already having a lunch of smoked salmon and her favoured organic crusty bread as we drop Jeremy off. I leave Steve in the car with the girls while I escort Jeremy inside so it's just he and I who stumble across Claudia's lunch guest and I realise that it is her writer. Woody Allen. Jeremy shows an extraordinary lack of guile, beaming a bright 'hello, Mum', as if this wasn't a man after his father's crown. But Claudia gives the game away, her cheeks flushing like she's had a bad glass of red wine, coughing like she's swallowed a stray fish bone.

I give Jeremy a squeeze of the shoulder and leave him with his adulterous mother.

To add insult to injury, as we are chugging out of Dulwich, I spot the wretched shoe-fitting student, Melanie. She is hand-in-hand with a tall, slim, cleanly-shaven young man, strutting towards the park. And if she notices me giving her daggers, she ignores it. She stares boldly ahead like she is the only woman in the world, and her newly-found partner is the only boy. How fickle are the young. How stupid the middle-aged.

Martin is sitting in our kitchen when we get back, a bag of garden peas strapped to the side of his face with Jeremy's old school tie. He has a black eye and dried blood on his cheek, right above the skanky beard. He glances up from his work and smiles as if he is the bountiful host, welcoming unexpected guests. 'Cup of tea, anyone?'

Rachel says: 'Wow, Uncle Martin, cool.' Then, seeing my face, backs out the room, joining Olivia who has gone straight to the telly.

Steve deposits Imo, asleep in her bucket, on the messed-up table and says: 'No, no, Martin, you sit there while I put the kettle on,' as if Martin has been mugged, as if he's been invalided through no fault of his own.

'Never mind the tea, Martin. What the hell have you been playing at?'

'Ask that... ignoramus next door.'

'So this is Bob's fault, is it?'

'Him and the Thai bride.'

'Leave Tamarine out of this.' Sexist, racist pig. Though, hang on... Tamarine? 'What's this got to do with Tamarine?'

Martin is quiet for a moment, weighing up how much to tell me, I know that scheming mind of his. He used it on Mum and Dad often enough. How much could he let on without getting into trouble? How much could he hold back without getting found out? He takes a puff of his inhaler to add to the invalid effect.

Steve leaves us, taking Imo with him. I have Martin to myself and I am going to let rip if needs must. 'Well?'

'Don't try your primary school teacher tactics on me. They won't wash. I'm not a naughty boy.'

'Exactly, Martin. You're an adult and yet you've been fighting. Would you care to tell me why?'

'It's all Bob's fault.'

'Really.'

'Yes, really. He reckoned I was chatting up his wife and told me to eff off. So I punched him.'

'You punched Bob? Haven't you heard of the concept of walking away or turning the other cheek? Even a Dawkins follower like you must agree that's a good way of avoiding confrontations.'

'Don't be ridiculous.'

'Me? Ridiculous? I'm not the one sat there with a bag of Bird's Eye on my head.'

Martin slouches further down the chair and removes the bag. I snatch the peas off him and put them back in the freezer; they're starting to drip. Without thinking I make him a cup of tea while he sits there sighing and moaning and taking more puffs.

'Have you got any painkillers? It's starting to hurt.'

I remove two aspirins from the packet in my handbag and hand them over with his tea. I have no words and the surprise of me not berating him does something to Martin. It gets him talking without me having to probe.

'I was only passing the time of day. She's a nice woman,' he says as if 'nice' and 'woman' are words that rarely go together. 'She was telling me she came over here to study for a masters and I only asked her how she ended up washing Bob's car and looking after his kid.'

'What business is it of yours how she lives her life? Maybe she likes washing Bob's car. And I know for a fact she loves Jessica like she was her own.' I pour myself a glass of wine, forget tea. I can't believe the cheek of the man. He barely knows Tamarine yet he expects her to live a life he's never let his own wife live, not without huge amounts of jealousy and fuss. 'And did Bob hear you say all this?'

'Not exactly. It was just bad timing.'

'In what way bad timing?'

'She dropped her sponge and I was picking it up and... '

'Stop.' I hold my hand up. 'I don't actually want to know any more details – it's all a bit too Carry On if you ask me.'

'That fat pillock made false accusations. I merely showed an interest in her academic career and suggested she give me a ring. I was only handing her my card.'

'You and your stupid cards.'

'You're just jealous you don't have any. Why don't you get some printed up? Mrs Vicky-Love, Patron Saint of Good Housekeeping and Smugness.'

'Believe me, Martin,' I whisper. 'If I had money to waste, it wouldn't be on stupid poncey cards. And as for smugness, you beat me there, hands down. You beat me at everything. Except for housekeeping. I'm a good housekeeper. You're right there. Nobody bothered when we were growing up. And I don't see anyone queuing up to do it now.'

Martin looks bemused. And then he says it; he says those words. Words he used to say all the time whenever I got het up about anything. He says: 'Why are you getting your knickers in a twist?'

And all those holidays in Worthing cramped into the B&B, all those Christmases sat watching Morecambe and Wise, enduring his running commentaries and eating all the best Quality Streets, all those Eurovisions, all those trips down the chemist, all my friends swooning at his big fat smelly feet, all these last few weeks running around, picking up after his responsibilities, all these images swim before my eyes and then merge and blur into one hellish red and I feel my arm swing back and then, for one glorious moment, my fist touches his face, bodily contact for the first time in our lives, Martin and I. One glorious second and then my brother is lying on the floor, curled up on his back like a swatted fly, his hands covering what was his good eye, a train of expletives filling the warm air of my kitchen. I go to the fridge, my fridge, to the ice compartment and, before leaving for the garden, I lob the peas at his horizontal body, sprawled on the kitchen floor. My kitchen floor. Ha!

Thoughts for the Day: I have no thoughts. My mind is empty. Blissfully, miraculously empty.

February 26th 1978

Martin is in trouble. Big trouble. A policeman came to the house and told Mum and Dad that Martin has been up to no good in the park. The parky caught him smoking. But then it gets worse. Ha, ha! Martin showed off in front of these fifth years from the Girls Grammar. He set fire to a rocket and it landed in the pond. Two ducks had a heart attack and were floating on the water.

The police are not going to lock him up in jail, worse luck. He has been given a warning. Boo. But Dad is really angry with him. He said that he always had a feeling something like this would happen. Der! I could have told him that. Martin has done stupid things all his life. It's just that he doesn't usually get caught.

And when Heidi finds out he's been flirting with the Grammar girls she will be cross. But I don't want her to chuck Martin because I like Heidi. She makes Martin less of a pig. At least some of the time.

Chapter Twenty-Six: *Tuesday 26th February*

We have been home nearly a week and in that time I have seen neither my brother nor my nephew. I miss one, certainly not the other. I feel no remorse for flooring Martin, just relief that I didn't do this in front of my children who I have told countless times that violence is wrong. I agree that violence is wrong but I also feel that on occasion, under duress or when there is no other choice, it is understandable, or even needed. The moment my fist came into contact with my brother's face was both understandable and needed. How else would he have known that what *he* did was wrong? Hitting on another man's wife and then hitting the husband? I had no choice. And one consequence of this is that he hasn't come near the place. My job here is done.

Rachel's assembly. A school hall, heady with the smell of musty plimsolls and yesterday's mashed potato. Steve and I have found two seats, next to Tamarine and Bob. We wait impatiently and somewhat anxiously, a child apiece wriggling on our laps, for the show to get underway. We never know if Rachel will join in or limply stand there, wearing her face of scorn. It is uncomfortable, squatting on the miniature chairs, brushed up against Bob's fat thighs, but I grin and bear it. Now is the time to be working on our friendship, sabotaged by my brother. These are our next door neighbours; they have to put up with the constant visitors to our house, with Imo's screams, with the general racket that goes on in our family. Admittedly we have to put up with Jessica's ball-kicking and Bob's ways but that's what you do with your neighbours. You learn to live with each other's idiosyncrasies and you are there when they run out of teabags or with a spare key. I never have to see my brother again.

Bob is at the ready with his camcorder. Yet again I have forgotten our camera. And I've given up with my phone because whenever Imo spots it she screams till she has it in her chubby little hands, desperate to try and cram it into her mouth. So I will have to rely on my memory but sadly it's not what it was. Though some things can never be forgotten.

At last the members of Class 12 file in, subdued, heads down. Only last year they still looked out for their parents, grinning and waving. Now they are on that cusp, feeling the burden of embarrassment. The girls blush and the boys slyly nudge each other. I want Rachel to be small again, wriggling on my lap, sucking her thumb and twiddling a strand of my hair. I knew what I was doing then – now it's all... scary... the teenage road ahead. I was a hopeless teenager.

Mr Jackson, Rachel's most hated teacher to date, welcomes us all to the assembly and tells us they've been learning about different types of family. I inwardly groan, wondering what sort of Pandora's box he has opened. They start with a few poems, haikus to be more specific. I'm not sure the Japanese had Penge in mind when they were first thought of but there you go.

Next up is the drama. The usual suspects have been chosen for this – the gobby, confident ones whose pushy parents send them to Stagecoach, an appearance on the *X Factor* glittering in the distance. And the token special needs kid – in this case Danny, one of the best escapologists since Houdini but so cute with his dark curls that he always gets the 'ah' Factor.

Then there's the kids like Rachel, the quiet, average, keep-your-head-down-and-stay-out-of-trouble kid. She never gets the roles, never quite gets her turn in the sunshine, always shunted to one side in the shade of ordinariness. But today Rachel gets to hold up an A2 portrait of her family. And this is where I squirm. Rachel, hidden behind her picture, is mute. Mr Jackson motions at Rachel to lower it. After a very long pause, she does as she's told and her red face glows for all to see. Absolute silence so we get the best chance at hearing her whispered description of her own modern family.

'This is my family.' She coughs. I send positive vibes to her in the hope she'll take heart. But my telepathy fails. She coughs again and after a nudge from Jessica who has sidled up to her friend, she finally gets going.

'This is my grandmother Dorota. She is a size 20 and comes from Poland. She has bright red hair. She likes bingo and the dogs. This is her husband, my grandfather, Roland. He likes whatever she likes.'

Laughter from audience, which deepens Rachel's redness if that's at all possible. Another nudge from Jessica coupled with an encouraging nod from Mr Jackson, which Rachel accepts like a lifeline.

'This is my other grandfather who lives in Worthing. He has a new friend. She is a lady. She has a tattoo.' Rachel points out the captured faded dolphin, 'even though she is really old, at least fifty.'

More sniggers.

'This is my dad. He used to be a plumber but now he's a vicar.'

People turn to stare at Steve who pulls that eyes-to-heaven look. Rachel is now in the zone, oblivious to the reactions of the parents and children and teachers all of whom are listening intently. She is talking to a parallel, unseen audience. This method works for her because for the first time in her life she has lost all sense of stage fright and has found her rhythm. Her voice is now so well-projected that it bounces off the climbing frame at the back of the hall and ricochets all around us.

'This is my cousin Jeremy who plays the cello and lives with us when his parents don't want him. This is my sister Olivia who likes cleaning toilets. This is my baby sister Imogen who takes up lots of my mum's time and this is my Mum. She does everything for us but she gets sad when she remembers my brother. He died when he was a baby. Oh yes, and this is my Uncle Martin. He lived with us for a bit because his wife kicked him out for getting off with his student and then my mum kicked him out because he had a fight with Jessica's dad.' All eyes switch to Bob whose camcorder is getting every last detail of this soliloquy so it need never be forgotten though even my memory is up to recording this moment for eternity. 'Oh yeah and Uncle Martin got arrested for breaking and entering and my dad had to go and get him out of the nick on New Year's Eve. That's my family.'

And that was the story according to Rachel.

Silence. Followed by a few outbreaks of applause. Gradually every member of the audience and all of Rachel's classmates join in. Olivia has leapt off Steve's lap and is jumping up and down. Even Imo is clapping, grinning wildly though she has no idea why, worshipping her big sister because she is just that: her big sister.

'Thank you, Rachel, for that... improvised description. It was... colourful and... enlightening,' Mr Jackson falters, smiling weakly, unsure if he should have intervened or whether this is quite possibly the best assembly he has ever done as the audience are still clapping like it's the last night of the proms. I look around, wondering if someone will whip out a Union Jack.

As the response winds down, the rest of the assembly continues, passing by without my attention as all I can do is stare at my knees. Knees that could one day go the way of my mother's if I keep on scrubbing the nave. I should be proud that my eldest child has received such accolades, but despite Rachel's words that I do everything, I can't help but wonder what must all the other mums think of my parenting skills, hearing our family summed up like that.

But then Steve nudges me, slyly, and I look up and see what he can see. Rachel has lost her customary glumness. She has lost her redness. Instead there is a pink sheen to her cheeks. And on her lips, if I'm not mistaken, is the merest, slightest, coyest, sweetest smile.

As Class 12 are shepherded out and back to their classroom by a visibly relieved Mr Jackson, the audience disperse. We shuffle out of the hall and emerge into the chill of the playground. We stand around for a bit chatting to various parents, mainly parents who have railroaded Steve, their shepherd, giving him parish updates or what would under other circumstances be classed as gossip. Olivia hops around with various other small children while Imo gets heavier in my arms. Tamarine and Bob catch up with us as we get rid of the last pushy mother. And Bob apologises for hitting Martin.

'You've got nothing to be sorry for,' I tell him emphatically.

This clears the air, Bob brightening a little, and fortunately Steve doesn't bring up the idea of turning the other cheek. But, being Steve, he does find something encouraging to say: 'Jessica did a great job of helping out Rachel.'

'She's good deep down,' Bob acknowledges, grudgingly.

'She's good all round,' I tell Bob. Despite the ball-kicking against my garden wall. 'Always cheerful, kind to others, which is really rare in this day and age.'

Tamarine stoops to pick up a crisp packet that has fluttered alongside us. She does that trick where you make an empty crisp packet into a ball and puts it in a nearby bin. 'The rubbish in this country is disgrace,' she says.

'I couldn't agree more.'

Before I can warm to the subject, Tamarine says something surprising. 'Jessica is not happy girl. I think she want her mother.'

'You're her mother,' Bob says, putting his arm around Tamarine's tiny waist. She looks nothing like Jessica's mother but I know exactly what he is saying and I am taken aback that Bob could say something so lovely.

But Tamarine is not easily won over. 'I am not her mother,' she says sadly. 'I do her mother's job but that does not change me to her mother.'

'Come on, Tam... ' Bob says, giving her a squeeze.

'She want Jackie.'

I look at Steve. I have no idea what to say. He seizes control. 'How about getting in touch with Jackie?' he suggests. 'Maybe it's time they had some contact. I could have a chat with Jessica if you like. You know, all four of us round your kitchen table?'

'You're alright, Steve,' Bob says, tightening up. 'This is family stuff. We'll sort it out. Jess is fine. Just a phase.' He pulls Tamarine closer to him and steers her away. Tamarine smiles a silent thank you at us and goes with her husband to his clean car, parked on the yellow zigzags. Normally I'd say something to anyone selfishly stupid enough to park on the yellow zigzags but now is not an appropriate moment so I let it pass, let them pass, Bob driving off at a skid while we strap our two girls into their seats of the Espace.

I'll have a word with Rachel, see if she knows anything. My Rachel.

Evening comes round quickly and I manage a few words with Rachel in between baths and stories and spellings. She says Jessica is fine, just going all soppy over Jeremy. Though she did say Jess had received a letter from Jackie, which Bob knows nothing about. Apparently she gets to the post first every day, in case of letters arriving from her mother, in case Bob would hide them from her. Which, knowing Bob, he most probably would. And one day there was a letter, which she snapped up. Apparently Tamarine saw her and asked her who it was from. Jessica said it was from a friend and Tamarine let it go. But, knowing Tamarine, she most probably knew it was from Jackie.

'Don't worry, Mum,' Rachel says. 'It's fine. Jessica's fine. You worry too much. And before you say anything about today, don't. It's all good.'

'And is everything alright between you and Jess? Only you haven't been playing with her much lately.'

'We don't *play*. We're not kids.'

'Well, you haven't been... *hanging out* with her much lately.'

'All she like talks about is Jeremy.'

'Ah, well, I can sympathise with that. My friends were always falling for Uncle Martin.'

'Really?' Rachel sounds amazed. She obviously can't see anything physically attractive about her Uncle Martin. But then I never could either. He was always enough to turn my stomach. I can't ever remember feeling pride that my friends found him fit. That Alice swooned whenever he deigned to speak to her. It was just embarrassing.

I manage to get in a very quick hug before Rachel picks up the opening bars of *Eastenders* and ducks away at top speed.

As I'm doing the last bit of clearing up in the kitchen before heading for bed, I open the back door. Let in some of the London evening. A train crashes past, lit up. People's heads are visible, floating like decapitated ghouls, and I wonder, as I often do, where they are going, what type of life they are leading. Are there mothers on there who have left their children? Why did Jackie leave Jessica? And is she regretting it? What mother wouldn't regret a decision of that magnitude? Maybe she wants Jessica back? Does she deserve another chance?

The front door goes and I feel a cold blast of air run through the house from front to back, Steve appearing in its wake, framed by the kitchen doorway, taking off his hat and scarf. He smiles, seeing me standing there at the other end of the kitchen. He makes his way around the table towards me. Holds me. I practise my breathing.

'Sorry I'm late,' he says, releasing his grip a little. 'I've lost my mobile. I've spent ages looking for it.'

'Maybe you left it in the vestry when you went in earlier.'

'Maybe,' he says. He kisses me on the cheek.

I feel his bristles. Breathe in his Steve smell. It's been a long time since I've thought about him, Steve, the man, my husband. We push each other to the back of the queue. Just as well we're British and good at waiting patiently.

But some men can't wait around forever.

'You should pray to that saint of lost things. What's he called... St Tony?'

'Have you ever considered an Alpha course, Vick?'

'Ha, ha.'

'Anyway, they're a curse, mobile phones. I'd be much better off without one.' His expression changes then, as he forgets his phone and notices me, Vicky. 'You're freezing,' he says. 'You'll get a chill with that door open.'

'A chill? How Victorian.'

He tenses, slightly, and after a few more seconds he lets me go, leaving me by the back door to go and fill up the kettle for his usual night time cup of Ovaltine. How 1950s.

'How was the Alpha?' I make myself ask him. The good wife. The curate's wife.

'Good,' he says, shoulders all relaxed again. 'We had a late-comer.'

'Anyone I know?'

'That Polish woman who asked about baptism. Karolina. With the hair. She decided she wanted to do an Alpha after all. Said she had questions that she needed answering. I said I couldn't promise – '

'She never said.'

He ignores my interruption and concentrates on measuring out his Ovaltine. 'Do you want one?' he asks kindly, sweetly.

I look at him, his hand hovering by a mug, waiting for my answer. How exactly has our life ended up here, like this? Where did this moment come from?

'No, thanks. I think I'll go to bed. I'm really tired all of sudden.'

He smiles his understanding smile and instead of welcoming his sympathy, I feel wretched. Confused. What do I care if Karolina goes on an Alpha course? What does it matter to me? Why do I feel... what do I feel? Did I think she was becoming my friend? She's not exactly friend material. And since when have I been good with friends?

The kettle boils and, despite the steam filling the kitchen, the icy blast rushes inside, wrapping itself around me. I shut the door and turn the key in the lock. There's a change in the wind. A cold front moving in. I don't like it.

Thoughts for the Day: Did I ever draw a picture of my first family: Mum, Dad, Martin, me? Did it get put on a fridge or tacked to a wall? Did it get slipped between the pages of a book to be kept as a memory of the way things were? And did it show how things really were? A distracted mother and father more interested in soil than soap. My tyrant of a brother. And me, gawky, buck-toothed, Vicky-Love. Where is that picture? Branded on my brain for eternity.

Chapter Twenty-Seven: Sunday 2nd March

Mothering Sunday

Fourth Sunday of Lent

I am woken up by heavy breathing. It is Olivia who has carried a cup of tea on a saucer all the way upstairs and is currently placing it, without spilling a drop (that's my girl) on my bedside table. My first thought is how could Steve be so reckless, allowing a three-year-old to risk a scalding? My second thought is how sweet, my daughter has brought me a cup of tea. And I make myself hold onto that second thought. My sweet daughter. I sit myself up and realise that Steve is actually still in bed beside me.

'I did it all myself, Mummy,' she breathes. 'Drink up.'

'What about me, darling?' asks Steve, jokey-serious, coming to. 'Don't I get one?'

'It's Mother's Day, Daddy.'

'You're right.' He kisses me on the head, that way of his, almost clunky and slightly jarring, but meant with affection. 'How about we wake Rachel and make some breakfast for everyone?' He doesn't suggest breakfast in bed because he knows I can't bear the crumbs but Olivia is already beaming at the prospect of a chore and is out the room before Steve can swing his legs to the floor. As I listen to them, to Olivia's excited whispers, Rachel's unusually ebullient voice, to the three of them clomping down the stairs, as I sit up in the bigness of our bed, drinking my tea, relishing each simple hot sip, I wish I could always feel like this, contented and peaceful. I wish I didn't live in the past... or somewhere in the future where a life of tranquillity must surely be lying in wait for me to catch up and join in. Why can't I live in the moment? Cherish each second of this life? Not even now, this morning, Mother's Day. I only managed a minute or so but now I'm aware, as always, of those who aren't here. And of those who will be joining us later.

Church. Looking round the congregation I can see mothers who are usually checking their watches wondering if they have to leave early to put on the potatoes. Today they are more relaxed, knowing they will be taken out to lunch or at the very least have lunch cooked for them. I, on the other hand, had the bright idea of asking people over and cooking lunch myself. I thought it would be nice to share the day with the other mothers in my life, namely Claudia and Dorota. This obviously means catering for Jeremy and Roland as well but both of these I am looking forward to having back in the house. But it also means Martin. Because if I didn't let Claudia know I'd invited him she might have snuck in Charles Dickens. I slip out early and enjoy a half hour of silence, alone in the house, my house, peeling parsnips to go with a beef casserole that is already slowly cooking, praise be to God.

A crash at the door lets me know my silence has been massacred. Martin. And he's not alone. Please, no, not Melanie. No. A man's cough. A familiar cough. Dad?

I rush out to the hall, wiping my hands on my apron and see Dad, standing there while Martin helps him out of his coat, taking care with the wrist.

'Dad. What a lovely surprise,' I give him a kiss. Pat hasn't managed to get rid of the potting shed scent yet.

'We've been down the off-licence.' He gently shrugs me off, his usual way, no fuss, straightening his cuffs. 'Shocking prices but there's a nice bottle of fizzy wine.'

Martin hands it over. '*Champagne*, Vicky-Love. Get your laughing gear around that.'

I mutter a thank you and lead the way to the kitchen where I sit Dad down and he fills me in on the surprise, that it was Martin's idea to fetch him for lunch. I am immediately suspicious of my brother's motives and yet begrudgingly thankful to have Dad here, where I can see him for myself, not via Pat's colourful descriptions down the telephone.

I hand him the peeler and a heap of carrots. 'Reckon your wrist is up to that?

Dad doesn't answer, turns the peeler over in his good hand as if it's a new invention, something he has heard about but never actually seen. I rummage around in the drawer and find another, which I present to Martin. 'You can do it between you while I make us a coffee.'

'I'll have a brown ale if you've got one,' Dad says.

'And I'll have a beer,' Martin adds.

Great. Once Dorota gets here with her sherry – unless she's stuck to her Lenten promise – we'll be in for an interesting ride this afternoon. A cultural cocktail of delight.

Half an hour later and the hordes arrive, bringing bottles and flowers and noise. First Roland and Dorota, then Steve and the girls, and finally Claudia and Jeremy. Claudia is dressed for lunch at Claridge's in a linen dress and her signature kitten heels (I can feel the tingling onset of bunions just looking at them). Dorota is wearing her usual baggy cotton trousers and tent-top but with a new ring on her wedding finger (Hallelujah).

All hands to the deck – apart from Claudia who has recently-done nails – as we sieve vegetables, warm up plates and carry food through to the back room which today earns the title of dining room, Jeremy's zed-bed neatly folded to one side, his belongings tidied into stacker boxes. I am more grateful than ever that Martin has not caved in and got a replacement cello, though there has been talk of renting one. Another reason to work on marriage mediation between my brother and his wife.

As we are sitting down and starting to pass round serving dishes, the doorbell goes. I run though a quick list of possible visitors in my mind when Steve says, 'Oh, yes, Vick, I forgot.' He smacks his forehead in genuine horror so I feel panic rising like bile. 'I half-invited Karolina and Natasha for lunch. They were at church and Amanda was about to ask them back seeing as they were on their own today and I intervened and said how about coming here if they fancied some company, thinking they'd be more relaxed with other children and she said they might but I didn't think they really would but that's nice isn't it, that she felt comfortable doing this but I'm sorry I didn't warn you, is there enough to go round... ?'

I don't get a chance to answer him as he has made this speech whilst getting up from his chair, squeezing round our assembled guests, backing out the door and disappearing from sight on his way down the hall.

The remainder of us, having broken off our conversation, listen as Steve opens the front door. Karolina's low gravelly murmur can be heard.

'She is Pole,' says Dorota, picking up immediately on a fellow countrywoman. 'I bet she has very bad-dyed blonde hair.'

Fortunately Martin is sitting opposite me so I am able to aim a sharp kick in his shin before he passes comment on the irony of this statement. But he does slip out, 'What odds would you give?'

'Dead cert,' Dorota replies.

Karolina appears in the doorway of the dining room, Natasha, eyes down, clutching her mother's hand. Steve ushers them in, does a brief introduction. Poor Karolina is blushing as she realises we are on the verge of beginning a family meal and says: 'This is bad time. We will come another day when you are less busy.'

'No, no,' I find myself on my feet, the good vicar's wife. 'There's plenty of food. We can add a couple of chairs. In fact, Olivia and Natasha could share that small table and sit on cushions. They'd like that. It'd be fun. Like a picnic.'

Natasha doesn't look like she would like that, or that she would find anything fun right now, especially a fake picnic on a plastic table in a stranger's house. But when Olivia gets up to greet her, Natasha willingly clasps her classmate's proffered hand. She follows Olivia to the little table, checking that her mother is in fact staying. Her mother is now seated between Martin and Steve, tight-shouldered and clutching her mobile phone.

'So you are Polish?' Dorota cuts to the chase, and her smug smile is intended for the rest of us that she was right about the blonde hair.

Karolina looks at Dorota, takes in her appearance, and says, 'You are Polish too?'

'How do you know this?' Dorota is amazed. She thought her heritage was a deep secret from her past, forgets so many things about her give the game away.

'You remind me of my aunt,' Karolina states neutrally.

Dorota frowns and gets back to her food.

I hand Karolina a plate, insisting she help herself to whatever she fancies and to tuck in, it's lovely to have her here, a nice surprise, wittering away to cause a distraction, make everything alright.

Martin does his gentlemanly act – and I'm almost grateful – passing our new guest the various vegetable dishes, offering them like delicacies. Karolina inspects each one rather too closely than is necessary before dabbing miniscule amounts on her plate. Martin's attentiveness has no effect on Karolina, no giggles, no flicking of blonde hair, no pushing up and out of chest. But her shoulders have loosened a tad; her phone has been placed next to her knife.

'What about us, Stefan?' Dorota asks her son. 'Do we get anything to drink in this house?' Her fat hand flits up to her throat to dramatically emphasise her thirst.

'There's that fizzy wine,' Dad announces.

'*Champagne*,' Martin corrects and scrapes his chair back before setting off to retrieve it from the fridge. My fridge.

The prospect of champagne makes everyone chattier, even though we'll have to stretch it now. Martin brings everyone to attention with the pop-and-fizz that he does in front of us, the show-off that he is. He makes a point of looking up and down the table. 'No champagne flutes, Victoria? Don't tell me we're going to have to slum it with IKEA's finest.'

I resist the urge to do the tablecloth trick, yanking it away from the table (ta-dah!), leaving the crockery and cutlery behind. I turn to Karolina and say, 'Forgive my brother. He has special needs,' which makes Claudia and Dad hoot and splutter. But for once I don't feel any pleasure in putting Martin down, not even with a receptive audience. It makes no odds to him what I say. And the thought of champagne mixed with casserole now makes me feel sick. I'm surprised Martin suggested it, other than to be flash. Surely it's red wine with beef?

I'm finding it hard to celebrate anything let alone being a mother. My new-found ability to be hospitable is already waning and as soon as the main course is eaten, and seconds consumed by the greediest i.e. Martin, I make my excuses, saying I've got to check on the pudding. Not that anyone hears me, they are all too busy glugging back the remains of the champagne and the beginnings of a bottle of Sancerre that Steve and I were saving for a special occasion, which I suppose this is. So no-one notices me leave, not even Steve, usually so keen to help, as he is deep in conversation with Karolina, no doubt filling her in on the meaning of life. I wish someone would fill me in.

I don't check on the pudding. The pudding is fine on its own, defrosting nicely on the side, just about enough to go round. I head upstairs instead, my feet taking me there rather than any intention on my part. As I reach the landing I hear Socks mew. A I'm-here-come-and-give-me-a-stroke mew. He is curled up in the box room, Imo's room, on her chair, where I sit and feed her before putting her to bed. Where I sit with her in the night, listening to the train on the tracks, the wind in the scrubby trees, the creaks of the house. Not that I've done that for a while, she is sleeping through now. But I'm not. Every night, at some point, I lie awake, resisting the urge to go and check on her, studying the monitor on the bedside table, listening out for the reassuring snuffles, watching the string of flashing lights.

I rub Socks behind the ears. He stretches his paws, pinging out his talons appreciatively. His winter fur is thick and slightly coarse from nights stalking vermin up on the cutting. Nothing changes in his life. He has food when he wants it, somewhere cosy to sleep and groom himself, his own back door, a world of small wildlife at his disposal. He doesn't care who's here, in his house, who's not, as long as there's someone with a lap when he wants it, a hand that can turn a tin opener, rattle a box of Go-Cat, scratch him behind the ears. Every night is the same.

He would have been out that night too, a warm summer night, in and out of gardens, prowling, fighting, hunting. As for me, I'd had a whole night's sleep for the first time since Thomas had been born. I'd fed him in this chair, listening to the shouts from the TV downstairs, Wimbledon, Rachel and Steve shouting *Come on, Tim*, basking in the evening sun, a precious moment. He drifted off and my arm became hot and heavy. He was piling on the weight like Imo. I kissed him on his fuzzy head, then got up carefully and carried him over to his cot, out for the count, reminding myself to phone Eileen in the morning and ask about his eczema.

I can still feel the shape of him in my arms.

He'd only been sleeping in the cot for a few nights, having been promoted from the crib in our room. It was going really well, though he'd had a blip the night before, a few snuffles, unsettled, a little hot, we guessed a new tooth, though at three months it seemed early. Steve and I were dead chuffed at how good he was. Rachel had been a shocker, waking every two to three hours till she was six months old. We couldn't believe our luck, having a placid, gentle, easy baby boy. Only I'd give anything now to have a loud, raucous, noisy boy. To have a six-year-old banging and crashing and kicking chips out of the skirting board. To be able to go back to that night and stop the morning from coming. But the morning came. I woke up next to Steve and checked the time. I could hear the telly drift up from downstairs, Rachel having gone down quietly and put it on. Her favourite video. Pingu. It was late. We'd overslept. But Thomas was still quiet. I knew straightway something was wrong. Something had changed.

I look at Socks sitting innocently in the chair. And then at the cot, the blanket ruffled from Imo's earlier nap. We had to get a new cot for her. I couldn't bear to keep Thomas'. I thought giving it away would help lay waste to the memory of going in that morning. Going in to the cot and leaning over. Seeing him blue and still. Sweeping him up in my arms. Feeling him cold. Screaming and screaming and screaming until Steve ran in and stopped still, his face panicked, knowing but not believing I was holding our dead baby boy.

I straighten up the blanket and as I am about to go to the cat, to earn myself a little more time up here away from the white noise downstairs, I hear the doorbell.

Go away.

I was half-hoping it would be Jessica, poor girl, today's not easy for those of us without our mother. But it's a woman's voice, strangely familiar.

I see her as I come down the stairs. She is standing with her fingers entwined in her long wavy blonde hair. Melanie.

She looks up at me. 'You're the woman who bought those ridiculous shoes.'

'You're the woman who sold them to me.'

Steve is standing there, unsure for a moment, then he says, 'Do you need to speak to Martin?'

'Steve?'

'What?'

'I don't think this is appropriate right now, do you?'

But whatever I think is irrelevant because Claudia has chosen this moment to do something unusual and has come into the hall with some dishes. Which she drops. We all look at the pile of broken crockery, maybe not Wedgewood, but mine nonetheless. The clatter brings everyone else out to the hall, including Martin, whose face drops to join the shattered fragments on the floor.

'Have you told her yet?' Melanie asks, looking at an ashen Claudia.

'Not now,' says Martin. 'Not today. Please Melanie.'

'Mother's Day, eh? Of course. How thoughtless of me.' The sarcasm is visible. I could reach out and grab it and bang Martin on the head with it if I could be bothered. But I am tired of all this. Sick and tired.

I leave the audience and climb the stairs, hearing Melanie's retreating footsteps and the front door slam. Then a deep and dangerous silence.

I should go back down and help my family sort out this mess but I don't. I go back to the box room, to the place where I shared those precious moments with Thomas.

There's a baby in the cot.

Oh.

For a split second my heart raised heavenwards in what I can only describe as joy. But it is Imo. Someone has put her down for a nap. Of course it is Imo. And how I hate myself for wishing it wasn't. She is here, living and breathing and yet the joy has gone as quickly as it came.

I make myself go to her and take her in. Her chubby form. Her delicate beauty. On her front, bottom slightly in the air as if she is practising crawling in her sleep. She is angelic and gorgeous. I pull her cover up around her and my hand knocks against something hard. A rattle or something. I pull it out. It is Steve's mobile phone.

'You found it?' Steve says, coming in the room, his sermon notes in hand, glasses perched on head.

'Looks like St Tony came up trumps.'

He laughs and tells me Martin and Claudia have gone to the shed for a chat. I picture Martin and Claudia in our shed and can't quite imagine a happy outcome.

I sit on the chair, shift the cat onto my lap, and feel his comforting warmth. 'Carry on,' I tell my husband, the vicar. 'I'll try and stay awake and you can practise on me.'

I listen to his words of surprising wisdom and make myself forget that downstairs is my family, my extended family. I try and forget the kids are playing virtual games instead of out in the fresh air on bikes and pogo sticks like we once were. I try and forget that my brother is being his usual pompous self, outwitting his wife in my shed. I try and forget my mother would be here sharing Mothering Sunday if only people had taken more care. I try and forget Thomas would be here if only I'd woken that night and gone in to check on him. I try and forget.

Thoughts for the Day: If I was allowed to believe in reincarnation, I would wish to come back as a cat in South London. Failing that I would come back as a behemoth. No-one would mess with Vicky the Behemoth.

Chapter Twenty-Eight: *Thursday 6th March*

Natasha has been absent from playgroup all week and I am fighting the fear that I somehow gave her food poisoning last Sunday, but when I asked Shelley yesterday, she said Karolina has got flu and can't manage to get to playgroup. So that is what brings me to their flat early this morning, armed with flowers, Lemsips and homemade chicken soup. That is when I am surprised to see the state Karolina is in and why I insist on phoning the doctor.

'No. No doctor,' Karolina is emphatic. Emphatic as she can be languishing on the sofa, under a duvet, surrounded by mountains of discarded tissues, screwed-up crisp packets, grubby toys, dirty tights, magazines, dog-eared books. 'Doctors do nothing for me. I must wait and I will be better.'

'Then let me take Natasha to playgroup. Give you a break.'

Karolina looks suspicious but cannot muster the energy to resist. 'Okay but do not give her sweets.'

I ignore her lack of gratitude and assumption that I will ply her daughter with sweets, reminding myself she is a dentist and too ill for niceties. But however ill I was, I would never let my home – even a home-from-home – slump into such a slovenly state. Really it is quite disgusting. The carpet, the patches of it that can be glimpsed though the rubble, is hairy and mouldy-looking. The hair – white and short – must come from Karolina because presumably they don't own any pets, living as they do on the third floor of this block of flats. I dread to think where the mould came from.

The coffee table is covered with the detritus of illness and general living: six mugs, four plates and an assortment of cutlery; Polly Pockets who reside in a world of chocolate wrappers (now, now, Karolina, cavities); junk mail, flyers, take away menus, nail varnish bottles, matches, lighters, joss sticks, tobacco, Rizlas, CDs, broken CD cases, orange peel, empty grape stems, broken pencils, earrings, coins, a mobile phone, an odd sock, toe nail clippings and a packet of pills.

I try to surreptitiously scan the label of the packet but Karolina spots what I am doing and, with a surge of energy, swipes them from the debris, saying, 'From the doctor, for my flu, antibiotics.' Hmm. *Doctors do nothing for me.*

Shelley is surprised to see me turn up with Natasha and Olivia. Not as surprised as I am, that both Natasha and Karolina have agreed to this arrangement. Or that I could do such a Christian act. Maybe Steve's goodness is rubbing off on me. Or Amanda's. Or maybe I am not such a bad person.

I watch them from the door on my way out. Olivia bypasses the cutting and sticking table, steadfastly ignoring her celebrity demons, and heads instead for the comfort of the book corner, pulling Natasha along with her. Once there, Olivia sits her new friend down and reads her *Spot the Dog*. She even allows her to lift a flap.

Seeing the confidence of Olivia, I can't help wonder how Thomas would have been as a boy. Would he be a noisy, messy six-year-old? Or quiet and pensive? At three months old it was impossible to say except that he was beginning to show us his personality.

'Where's the baby?' Shelley asks, knocking me out of my daydream.

'The baby?'

'Your little girl.'

'Oh. Yes. She's with Steve's parents.'

'You're lucky to have them,' she says. She knows nothing. I'd rather have my own mum. But I can't be bothered to say anything. 'Yes, I'm very lucky.'

Luck? Is that what this is all about?

I want to tell her all about Thomas, all about the ambulance, the hospital, the aftermath of the funeral, having to cope with Rachel missing and mourning her baby brother, with Steve, my rock who was eroding into rubble day by day.

And me, I was Strong Vicky. I was Capable Vicky. I was Isn't-she-amazing-the-way-she-carries-on Vicky. I was coping. And then one day Steve gets a call to go to Dartford and our lives, which have already been thrown up in the air and scattered into the winds, fall back down to earth and land in a different pattern, the holes that were there before bigger, the gaps deeper and more treacherous, liable to widen at any second and topple me in, swallow me up and down. Down, right down until there is nothing.

Only, when you get to that point of nothingness, you start to kick your feet and push with your arms. You start to pull yourself up towards the light until one day you are breathing air again. You begin to live and make plans and try new things and have more babies. But that doesn't stop you yearning backwards or wishing yourself forwards. It doesn't help you live and enjoy each moment. It doesn't stop you wondering what if... ?

I should be telling Steve all this but he knows it already. We were in it together, only we came out of it differently. He found his life. A new life. And sometimes I hate him for it. And then I hate myself for hating such a good man. I don't tell Shelley. I don't tell anyone. I've only just got round to telling myself.

Later, a rare hour on my own at home, after I have cleaned the loo and done the washing and am about to hoover the stairs, there is a ring at the door. There's something about the ring that suggests Amanda. When I approach the door I can see an Amanda-shaped head through the frosted glass.

'Hello, Amanda. Come in.'

'I will if you don't mind, Vicky.'

She bustles through the door, scarves swaying, bringing in a bundle of cold with her.

We go through to the kitchen where Amanda accepts a glass of water after much persuasion. She asks after the feeding and I reassure her it is going fine, just the one at bedtime now since Imo has discovered the delights of strawberry porridge for breakfast. But I don't think that is why Amanda is here.

'Is there anything in particular I can do for you, or is it just a social call?' I join her with a glass of water only I indulge myself and have a splash of Ribena in it.

'Actually, this is a pastoral visit.'

'Oh?'

'I wanted to check all's well with you.'

'I'm fine. The kids are fine. Steve's fine.'

'Where's Imo now?'

'Out with Roland and Dorota.'

'It's good that you let them help.'

'Why wouldn't I?'

'Well, I know you found it hard to let people take care of Olivia when she was a baby.'

'I liked looking after her.'

'We all need a break.'

'I'm fine.'

'That's good. Only, how's the whole... curate's wife thing. I mean, I know it can be a bit of a culture shock.'

'I'm still trying to get used to it. There's a way to go.'

'A marathon not a sprint.'

'Something like that.'

'And Steve. Is everything alright with him?'

'In what way alright?'

'Well, you know, it's hard, this new life,' she sips at her water. 'You must let me know if I can help. And make sure Steve talks to Desmond if he gets in too deep with anything.'

'In too deep?

'Some parishioners can be overbearing. They can demand too much attention.'

'Tell me about it.'

'Just watch who you spend time with.'

I remember the young girl that haunted Amanda and Desmond's early marriage. I remember the warnings but that was then, a different time. 'I don't think either of us would put ourselves in a vulnerable position.'

'Well, then,' she says. 'That's good.' She finishes her water, the hedonist, and wafts back down the hall, off on another mission. On the doorstep, she turns and says: 'Don't let the Devil get to you.'

I look at Amanda for a moment; her earnest rosy face. 'He'll have to join the queue.'

She manages a smile and then is gone, swaying down the street in a haze of clashing colour.

When I return to the kitchen I notice one of her scarves draped across the seat. I pick up it up and fold it neatly. The smell of Charlie is so overpowering I feel quite nauseous.

Thoughts for the Day: Do I leave a smell behind me when I leave the room? Is it Harpic? Flash? Cillit Bang? Is that my legacy?

March 5th 1978

Martin has gone to tea with Heidi. He brushed his hair because Heidi's parents are posh and live in a big house in Blackheath. Heidi's mum does French cooking because she is French and they are having orange duck. We are having shepherd's pie (my favourite!) and there will be more to go around. Hurray.

Heidi's dad came to pick Martin up. He beeped his horn. Mum said ask him in but Martin said there wasn't time and ran out the house. Mum, Dad and I watched out of the window as the car pulled away.

Nice motor, Dad said.

He should have introduced himself said Mum. He couldn't wait to get off.

Martin has fallen on his feet there, Dad said.

Mum went into the garden to empty the potato peelings.

Chapter Twenty-Nine: *Monday 10th March*

The story according to Steve:
It should have been like any other Saturday. A day off from plumbing, unless I got an emergency call-out. Vicky would usually have a list of jobs for me – a wobbly door handle, a blocked waste. Then we'd go out somewhere. The park. Swimming. A trip to Bluewater. We hadn't done much of that yet, what with a new baby, but we could always manage the park. Pushing Rachel on the swings, feeding the ducks. Crystal Palace or Greenwich. Sometimes we'd drive over to Dulwich and see Martin and Claudia but that could be stressful. Martin was always pleased to see me, some job he needed doing, too tight to call out a plumber and pay the going rate. I didn't mind. He's family. I just wished he and Vick didn't argue so much.

Sometimes we'd go down to Worthing for the day, though that would usually be on a Sunday. Saturdays were better off staying in London where we only had to battle with local traffic and we could do all the stuff that needed doing – shopping, washing, all of that. Vick was on maternity leave but I did my fair share. It's not easy with a new baby and a three-year-old but we were getting into a routine. Thomas was great, fitting into our family, and we were chugging along quite nicely.

We woke up late. I was checking the time on the bedside clock – 8.43 – when Vick sprung out of bed like a ghost was after her. She leapt from the room, her feet barely touching the carpet, the door rattling behind her, an empty coat hanger on the back of it. I hate that; the clanging gets you right in the stomach. A few seconds later and I heard her scream. A terrible noise. Far worse than any stupid coat hanger. Animal-like. It went on and on and I never want to hear that sound ever again, as long as I live. But what was to come... I found her in the box room, the pink nursery. I was supposed to paint it. Blue for a boy. It was on the list. I'd almost made a start the week before but got a call out to Lewisham. A leaky loo. Not an emergency at all. It could just have easily waited till the Monday but it was an old dear and not wanting to make a drama out of a crisis I fixed it in ten minutes. But then there's your travelling time, there and back, and sorting your stuff out, getting changed and washed up. It all takes time, precious time, so I never got started but we decided, because he was doing so well, we'd put him in the room anyway, in his cot, and we said the painting can wait, let's go with it, go with him on this one. And as I went into his room that morning, I was telling myself I'd make a start today, I'd make it all right, all good, but then Vicky's scream was still echoing, colliding off the pink walls and I saw her, standing there but her face belonged to someone else and she was holding someone else's baby. A blue, still, dead baby. Not our Thomas. It couldn't be him. Surely he was still sleeping in his cot. I couldn't help myself: I looked in the cot. It was empty. Did I really have to touch the place where he'd been lying? Did I have to pull back the covers and check he wasn't there, hiding? I went to Vick instead, and touched the boy in her arms and he just lay there. Not the usual gurgle or frog-kick of a leg. His eyes were all wrong, half-open and staring at nothing.

I can't even bring myself to talk about the next part. Except that Vick had calmed down somehow. She handed him to me and went to phone an ambulance because that was what had to be done, she knew that somehow. He was cold. Lifeless. It was clear that Thomas, the Thomas we were getting to know, had left his little body behind and gone somewhere else. And in the slow, agonising days that followed, that was the part that was killing me: I had no idea where he had gone.

Two weeks later, after the funeral, after the endless official stuff, after we'd had a few days away in Worthing to give Rachel some support from her grandparents, I had to go back to work. We had to try and get back to some kind of pretend normality but I suspected that was never going to happen for me. Vick was so strong, getting on with things, making food for us, making me eat, making herself eat, though I could see she was losing weight and her colour wasn't right. But she was carrying on, getting Rachel to and from preschool. It was all I could do to drink a cup of tea or get in the shower. But she told me I had to go back to work. It was the holidays so Vick didn't have school for a few weeks, back from maternity leave, with no baby. She said it wasn't good, both of us moping around the house. I needed to work. So I accepted a job. A callout to Dartford. What happened next changed things again. Changed things completely.

Steve tells Karolina this as she calls round for a cup of tea and a chat, an Alpha follow-up, because she's still got questions. (Haven't we all?) I leave them to it and go and sort out the airing cupboard.

The story according to Rachel:

They don't talk about him. Sometimes I wonder if he was like really here or whether, for a bit, I just had this imaginary friend. But deep down I know he lived. I remember how he smelt of cream. Uncle Martin uses it for his scaly skin. I've seen him rub it in his hands, round his wrists. I smelt it when he wasn't looking. He'd left it on the coffee table and I unscrewed the lid and sniffed it and Thomas like floated back to me so I knew he'd really been here, in our house, up in Imo's room and lying on his mat on the carpet under a baby gym, a different one to the one we've got now. Where Imo's

218

always getting wedged cos she's like so fat.

Rachel tells Jessica this in our front room, after school, while they are playing a game on the laptop. My laptop. A laptop that I almost forgot existed. An old, clumpy paving slab of a techno-thing that used to be so precious to me. They are playing a golf game. Yes, golf. Jessica is a big fan of golf and drags Rachel down with her.

I am unseen to them, behind the half-opened door, scrubbing – as quietly as possible, not easy – at a patch of hall carpet where Jeremy has trodden in dog poo. But I can hear their every word. And I scrub all the harder, not caring if I am detected, not caring about anything except stopping the tears, stopping the pain in my chest, the sick in my stomach that threatens to pull me over and knock me into a ball, like a hedgehog. A prickly, stupid, flea-ridden hedgehog.

The story according to Dorota:
I may not do church but I do God. He is there when you cry out, listening, even if you think he is far away, stuck on a cloud. He hears you and he feels your pain. But you cannot lie on the carpet in the hallway. Your children will see you and think you have gone round the bend. And it smells of dog mess. Where is your 'Shake-n-Vacky, Vicky?'

Dorota tells me this while sitting me down at the kitchen table and pouring me a glass of her sherry, the bottle still untouched from Shrove Tuesday which shows she does 'do church', keeping those promises.

She and Roland have called by on some pretext, hand in hand and all loved-up. Is she checking up on me?

'Are you checking up on me?'

'Yes.'

'Oh.'

My heart, now calmer, has another blip. So. I need to be checked up on, do I?

The story according to Jessica:

I remember your baby brother. He was so cute and your mum let me hold him once on your sofa, the old one with the flowers. We were watching Dick and Dom and your mum was looking after me because my mum had a headache and Dad was at work. I remember holding onto him really tight because I didn't want to drop him on the floor and you told me to be careful, I was squashing him and your mum said I was doing good. I was dead jealous of you cos you had a baby and I didn't. I was jealous of your mum cos she never shouted. And then Thomas wasn't here anymore and I wasn't jealous. I was really sad. But then my mum left and I was jealous again that you had a mum and I didn't. But then I got Tamarine. She can be bossy sometimes but that's just cos me and dad are slobs.

Jessica is sitting at the kitchen table drinking milk with Rachel, and eating her way through a packet of Rich Tea. Imo has gone up for a bit of shut-eye and Olivia is glued to *Raven*, along with Jeremy, who has taken a liking to his younger cousin as she tidies up after him. So this allows me, once again, to eavesdrop on a private conversation, on this occasion under the pretext of changing a hoover bag outside in the poky hall. But I feel justified in my snooping if it gives me such insight into an otherwise closed shop. On hearing her words, I want to wrap my arms around Jessica but then she and Rachel will know what I've been up to.

Dorota has left, taking Roland with her, still hand in hand, feeling she has put the world – my world – in order. But there is only one way I know how to put things in order and that is with my hands, a cloth and some kind of cleaning implement, electrical or otherwise.

As I put in a new hoover bag, I wonder about three things:

If I had been a passenger in Steve's van that Saturday morning he got a call-out to Dartford, would I have shared in his life-changing experience? Or would it have affected me differently? And I know it is stupid to wonder that, because I wasn't a passenger in Steve's van that Saturday morning. I was here, at home, with Rachel, changing a hoover bag or the sheets on a bed. I was carrying on my life as normal, as normal as it can be when you are recovering from the death of a child. If you ever recover. Steve says he is in recovery, like an alcoholic. It will never be over but it will get better than it was. Life without a drink, without Thomas, will be more bearable. Because of what happened that day, and what has been happening to him every day since then on his new walk with God.

Shall I go in the kitchen and ask Jessica if she wants to see her mother? Shall I talk to Bob or would he be offended? I don't want to aggravate neighbourly relations. Maybe Tamarine.

Shall I get a Dyson and be done with bags?

The first of these three things I can't do anything about. The second and third will have to wait.

Thoughts for the Day: Where do hedgehogs catch fleas from? Why aren't fleas put off by those spikes? I wish I had the tenacity of a flea.

Chapter Thirty: *Tuesday 11th March*

So where is Martin? Bill (or his wife) has kicked him out and he has crawled back home. Not to Claudia. Not to me. But down to Worthing, to Dad. The term is over for him and he is taking advantage of the break to crack on with his research. Only he does find time to come back to London for a night, squeezing in a visit to his son as an afterthought. The main reason he comes is to attend tonight's Alpha meeting.

'I couldn't believe it when I saw him there, Vick. I never thought the day would come when Martin willingly stepped foot inside a church.' Steve is making Ovaltine while I sit at the table darning socks, one of my gifts that few people in this country still have. But at the mention of Martin's name I stab myself in the finger with the needle, cursing inwardly.

'Don't tell me it's a miracle,' I sigh, sucking on my finger.

Steve gives me a sympathetic look. 'Poor Vick.' He rummages in a drawer for a plaster and once found takes off the wrapper and wraps up my finger. He is gentle but my finger throbs, its very own heartbeat. 'I wouldn't dream of using that kind of language with you, Vick. But God is working here somehow.'

'What did he say?'

'God?'

'No, Martin, you muppet.'

'Ah, well. Not a lot. He was making notes.' Steve hands me

a mug, sits down opposite me. It's a quiet evening. No wind, no rain, the kids sleeping peacefully above. The monitor blinking on the dresser.

'Notes?' I remember Martin that day in church, creeping in at the back, scrawling in his book. 'And did he give any clues as to what he was doing there?'

'He made the odd flippant comment to try and put a spanner in the works. There's always one like that. And that's good. That's what Alpha's about, daring to throw up questions and admitting we don't have all the answers. Only God has all the answers.'

And where's Martin now? He has left his son, and whizzed back down the motorway to his father. Our father. Who lives in Worthing.

I'm simmering over this when the phone goes. I barely hear it, barely register that Steve has left the room. He re-enters a couple of minutes later and I switch back on.

'Who was that? At this time?' According to the clock it's gone 10.30, the cut-off for being worried when the phone goes and my heart doesn't even jump. I don't know what I should be more worried about, the call or my non-responsive body.

'That was Desmond.' Steve sits down quietly at the table and takes a deep breath, practising what he preaches, inhaling and exhaling, from his stomach not his chest, to maximise energy, to keep calm and focused. His face looks slack, loose, like it's struggling to keep its shape. Its Steve-shape.

'What is it?'

'Desmond's had a call.'

'Who from? Has there been an accident?'

'No, no. No-one's died. Nothing like that.' He takes my hand; to reassure me or himself, I'm not entirely sure. 'It's Karolina.'

At the sound of her name, I get a flash of her languishing on the sofa, surrounded by all that gumph and wonder if I should have done more to help her. Maybe she's got really ill and turned to Desmond and Amanda. Maybe she's in hospital. Maybe... what... ?

'... Why would Karolina phone Desmond?'

Steve breathes in and blows out his breath so I feel its warmth in my face, smell the malt of his Ovaltine. 'You're not to worry when I tell you,' he says, worrying me straightaway. 'It's all a bit weird. I only saw her tonight.'

'So she came? She's not ill?

'She looked a bit dishevelled. Loads of make-up, like a Goth sort of thing. A blonde Goth. She was very quiet, subdued and I'm not sure Martin helped. He was sat next to her and snorted when she did speak up once about suffering.'

Martin.

'What's Martin done? Has she made a complaint about him?'

'No. That's the weird thing.' He shakes his head. 'She's made a complaint about me.'

You.

'You? What do you mean, "a complaint"? Was the church hall not warm enough or something?'

'She told Desmond I... made inappropriate advances.' He says this like it's something he's read in the paper. Something one of his parishioners has told him.

We sit there in silence for a moment. The train trundles up the track and I wish I was on it, going clubbing in town, going for a night walk along the Thames, watching the lights of London reflected in those dark waters. I wish I wasn't here. I wish this wasn't happening.

Steve doesn't ask if I believe what Desmond has said to be true. He and I, we go back too far, we know each other too well to question this. I know she is lying. Without any doubt whatsoever. She. Is. A. Liar. And I know Desmond is phenomenally stupid to be phoning at this time of night and worrying us. For I am worried. Not about the integrity of my husband but for the repercussions of what Karolina has said.

The lies she is telling. The story she is weaving.

He stares ahead, trying to piece together the events of the evening, trying to get his brain working. 'She left her purse in the church hall. We were all outside in the car park, saying goodbyes, going home. She said she had to go back in to look for it, the purse. So I unlocked the door to let her in, switching on the light. I waited with Martin, chatting through some stuff. He has some interesting theories. Then he said she's been a long time. Nearly everyone had gone by now. It was getting cold. So I went in after her, to see if I could help. She was at the other end of the hall, reading a leaflet. I asked her if she'd found it. She said: 'Found what?' I said: 'Your purse.' She said: 'Yes, I have my purse,' and she patted her coat pocket. Then we left the hall. Martin was getting in his Saab and he offered her a lift. She accepted. I said goodnight to them, got in my car and drove home.'

'So you were alone with her.'

'Only briefly. Just a couple of minutes, not even that, and the hall door was open, there were people in the car park. Martin was still in the car park. I didn't think for one minute I was putting myself at risk.'

I feel sick. I have taken my eye off the ball. Shelley warned me about her. But that was Shelley. And then Amanda, here, in my kitchen, warning me of this. She had a feeling. I had a feeling and I never spoke to Steve about it. I never said a word because I dismissed it. Stupid, stupid idiot. I dismissed it. I forgot about it. I thought Amanda was being overly dramatic. I thought Shelley was being her usual gossipy, big-mouthed, fascist self. 'I should have warned you. Amanda told me she had worries about... well, she was a bit vague about what exactly. Suspicions. And Shelley. She said Karolina was a man-eater. I should have told you.'

Steve says nothing so I don't know if he agrees or not. I don't even know if he has heard me. He has on his thinking head. That distracted look that tells me he is deep in contemplation, processing all sorts of stuff that would never even occur to me. Surely no-one will believe this? Surely she's got a screw loose. And I remember the packet of pills and wonder... I should have listened to people. Amanda. Shelley. Myself. I should've known she'd pull a stunt like this. But I thought she was actually possibly maybe becoming my friend.

'She planned it.'

Steve shakes his head again, like he's trying to clear it of bad thoughts. 'No, Vick. No. I don't think so. She's just messed up.' He puts his head in his hands, exhales, then looks up at me and takes my hand again. The hand that is always there, ready. It is cold. I expect him to thank me for believing absolutely in him. I do not expect this: 'Poor Karolina,' he says, simply. 'She needs help.'

I could scream. I do scream. And then when I have stopped screaming, I can hear Imo scream.

March 9th 1978

When I got back from Guides tonight (hurray! I don't have to be a Brownie anymore) Heidi was around watching Top of the Pops. I peered round the door and they were snogging. Gross. Martin had his hand on one of her enormous wotsits. I felt a bit funny so I went to find Mum. There was a note on the kitchen table. Mum and Dad had gone to the cinema. Anniversary treat. I made myself some cheese on toast, learnt my spellings and polished the brass.

Chapter Thirty-One: Sunday 16th March

HOLY WEEK

Palm Sunday

We have lived under a cloud this week, a cloud spitting rain on our family, threatening to split open and pour its dark, wet contents over us. I think of the wise man and the foolish man and wonder if our life is built on rock or sand. What is going to happen to us? Will Desmond sort it out? Will the Bishop be called in? Will Steve be believed, his word against hers? Will he be suspended? Lose his job? Go back to being a plumber? And will this be what I have longed for?

As my family sits it out at home, having a quiet, low profile day off, and as people sit in church, unaware of what is happening, with their palm crosses, remembering and celebrating Jesus' triumphant entry into Jerusalem, I crawl across the level crossing into Worthing to meet Dad and Martin, my other family, for a pub lunch. No celebration. No hope of better things to come. No sense of destiny about to be fulfilled. But with a heavy heart and hammering headache.

Go, Steve said. *Get away. Stop fretting. It'll be fine.*

And I felt guilty, leaving him to it with all the kids, Imo, the bottle, the fallout from Karolina's revelations.

Martin's going to love this.

Martin takes me by surprise. He hands me a large glass of red wine despite my protests and makes me drink it, saying I should stay overnight and have a break. Of course my first thought is Imo's nighttime feed. And the fact I have no clean knickers or toothbrush. But there is the milk I expressed in the fridge. Just in case. Maybe this is just in case. Maybe a night in Worthing would do me good. Bizarrely. With Dad. And Martin. And that's my second strange thought: that I'd quite like to spend time with them.

Meanwhile there's a carvery to be gathered and eaten. A glass of wine to be drunk. No washing up.

Late. Dad's front room. A cup of tea and the remains of crumpets and jam on a tray by the fire. A black and white film. Violins and ladies in box hats. Dad snoring on the dust-free dustbowl. Martin battering away on his laptop in the armchair. Me, on the pouffe, with Mum's tin on my lap, going through the contents.

'Have you still got your old tin?' asks Martin, cutting in on my reverie.

'Have you?' I have learnt this technique from Steve, turning a question back on the questioner.

Martin falls for it. 'I have actually. It's in the attic somewhere. I hope Claudia hasn't chucked it out. No. She won't have. She doesn't know how to get down the loft ladder. Not with her nails.'

I find myself smiling.

He stops battering, puts the laptop on the coffee table and stretches. 'So... what's in Mum's tin? Any secrets we should know about?'

I hold up some of the items which he takes off me to inspect: Mum's birth certificate, marriage certificate, a christening card from some long-forgotten godmother of mine who failed at her job. Some photos. Martin and me on our bikes in the back garden. Martin's Chopper, his pride and joy. My three wheeler.

'I loved that bike,' says Martin, wistful, examining the photo closely. 'I can still remember the sound the bell made. The way the pedals felt when I was going uphill.' He sits back and holds the photo for a moment and I catch a glimpse of nostalgia that I thought I would never see in my scientific, rational, logical brother. All over a bike.

Then I dig out the photo of Dad and Uncle Jack and hand it to him. 'Do you remember this one?'

'Never seen it before,' he says.

'You've probably forgotten.'

'No. I've definitely never seen it. I remember the name, not the face.' He straightens his arm, to get a better look (someone needs to go to Specsavers). 'It's not exactly expertly taken. You can hardly see his face; he's squinting into the sun. Must've been one of Mum's. She was a lousy photographer, always lopping off heads, if she even remembered to open the shutter.'

We laugh at this, kindly, remembering our ditsy mother, the one who always had a smile for us, a kind word, if she actually noticed us coming into the room. She was so often in a dream, somewhere else. Knitting wonky socks. Sowing seeds for Dad.

We look at Dad, dozing on the dustbowl. Hard to imagine how he carries on without her. But he does. And he's made room for Pat in this life, back-filling the space left by Mum. People say men move on quicker than women; they can't survive on their own. Maybe that's true... and what about Steve? If I pegged out here and now on the freshly hoovered carpet, would he find someone else? Would Amanda have to beat off crowds of needy women rampaging after their widowed priest? Would Karolina step in?

Some men can't wait around forever.

Karolina.

The echo of her name, her words, rattles around my head, makes me feel nauseous. I can taste the strawberry jam at the back of my throat. The tin feels heavy on my lap and I pass it over to Martin.

'You alright?'

'No.'

'Want to talk about it?'

Want to talk about it?

I have never heard Martin utter that particular collection of words in that particular order and somehow this makes me start babbling. I tell him everything that has happened over the past week. The accusation. The suspicions. The uncertainty. He doesn't snort. He doesn't comment. He doesn't once say 'Vicky-Love'. He just listens.

'I wouldn't worry about it,' he says, after a few minutes silence when I believe I have finally found a way of pulling the rug from under his big fat feet. 'It'll get sorted.'

Profound words from Professor Martin Bumface.

'Shame about Uncle Jack,' he says, re-examining the photo. 'He would've been company for Dad in his old age.'

It's then that we notice Dad's eyes are open. He has this odd expression, hurt mixed in with something darker... He sits up and reaches out to Martin who hands over the photograph wordlessly, a boy returning something he shouldn't have. And I remember the look on Dad's face, up in his bedroom, when Rachel held the same photo in her cold hand.

'I don't know why your soppy mother kept that old picture. It's years old.' He stares at it, the first time in a long time, and I wonder if he might actually lob it on the fire.

'He was your friend, wasn't he, Dad.' My voice sounds patronising even to my ears, like I'm talking to Rachel about Jessica.

'Yes, he was,' he mutters.

And to our horror Dad starts crying. I've never seen him cry like this and it snatches the breath out of me, swirls it round the room and shoves it back in so I feel sicker than ever.

'Dad?' I go and sit next to him, take his hand in mine.

It feels smaller than it should, the skin tissue-soft. I hold it gently, no hand-patting. 'What's wrong?'

'She wouldn't want you to know. But maybe you should know.' He brushes me away, the way he always does, and takes out a grubby hanky before comprehensively filling it with the contents of his nose. This calms him down a bit.

But not me. 'You're ill, aren't you, Dad? The anaemia... ' I want Martin to help me out but he is staring at the fire, like a soothsayer or something, trying to work out what is going on around here.

'I'm not ill.' Dad is firm, dismissing his neurotic daughter. 'I wasn't eating properly. My blood's fine. Pat's sorted me out, got me back on the veg. She's got an allotment.'

'Pat?'

'You shouldn't judge a book by its cover, Vicky-Love. Didn't Jesus say that?'

'I don't know, Dad, I'm not an expert. So you're alright?'

'A bit doddery, that's all. Getting old, aren't I?'

I don't answer this. It seems rude. But the relief makes me light-headed – it's not cancer! – and I breathe deep, from the stomach.

Martin is up on his feet, pacing, giving up on the psychic properties of the fire, which is fizzling out. I should get up and add another log but I don't want to break the moment.

'Sit down, son,' Dad says. 'You're making me nervous.'

'She wouldn't want us to know what?' Martin slumps onto the pouffe, stares Dad outright. 'It is Mum you're talking about, right?'

Dad caves in, quickly, as if he's been waiting for this moment. This is it. His time to tell us something. 'It's your Uncle Jack.'

'Is he still alive?' I ask, flailing around for ideas, recent relief so quickly usurped by confusion.

Dad shakes his head, almost smug. 'He's dead as a wotsit.'

'What then?' Martin fires at him. 'What did you want to say?'

Dad sniffs, pulls at his cuffs, studies his knees, looks up slowly at Martin. Then he goes for it. 'Hesyourfatheryourrealfathernotme.' One breath so he can get it out quick, before he changes his mind and pulls the words back into him. Because he knows that once they are out, the words, things will be different round here.

He's your father your real father not me.

I say nothing. Martin says nothing. His eyes are blank. His face empty. And then he laughs. A dry laugh that swamps the room, sucking everything in its path so that's all there is: his laugh.

When at last it fades, he gets up and leaves us. Leaves the room behind with all the unspoken questions and explanations. Walks quietly down the hall and out of the house.

We listen to the door click.

'That shut him up,' Dad says. 'Thought he'd never give it a rest.'

That's when I decide I'd better go after my brother.

He's your father. Your real father. Not me.

I'm pretty sure where he'll be. So I wrap up well, despite the mild spring day because it's flat, windy Worthing and knowing Martin, he'll be on the seafront. I walk through Marine Gardens, past the bowling greens and the old-fashioned cafe, reminiscent of an earlier era, of women in hats and men in flannel trousers. A time when you addressed your parents' friends by their formal names. Or, if they were better known, by Auntie or Uncle.

Uncle Jack.

Was Dad making some kind of joke back there? Did he really mean that Uncle Jack was Martin's father? Which means... Mum and Uncle Jack? Our mother, the daydreamer, in whose eyes you sometimes glimpsed other lives. Other possibilities.

Other men?

Uncle Jack?

Over the road and onto the prom, past the beach huts – a quick check in the shelter – and then onto the shingle. Tide out and a vast stretch of grey beach beyond the pebbles, the waves reticent and far off. The fresh smell of seaside. Vestiges of burnt wood. Gulls dive-bombing, squealing, in search of chips.

I trudge along the sand, firm under my sensible-Vicky shoes, Marks and Spencer's, wide-fitting to allow for bunion growth, and it's not long before I spot him: a tall, substantial figure lobbing stones into the retreating tide, aimlessly, aimless.

I decide to join him, first retreating up the shingle to retrieve a fistful of stones, shoving them in my jacket pockets. When I catch up, I offer him a pile and chuck one myself for all I'm worth, till my shoulder hurts. It disappears into the water, without a sound, the merest splash.

'Call that a throw?' He has a go himself, stretching his arm right back, like it's serious, a competition. Which, of course, it is. There's nothing I can beat him at. After several minutes of exertion, he turns away from the sea and starts striding away along the tide line, kicking at random bits of wood so I have to jog to keep up. Eventually I go for it, in between gulps of cold air: 'You alright? Want to talk about it?' I realise I have never uttered these words to him in that order either, and we both laugh, both of us dry, but because we are out in the open, the sea and the sky stretched before us, there's more freedom, more emotion.

'Is he winding me up?' Martin stops, pinning me to the sand with a look, a possibility.

I consider this. I wouldn't put it past Dad. He can have a cruel streak to him. Maybe he's losing the plot. But my gut instinct is that this is the truth. And the photo backs me up. Though you can't see Uncle Jack's face there is something about the presence. I always thought that Martin took after Dad, with that presence, going in a room and holding court. But the two of them together, friends captured in time, you can see something hanging around Jack. An aura or something. I don't of course say this to Martin, whose aura has always cast a shadow over me. Stunted Vicky. 'I reckon he's telling the truth.'

'Right.' He grabs another stone off me, grappling in my pocket the way he used to hunt out my Hubba-Bubba and he throws the stone so hard it almost hits a gull, but the crafty thing gets away and perches on a groyne, its small, pebbly eye fixed on my brother. 'Let's get some chips,' Martin says, surveying the bird. 'I'm starving.'

Much later, after chips, after miles of walking in the gathering dusk, after I've been to Boots and BHS and got my toothbrush and a packet of knickers and tights, after I've called home and cleared it with a curious Steve, we get back to find Dad in the kitchen with Pat. I say hello politely – Martin lingering in the hall – and leave them to their scrambled egg on toast, while we set ourselves up in the front room, Martin constructing the mother of all fires, me getting out the Scrabble and a bottle of Teacher's. It's going to be a long night.

Martin thrashes me, trebling my score, making me feel like I've never read a book in my life. It's been a while (must go to library).

The fire is dying down and the whisky bottle much depleted by the time Pat puts her head round the door. 'I'm off,' she says. 'Your dad's tucked up in bed, should be fine till morning.' She disappears, clattering into the night.

How much does Pat know? Has Dad told her? Is she colluding in all this, keeping Dad out of the firing range? Not that Martin's fired anything, apart from those pebbles on the beach and the towering inferno in the grate. Nothing at Dad. He's said nothing to Dad.

Then Martin says something, *in vino veritas*. 'Do you ever wonder what it's all about?'

'You sound like an advert for Alpha.'

I don't really expect him to laugh at my little joke because he never does laugh at anything I say, unless it's not intended to be funny. But I don't expect him to cry. Him and Dad in one day.

'Martin?'

He keeps on crying, his shoulders shaking, his eyes wet, no sound apart from phlegmy sniffing. I hand him a hanky from up my sleeve, assuring him of its cleanliness. He blows his nose (must boil on my return). Feel bad about my thoughts. This is my brother. Crying. Because he's been told our dad is not his dad. Which means he's not technically my whole brother. Which would usually thrill me but I feel myself well up and a fog of confusion wrap itself around us. But one thing is clear. I will be Vicky the Comforter.

So I reach out. I put my arms around my big brother and I hug him.

It is a very strange sensation. Unnatural and awkward at first but after a few seconds, his shoulders stop moving. I don't know whether they are tensing up because he is embarrassed or whether my arms have had a soothing effect on him. But I carry on regardless until Martin stops me.

'Vick, you're choking me.'

I let him go, move apart, trying not to feel slighted. But he smiles at me, a lopsided smile, and rubs his beard.

'Are you alright?'

'My tooth hurts. Despite all the whisky. People keep hitting me in the face for some reason. Pot Noodles and fists.'

'Funny that,' I smile back. I can't help it.

'I'm going to have a bath.'

'Good idea,' I say. 'You stink.'

He smiles again. And then he pats my hand.

It is late. Very late. I am sitting by the dying fire, sipping Horlicks, going over my phone call to Steve where I gave him the latest news, which, as ever, he took without blanching. The day's revelation banged about my head but he said these things were more common than one could ever imagine. We're not always who we think we are. I didn't want to get into all this over the phone so I asked him about the kids. He had nothing to report other than they are fine; Imo's had her bottle and gone off happily. It is only when he mentioned her name and I pictured her with a bottle that I realised: no let-down, no tightening, no leakages, no pain. Was this it? Had we done it?

And now, sitting by the fire, I know that whatever the achievement, it is just one battle won. For there is still a war brewing ahead. Karolina. Steve never mentioned her name, so I didn't either. If there was any worrying news I didn't want to hear it. I don't want to hear it. Not here. Not now. All I want is Horlicks. A dying fire. Bed.

Martin went to bed long ago. Never came back downstairs after his bath. I put the Scrabble away, made myself a fish paste sandwich and watched some costume drama. Bonnets and petticoats. Then sat here in the quiet, pondering all that has happened to me. Why is it I never do anything? Why is it always done to me? I am feeling rather sorry for myself when Dad shuffles in, cuff-fiddling.

'Has he gone up then?'

'I think so.'

'Is he upset?'

'What do you reckon, Dad? You dropped a rather large bombshell on him, didn't you?'

'I never meant for him to know. Me and your mum, we agreed. Best that way.'

'Best that way as long as you didn't let it slip.'

'I know. Me and my big mouth. But I got this urge. To spill the beans. I couldn't help myself. I've been lying in bed going over and over it. Do you think I should wake him and have a chat? Check he's alright?'

'I should let him sleep on it, Dad. He's most probably done

237

in. Maybe in the morning.'

'Things always look better in the morning, eh?'

I smile in agreement though I don't go along with that assumption. Your problems are still there when you wake up. Following you around. Pestering you. 'So, Dad.' I take a deep breath. Hold it. Let it go. 'Want to talk about it?'

Chapter Thirty-Two

The story according to Dad:

We were the best of friends. Went to school together. Left school together. Soon as we could. Fourteen we were. Jack got an apprenticeship with an engineer. He had a brain but hated school, wanted to earn. And me? All I'd ever wanted was to get my hands dirty, roll around in the mud, see what Mother Nature had to offer. I knew there was more than bombsites and grey streets. There was a whole other world out there. Ever since that visit to Kew as a young lad with my gran, pointing out all the trees. She knew all the names, some of the Latin. It was exotic, colourful. That's what I wanted: colour.

And then when I got older, and Gran had passed on and I was earning some money, working for old man Lewis down at the parks, I'd go out on a Friday with my mates Charlie and Jack up in town sometimes, or down the pub. But best of all we liked the pictures, the Odeon, and that's where I met your mother, queuing up outside, on her own. I was impressed with that. She didn't look lonely or awkward. She looked self-contained like she was all she needed. She looked like something off the films, not Hollywood, one of them British films. Black and white. Serious. Kitchen sink. She had her hair swept up in a kind of bun thing but it was a bit messy, strands of hair falling over her face. I thought about going up to speak to her but, well, Jack cut right in and talked to her first. And that was that. Or so I thought. They started going steady and a few months later they were engaged. There was a party at her mum and dad's and we were invited, Charlie and I. I tried to say congratulations as I turned up on her doorstep. She answered the door and I'd planned to kiss her on the cheek but I grabbed her by the hand instead and gave it a shake. What a fool. If Jack had been me he'd have managed the kiss. He was so easy-going, so relaxed, everyone loved him. And there he was in their front room, his best suit, looking like a king, smiling and blonde and fresh-faced. And then there was this announcement, your Granddad Tom chinking his bottle of stout with a spoon. A wedding. Two weeks time. Lewisham Register Office, followed by a buffet at the house. But your grandma didn't look too pleased. She never said a word. Never said anything to Jack. I caught her looking daggers at him. Couldn't work out what he'd done to upset her. He never upset anyone. Though he'd upset me that day, outside the pictures, talking to your mum before I got up the nerve.

But it never happened, the wedding. Within a week Jack was dead. One of those freak accidents. There'd been a delivery at the workshop. A truck. It crushed him against a wall. Horrible. Makes you shiver to think of it. His life gone, just like that. And so instead of a wedding there was a funeral. Your mum looked pale and fragile as a snowdrop, standing there in the winter sun, throwing a red rose onto his coffin, her hand shaking. It fluttered to her stomach. I don't think anyone noticed, except for your gran. And then I twigged. Jack had left a baby. That was what the rush had been about. Not just the rush of love. But the rush of time. Getting in quick so there was no tongue-wagging.

The tongue-wagging followed. That day, by the graveside, seeing her small hand flutter to her belly, I knew I would do my best to take care of her. And soon, she was my girl. It's what Jack would've wanted. He knew about the baby, was pleased about it. Wanted to do the right thing. And that's what

I wanted. To do the right thing. Take care of her. And the baby. Martin.

When he was born, we'd walk the streets together, your mum pushing the pram and me linking arms with her. Men didn't push prams then but I would've. I'd have done anything. We could see people muttering, but they never said it to our faces. This happened all the time, our predicament. It was part of life. A man would step in where another had left, for whatever reasons. That's what I did: I stepped in. Not out of a sense of duty, though maybe there was something of that. But I loved your mum, had done since that first day, outside the pictures.

And I loved Martin, from the first time I held him in my arms, wrapped up in a blue woolly blanket, a smattering of blonde fuzzy hair, pumpkin face, chubby legs that you wanted to squeeze. He was my son.

Dad tells me this over the fading embers, a blanket on his knee, scrunched uncomfortably on the pouffe, me at his feet, the pair of us trying to keep warm.

'You need to tell Martin what you've just told me. In the morning. Promise me, Dad?'

'You sound like your mother,' he says. 'Always wanting what's best for him.'

'Isn't that what you want too?'

He nods. 'It's what any father wants for his son.'

I get up then, exhaustion getting the better of me. 'Time for bed, Dad.' I reach out my hand to help him up but he waves it away.

'Let me sit here a while longer. You go on up. I'll be fine. I can get myself to bed.'

I stoop down to kiss his cheek and leave him, too tired to worry enough to argue with him.

I'm sunk in the deepest of dreams when I am shaken awake, my brain immediately kick-started into anxiety. Dad? Steve? Kids?

'Martin?'

'Ssh, Vick. Don't wake the old codger.'

I pull myself up to get a grip on the situation. 'What is it, Martin? What's happened?'

'Have you forgotten Dad's little revelation?'

'No, no, of course not.'

'I couldn't sleep.'

'No, of course not.'

'It's not the sort of information you have to process every day.'

I shake my head in sympathy but then I see something odd. His face. 'Martin, you've shaved off your beard.'

He rubs his new pink skin. 'It was getting too itchy. I had to get rid of it.'

'You look much better.'

'My skin's going to kick off though. I forgot my moisturiser. Have you got any?'

I lean over and retrieve my handbag from the floor and dig out some Nivea. He grabs it off me, a cream-junkie, and helps himself, liberally. Then he flops down on the bed like he's lost his bones. I don't ever remember him sitting on my bed, even as a child. He steered clear of my room; it was beneath him. Sindy dolls and posters of Starsky and Hutch. Lilac woodchip and flowery curtains. His room was a homage to masculinity. A dart board on the back of the door. Led Zeppelin and Black Sabbath posters covering the black – yes, black – walls. A drum kit. A rugby ball. Dirty socks on the floor. A smell hanging in the air. I gave it a wide berth but sometimes Mum made me go in and wake him up. Sometimes, rarely, she handed me a pile of ironing to take in and leave on his bed with the orange grungy sheets. It was creepy in there and I darted in and out like a member of the SAS.

This is all a bit weird.

But seeing him smooth skinned takes me back there like it wasn't all those years ago. Like it's a Sunday night before school and he's up late doing his homework and I'm polishing everyone's shoes.

'You need to talk to Dad in the morning. Son to father.'

I'm contemplating the wisdom of that phrase when there's a knock on the door and it slowly opens to reveal Dad, in his dressing gown, clutching a tray of Horlicks balanced on his cast, and the dregs of the whisky bottle. He shuffles in and half-drops the tray on the bed. The three mugs stand in a pool of frothy liquid.

'We need to talk,' Dad says. And there is no way I can escape, trapped as I am in the bed with both Martin and Dad sat on it.

And so Dad begins again on his story.

Thoughts for the Day: Steve likes to quote Kierkegaard at me: *Life can only be understood backwards; but it must be lived forwards.* Maybe that's true. But I've learnt to my cost that the past is a dangerous place. I've dwelled on Mum's death. Like Thomas, it shouldn't have happened. She still had time to go, a life ahead, but it was taken from her when she wasn't looking. I've given no thought to how she was before Martin and I arrived, before our arguments, our personalities, came into her life. No wonder she disappeared so often into her own world. She must've needed that to survive. The way I need to clean and scrub and hoover and iron and...

March 15th 1978

*Mum and Dad are up the allotment. I am a latchkey kid.
Martin is in his bedroom with Heidi. He is not allowed to go
in his bedroom with Heidi, especially with the door locked. He
told me to keep my mouth shut or he will cut my fingers off.
Even Martin wouldn't do that to me but he had a bad look in
his eye so I won't risk it.*

*I want Heidi to come out and watch telly with me because
she talks to me about what's going on instead of shouting at
the screen like Martin. He is better behaved when he is with
Heidi. When she has gone he becomes a caveman again.*

I arrive back home at noon to a chilled-out house, Imo propped up with cushions in front of CBeebies, Olivia squatting companionably next to her baby sister doing a floor puzzle of Maisie the Mouse, Jeremy and Rachel in the garden with Jessica, armed with Bob's camcorder, Steve at the kitchen table reading one of his hefty theological books, making notes with exclamation marks and much underlining.

My family, this family, greet me like the prodigal mum, but soon return to their tasks, getting on with stuff as if I'd just been down the shops. It feels like an age to me that I've been away, though it's only been twenty-four hours. It's good to be home with them, going about ordinary tasks, the washing up, picking up stray items of clothing, but I keep hankering after Worthing, being back with Dad and Martin who are still holed up together, talking things through.

We got up early, the three of us, considering the very late night. Over breakfast, at the cleared table in the kitchen, we sat together, what was left of my family, my first family, Mum's place emptier than ever, not being there to tell her version of events of how Martin came to be on this earth. Then I left them, to come home.

I empty the bins and put on a wash.

I am gathering the children for lunch when I realise that Jeremy is absent. They came in from the garden, the three of them, whispering and behaving oddly, something to do with their project, the film they're making. Then, when Tamarine called Jessica back home, Jeremy must've slipped away somewhere. Probably back outside in the shed. His shelter and refuge. So it's back over the steeping stones, through the drizzle that has decided to cling to Penge today.

'Jeremy?' I knock on the door, wondering how Martin will break his news, if he will do it soon or if, like Dad, he'll wait for it to slip out in its own time.

'Hang on a sec, Auntie Vicky.' He sounds breathless.

'Lunch is ready.'

'Alright, I'll be there in a minute.'

I decide against going into the shed and hop back inside. In the two minutes of my absence everyone, including Martin, is sitting at the table, helping themselves to bread and cheese. They seem quite self-sufficient all of a sudden, like they know they can manage without me. Which is ridiculous. They're only eating bread and cheese. Who'd know how to clean a toilet around here? Apart from Olivia.

'You're back,' I say to Martin. Profound as ever.

'So it seems.' He heaps the Branston on a slab of Cheddar.

'How's Dad?'

'With Pat.'

'Oh yeah, Vick,' says Steve, smacking his forehead, before I have time to consider Dad with Pat. Her tattoos and his green fingers.

'What's wrong?'

'Nothing. It's just I forgot to say.' He looks shifty, like Rachel when she's not done her homework. 'Mum and Dad are coming tomorrow for a few days. They want to take the kids out seeing as it's the holidays.' He smiles, the relief of confession. 'And they have eggs. Lots of eggs.'

If Martin weren't here I might tell Steve how I feel about eggs, but Martin most definitely is here, eating his way through my food and breathing my air so that all the sympathy of yesterday is sucked straight back into me, cleaned up like a Dyson. So I keep quiet about the descent of the in-laws. I don't want to be mean to Steve in front of Martin. Won't give him the satisfaction. And, to be honest, I don't really care. Dorota and Roland are the least of my worries. Let them take the kids out. Let them eat eggs. Then maybe Steve and I can get to the bottom of all this Karolina nonsense.

'Have you heard from the Polish psycho?' Martin says, picking up on some heavy vibes. He looks from Steve to me and back to his sarney.

Steve says it's all gone quiet on the western front and I am about to change the subject before Olivia asks who the Polish psycho is when the door goes. We all stop eating, like in one of those bad dramas, but there's no need to worry. It's not the Polish psycho or Desmond; it's Roland and Dorota, all bouncy and full of the joys of Penge.

Great.

'Surprise! We come early!' Dorota beams at us, expecting a standing ovation, a round of applause at the very least. Imo obliges, banging her high chair with her beaker. Dorota spots the beaker, her green-lidded eyes sharp as a young girl's and with all the tact of youth asks, 'So, tell, me, Vicky. How are your breasts?'

Martin snorts but, try as I might, my foot will not reach him under the table. If I didn't feel sorry for him at the moment I would gladly aim the jar of Branston at his newly-shaven face.

'Martin,' Dorota says, fluttering her mascara-matted lashes at him. 'You look so young without your beard. Like a teenager.' She giggles. 'And with those strong muscles you can help Roland carry the luggage. I have lots of Easter surprises for the kids. And who knows, if you behave... ?' She winks at him. It is unbearable.

I collect up the plates and plunge them in the sink.

But I am thankful later for the early appearance of my

parents-in-law because they take the girls and Jeremy off to the park, wrapped up like rolls of lagging, in jumpers, coats, hats, scarves and gloves despite the hint of spring in the air – Dorota doesn't take any chances with London weather because it can jump on you from nowhere. I watch them leave, from the window. Jessica, as usual, appears from next door and trails them up the road, camcorder in hand, aiming it at anything that takes her interest, including Dorota's big bottom.

It is then that I notice a serious-looking Desmond pull up in his dirty car. He catches my eye and smiles weakly. A smile that holds all sorts of unspoken words and feelings. I step back from the window and go and find Steve. It takes me a while, even in our poky terrace, but I stumble across him in the downstairs loo, lying awkwardly on the floor. I try to say his name but it's lodged deep down and won't come out. Has he had a heart attack?

The doorbell. Desmond. I am about to drag in the vicar to help administer CPR when Steve, alerted by the bell, sits up, spanner in hand. 'Alright, Vick? I was just fixing that drip. Thought you'd be pleased.'

I am of course pleased. I am in fact ecstatic that Steve hasn't conked out. So I am smiling inanely when I answer the door and usher Desmond in.

'What's all the fun about?' he asks, like he's Oliver Cromwell.

Steve emerges from the loo, drying his hands on a towel, caught out by his boss who today is unusually smart in his dog collar and black suit, armed with a briefcase. Smart and sombre and efficient, like a JW or the man from the Pru.

'Can we have a chat,' Desmond says, not asking, not smiling, going on through to the kitchen, scouting for children with flapping ears. He stands upright by the back door and motions for us both to sit down, which we do.

'It's Karolina,' he says, straight to the point. 'The church wardens and I have had a meeting with her and she has given us her version of events. She's going to go away and write it all down, in a formal statement.' He leaves a gap in case we want to say something but we are both silent, waiting for more information. 'We need to begin the process that investigates whether you, Steve, have engaged in conduct that is unbecoming or inappropriate to the office and work of the clergy. If Karolina wishes to pursue this accusation she must write a formal complaint, which will be made to the Bishop. She'll have to produce written evidence in support of the complaint, and verify the complaint by a statement of truth. The Bishop will then refer this to the diocesan registrar for advice on whether the allegations are of sufficient substance to justify proceedings under the Measure.'

He takes a breath, scans our faces. 'I won't go on. I've printed all this off for you. Read it through and we'll talk later when you've had a chance to consider.' He lays a bundle of officious-looking paper on the table.

Steve doesn't move.

'It's difficult, Steve. I know you are a man of integrity but maybe you've let yourself get in a vulnerable position. It's easily done. Spending time counselling her. Some people can get attached and imagine all sorts of things.'

'I haven't spent any time counselling her,' Steve shakes his head. 'Only the odd conversation after church, or at Alpha, when there have been others around. And confirmation classes... '

'So you've seen a bit of her then?'

'Nothing beyond the call of duty.'

'No phone calls.'

'I don't even have her number.'

Desmond takes out a grey hanky form his trouser pocket and coughs into it. After a moment, he says: 'She showed us her mobile. Your mobile number came up several times in her incoming calls box.'

I daren't look at Steve. I don't want to see his face. I don't want to see his reaction to this revelation. I don't want to know if he phoned her. Why he phoned her. Why he said he never phoned her.

'As for tonight's Alpha, I'm afraid I have no option but to take over,' Desmond goes on. 'Have a night off and talk things through.' He gives the slightest of smiles and nods his head, saying he'll see himself out.

Steve and I sit together, apart, listening to the door shut, the car pull away. The papers stay on the table, waiting to be read.

This is really happening. It won't be resolved today, overnight. It is going to drag on, judging by the papers on the table which no doubt outline all stages of the process. It'll all be done by the book, as it must be. But I hate it. It's not fair. Steve doesn't deserve this. He doesn't. They'll be a reason for the phone calls. And what about me? Has the witch once thought about me?

I remember her languishing on the sofa, the table strewn with rubbish, the packet of pills. I remember her looking at Imo in the surgery telling me she was a lovely baby, making me feel better. The conniving cow.

'Did you phone her?'

'Never.'

'Right, well, okay then. We'll work this out. But we've got to be smart. She's cleverer than we think. And far more dangerous.'

Thoughts for the Day: You will not beat me, Karolina. I am Vicky the Conqueror. Vicky the Victorious.

Chapter Thirty-Four: Thursday 20th March

Maundy Thursday

Martin, surprise, surprise, is staying with us once again. Dorota and Roland are going back later today, what with it being bingo night. So no bed issues.

Martin has toothache, man-toothache, growling at anyone who comes within range. Dorota rummages in the larder and finds a half bottle of brandy left over from Christmas. She puts a generous snifter in his cup of tea and urges him to avoid the dentist. Martin is happy to go along with this treatment but I am not. I won't be shouted at in my own house for cleaning windows, however much pain he is in, physical or otherwise. I won't be told to stop the bloody squeaking because it cuts through him, the poor diddums.

So I phone around and get him an emergency appointment at a local surgery seeing as he doesn't have a dentist of his own in Dulwich. (Too expensive. Too tight.) I scribble the appointment time on a post-it note and stick it on the brandy bottle dwindling in front of him on the kitchen table. My kitchen table.

'Four pm. Can you wait that long or will you be rolling around drunk on the floor by then?'

'What a good idea,' he says, winking at Dorota and taking three consecutive puffs of his inhaler.

My mother-in-law giggles in a sickening manner and I harbour unchristian thoughts, which include smashing the brandy bottle over her hennaed head. Breathe deep, Vicky-Love.

And where is Steve? He has left me with his parents and our children to spend some reflective time in the church. Which is good. Which is right. So why do I begrudge him a simple thing like that?

The last few days and Olivia is still holding her Lenten fast. She has resorted to making sculptures out of bubble gum. Chewed bubble gum that Jeremy has stuck under the zed-bed. She was in the back room earlier, organising his stuff for his return tonight – Claudia has a date – and decided to clean under his bed. That is when she found the discarded bubble gum. She thought it was some kind of pink Blu-tack and has made a small collection of farm animals. I try to hide the horror in my voice, suggesting she use the playdough in the kitchen instead. At the table. On a tray. With an apron. She skips ahead of me, her animals forgotten so I can wrap them up in paper and dispose of them surreptitiously in the bin.

Martin and Dorota have disappeared to the front room to watch a DVD with Rachel and Jeremy. This is Martin's first encounter with *High School Musical* and, when I peek around the door, he is deeply engrossed, a discarded packet of painkillers on the table and a hot water bottle held to the side of his face. I have an hour before I have to get him to the dentist. Possibly half an hour before Imo wakes from her nap. I catch Roland coming out of the understairs loo and urge him to hold the fort.

'Going anywhere nice?' he asks in the manner of one knowing the answer: that I rarely go anywhere nice.

'To the church.'

'Right,' he says, enigmatically. Roland is a man of few words but much subtext.

The door of St Hilda's is open. I stand in the porch and wipe my shoes, like all those people before me from the end of the war until now. And preceding them, when the old church stood here, many shoes would have been wiped before entering this sacred place. (If only Desmond remembered to do likewise, it would make my job a lot easier.) I am following in the footsteps of thousands of believers who have worshipped here, inspired by St Hilda herself who'd probably never been to London herself being a northern lass. And if she had, it's doubtful she would've ventured as far as Penge. The weight of history is upon me as I enter the nave and spot my husband seated near the front, gazing up at St Hilda herself, the stained glass seagulls dipping their wings in honour of the lapis lazuli clad figure, her golden halo shining with Penge's new-spring sun.

'Steve?'

He jumps a little, so lost in thought, not hearing my approach. But he knows my voice and, when he turns to look at me, he is smiling his Steve smile. His everything's-going-to-be-alright smile. It is at once comforting and infuriating. 'She must have been an awesome woman,' he says.

'St Hilda?'

He nods, patting the pew beside him.

I force myself to ignore the cumulus of dust powder-puffing from the cushion. Amanda's responsibility. I ease myself into the pew, next to my husband and we both look up at her. St Hilda.

'Bede says she was a woman of great energy.' Steve says this little gem after a few moments of companionable contemplation.

I try to stifle an all-encompassing yawn; this is the first time I've sat down all day and tiredness settles on top of me, sinking me down into the pew. 'I wish she'd give some of it to me.'

Steve ignores my attempt at humour, not that it was said

without an element of truth. I'd happily take on some heavenly vibes from old Hilda. Instead he carries on with his theological ruminations. 'Bede said: *All who knew her called her mother because of her outstanding devotion and grace.*' He sounds wistful, dreamy. 'He also said she was a good teacher. And very wise.'

I'm not altogether sure where he's coming from right now. Shouldn't he be thinking of Karolina? Of me? Even of Jesus? Why is he fixated on a nun from the Dark Ages?

He gazes up, searching for God up there, while I am searching for cobwebs. 'Have you ever noticed her feet?' he asks.

'Her feet?' I look at the dainty blue slippered feet of St Hilda and think of my own feet, clad in my favourite Clark's. I think of all those other feet again, the ones who have trod in here before me. All of these worshippers gazing up at this window, a window somehow salvaged from the ruins left by the Luftwaffe, brought back to life in the new church, so St Hilda could once again offer words of wisdom to those with open ears.

'Look at the snakes, Vick,' Steve says, pointing them out, a tangle of serpents writhing around her feet. I've never really considered them before, the snakes, preferring the seagulls above her, memories of Worthing. 'She turned a plague of snakes to stone.'

'A plague of snakes? In Whitby?'

'So legend has it. They say that's why ammonite fossils have been found on the beach there. Hence the ammonite genus *Hildoceras*.'

What is going on inside my husband's head, going off on one right when he should be firmly on the ground? 'Have you been Googling again?'

'Wikipedia.'

I can't help letting out a sigh. I sense Steve stiffen beside me, bristling at what he can only take as criticism. 'It's all very interesting, Steve,' I start, pushing myself on. 'But I was kind of hoping your time-out for reflection might've been more productive.'

'What do you mean?'

'I was kind of hoping you might have worked out a way of solving our little spiky haired problem.'

'Karolina.'

'Yes, Karolina.'

He sighs this time. A mighty sigh that comes from deep within. 'I suppose I was hoping,' he looks up, 'the old girl might pass on some of her legendary wisdom to me.'

'Shouldn't you be relying on God for that?'

'Shouldn't you?'

'This isn't about me.'

'But it isn't about me either.'

'What about the phone calls?'

'There were no phone calls.'

Silence. Deadlock. I forge on. 'And what about Desmond? Have you spoken with him today? Or have you been waiting for St Hilda to step down from that window and chin Karolina.'

'I'm not sure chinning will get us very far.'

'It helped me with Martin.'

He shakes his head, at me, at the world.

But I've said that word. That name. Martin. It hovers in the hushed air of the church and I have to do something about it. A quick glance at my watch tells me I need to leave my husband here, with the old girl. It's quarter to four. Time to get back to the real world.

'Just how much have you put back?'

'Unlike you, Vicky-Love, I can hold my drink. You only have to sniff a wine gum to get trollied. And anyway, your mother-in-law has fuelled me with a tanker load of coffee. I'm fine. It's all good.' He takes a puff of his inhaler and lights up.

I pull away from the street, leaving my family, my shelter

behind me, stuck in the Espace with Martin and his smoke and his man-toothache that is the worst toothache since the beginning of time. Since Adam and Eve trod happy-go-lucky through the Garden of Eden, not a care in the world. Before cares even came into the world. Before Adam gave in to his stomach and ate that stupid apple. That stinking rotten apple disguised as a luscious Granny Smith.

The waiting room. Eerily quiet, which straightaway makes Martin fret over his health, cupping the side of his face and groaning like a Premier league footballer. 'Never trust a quiet dentist,' he says, barely audible as he won't open his mouth. A ventriloquist's dummy. A dummy anyway.

'You've spent too much time with Dorota.' I find a chair and swipe a dog-eared magazine off the heap on a table.

'Don't diss your mother-in-law,' he whispers. 'She saved my life today.'

Today's not over, that's what I want to say but I restrain myself, breathing deeply and reminding myself that Martin has had a mega week. I should be supportive. Kind. The good sister.

I'm halfway through the latest *Chat*, catching up on my celebrity 'news' so that I can be one step ahead of Olivia, when Martin is told to go in by the receptionist, who he has been blatantly eyeing up ever since we arrived. (Nothing stops him.) He shuffles off and I get back to *Chat*.

Ten minutes later and I am fully up-to-date on Tom Cruise and his young wife. Just as I am moving on to a minor Royal, there is a scream. High-pitched and panicky. Followed by a muffled crash of scattering metal. The receptionist snatches her blonde little head away from the computer monitor and looks at me as if it's my fault. A passing hygienist stops in her squelchy Croc-tracks and looks at the receptionist as if it is her fault. The magazine slips from my lap and falls, splayed, Tom Cruise face-down, to the floor. We all look at it. And

I know exactly who is to blame. Who else? I feel my face heat up as quick as a halogen cooker. A menopausal flush that reaches up my nose and into my ears. What's Martin done now? Has he made a pass at the dentist? Please tell me no.

The three of us, united in worried curiosity, listen out, alert. A moment of silence. Just a moment. Then the door flings open and we can see into the surgery: Martin prone on the chair, his arm fallen to one side, hanging limp, metal instruments strewn across the floor.

He's fainted.

The wuss.

But where's the dentist? I can't see the dentist. There's the dentist. That's the dentist, coming out of the room, panic stuck to her face. Shouting. Wild-eyed and spiky-haired.

Karolina?

Yes, Karolina is the dentist, who else, I might've known, and she's shouting for help.

'Somebody call 999!'

Meanwhile another dentist emerges from the staff room, brushing off the crumbs of a sugar-free snack with each rushed step, and they disappear, the two of them, Karolina lagging somewhat behind, back into the room. The door slams shut. Bang. Boom.

More silence. Louder than any noise. I can hear the cogs clicking in the receptionist's tiny head. She's been joined by the hygienist, priest-like in her white uniform; they are whispering to each other, glancing from me to the closed door behind which carries on a drama involving my brother.

Two brief thoughts.

Why, out of all the dentists in South London, did Karolina have to be the one to deal with Martin?

Has the Polish psycho killed my brother?

These thoughts jostle for supremacy in my head but I am beyond sorting them out. I am beyond thinking. I am reacting, up off my feet and barging into the room, ignoring requests to stay outside, ignoring the receptionist and the hygienist's dual attempt to pull me back, an overpowering urge to help Martin.

And there he is, Martin. Out cold. Blood trailing down his nose, like he's been hit. Again. The second dentist is stabbing something in his leg. Through his trousers. His thigh. My brain cannot work out what is going on. I look to the dental nurse who is on the phone to the ambulance. Then I spot Karolina, standing with her back to the wall, staring blankly ahead, quite still. What the hell has happened? I speak to the room, to anyone who'll listen:

'Will. Someone. Please. Tell. Me. What. She's. Done. To. My. Brother?'

'Apparently it was the latex gloves that did it,' I tell Claudia much later as she finally answers her phone and drags herself away from William Shakespeare to visit her husband in hospital.

Her husband, my brother, is sitting up in bed, calmly watching the News, with a red nose, a drip in his arm, and wires on his chest hooked up to one of those heartbeat monitor things. Nurses swarm around him, taking his blood pressure, scribbling notes, and generally fussing.

Jeremy is perched on the bed eating his father's untouched supper, something involving mashed potato and beige meat. He picks out the diced carrots and lines them up on the side of the plastic plate like the victims of a vegetable firing squad.

Claudia and I sit opposite each other and talk over Martin's long legs.

'It was an anaphylactic shock,' I tell my sister-in-law who has still managed to leave home with coordinated accessories. 'When Karolina hit him in the face, that must have triggered it.'

'Why the hell did the dentist hit him in the face?'

'That's the bit I'm not sure of. Martin, would you care to elaborate?'

Martin continues to watch the News. 'Drop it for now, will you? I've had a day of it.' He turns, appealing to the nearest nurse for rescue from these two pestering women. The nurse is only too pleased to administer a stern shake of the head to both Claudia and me. I want to kick her in her stockinged shins but instead I stare pointedly at my watch, waiting for her to drag herself away, which she eventually does when Martin hands her his empty mug.

'I'll get you a refill, cheeky,' she simpers, reluctantly swaggering away.

'So how long do you have to stay in for?' Claudia asks.

'They haven't said.' He looks at his wife, mustering up an expression of misery. 'Till my heart rate settles.' He points to his heart, a gesture laden with symbolism, which elicits an expression of worry, a delicately crinkled brow, from his estranged wife. 'I had a funny reaction to the adrenaline. The very thing that saved my life almost killed me.' He smiles weakly and we can see a gap where the troublesome tooth once was.

While we contemplate his words, forgetting the bit about Karolina punching him, he asks: 'Where's Steve? Can you send him in?'

This is when Claudia's eyes well up and her little pixie nose pinkens in sympathy with her husband's red hooter. 'But Martin, surely it's not that serious you need a vicar?' She extracts a delicate lace handkerchief from her clutch bag, perfecting the hospital bed scene.

I know he's had a scrape with death but Martin is perfectly alright. He's going to be fine. So I will not buy into this melodrama. 'Why on earth do you want Steve?'

Martin drags his eyes away from Claudia and lands them on me. 'I've got some information.'

'Information? What are you talking about?'

'Information about our Polish friend.'

'The one that decked you?'

'The very same.'

'Why did she hit you?'

'That's what I want to tell Steve. Can you get him to come in?'

The story according to Martin:

When I was a kid I had this shocking eczema. Scaly red patches behind my knees and in the crooks of my elbows. Bad in the heat. Worse in the cold. My skin would be cracked, oozing pus and itchy. So itchy. I had to have oily baths and plaster myself in cream or else my skin would be so tight it would split. Mum used to fuss over me, spent ages applying greasy emollients, gently, methodically, the way she'd rub milk into the ficus leaves to make it shine.

It got a bit better when I was a teenager though there'd be outbreaks at times of stress like my O-Levels. Then when I got into my twenties I had this funny turn. It was a colleague's retirement do, this crusty old academic who'd been in the department since the time of Aristotle. There were drinks and nibbles one Friday afternoon in the senior common room. Warm white wine. Dry, salt-flecked pretzels. Crisps. Peanuts. I ate great handfuls, anything to soak up the Liebfraumilch so I could get away sharpish and avoid the rush hour. Claudia had a dinner party planned. Her first, and I didn't want to let her down. I felt a bit odd, was in a trance-like state listening to Hugh bang on about his latest research project and the huge lump of funding he'd somehow blagged, when I thought I was going to be sick. Blamed it on the gut-rot wine, excused myself and went to the loo. Sitting there I felt steadily worse. My stomach was heaving and I felt giddy, like I was on a ferry sitting in the bilge. I went to get a drink of water from the tap, and then glancing in the mirror above the sink, I saw my face was distorted. My eyes and lips had swelled up and suddenly I found it hard to breathe. Needed a puff of my inhaler. And another. And another. I could feel my airways constricting, my tongue swelling. It was like I had a sock stuffed in my mouth and then I had this overwhelming sense of doom, as if the world was falling down on me. That was the point at which Hugh came in and rushed straight back out to call an ambulance.

I had these tests done and they decided I was allergic to nuts. So I avoided nuts. I didn't seem to be quite as bad as some people who couldn't even be in a room with nuts without keeling over. I just don't eat them. So it hasn't really impacted on my life.

And then there's my tooth. I should've gone to the dentist sooner but to be honest I hate going. Haven't been for years. I've spent so much time with doctors, in hospitals, with my eczema, asthma and all the rest of it that I suppose I've avoided the dentist. My teeth have never given me any problems. Until recently. This tooth has been aggravating for a while and then I got walloped by Bob. And then by Vicky. Then Karolina extracts it. Once I see it, my tooth, held up to the light, its long pointed root, clasped in the grip of her shiny dental implement, I confront her. The dental nurse has popped out for something, a sticker maybe because I've been such a good boy and not cried a drop. I tell her, Karolina, that I know she has made up stories about Steve. I tell her that she needs to retract everything she has said. She stares at me, her mouth open, nothing coming out. She starts to cry. I tell her I know she made those phone calls, I know she stole Steve's mobile and made those calls herself. I worked it out. It's a no-brainer. She stops crying then, as suddenly as she started, the proverbial tap, and comes over all serious and quiet. She is very close to me. Her hands are right by my face. I can smell the latex. It makes me feel queasy but maybe that's the tooth, the blood I can taste in my mouth. Her musky tobacco scent. I'm biting down on this swab and I wonder if she can understand what I am saying to her, muffled as I am, and English not being her mother tongue. But she understands alright. She gets up from her swivel chair. She gets up and she punches me. A third time. Only at least she has the decency not to punch me in the mouth. She goes for my nose. It hurts. But not for long. Soon I feel drowsy, like I'm wafting up out of the dentist chair. I am stuck to the ceiling, looking down at this spiky angry head. I hear a scream and then I see me, myself, Martin, in a deep, deep sleep from which I may never wake. It is not the punch that has done this. It is the gloves.

Martin tells this to Steve, Claudia and me. Jeremy has disappeared with a can of Pepsi, courtesy of a nurse, to the TV room as it is time for *Eastenders*. A Maundy Thursday special.

Martin is peaky, his face dotted with patches of pink eczema and strange red bumps. Stubble is creeping back and he has a George Michael look about him. The porky middle-aged George, not the gorgeous Adonis of the Wham! years. I have to stifle the desire to sing 'Club Tropicana' and focus on what my brother is telling us. About his spiritual moment. His epiphany. I am finally about to discover what this word actually means.

As I am floating on the ceiling watching the new dentist seize control of the situation, grabbing a medical pack from the wall, the nurse shouting down the phone... ambulance... emergency... as fast as you can... I can see that this is quite serious; I am separated from my body and there is nothing I can do about it. But it isn't me I think about. It is Karolina. I realise that she is actually a crazy woman. A crazy woman who is actually very clever. But not clever enough; I have found her out. And I can't die because I have to tell Steve what I suspect. That she stole his mobile and made those calls to herself from his phone. I have to tell Vicky that her family is safe. Her husband is a good man – not that she would ever believe the accusations to contain a grain of truth, she's not that stupid (a back-handed compliment if ever there was one).

And I have to see my son and tell him that I love him as I can't remember the last time I did this, possibly when he was a baby and not able to comprehend those words.

And then I think of my wife. I think of you, Claudia, and I know I have to tell you I love you and I'm sorry for not being honest and if it takes the rest of my life, which I'm hoping is going to be longer than the few minutes it might take before my body shuts down completely, I will make sure you know I love you.

And then I think of God and the Alpha course that was supposed to help me gather evidence for the God gene... only I ended up being less sure of anything.

An epiphany.

And then I feel a prick in my leg... far off and faint... after a few more moments I see another head appear beneath me, so frizzy-haired and wild I would know it anywhere. It belongs to my little sister, Vicky. And I remember how she used to skip along the road ahead of me, off to the newsagent's. I remember how once she fell and had a bloody knee and I had to carry her all the way there to get her sherbet pips and all the way home again, and her legs rubbed my eczema something chronic but I wouldn't let on because she was my little sister and I had to take care of her. And it doesn't matter if we have a different dad. It doesn't matter because the same man brought us up, the same man and the same woman and I will do anything now to help my sister grieve properly. And there she is, Vicky, standing over me, her hand reaching out to touch my face... and then a surge of something running through me... energy. A life force. Something medical yet supernatural. And I float back down off the ceiling and am aware of a bright light shining in my face, not heaven's glory but the dentist's light. The light is moved away and, once my eyes adjust, there is Vicky, smiling at me. Vicky-Love.

Steve says: 'Do you want me to pray for you?'

Martin says: 'Don't push it.'

There is a slightly awkward silence as we come to grips

with Martin's revelation and all its repercussions. Then Martin asks Steve to bring in Dorota tomorrow. He needs her help.

I suspect the help he 'needs' will be contained in a hip flask, but I let it pass. I pat my brother's hand and tell his audience I need some fresh air.

I keep my head down till I get outside, following the yellow line on the floor that guides me through the warren of corridors, back to the main entrance. And there's the hand gel. The very thing that's supposed to prevent what happened to Mum. It is impossible not to remember.

The last time we saw her was in hospital. The night before her knee op. Martin and I came in to visit her. He'd picked me up in his Saab and was still smarting over the expense of the car park ticket and was huffing while I gave Mum a *People's Friend* and a Fry's Turkish Delight. She wittered on about everything she was going to do once her knee was repaired: the allotment, a keep-fit class, swimming. Martin, calming down after a few soothing glances from appreciative nurses and a junior doctor, joked that she'd be bungee jumping next. Mum said, oh, no, she didn't think her stomach would put up with that malarkey, it wasn't natural to be bouncing upside down on a large elastic band. We laughed and, after another half hour or so, gave her a kiss goodnight and said we'd be in the next evening. She reached up and gave each of us a squeeze of the hand. And that was the last time we talked to her. The next day, Dad called Steve. He was in a state. Steve had to sit me down at the kitchen table and explain to me that my mother had caught an infection. We couldn't see her because she was in an isolation ward. It was serious. Ferocious and quick. The germs had marched in and got hold of her. They wouldn't let go. Two days later she was dead.

My brother could have died.

It is late and I need to see my children.

The box room. A sleeping angel, cherubic and snoring, moonlight pooling over her curled up body, her snuffles reassuring. Bunk beds, two sleeping girls, heavy breathing and dreaming, the pink nightlight making them glow healthy and well.

Thoughts for the Day: When will I get an epiphany?

March 20th 1978

We were out shopping, Mum and me. It was really embarrassing because it was for my first bra. Mum said it was about time. I was a bit young but I needed to look after them (my wotsits) because when I was grown up and married and had babies I would be grateful for taking care of them. I told Mum I would never have babies. They smell. She laughed.

We went to the Army and Navy in Lewisham. The lingerie department. And there looking at the Triumphs was Heidi and her mum. They didn't see us at first. I heard Heidi's mum say honestly, Heidi, you're getting bigger by the week. And Heidi looked miserable. I would be very happy if I had wotsits the size of Shooter's Hill. Instead of the size of Dad's cherry tomatoes.

Then Mum spotted Heidi and shrieked heelllooo. And she introduced us to Heidi's mum who is called Francoise. She owns a boutique in Blackheath but they don't sell bras. She said it would save money if they did because they are always in here. But I don't think she needs to worry about money because Heidi's dad is rolling in it.

Heidi didn't say a word. Just looked at her feet. She had new shoes. She was always getting new shoes.

Chapter Thirty-Five: Friday 21st March

Good Friday

I am re-hanging the front room nets when I see a dangerous-looking Campervan bump up onto the pavement outside. I am curious as to who will get out of it. I certainly don't expect it to be the tattooed lady. But it is, tottering out of the driver's seat. In those sling-backs. And I know who'll be getting out the passenger side.

Dad bounces up the front path like a schoolboy, while Pat empties a bag of rubbish into my wheelie bin.

I meet them at the door. 'What a surprise.'

'We heard about Martin's latest adventure. Pat said we should come and see him. Thought we'd pop in here first and have a cuppa. Put the kettle on, Vicky-Love.'

Two pots of tea and a packet of Ginger Snaps later, with the kids occupied in front of *Grease* (a gift from sunny Worthing), and Imo sitting on Pat's scrawny lap, I've recounted the events of the past twenty-four hours as regards Martin, including the background to Karolina. Dad still hasn't got over the Dulwich College incident but he softens now. I can see it in his watery eyes – a murky depth of compassion for his son who's not his blood-son but who's as much a son as he could ever be, had Dad got to Mum before Uncle Jack.

'How is he?' Dad asks.

'I've just told you. He's fine. They've sorted his heartbeat. He'll be back later, unless... '

'Unless Claudia takes him back?'

'Well, this might do it for her.'

'And what about the other stuff?'

'Stuff?'

Dad looks sideways at Pat and I catch a facet of their relationship, a conspiring closeness I'm not quite ready to think about. She nods at Dad, encouraging, before dunking another biscuit in her tea.

'I mean Jack,' Dad says.

I know he means Uncle Jack. Uncle Jack, squinting into the sun, his blonde fringe, his easy smile. And Dad, gawky and upright, grinning like a kid on holiday. Not much older than a kid. Either of them. And tragedy just ahead...

'Vicky?'

'We've not really had the chance to talk that through, Dad, what with one thing and another. And besides I'm not sure there's anything I can really say. I reckon we should give him some time to get used to the idea.'

I don't tell him about the epiphany. I'll leave that to Martin. It might have worn off by now anyway, washed away with the adrenaline. He might have shrunk back to his usual angry Dawkins self. And part of me hopes that he has.

I am in the garden. A few moments of fresh air and head space. I walk across the stepping stones, dappled with pale sunshine, and stop a few paces short of the shed. Above me are the scrubby trees, the embankment. Pigeons. Fox wee. In a few weeks the nettles will be rife, the bindweed suffocating but for now it is enough to see the bulb shoots poking up through the heavy clay soil of my beds. It's been a long winter.

The shed. No longer a place I can enter without knocking.

'Who is it?' Rachel asks. There is rustling but none of the whispering that has been going on of late.

I let myself in, without waiting for an invitation. My eldest child is sitting cross-legged on a tartan picnic rug playing solitaire. The two camping chairs are vacant, apart from an abandoned pen and a set of stationery, what looks suspiciously like my expensive Basildon Bond stationery usually reserved for the thank you letters I have to browbeat out of my ungrateful children. 'Where's Jeremy?'

'With Jessica.'

'Next door?'

A pause.

'Think so.'

'What are they doing? More filming?'

'Maybe.' She deals the cards, carrying on with her game.

Despite the effort made by Jeremy to kit out the shed, it is draughty. There is a hole low down in the side (must get Steve to patch it up). A fierce draught blasts through, catching the back of my legs. 'I need the rake, Rach.'

Rachel pushes herself wearily up from the floor and reaches for the rake – one of Dad's cast-offs – hanging from a nail behind her. 'Here you go, Mum.' She hands it over, a half-smile, slightly coy, evasive even, like she's up to something but I won't press her now. I leave her to her game. Sometimes she needs some peace and quiet... but I do hope Jessica isn't leading my 'sensitive' nephew astray. 'Don't stay out here too long. Granddad will think you're avoiding him.'

'I am avoiding him.'

'Ra-ch?'

'I'll be in soon, Mum. Don't fuss.'

I shut the door behind me, before I get embroiled in a pointless argument, and hop back up the patio where I rake a few leaves.

My Garden of Gethsemane leaves.

Dorota and Roland are now sitting at the kitchen table with my father and Pat. An interesting foursome.

'Vicky, I have seen your brother. I got rid of the nurses and we talked. Sit down and I tell you.' Dorota pulls out the chair next to her. 'How about a nice glass of sherry? It is Good Friday. That's near enough to Easter, isn't it?'

'I think technically, in the Church of England, Lent ends tomorrow. But, like you say, it's near enough.'

I have never seen my mother-in-law move so fast. She conjures up glasses and pours them to the brim, but I try not to be distracted. I need to know what's going on. 'What is it, Dorota? What's happened now?'

She takes a sip of sherry, subverts a smile with a serious shake of the head. 'Your brother has a job for us to do. Just you and I can sort this mess out.'

Dorota and I stand in the cold corridor outside Karolina's flat. Rubbish skids along the concrete floor, pushed by the insistent wind. She looks at me and points to the bell, willing me to take control and ring it. Not because she doesn't want to but because she knows I need to. I need to do something. I am not entirely sure what it is that I am going to do but, for once, with Dorota's comforting bulk beside me, I will wing it.

I pull my coat tighter and ring the bell. It doesn't seem to be working. So I knock on the door. It needs a good lick of paint. Dorota and I look at each other. It is quiet within, very quiet. But then we hear a small child's voice. Followed by a low urgent hush. I bang again, annoyance bubbling up within me. How dare she do this to my family? How dare she hide? I am about to bang again, harder, when the door creaks, slowly opens, slightly, and we squint into dead space. As our eyes adjust, and we look down, we see her: Natasha. She says nothing, stares up at us with those mournful eyes.

'We've come to see your mumia, Natasza,' says Dorota. 'Can we come in?'

The little girl says nothing, turns her blank face away from us and walks off down the corridor. But she has left the door open so we take this as an invitation to come in, whether it was offered or not. We follow her to the sitting room. It hasn't been cleared up since my last visit. If anything it's worse, a stale smell hanging thickly in the heavy air.

'It is pig sty,' Dorota whispers to me, as we hover on the threshold. 'Karolina is dirty slut.'

Natasha has sat back down in front of the telly, close up as if she needs glasses. And there is her mother, lying there on the sofa, like a dead woman. Though of course she is not dead – that's not what the smell is. The smell is last night's Kentucky Fried Chicken. Does she even know we are here? Should I say something?

'You shouldn't be here,' Karolina says, beating me to it. 'I have complaint against your pervert husband.'

I feel Dorota flinch next to me and put my hand on her arm, to keep her from launching herself onto Karolina and squashing the life out of her, tempting though it may be to let her try.

'A pervert is someone who strays from what is acceptable,' I hear myself say, matter-of-fact. 'Everything my husband does is good and honourable and from the best will in the world. What *you* are doing is perverted. *You* are trying to disrupt a family with lies and fabrications. *You* are living in a fantasy world and dragging us into it. *You* are the pervert.'

Karolina continues to watch some film or other and doesn't appear to have listened to one word though I have been speaking loud and clear. 'I don't understand you,' she says, at last, slowly, her eyes finally open and aimed in my direction. 'I have very bad English.'

At which point I look at my mother-in-law. Dorota strides over to the TV and turns it off. Then, in her mother tongue, she repeats what I have just said, I presume, though she could be adding all sorts.

Karolina shrinks as she lies there on the sofa, so she looks hardly older than her daughter and I have to fight this ridiculous urge to feel sorry for her.

Dorota has no compunction. 'You are crazy woman and yet not so crazy you can't listen to us talk sense to you. We know your game. We know you tell stories to make trouble. I don't care why you do this but I want you to stop. I want you to think what you are doing to my daughter-in-law. She is best daughter-in-law I have. When you hurt her, you hurt me. We have had enough hurt in our family. Maybe you have had hurt in your family but that doesn't mean you lash out at us.' Dorota takes a deep breath and sits herself down on a chair, after sweeping a mound of papers to the dirty floor.

This is where I decide to wing it, looking at her struggling for breath, puffing on her inhaler, seeing her upset. Her hurt. It is my turn to do something. And actually once I start speaking I know exactly what I want to say, what I want to happen. And I can make it happen. I can insist it happens.

I take a step closer to Karolina, to the sofa where she still languishes, eyes tight shut once again. 'I want you to go to Desmond and tell him the truth.'

A pause.

Natasha turns the TV back on but all I can hear is my heart beating. I feel this enormous surge of power boiling up in my guts, but I don't know if I am in control. I don't know if I can do this. I am looking so hard at Karolina's closed lids that I wonder if the force of my stare will make her eyes ping open.

And they do. They hold my gaze for a second and then they turn to the ceiling. Then she speaks. In a tired voice. In Polish. Dorota listens and then Dorota laughs, theatrically, and puts her hands on her ample hips, before replying in a steady voice. The conversation goes on for a while, quite a while, and I feel the old familiar frustration build inside me again. I wanted to do this. I wanted to sort this out but Dorota is the one with the knowledge, with the steering wheel in her hands. Eventually, as Karolina drags herself from her lair and staggers to the kitchen, Dorota turns to me and translates. 'She says if I weren't old woman, she would throw me out of the window. I said she should try it. She wouldn't get very far. Then she offers me vodka and I say okay, if she listens. And I tell her. I tell her about the effect she has had on my family. I tell her about Thomas.'

Dorota reaches out to me but all I can do is collapse onto the sofa, still warm from Karolina who is now clanking around in the kitchen, emerging with a tray, a bottle and three glasses. She balances the tray on top of her mess on the coffee table and begins to pour. As she pours, she sniffs and I can see that she has been crying, that she is still crying, tears sliding down her face, into the corners of her mouth. But her tears leave me cold. They mean nothing. They are a drop in the ocean of my grief. Then she hands me a glass of vodka.

I pick up the glass slowly and smell the vodka. I swill it around, taking in the clear liquid, and then I knock it down in one and feel the warmth of glorious relief spread up from my toes to my brain.

'We're going to see Desmond now,' I tell Karolina.

And she nods.

Finally, I have winged it.

The vicarage. Amanda takes Natasha to the kitchen for a glass of milk, while Desmond, Dorota, Karolina and I sit together in his book-lined study. It smells of old dust and heavy learning.

'In your own time,' says Desmond, spidery hands clasped together in a prayer-like grip. 'No one wants you to feel pressurised to say anything other than the truth.'

Oh, yes, the truth. That's what we'd all like to hear.

Karolina juts out her chin and the gesture makes me scared that rather than giving us the truth, she will return to her fantasy world. I hold my breath while she begins to speak.

The story according to Karolina: *I always want to be dentist. I like teeth. It is first part of body I look at when I meet somebody for first time. My mother died when I was twelve-years-old. When my father goes away to work, I go to live with my aunt in Kraków. Very small flat. I cannot wait to leave there and have my own life. My own flat. But it will take very long time. I study hard for six years at medical school. For the last two years I work with patients under supervision. Then I can register with Polish Chamber of Physicians and Dentists. I get a permit and so I am allowed to practise.*

But then I find out that I am pregnant.

I do not want to marry my boyfriend. He is not the one. He is dental student too and not yet grown up. My father and aunt are not happy with me. I cannot afford to leave home but the idea of staying is too horrible. I get fat. I get stretch marks. I have baby, Natasza. My aunt looks after her when she is only a few weeks old so I can go back to work. I want to be able to look after Natasza, not my aunt, but what can I do?

I get depressive.

I see doctor who says dentists are often depressive, but it could be post-natc depressive. She gives me pills and I am okay for a while. When Natasza is one-years-old, I hear about England. UK need dentists and they come to Poland to recruit. It is 2006. One third of all new dentists who join NHS are Polish trained. So I think it will be good opportunity for me. Somebody needs me. So I go on visit and have interview and they want me. I go on language and adaptation course. Then Natasza's father gets back with me. He wants to come to England. So we come to London, together, a family. A new life.

I stop my pills.

We have good job and flat and Natasza goes to nursery and speaks English. And then my boyfriend decides it is not such good idea and he wants to go back to Poland. But I will not go. I stay with Natasza. But then I get depressive again. I get new pills but I think they do crazy things to my head. I start dreaming about home. About Polska. About my mother and the church where she took me when I was a girl. Where I felt safe. The candles. The incense. The black Madonna. I want to go somewhere like that and I find St Hilda's down the road, near my flat. Ugly building. Not like a church. No statues. No candles. No incense. But it has same feeling. I feel safe.

And then I meet the priest.

He smiles at me and shakes my hand. He is kind. He asks me questions like he wants to hear my answers. He explains he is curate, what this means in his English church, and I wonder if he could be the one to cure me from my sickness. And I see his wife with all her girls and she tries to be nice to me but I don't want her to be nice. It is okay for her with her family, her easy life. She has husband. She has church. She has everything. And one day, during Alpha, he talks about suffering. How the world is not the perfect place because we are not perfect. After, when they stand around drinking tea, always drinking tea, I see his mobile phone on a chair and it is so easy. I take it and I put it in my bag.

Over next few days I make calls to my phone. Then I leave phone here in your house when you ask me for mother's lunch. I go upstairs to put your baby in her cot because she is tired and no-one seems to notice her in the busyness, this Melanie girl making trouble. I put the phone in next to baby. She likes it. She holds it in her hand and falls asleep. It is easy. I know it will be found. But I didn't think about the baby boy. Or how Vicky has worse life than me. Dorota – she is so like my aunt – makes me put on Vicky's shoes but I do not want to walk around in them.

I make it all up. Stefan never touched me. Never spoke to me. Except as a priest should speak.

I am sorry. I am sorry for your Thomas and I ask you to forgive me.

Karolina has been addressing the ceiling (have they never

heard of feather dusters in this house?) while the rest of us sit still, open-mouthed, holding our collective breath. A public confession with no confessional box to hide away in. But Karolina is looking at me when she asks for forgiveness, me alone, and it is within my power to give it to her. So I do. It is free. I let go of my anger and it floats out the crack in Desmond's window, up the garden path, where it can cadge a ride on the bus that is trundling past, away from Penge, out of my life.

And then what do I do? If I was at home, I would go and put the kettle on. But I am not. So I get up and, ignoring Desmond's gob-smacked mucky face, and Karolina's empty one, I kiss Dorota on the cheek, telling her: 'You're my favourite mother-in-law.'

Later, back home, I sit in the quiet of my kitchen and breathe deep while Pat and Dad, Dorota and Roland toast a happy outcome with tea and biscuits. Martin and Claudia suddenly appear. I am so engrossed in re-living the morning's developments that I barely noticed the usual banging and crashing that accompanies Martin or the gock-gock of his wife's stilettos. He is treated regally, people jumping up to offer chairs and make tea while Dad sits quietly, contemplating his son. Martin sneaks a cock-eyed glance at him and earns a small, encouraging smile and a tilt of the head. Claudia asks after Jeremy and I tell her he must be next door with Jessica. Martin says, 'That's my boy.' Claudia goes to wallop him but remembers at the last moment that her husband is an invalid, which wouldn't necessarily stop me. Then Martin and Dad disappear to the garden for a man-to-man, more handshaking and back-slapping. Pat announces their intention to stay a couple of days in the camper outside. I try not to think about this. The double bed. The very small rickety pull-out double that looks like it's seen some action over the years. But... why begrudge Dad some company in his old age?

Then, while Claudia jigs Imo up and down, with some effort, on her petite lap, while Pat quizzes Dorota on what it is like to be the mother of a priest, while Roland disappears to watch *Seven Brides for Seven Brothers* with Olivia and Rachel in the front room and after I have checked everyone is alright, praying (am I praying?) for Steve to get back from the Good Friday service and help me hold this strange band of people together, I head out into the garden. My garden.

Much later, with a mound of mouldering garden waste and a mug of tea in my hand, I survey the last two hours' work and revel in the fact I've been left to it. No children. No family. No annoyances.

I try to enjoy my relief. But it is spoiled by this nagging feeling, wriggling around my gut like a case of threadworms. I can't quite work out the cause of this worry: is it Dad and Pat canoodling in the campervan? Is it Martin and Claudia who have shut themselves in the back room 'to talk'? Is it Melanie or Geoffrey Chaucer, both of whom could still scupper these delicate marital negotiations? Or is it Karolina and the way she duped us? The friend I lost before I even had her... It could be any number of the holes in my life.

As I stoop to pick up a stray football – Jessica's – I get a flash of memory: Martin trying out his card tricks on me. *Shut your eyes and pick one.* But I'm still none the wiser to what exactly the niggle is.

Then I hear Bob calling out in his soft baritone: 'JESSICA!' Jessica?

Bob pokes his fat bald head over the loose fence panel (must-get-Steve-onto-it). 'Have you seen her? Is she with you?'

'I thought she was at yours. With Jeremy.'

'Haven't seen either of them for a couple of hours.' He checks his watch. 'At least.'

Tamarine appears next to him, barely visible over the fence.

'You better see this, Bobby,' she says, eyeing me up sideways so my heart goes cold and the nagging feeling springs right up out of my body and hangs there in the Penge air in front of me. Why didn't I acknowledge it earlier? 'I found it under Jessica's pillow.'

Tamarine hands Bob an envelope. One of my blue Basildon Bond envelopes that my children are always pilfering to play post offices. The ones I spotted earlier in the shed. On the vacant camping chair.

Bob holds the envelope in his hand like it's a letter bomb. I can make out the word 'Dad' in bubble writing.

'Open it, yeah,' says Tamarine gently.

So Bob opens it and scans the letter inside. He says nothing but the letter floats to the ground as he spins on his foot, as deft as an ice-dancer, and runs off in a way I have never seen him run until he disappears inside, leaving Tamarine scrambling on the other side of the fence to retrieve it. Tamarine's hand quivers as she hands the letter over for me to read and in that movement I can see how much she loves Jessica.

Dear Dad
I am going to find Mum. I didn't ask you
if I could go becurse I knew you wold say
no I cant'. I will be OK. Jeremey is coming
with me. Dont' worry. I will phone you soon.
Love Jessica XXX

It is a few moments before I realise that Tamarine is urging me to tell Martin what's happened. Before her Bobby goes round and hits him. Because her Bobby will blame his Jeremy for leading Jessica astray. Because her Bobby has no sense when it comes to Jessica's mother. Tamarine goes in then, after the man she loves. And I go inside to face Martin and Claudia with this news. If ever a prayer was needed it is now.

Chapter Thirty-Six: Saturday 22nd March

Easter Saturday

It is quiet and peaceful in St Hilda's, barely any traffic outside as it's so early, but I can still make out the rain falling, tapping on the roof like fingers drumming on a table. Fingers battering a laptop. In this sacred place, on your own, it can be possible to forget the world. You can leave your troubles in the porch, as you wipe your feet, and pick them back up on your way out. For a while it's like you have fallen through a crack in time and space and ended up somewhere... other.

But not today. Today it is all pervasive. I look at St Hilda, her blue gown exquisite, too outwardly beautiful for a nun. But it is symbolic, I suppose. The beauty on the inside reflected on the out.

Reflection. That's what today is supposed to be: a day of waiting and reflection. The end of Holy Week though this holey week is far from over. For Jessica and Jeremy have still not been found.

The police have searched our houses, under beds, in attics, the garden shed, the cutting, but they are taking Jessica's letter seriously, that she and Jeremy are trying to find her mother. They're searching the airports and ports, the coach stations and train stations, anywhere they can think of that Jeremy and Jessica might go. Their passports are missing but how the pair of them thinks they'll get to Lanzarote without adults is a mystery. And a worry. There are those out there who would gladly offer their 'assistance'.

Poor Bob. He's beside himself, taking the blame for everything. And Claudia, just sitting there in a trance. Martin meanwhile is surprisingly calm, even apologising to Bob for the fight. And Tamarine's quiet presence, making herbal tea and offering morsels of food to tempt us to eat.

I had to get out. I felt sick with tiredness, up all night with a police officer, waiting for phone calls, an echo of *The Bill,* but this is real life.

But no news yet. No CCTV images. No mobile phone tracings; Jessica doesn't have a phone; Jeremy has left his behind. They have some money, pilfered from Tamarine's latest car boot takings, and two packets of Penguins, smuggled from my larder. They even thought to pack their toothbrush and pyjamas. It would be sweet if it wasn't so heart-breaking, so... devastatingly worrying. A whole night. I thought they'd show up as it got dark, at teatime. But no. Not a word. It's some comfort to know they left of their own accord; they weren't taken. But it is awful, this not knowing. I feel sick and faint with it all. Who knows what will happen to them out there?

I never had the chance to worry over Thomas. Everything was fine, sitting in the box room with him, listening to Steve and Rach cheer on Tiger Tim. Laying him down in his cot as soft rain started to fall. I touched a kiss to his forehead, thinking how a cooler evening would help his skin, and crept out the room. When I got downstairs, Tim Henman had come off court. Rain stopped play, just as he was in the zone, on the verge of beating Goran Ivanisevic and getting to the final. There'd been hardly any rain that Wimbledon. So when it came, at such a moment, Ivanisevic believed God had intervened. Henman was steaming ahead and this was the Croatian's chance to alter the rhythm of the match. It was his destiny. He came off that court and he got himself together.

On and off they played over three days of rain stoppages. But Ivanisevic crawled his way back and finally he won. And Henman lost.

Someone has come in. The door creaks and clangs shut and I hear heavy footsteps. I turn and see Amanda, swaying up the aisle like a scary bride, sweeping aside thoughts of tennis. She sits down and squeezes my hand. Hers is warm and I realise how cold I am.

'Any news?'

She shakes her head. The tinkle of bangles. The waft of Charlie. 'I came to see if you were alright.'

I check my watch. Gone seven o'clock. 'I must've been longer than I thought. I'd better get back, sort out breakfast for those who can eat.'

'Sit a while longer,' Amanda says, though I haven't the energy to do anything other than be surprised at how comforting her voice is. Not the tiniest bit annoying. 'Today is the time of weeping that lasts for the night while awaiting the joy that comes in the morning,' she says.

'Pardon?'

'Psalm 30.'

'Well... I hope you're right.'

I hope there will be joy. But joy is so elusive, even the odd snatches of it flutter through your fingers, so hard to pin down and name as joy. So hard to recognise because once you examine it, the joy has gone, blown away on the wind.

I look up at Hilda. The blue dress. Blue. And I think of that other blue, that pale Basildon Bond blue. And I think of Rachel, dealing cards on the picnic rug on the floor of the shed. I think of the police gently questioning her and I wonder if she knows more than she is telling. I turn to Amanda. 'Where's God in all this?'

She doesn't reply straightaway, deciding how to word such a delicate answer, or maybe praying for divine guidance.

I wait. I put my hands in my lap and wait.

'He's sitting here beside you,' she says, so faint I can hardly make her out, her usual strident tones quite dissipated. 'And He'll go with you when you leave this place. You simply have to trust that He is there. Always there. Especially on a day like this.'

I look next to me, I can't help it. But all I can see is the empty pew. The dusty, empty pew. 'Have you ever thought about trying beeswax, Amanda?' I hear myself say, joking, nudging Amanda in what could be seen as entirely inappropriate under the circumstances though I suppose I'm trying to find some let-up from this heavy worry.

Amanda looks surprised, briefly, but then for the first time since I have known her, she digs deep and excavates a slither of her deep-buried sense of humour. 'It says in Ecclesiastes, *Let thy garments be always white*. But you don't have to take this literally.'

And then she surprises me further.

'In the Epic of Gilgamesh – do you know it? No? – well, Siduri, a woman of the vine, a wine maker, tries to stop Gilgamesh, this king, in his quest for immortality, urging him to enjoy the life he has.' Amanda shuts her eyes and they move behind her closed lids as she quotes: *As for you, Gilgamesh, fill your belly with good things; day and night, night and day, dance and be merry, feast and rejoice. Let your clothes be fresh, bathe yourself in water, cherish the little child that holds your hand, and make your wife happy in your embrace; for this too is the lot of man.'*

'In memento mori?'

'More than that. Jesus said not to worry about tomorrow, for tomorrow will worry about itself. Each day has enough trouble of its own.'

'But what about today?'

'He also said: *Come to me, all you who labour and are burdened, and I will give you rest. Take my yoke upon you and learn from me, for I am meek and humble of heart; and you will find rest for yourselves. For my yoke is easy, and my burden light.'*

'How do you remember all this Amanda?

'The same way you remember to sweep under rugs.'

Rachel is lying on her bed, a plate of uneaten toast beside her, making a friendship bracelet. She doesn't look up as I walk in, concentrating hard on her handicraft.

'Who's that for, darling?'

'Jessica. When she gets back.'

'Do you know when that might be?'

'Why does everyone think I know where they are?'

'Well, I'm surprised they didn't tell you where they were going. I thought you three did everything together.'

She carries on plaiting, still on her back, knees up, holding the bracelet close to her face so I can't make out what's going on inside her head.

'They did ask me if I wanted to go,' she says casually, as if they'd asked her down to the newsagent's to get some sweets.

'Oh?' I put all my effort into this one word, restraining myself, holding back all the questions.

'I said I couldn't leave you,' she says. 'You'd worry too much. You know, cos of him.'

'Him?'

'Thomas.'

Thomas.

A wave of anguish threatens to topple me so I sit down quickly on the bed. Is that how she sees it? That she needs to protect me? What kind of burden have I loaded on her young shoulders? She was so young. A three-year-old. A little tot just out of nappies and starting playgroup. We were going along quite nicely...

I need to be the grown up here. Now. I need to see if there's anything I can do to sort this mess out. 'Martin and Claudia are worried,' I say gently, calmly. 'Bob and Tamarine are worried.'

'Bob and Tamarine don't care about Jessica,' she says automatically, repeating stuff she's heard, not really thought through.

'Is that what Jessica told you?'

'She only wanted to see her mum. Her dad won't let her. Because of Tamarine.'

'Bob doesn't want her to get hurt, that's why. He's not being spiteful or mean. And it's certainly not down to Tamarine. She's tried to get Bob to give in on this one but he's too scared.'

Rachel stops plaiting and lays her friendship bracelet on the bed, next to her. A woven bracelet of red and blue, Palace colours, set against a background of pink and purple striped duvet. I wish it was still Pocahontas but she is beyond all that now. She sits herself up, untangles her legs, unbelievably long, and gets off the bed. Crouching down beside it, she reaches underneath for something.

It is Bob's camcorder. She holds it in her hand, gripping it tight, and then says: 'You'd better watch this.'

Once Bob has got the camcorder connected to our TV, we all sit down to watch the film, an odd time to be seated together doing such a thing, Steve and I, Martin and Claudia, Bob and Tamarine, Roland and Dorota, Dad and Pat, and our delegated police officer who lurks on the arm of my sofa, notepad in hand. But this film is not *High School Musical*, *Grease* or *Seven Brides for Seven Brothers*. It is the film that our children have been absorbed in making these last couple of weeks, so absorbed in creativity that we have left them to it. It is so rare for them to get on and do things without squabbling or the constant need for adult intervention that we let them. No questions asked. So we could get on and do things ourselves, things we thought were more important. But what can be more important than spending time with your children? Cleaning loos, polishing pews, raking leaves? Are these important? Are they?

The blank TV suddenly turns into Jessica's face. It is such a surprise to see her that some of us actually gasp. Bob puts his hand to his head and rubs it, that way of his when he is lost for words. I've seen it often enough as Jessica does something that exasperates him.

It is an extreme close-up of Jessica, jerky at times so it looks like she has hiccups. You can see her freckles, the deep brown of her eyes. The collar of her precious football shirt.

'When did she pluck her eyebrows?' Bob looks at Tamarine.

'I did it for her two weeks ago, Bobby,' Tamarine says. 'She ask me. She want to look nice. Like young lady.'

Bob lets out a noise I have never heard him make before. His eyes are wet and he swipes at them with the back of his hand. 'She's ten-years-old,' he whispers. 'Ten.'

Then Claudia, quiet and contained for so long, starts to cry and moan and Martin puts his arm around her and she lets him, too weak to fight him off. Maybe she doesn't even notice; she is so focused on that screen, waiting for her son's face to appear.

Dad keeps looking over his shoulder at the door, anticipating the return of his grandson, banging and crashing his way to join his family in this communal viewing. But no-one comes in. Those of us here, including Olivia and Rachel cross-legged on the floor, consume the heart-stopping film, none of us more deathly quiet than Martin, whose arm remains round his wife's shoulder, still and limp, the way it lay on Thursday, (was it only Thursday?) hanging over the dentist's chair.

The children have made some kind of documentary, a project for school. 'What is family?' It sounds like a feature you'd get in Martin's *Observer* but this is much more profound, much more unpredictable.

Jessica introduces the project before her face fades to black. Then there is a shot of the playground at the park, children of all sizes, from toddlers on slides to teenagers messing about on swings and, dotted about, mums chatting, offering biscuits and shouting warnings. And the odd dad, standing around, awkward and out of place, or overly-confident, chucking their sons around like rugby balls. A general hum of noise and activity, nothing unusual, what you see in any London park, on any day of the year.

Cut to: Jeremy sitting on a wall down our street, outside the Khans' house. Jessica's voice asks a question off screen and Bob flinches. 'What is family?' Jeremy bites his lip and leans back on the wall, swinging his legs so he's on the verge of falling back onto Mr Khan's crazy paving. 'It's the people who look after you,' he says. 'That's not always your mum and dad though they're supposed to. Sometimes they can't. Not all the time so someone else helps out. They are family too.'

I dare not peek at Martin or Claudia, knowing how they must feel hearing that, wondering if I could have done more to mediate but I was so wrapped up in my own stuff that I couldn't. I just couldn't.

Cut to: school playground. End of the day. Parents standing around chatting, loaded down like donkeys with PE bags, reading bags, backpacks, drink bottles, letters, while their children, unencumbered and light-headed after a day indoors, skip around and jump up and down, squawking and squealing.

Cut to: Rachel, hop-scotching over the far end of the playground, speaking breathlessly with every jump. 'Family is the people you like live with. The ones you argue with and don't have to make up with cos you have to just get on with it. And family is your grandparents cos they come and treat you and spend time with you and talk to you which is good cos your parents can be like busy with stuff, all that washing and meetings and rushing around. And family is your brothers and sisters and my sisters are a pain in the butt but I love them just the same.'

She stops and grins briefly at the camera, embarrassed at that word, 'love'. And then turns her back, throws the stone and jumps off. The camera gets a bit wobbly at this point and you can hear Jessica mutter under her breath at a child who has come up to her. Then it goes dark. A moment later the screen is back, Rachel's feet, scuffed shoes, hopping towards the camera and stopping. She has been asked a question but we don't hear what it is. As the camera pans up to her face, we can see her expression while she considers her answer.

'I had this baby brother. He was like small and wriggly and cried quite a lot. I used to hold him sometimes sitting on the sofa. He was warm and heavy. He felt nice. When Mum laid him on the changing mat, he used to wee and it would like squirt everywhere. And we'd go out, Mum, Dad and me, to the park, and Dad would push me on the swings, really high so that Mum used to panic and she'd push Thomas round the edge of the playground in his pram to like get him off to sleep and that. And then one day we went to bed and in the morning he was gone. To heaven. But I'm not sure where that is or if I'll see him again. And now I've got Olivia and Imo and they are well annoying. And sometimes they're nice. And that's it.' She turns and hop-scotches out of shot.

Cut to: St Hilda's church hall. Tea and coffee after a Sunday morning service. People of all ages and backgrounds, all those people from the community, so diverse and yet gathered together in a squat ugly building, drinking tea and squash and biscuits, even a few young people who don't think church embarrassing. You can hear Jessica breathing as she walks around the periphery of the room, filming the people in her path, dodging Desmond – the shot goes to the floor for a while as she tries to hide the camera from him, in case he asks her why she's filming. She stops when she reaches Karolina who is scowling. Jessica perseveres. Karolina takes out her lipstick and slashes it across her mouth. Then she smiles, says hello in Polish. *Dzien dobry.*

Jessica: D'you like living in London?

Karolina: Is grey and dirty. Penge is very boring. But is

okay. I get used to London one day I hope.

Jessica: D'you miss your family?

Karolina: (Sneers) No. I have my family here.

The camera pans down to Natasha, clutching onto her mother's denimed leg.

Cut to: Interior of the shed. Two camping chairs set out like the set of Parky, Jessica sitting on one, Jeremy on the other. Rachel must be holding the camera.

Jeremy: Who is the most important person in your life?

Jessica: My dad I suppose cos he's like around all the time. Tamarine nags him to get off his backside sometimes and make some more money but Dad says he'll work when he wants to work. But at least he's around a lot. When I get back from school he's usually there and he asks me about my day and stuff and if everything's alright. And I always say yeah, it's alright even though sometimes I want to say, Dad, school was a load of pants, my teacher's a muppet and I miss my mum.

Jeremy: And what's it like being an only child? For the purposes of the tape.

Jessica: It can be boring. It can be a pain cos you don't have no-one going through the same things as you. Not like her. (She points at the camerawoman.)

Jeremy: And what would you ask your mum, if you got the chance?

Jessica: (after a long pause) I'd ask her when she is coming back.

Fade to black.

Later. In the back room I come across Martin and Claudia sitting side-by-side on the zed-bed, his arm around her fragile shoulders. She is nursing Jeremy's old school tie, scratching away at a Tipp Ex stain with her chewed fingernail. They look up as I come in, faces hopeful for a moment, then scared.

'No news,' I tell them straightaway.

But they are not looking at me; someone else has entered the room. Rachel. She stands awkwardly, the friendship bracelet on one wrist, her other arm behind her back. She says in a strange voice, like she's in a school assembly: 'People run away *from* something or *to* something.' She sniffs. 'That's what I heard the police woman say to Bob. She was trying to get him to think where they might have gone. Bob wasn't very helpful. Said Jessica would never run away from home. She was happy. He never hit her if that was what they were getting at.' A pause while we wait for Rach to get to her point which I know is coming.

'Anyway... ' She reveals what is lurking behind her back: an envelope. 'I should give this to Bob but he's crying and I don't want him to feel worse. It was in the shed, in a seed packet. Runner beans. It's time to plant them soon, Granddad reckons. I knew it was there all along and I thought the police would have found it but I suppose they were like only looking to see if Jess or Jeremy were hiding in there.' She hands it over to her uncle. Not a Basildon Bond blue envelope but a scruffy, brown one.

Martin carefully takes out the folded letter inside, a grubby piece of lined paper torn from a pad. He holds it so that Claudia can read it. Then he hands it to me. It is from Jessica's mother. It is from Jackie.

Easter Saturday may be a time of waiting and reflection but today requires action. I am no longer happy to have things done to me. I am going to do things myself, like the little red hen. I am Vicky the Do-er.

It is dark by the time we hit the A303. No Jazz FM today. No music at all. Martin and I sit in silence, his Saab doing the work. I don't know what is going through his mind; it's hard enough working out what's going on in mine. I clutch onto the hope that we will find them. They weren't snatched. They decided to go. But...

The wheels keep turning, taking us nearer to the West Country, to Devon, to a small seaside town famous for its black swans and Brunel's railway. A long way from Lanzarote. How did Jackie end up there? Why did she never come back for Jessica? Which I suppose is what Jessica needs to ask her.

I say nothing to my brother. It is my job to sit here quietly, to be next to him and to do whatever it takes to get his son back.

Nine thirty and we arrive in Dawlish, Martin's sat nav wrestling with its one-way streets and narrow lanes. Finally we pull up outside a small painted terrace house. It looks quaint and authentic, only the Sky dish out of place. A dim light gleams within and I take that as a ray of hope. Martin switches off the engine and instead of tearing out the car and hammering on the door, he waits. And now I know exactly what he is thinking: What if that ray of hope is darkened?

'Come on,' I say. 'Let's go.' I open my door and clamber out, stiff and tired and anxious, into the cold evening. The sea sighs, a few streets away. And then I hear Martin get out and click his door closed.

'Let's go,' he agrees.

I follow him to the house and while he rings the bell, I try to peek inside the window, hoping for a pair of familiar shadows but there is nothing to see. The closed curtains give away no clues.

We don't have to wait long.

'Just coming.' I hear a voice that I haven't heard in a while. Jackie. So she lives here still. Rachel has done well. Unless... but I don't want to think about 'unless'. I won't. They will be here. They will be here.

As she battles with the lock and then pulls back the door, we can see her face, slightly older, but still definitely Jackie, though she's lost her brassy blonde hair and appears altogether more conservative than I remember.

'I was expecting Bob, not you Vicky. And Martin, isn't it? You'd best come in.'

We say nothing, but go in the door, straight into her living room and there in front of *Friends* are Jessica and Jeremy, side by side on a wicker sofa, the remains of a fish and chip supper on their laps. They blink up at us, guiltily, but say nothing, waiting for the telling off that must be coming their way any second now. But Martin surprises us all and swoops over to his son and does something I have wanted to see him do for months. He kneels down in front of Jeremy and clutches hold of him in a hug that might possibly go on forever.

Jessica looks up at me and says simply: 'Don't be cross with him. I wanted to find my mum and he helped me.'

Her mum, Jackie, is fighting back the tears, saying how sorry she is, that she was going to call us as soon as they'd finished their tea and gone to sleep. She just wanted Jessica to herself for a short time, before she was taken back to London.

'But you can come too, Mum,' says Jessica, with a child's simplicity.

I have to be the grown-up. I have to be hard. 'We'd better call Bob. He's out of his mind.' I don't tell them he didn't come because he was so distraught, blaming Jackie, blaming himself, and unfit to drive or come with us, that we'd persuaded him to sit tight at home with Tamarine.

And so I make a phone call that I know will give a father the best news of his life, but knowing there is no such thing as a simple, uncomplicated happy ending, whatever Steve might say.

March 23rd 1978

Martin is being a pig. A bigger pig than normal. He shouts at me all the time and tells me I'm a stupid little girl whenever I open my mouth.

Mum came to see me in my bedroom. She said gosh it's tidy in here and I said thank you. She said that Martin was upset because Heidi was moving away. I asked her where and she said to boarding school so she wouldn't be able to see Martin anymore. Martin had said they could write to each other and see each other in the holidays but she had said don't bother. She said it was easier if they finished. So they are finished and I am sad because I liked Heidi. But I can't tell Martin that because he will say I am a stupid little girl.

Chapter Thirty-Seven: Sunday 23rd March

Easter Sunday

Very early in the morning and I am in the garden. In my nightie. I am Vicky, the Easter Bunny.

And why am I hiding cheap chocolate eggs behind drain pipes and under bushes? Because there's an egg hunt this afternoon. In honour of the prodigals' return. We will kill the fatted calf (pre-killed actually, from Waitrose courtesy of Claudia) and we will hang out the bunting (a packet of balloons from the corner shop).

Dad appears suddenly beside me in his dazzling white dressing gown. My dad, the gardener. Seeing him there, his knobbly knees, his frailty, I start to weep. Big, fat, snot-bubbling-out-of-nostrils, wet-faced, beyond-embarrassing sobbing. He opens his arms to me and I go to them, like a child, a little girl. I let him wrap me up and hold me until, much later, I am still and quiet and relieved.

He offers me a hanky from his pocket and, after a quick inspection, I give my nose a good blow. 'I often think that relief is the best feeling in the world.'

'You could be right, Vicky-Love.' He's managed to extricate himself from me and is passing a critical eye over my beds. 'I'll give you a hand later. Get them dug over for those runner beans.'

'With one hand?'

'It's surprising what you can do with one hand.'

'Dad, please.'

'I'm famished. You got any bacon? Pat's doing a fry-up and she can't find any.'

The story according to Olivia: *I am Olivia. I am three-years-old. I live in Penge with my mummy, my daddy, my big sister, Rachel, and my baby sister, Imogen. I go to pre-school and soon I will go to big school when I am four. When I am at big school Rachel will be at a more bigger school. We have a cousin called Jeremy. He lives with us sometimes but mummy says 'it will all blow over'. She says Uncle Martin should grow up. A long time ago, before I was born and came out of my mummy's tummy, I had a brother called Thomas. He died. That makes me sad. He is in heaven. So is Grandma. I don't remember her neither. She looks after Thomas. She takes him for walks on the clouds in a shiny silver pram. I wish he was here with us in our house. I would like a brother I could talk to. It would be like having Jeremy all the time. He might play the guitar or the drums or the recorder. When I am five I want to play the organ like Mrs Filler. Mum said I'd probably be as good as Mrs Filler. I think she was making a joke but she wasn't smiling when she said it. She'd had a busy day. She's always having a busy day. She says 'hang on', 'in a minute,' 'give me a chance'. When I am growed up I don't want babies. Unless Mary Poppins comes to help out. But Mary Poppins isn't real, she's made up in your imagination like the bogey man. I think Father Christmas might be made up too but when I asked Jessica last Christmas, she said I better watch it or I won't get as many presents. So I didn't say nothing. Jesus isn't made up. I know he is real because I just do. I said a prayer for Jessica and Jeremy to be found, all safe, and they were. Uncle Martin will be cross with Jeremy. But they might buy him a present. They said he can have a new cello but I know* *he wants a tent so he can go camping with Jessica. Jessica is his girlfriend. Uncle Martin had a girlfriend but that was very naughty because he has a wife as well. That's my Auntie Claudia who is the prettiest lady in the whole world and she has lots of shoes...*

Olivia is sitting at the kitchen table, doing a sticky picture, chattering away to the police officer while I clear up after a mammoth breakfast session. Martin and Claudia and Jeremy are due round any second and Jeremy will have to be interviewed to find out why they went, as well as everything else, but the police officer says she won't keep us long. I tell her she's welcome at the Easter service that Desmond, is taking – his last one as he's just announced his impending retirement.

The officer looks doubtful, says she needs to get home as her shift is over. Then she says: 'I've often wondered about doing one of them Alpha courses.'

I manage to smile and it doesn't hurt.

I leave them to it for a moment, to check up on Imo who has managed to roll over onto her stomach. She is huffing and puffing, trying to keep her head up, like she's Private Benjamin. I grab her up off the floor and tell her what a clever girl she is, though life will be quite different from now on, now she is beginning to catch up with her sisters.

'For you,' Olivia says, as I lug Imo back into the kitchen for her bottle. She hands over the picture. PC Wilson blushes, gushing a thank you, that's really kind.

I can make out the cast of *The Bill*, hacked out of Pat's *TV Times*, drowning under a deluge of PVA.

'And talking of families, what about your mummy?' PC Wilson whispers conspiratorially, winking at me in a way that would make me want to brain her with my iron had she not been so helpful over the last twenty-four hours. 'What's special about her?'

'Well,' says Olivia as I wait for the longest time. But I should fear not. She is an angel. 'She's the best mummy in the whole world of course.' She folds her arms, her angel wings, in an amazingly patronisingly way for a three-year-old, as if she pities PC Wilson, whose mother, if she has one, must be of an inferior quality.

But I can't stay smug for long. I have a feast to prepare. The fast is over. And the fatted calf – a sumptuous-looking sirloin of British beef – must go in the oven if we are to eat before sundown.

I have a family. It isn't perfect but it is mine. I will cherish them all – those that are here, and those that stay quiet in my heart and memory – and be thankful that it never got as bad for me as it got for poor old Job.

But then, as Steve likes to say, look what happened to Job in the end. So I did. It's all written down, helpfully in the Book of Job, in the Old Testament, nestled between Esther and the Psalms.

But that's Job's story. What about Steve's?

The story according to Steve: *It was the call-out to Dartford that did it. I didn't really want to go, it was quite a way but it sounded like a genuine emergency and Vick was keen for me to get back to work so I got in the van and I went, a tortuous journey, Saturday morning. But I never got there. Had to ask Craig to get that one in the end.*

Steve tells this to PC Wilson who is still hanging around our kitchen, unable to drag herself away. 'Go on,' she says. 'What happened next?'

I get to the A2. Past Bexley. There's a lot of traffic and the rain's coming down. I'm in the fast lane, behind a pick-up, piled up with all sorts of gardening junk, like they're on their way to the tip. It looks a bit dicey, the way it's shoved on, a wheelbarrow at the back of it all. I keep half an eye on the wheelbarrow, wondering if we should get one and then I get annoyed at myself for thinking such a thing. How can I be considering a new wheelbarrow? How can I be getting on with life? So soon? It's only been a few weeks.

The rain comes down faster, there's splash-back from the pick-up, and I put the wipers on full whack.

*Then I hear a voice. Clear as if someone's in the van behind me. I check the mirror but there's no-one there, course there's no-one there. The voice says: **Move over**. I reckon I must've imagined it, the wind whirling through a gap in the van, tools shifting in the back. But it doesn't sound like any of those things. And it can't account for this feeling I'm getting. Then the voice says it again, louder, more insistent: **Move over**. And this time I don't think. There's no time for thinking. Instead I feel my hand move to the indicator, my eyes flick to the mirror, and I am moving over, to the middle lane but I don't drop back like I should, my foot stays down on the pedal and I keep even with the driver of the truck, the rain pouring so I can't hardly see out the window.*

Then there's this loud bang.

I look from wing mirror to rear view. The wheelbarrow has flown off the pick-up. It's taken off, rising above the road, bouncing backwards through the space where I was, just a moment's breath before. My heart's like a frightened budgie trapped in my ribcage, beating about, trying to escape. Where the hell is it going now? But I can't think these things. I can't speak them. There's no time. The wheelbarrow, a huge metal bird, carries on bouncing, skidding and sliding sideways, backwards, dodging a burgundy Vauxhall Cavalier, a red Micra, obstacles in a bizarre It's a Knockout *race. It skids all the way across the lanes and ends up like a twisted sculpture by the side of the road. All these thoughts, all these movements pass in a matter of seconds. The traffic carries on as if nothing's happened, as if it were a dream but the clang of metal, the sight of the flying wheelbarrow, the voice, all repeat over and over until I can get off the road at the next exit.*

I find a pay phone, by a row of shops, the rain easing up

by now. I call the police. Tell them about the pick-up, the wheelbarrow, giving descriptions and locations and my address. Then I sit back in the van. I sit still, the window open to help me breathe, and I wonder at what just happened. My heart's settled down but all my senses are fired up. I notice the drops of rain on my windscreen, no longer falling but sliding down. Each one stands out, unique and clear. I hear the sound of a man and woman passing by, her heels on the pavement, his deep voice asking her something. I smell the newly-cleaned pavements, the heat washed off. The washing powder waft out of the launderette. I touch my face with my hands, to check I'm still here. The heat of my cheeks. The stubble poking through my skin. The taste of blood in my mouth, where I must've bitten my lip. And this other feeling. A sixth sense maybe. A gut feeling. That something has happened. Something I can't define. Something supernatural. But I shake off the feeling, switch on the radio, try to pull myself together, wonder what I'm doing here when I have a job to get to.

    Then.

    I look up, out of the open car window and see a young woman coming out of the launderette pushing a toddler, maybe eighteen-months-old, in one of those umbrella buggies. She's carrying a big bag of washing, a stripy plastic zip-up bag you get in the pound shop and the boy is clutching a rubber ball. She stops outside and murmurs something, more to herself than the child. She swipes at her hair, which has come loose from a pony tail and puts down the bag. Then she leaves the toddler in the pushchair while she darts back inside to get whatever it is she's forgotten.

    But the toddler isn't buckled up properly. I watch him shrug his arms out of the shoulder straps. He looks surprised, like he didn't expect that to happen so easily. Then he inches forward on his bottom and sits on the edge of the pushchair, swinging his legs, looking behind him for a glimpse of his mother. But she hasn't re-emerged from the shop. I will her to hurry up.

Hurry up. I know I'll have to do something if he gets himself out the buggy.

He drops his ball. We watch it bounce across the pavement. He jumps down onto the pavement and I get myself out of the car. But he's quick. He toddles with surprising speed and determination after his ball. Towards the road. Not a busy road but there's this sharp bend. I have to be faster. I'm running towards him and right then I hear a shattering scream. A mother's scream. That sound I never wanted to hear again. I've nearly reached him, watching his little body bent forward in concentration. The scream makes him stop and turn round, balanced on the edge of the kerb. He wobbles, like in a cartoon, teetering on the brink of a cliff. Which way will he go? He falls towards the road. I lurch forward like I have super human strength and speed.

I can do this.

I can save him.

His coat is in my hand. I pull and he falls backwards onto me, just as a car speeds round the corner. The driver has no idea, carrying on as if nothing has happened. But my life will never be the same again.

The mother cries and thanks me and the relief in her eyes makes me cry too, like I've not cried since Thomas' death. She looks at me as if I am unhinged and asks if she can do anything to help, all the while clasping her son to her like she'll never ever let him go.

I get back in the car and call Craig. Tell him he'll have to take the job. I'm going home. I drive away, Dartford behind me, back onto the A2, and then ahead –

– a rainbow...

I let the car take me back to Penge. But when I reach the high street, the car doesn't take me home – that sounds stupid, I know – but I have switched off, gone on automatic. I end up in the car park of St Hilda's, my hand taking the keys out of the ignition, my feet getting me out of the car and across the car park and into the church which happens to be open so that one of the ladies can do the flowers. She's sticking long yellow crysanths into a huge vase, lots of tangled greenery and the smell is the most beautiful thing I have ever breathed in. Like I've entered heaven on earth.

And there's the vicar. There's Desmond turning to welcome me.

This is what I will come to know as my mountain top experience, though it happened in the London Basin. Desmond knows me from the funeral, from our children's christenings. He sits me down as he can see I am shaking. He tells me I've had an epiphany. I say that sounds painful. He says, with a simple lack of humour, such moments can be painful but they can lead to great peace and a wonderful joy.

Revelation: If I hadn't survived the wheelbarrow flying off the back of the pick-up, then I wouldn't have been there to save the boy. It is not all random – a pack of cards thrown into the air to fall where they will. A load of timber washed ashore. This was planned so I would be in that place at that time. I moved over when I was told to move over. And I survived. So did the occupants of the Vauxhall Cavalier and the Micra. So did the little boy. Another set of parents didn't have to go through what we've been through. If Thomas hadn't died it is quite possible that I wouldn't have gone off to Dartford that Saturday morning. We would have spent the day together. The park, shopping, a day out to Worthing. Other people would have died in his place. Other sons. He didn't die in vain.

*I didn't change immediately but there was a shift. I came to realise that God doesn't want bad things to happen. God listens when we cry out. Even Jesus cried out. **Why have you forsaken me?** God knows what it is like to lose a son. My pain is His pain. The cross is His way of saying: I know how you feel. People say it's all part of God's plan but that's not exactly a great comfort when you're in the deep dark pit of depression. But I began to see there was something beyond me and bigger* *than me. I began to think of all the things that have happened in my life that might not have happened. All the disasters in the world that have been divinely averted. And I began to feel that peace seep into my bones and spread throughout me. And peace was followed, surprisingly, unexpectedly, by joy.*

PC Wilson shifts uncomfortably in her chair. Steve remembers he has an audience. For a while he was back in the van, driving across his mountain top. Now he's back in our kitchen. 'I'm sorry, Vick,' he says, out the blue.

'Sorry? What've you done now?'

'I'm sorry my experience changed your life. I don't think I took you into consideration in this, not like I should have done. I mean I thought this would be a better life, for all of us. I still do. Only I haven't thought enough about you... You know, you don't have to do this curate's wife thing. I'll stop it all now. Go back to plumbing. I can be a lay preacher. There's all sorts of voluntary work I can do in the church. I want you to be happy. And I want to honour you.'

'Honour me?'

'I don't think we do half enough honouring these days.'

'You'd really give it all up?'

'Well, obviously not all of it. Just the vicar bit.'

'But what about Desmond? He's retiring.'

'I admit it may not be the best timing, both of us going together, but like I said, there's someone else in control here. It'll work for the good.'

PC Wilson coughs. 'I think I might just head off now.'

'Hang on a sec,' I say, pushing her back down. 'Steve, I don't want you to give it up. I think you should be vicar. I mean, who else could do it as well as you? Who else knows St Hilda's like you? Who else knows the community?'

Steve is silent.

'Don't you think that'll mean more work?' PC Wilson chips in.

We look at her. Steve says, 'more responsibility, not necessarily more work.'

'And what about a vicar's wife? What does that mean for Vicky, here?'

Steve looks at me. 'It's what you make of it,' he says. 'You can go back to teaching if that's what you want.'

Teaching? Do I really want to leave my kids to go and teach other people's kids? Or do I want to be a fully-fledged vicar's wife?

'Shouldn't you be getting off home now? We've kept you far too long. Or would you like to stay for lunch?' I check my watch, 'Well, a very late lunch. It's roast beef.'

PC Wilson gets up reluctantly from our kitchen table. 'I'm tempted but I'm needed at home,' she looks around the room. 'You're a nice family set-up here,' she says. 'I wish they were all like this.'

I show her to the front door. She puts on her hat and says to me: 'We don't all need a title to make us happy. I've been in the force and never bothered about going for sergeant or promotion or anything. I like what I do. I'm good at it, I think,' she coughs again. 'But sometimes we need a status of our own. Something of our own. Do you know what I'm saying?'

I know exactly what she's saying.

We are gathered in the back room, the dining room once more, as Jeremy is returning to Dulwich tonight – along with Martin, the jammy dodger. Steve lets Martin carve the beef, a gesture full of grace and humility that ignites a surge of love for my husband. I want to honour him. I want to do the best for this family. My family.

I look around at them all, cramped round the table in the poky room: baby Imo in her high chair, a cocktail sausage squeezed in her chubby hand. Rachel, next to Jeremy, listening intently to his adventures, on the train to Dawlish, dodging the guard the whole way, finding Jessica's mum in her painted cottage, screeching with joy to see her daughter,

Jessica hugging her, how it was worth the aggro and maybe he's right. Dorota and Roland side by side, quiet, watching the people around them, but mainly watching each other, offering vegetables, passing gravy, spooning horseradish, a choreographed dance learnt long ago in their youth. Dad and Pat yabbering away, about the food, the campervan, plans for the garden, for next week, and though it hurts like hell, thinking of my missing mum, this pain is mixed in with – yes, it has to be said – relief.

And then Claudia, on the other side of her precious son, sneaking looks at him, checking he's still here, he is real, alive and kicking the table leg.

In rushes another wave of pain, but on the crest of this, a revelation: This is fine. This is life. It is okay to cry out. My family will help me. And God will hear me. He is not hidden away inside a fluffy cloud. He is there, to be found. And this might be in unexpected places. Steve found Him in Dartford after all. And I never thought I would find Him in Penge. But maybe Amanda's right. Maybe he's been here all along, only I never realised.

Then I look at Martin, piling my divine Yorkshire puddings onto his plate, my plate, as if he hasn't seen food since 1987. And I have another revelation: I actually quite like him. In small doses. When he's not living with me.

But this feeling soon wears off. There is another ring at the door. Olivia dashes off to answer it and escorts the uninvited guest along the poky hall and into the back room, announcing in a loud, clear voice for all to hear: 'It's the lady from the shoe shop.'

Chapter Thirty-Eight

The story according to Melanie: *My mother owned a shoe shop. My grandparents bought it for her 'to start us off'. They had stacks of money and they said after what she'd been through, they'd do their best to help. They said she could have this sum of money and do what she wanted with it.*

She chose a shoe shop. Not the one I help out at. This was in Greenwich. Her first one. And we lived in the flat above it. We could've stayed with my grandparents, their house was big enough, but Mum was desperate for independence, to be in control of how I was brought up. And even though it was hard, really tough sometimes, bringing me up on her own, so young, she preferred it that way.

My grandmother helped out a lot. She was in retail so she showed Mum some tricks of the trade. But mostly she took care of me while Mum was in the shop. Then, when I was four, about to start school, Mum met someone, Mike, and all her plans for independence went out the window.

They got married. Mike was great. He treated us both really well. Not that we were a burden to him financially; he was a self-made millionaire, carpets. And even though Mum hadn't been looking for a cushy life, that's what she got. But she carried on working and with Mike's encouragement she opened a shop in Crystal Palace and then another in Dulwich. And that's where we moved. The Village. Into that huge place.

We were a proper family.

Mike brought me up. He was my dad. He would've been at my graduation and walked me down the aisle at some possible point in the future, but it wasn't to be. He died when I was twenty. A heart attack. I was at university, caught up in finals, so I couldn't really help Mum at the time. I don't know how I sat through those exams. But I didn't get the predicted first, just an upper second. Mum went abroad for a bit. She ended up staying a few years. Finally came back six months ago. And now we're together again. I'm making up for it, back at home, in the shop, doing my PhD to make her proud.

We have adjourned to the front room and Melanie tells us her life story, poised on my not so new leather sofa, where Martin passed out not so very long ago. Now he sits on the armchair, raspy-breathed, Claudia perched beside him, proprietorially. Steve and I are squished together on the other armchair. Melanie has a captive audience as the remaining adults have made a discreet exit, joining Bob and Tamarine in a trip to the park, taking all the kids, including Imo in her pushchair.

'Only that's not the whole story. Is it Martin?' Melanie looks at Martin. We all look at Martin. He is pale, still blotchy after his traumas, and rubs a beard that is no longer there, the way an amputee can feel a limb long after it has gone. He doesn't say a word, shut up for once, so Melanie carries on.

I found Martin on the internet. It was easy. Mum had already tried to help me when I'd said I wanted to meet him. She went onto Friends Reunited but he wasn't there. But all I had to do was Google his name and I found him. A few clicks and there was his department. Another and there was a photo of him. Pretty much as Mum had explained. Pretty much as I'd imagined. So I sent him an email with a research proposal. He asked me to come in and have a chat about it. And that's what I did.

He had no idea that first time we met. He assumed I was just another student hawking my ideas around. Only he seemed interested. I'd done my homework. I knew exactly what his specialism was. I knew he'd be able to supervise me. And the thing that was most worrying me, never happened. I was afraid I'd catch that look in his eye that I get off older men. My blonde hair and my other major assets do something to their already programmed brains. But I didn't do it to him. It was weird. It was a relief. He said my proposal was excellent and he'd get back to me as soon as. And then he did give me a look but not the sort I was concerned about. An unsure look, like he'd seen me somewhere before and couldn't quite place me. He asked if we'd met previously. I said no, we hadn't met previously. He said you must have a doppelganger. I said perhaps we'd met in a different space-time continuum. We agreed that it must have been around the Village. He said he and his wife had moved there about eight years before and even though I'd been away a long time our paths may have crossed.

I wanted to tell him then but I didn't.

The following week I met him for coffee to talk details. He wanted to grab some lunch so we went to Starbucks. It wasn't slimy. It was just nice. And then I told him. I told him he was my dad.

Claudia is on her feet, so fast she almost goes over on her heels. 'Don't be ridiculous,' she says. 'I know you're young but how could Martin possibly be your father? Martin, why are you letting this woman say these things? Can't you see she's deranged? What is it with all these crazy women? Tell her to go.'

'Sit down, Claudia.' Martin is firm, his big hand on her tiny arm. 'I should've spoken to you before.'

Claudia stays on her feet, wobbling, swiping his hand away. 'What do you mean?'

'I mean, listen to Melanie.'

Claudia is fuming but she does as she's told, shaking, and

she, along with the rest of us, listen to Melanie.

'I'm twenty-eight,' Melanie says. 'I look younger, I know. But you should see my mum. She's only forty-five. Sixteen years older than me.'

Martin has taken Claudia's hand in his. She is shaking but trying to calm down, trying to find out what the hell is going on – which is what we all want to know. Why has another crazy lady gate-crashed a family gathering? And the repercussions of this? If this is true, there was no affair. Martin has not been unfaithful to his wife. But he *has* been dishonest. If he had told Claudia about this, that he has a daughter, then she would never have got involved with Graham Greene. The idiot. The liar. The bumface.

'Did you know you'd fathered a child at... sixteen? Can this be proved?' Claudia asks her husband, her eyes fixed on Melanie.

Jeremy Kyle comes to mind. DNA tests and paternity suits. But seeing Melanie and Martin together, it is clear there is no need for any of that. The truth was there all along but we missed it. We made assumptions. We didn't delve deep. We didn't ask.

'I had no idea, no.' Martin shakes his head. 'Well, maybe I wondered. From time to time. Because she went away so suddenly, never answered my letters. It was like she'd disappeared overnight from the face of the earth. And then, once, years ago, I saw her. In the supermarket. I knew it was her straightaway. She was with you, Melanie. You must have been about eight or nine. And I hid behind the toilet rolls. Like a coward. My heart going like the clappers because I wondered. I really wondered. And I stayed there for ages, clutching a bottle of wine, panicking. I didn't know what would happen if she saw me. I didn't want to hear the truth. I was ashamed. Not of you, Melanie. Of myself.'

'So how did all this happen? I mean, when? Who?' I realise I'm making a fool of myself but I have to know. I think I already do know.

'Mum used to go out with Martin. For a few months. Then she got pregnant and was sent away to France to have the baby. Me. When I was a few months old we came back to London and I've told you the rest.'

Claudia is looking at me now as if I might be the one to tell her the truth. A truth that she had no idea about until Melanie turned up on our doorstep. She thought she was a trollop. But she is my niece. Her husband's daughter. A sister for Jeremy. A cousin for my girls. And I know who the other mother is. Of course I do.

'And where's your mum now?'

Melanie gets up and moves to the window, lifts the nets. 'Waiting in the car out there.'

Claudia and I join Melanie at the window.

'I know her,' Claudia says after a deep and heavy pause. 'I've seen her in your shoe shop. I didn't know she owned it. I've bought countless pairs from her over the years. She has divine taste.'

Standing outside, dressed from head to toe in expensive clothes, leaning against a fancy sports car, is a woman I haven't seen in years. She was a girl the last time we spoke. A girl in a lingerie department in a new pair of shoes.

It is Heidi.

... And Finally: Sunday May 11th

Pentecost Whit Sunday

In two weeks we are going to have a Eurovision party. Eurovision might not be what it once was, when you had to sing in your mother tongue and didn't vote for your allies, but that's life. Life is all about change.

We're inviting all the usual suspects, including our neighbours and even some parishioners. And we've invited Melanie and Heidi. They have met up with Claudia and Martin and it is all very civilised. Very Dulwich Village. And we've even invited Karolina who, along with Dorota, can support Poland. Let's hope for a better party than New Year's Eve. I couldn't stand another evening of Gerry's dovetail joints.

But today is a family party. A celebration. Today is Imogen's christening. We are meeting afterwards, for lunch, in our house, here, though Amanda has offered the vicarage. She says it will be ours soon enough, which it will be, once Steve takes over as vicar in the summer. I've coveted that vicarage for so long and now it is almost mine I am already hankering after the poky terrace. I'm not sure I can bear to leave it. To leave him. But I have to think of the girls. The space. The room they will have to grow and thrive and flourish.

Not to mention the cleaning that lies ahead. It'll take weeks to cut through the layers of ground-in grime and grease. (I'll use that Sanctuary voucher when it's all done and dusted.) And as for the jobs that need doing – Steve will never get round to them so I've booked to go on a home-maintenance course. Because maintaining a home is what is important to me. I don't need a job title. I don't need status. I know what I do is vital. And I know who I am. I am Vicky. And my life might be holey, not holy, but that's okay. It's not a race. It's a journey. And I will make the journey in bare feet, if I have to.

We will gather in St Hilda's today, together, to witness that this is a special moment for the family. A time for a photo. For a camcorder. For memory. And now, as we are about to leave, Steve and I and our girls, the Saab pulls up outside the poky house, squeezing between the campervan and Bob's woebegone Rover. Martin gets out and I join him on the street. My street.

He hands over a box. Not a biscuit tin or a shoebox but a small, expensively wrapped oblong box. It is a gift. For Imo. 'For my niece,' he says. 'Open it.'

So I open it. Inside is a silver christening spoon. I look at my brother.

'We can't all be born with a silver spoon in our mouth so here's one I bought earlier. Well, Claudia did, that's her department. And a very expensive department it was too. In Selfridge's.'

I look at the car. Claudia waves at me from within, like the queen.

'We don't know what we're going to be born into,' he goes on, a dangerous note of wistfulness lurking in his voice. 'And sometimes we think we know but it's not like that at all.'

Profound words from Professor Martin Bumface. And this time, he's right. Uncle Jack. Melanie. Thomas. Mum. Life is uncertain. Fragile. Precious.

'And I don't know about God. Or genes. I've still got a lot of questions. A long road ahead. But there's one thing I know, Vick.'

He pauses dramatically for this is a dramatic moment.

'You're my sister. Through and through.'

I wonder if he's going to kiss me but he doesn't. Instead, he gets back into his car with his own family, Jeremy in the back on his Nintendo wotsit, Claudia redoing her lipstick.

I am turning back to the house when I hear my name called.

'Vicky-Love?'

'What now, Martin?'

'Before you get to church you might want to take your skirt out of your knickers. It's not a good look.'

St Hilda's. Pentecost. The congregation dressed in bright colours. Reds and oranges. Tongues of fire. The Holy Spirit hovering as He did over the water at the beginning of time. Imo, dressed in white lace is held up by her father who looks slimmer, more like the old Steve. She is staring with her big greedy eyes at Desmond, resplendent in red chasuble, as he dribbles water over her fuzzy nest of hair. She tries to catch the trickles in her podgy hand, her happy shouts echoing, making the packed house laugh out loud. And then, because it is Pentecost, Desmond anoints her head with oil, a sign of the outpouring of the Holy Spirit and I try to see the symbolism, not the oil stain on her delicate robe. Imo heckles some more, gurgling infectiously. Not like Rachel who screamed her little head off. Or Olivia who looked mortified, her bottom lip quivering. Or Thomas, who slept the whole way through, an angel. For this public act is something Steve and I have done for all our children. Long before Steve had his Dartford moment, we both wanted to celebrate the birth of each child, and give thanks. To someone. To anyone who'd listen.

Desmond says: 'May God, who has received you by baptism into His Church, pour upon you the riches of His grace, that within the company of Christ's pilgrim people you may daily be renewed by His anointing Spirit, and come to the inheritance of the saints in glory.' He hands me a lighted candle, spilling wax over his red stole. The flame flickers briefly but I keep quite still and it stays alight, burning bright and I know now that this is what I have to focus on: the light shining in the darkness.

The grandparents take a back seat, watching on – Dorota, Roland, Dad. And Pat. They share a packet of Polos and click away with cameras and I look up briefly, at St Hilda, wondering what she reckons to all this.

For this is my life. Here and now.

And here I am, standing tall, as tall as I can in my bare feet, the cool floor firmly under me. Here I am, next to Steve and Imo, the girls between us, Rachel dressed like a Sugababe, Olivia as Tinkerbell. Next to our family are the godparents – Claudia, Melanie, and Martin. Claudia and Martin stand arm in arm, her Elizabeth Taylor to his Richard Burton. Melanie looks even more glamorous, her long blonde hair glossy and coiled into a sculpture on the side of her head, a satin dress with a slit up the side that is bordering on indecent.

And in a circle around us, there is a smart(ish) Bob with a gorgeous Tamarine, Jeremy in a ridiculous suit, next to Jessica Talbot in a dress (hallelujah). Jessica is holding the camcorder steady, capturing the hushed moment for future generations (or *You've been Framed* if someone slips and bangs their head on the font).

For there will be future generations. Feet will tread over the threshold, in kitten heels, in sling-backs, in Crocs, in sandals like Mr Maynard's, in plastic Cinderella slip-ons, in Marks and Spencer's wide-fit. People will seek, people will worship, people will knock over flower arrangements (thank you, Jeremy). They will enter this sacred place for comfort and for refuge, for celebration and for joy. They will look up at St Hilda, shining away in her own blue slippers. And they will look further, beyond, to eternity. Knees will bow, tongues will confess, souls will sing. Now in Penge. And forever more. Amen.

If you enjoyed This Holey Life, don't miss the brilliant debut novel by Sophie Duffy,

The Generation Game

The Generation Game

Life is the name of the game
Bruce Forsyth

2006

Oh dear. How did that happen?

Last time I looked, I only had myself to worry about. Now I've got you. Another person. Yesterday you were hidden away, tucked up inside me, completely oblivious to what lay ahead. Now here you are, floppy and exhausted, the biggest, scariest journey of your life over and done with. All screamed-out and sleeping the way babies are supposed to on a good day.

So what now? Where do we go from here, you and I? Backwards, I suppose. To the beginning. While you are quiet and still and here in my arms. Before they chuck us out and send us home.

Home.

But where to start? Where is the beginning exactly?

Long before the bags I packed full of nappies and cream and teeny-weeny babygros. Before the hairy ride in the taxi over the speed bumps of East Dulwich banging my head on the roof while the Irish cabbie recited his Hail Marys. The tracks I played on my iPod, full blast to drown out the noise I couldn't help making. The Best of The Monkees. Hearing those voices and tambourines took me back to a time when I had a best friend in all the world who I thought I was going to marry. Who I thought would be there forever. Who taught me that everything changes. (A Monkees compilation was as far as your father got involved in your birth. That and the quick leg-over that was lost somewhere amongst the ravages of my fortieth birthday.)

Long before then. Right back at the beginning, my beginning, way back when I was held for the first time in my mother's arms.

Were my fingers ever that small? My toenails? Was my skin ever that smooth and wrinkled at the same time? My hair that fluffy? My grip that tight? My nose that squashed?

Did my mother hold me and wonder these very same things?

I can't answer these questions.

And try as I might, I can't tell you everything that went before. Everyone I could've gone to for help, for answers, has gone, is lost – in one way or another. But I'll tell you what I can. I'll tell you about the people who loved me. Who brought me up somehow, against all odds.

I'll tell you about Lucas, the boy I was going to marry.

I'll tell you about your father (though I'd rather not).

And I'll tell you about a little fat girl called Philippa.

I'll tell you my story. Our story. Because there's nothing worse than wondering. Knowing is always better.

Chapter One: 1965
Family Fortunes

On the 29th day of July, 1965 I arrive in the world – a brightly-lit poky delivery room high up in St Thomas' Hospital – amid a flurry of noise. The doctor is shouting at the midwife, the midwife is shouting at my mother and my mother is shouting so loudly, her screams can probably be heard across the Thames by the honourable gentlemen in the Palace of Westminster, possibly even by the Prime Minister himself, if they weren't on their holidays. In fact, my mother is so busy screaming, she doesn't seem to have noticed that I am already here. But I am. I have arrived in style, waving a banner, heralding my birth. I am happy to be here even if she isn't so sure. I'd put up some bunting and have jelly and ice cream if I could.

(It is years later before I find out the truth: that I am in actual fact yanked out of my mother with a sucker clamped to my head, her (ineffective) coil clenched in my tiny fist. I am lucky to be here at all.)

I spend the first week being manhandled by stout nurses in starchy uniforms. They poke me and prod me and tip me upside down for no apparent reason. They bring me to my mother every four hours ('Baby's feed, Mrs Smith! Left side first!') and whisk me away again to be comprehensively winded and gripe-watered before I've even had the chance to take a good look at her or to have loving words whispered in my newborn ears. Instead I have to lie on my tummy in a little tank in a large room. I am one of many. The others cry a lot. I give up and join in.

When I am seven days old, I am brought to my mother's bed. It is empty. She is sitting in a chair next to it, reading a magazine. She looks quite different fully clothed. She has long legs and red lips and green eyes and smells of something other than the usual milk. The nurse hands me over hesitantly, as if I might explode in the wrong hands. But these are the right hands. My mother's hands.

'Time to go,' she whispers to me after the young nurse has gone. 'You've been here long enough.' And she embarks on her plan to smuggle the pair of us out of St Thomas', swaddling me in a yellow blanket despite the sweltering August heat ('Always keep Baby warm, Mrs Smith!'). Not an easy operation as the sergeant major of a sister is of the belief that new mothers are incapable of doing anything more strenuous than painting their fingernails.

But my mother, I am already discovering, is a skilful liar. She convinces a stranger in a pinstripe suit – lost on his way to visit an elderly aunt – that his time would be better spent posing as her husband and my father (the first in a number of such attempts). He is only too happy to oblige and, at a carefully chosen moment when Sister is on her tea break, the young nurse relinquishes Mother and I into his control. We follow meekly behind him, down squeaky corridors and ancient lifts until at last we are out through the front doors and into my first gulp of fresh air (well, semi-fresh, this is London after all).

Mother gives the poor chap a cheery wave and a dazzling smile that makes it quite clear his assistance is no longer required and makes for Westminster Bridge, in her Jackie Kennedy sunglasses and killer stilettos, clutching me to her breast, like a fragile parcel she has to post. She hails a black cab all too easily and bundles me into the back of it while the cabbie deals with all our worldly belongings: a Harrod's bag full of nappies and, more importantly, my mother's vanity case.

Inside the Cab we are bumped and swayed along the London streets at unbelievable velocity. It is not as comfortable as my little tank. Or indeed my mother's womb where I was safe and happy, swimming about in her amniotic fluid sucking my thumb, listening to the drum beat of her heart, not a care in the world.

At last we come to rest at Paddington Station. My short life as a Londoner is almost over.

Some time later, I lie in my mother's awkward arms on the train, hot and fidgety. We have a carriage to ourselves. She is feeding me from a bottle. I preferred it when she fed me with her own milk which tasted of grapes and hospital food, each time slightly different. It is all the same out of these bottles and I keep leaving pools of curdled cream on her shoulder as she pats me rather too vigorously on the back ('Come on, give me a good one, pleeeasse,'). I have the hiccups and tummy ache. Doesn't she know I am too young to be on the bottle? Doesn't she know that breast is best? My mother tuts, wiping her eyes with her sleeve. Maybe she is a hay fever sufferer. I know so little about her. This is the first time we have been on our own together.

Over her shoulder the world whizzes past the window so fast it hurts my little eyes, spins my tiny head. Maybe I am drunk. Maybe she's given me too much gripe water to try and staunch the crying. She could probably do with a gin and tonic herself.

After a fitful sleep the train jolts me awake as we pull into a hazy greyness otherwise known as Reading. Heavy doors bang and crash but we stay where we are, trapped together in our carriage. Mother's green-lidded eyes are closed but it is unlikely that she is sleeping as her fingers appear to be playing an invisible piano. The journey continues as does the winding and the curdling and the sniffing.

We do not get off at Swindon either, a new town with

new hope. We carry on, via Bristol, heading south through Somerset and into Devon until we reach the coast. Sandy beaches, coves, and palm trees. The English Riviera. Torquay.

'Our new home, Philippa.'

My mother sighs – whether from relief or regret is anyone's guess – before lugging me and the bags out of the carriage and onto the platform, where she stands for a moment looking wistfully back up the track. Then she turns her face to the sun and lets the warm breeze brush over her. She sighs again, taking in this new air. Air that will thankfully make me sleepy over the weeks to come.

'Right then, Philippa, let's go.'

I don't know where we are going. Of course, I don't. It could be to one of the hotels on the cliffs or to one of the painted Victorian villas overlooking the Bay. Our lives are all set out before us and we could do anything. I could be destined to attend the Girl's Grammar. To have tennis lessons. Elocution lessons. Cello lessons. I could be part of a happy family...

Unfortunately it is 1965 and my mother is unmarried.

So my first home turns out to be two rooms above a garage. Nothing flash – not Rolls or Daimler or Jaguar. No. The cars in the showroom below aren't even new. There isn't a showroom to speak of. Just a 'Lot' out the front, full of second-hand cars run by a bloke called Bernie from Wolverhampton. 'Sheila and me came on our holidays here in 1960 and fell in love,' he informs my mother, with a misty sheen to his eyes as he holds open our shabby front door to show us into our home. 'We've never looked back.'

Advice we should all take on board.

(Too late, too late, I've started so I'll finish.)

Come and visit us at

www.legendpress.co.uk

www.twitter.com/legend_press